D0191923

The Best
AMERICAN
SCIENCE
FICTION &
FANTASY
2022

AMERICAN SCIENCE FICTION & FANTASY™ 2022

Edited and with an Introduction
by REBECCA ROANHORSE

JOHN JOSEPH ADAMS, *Series Editor*

MARINER BOOKS
New York   Boston

FIRST EDITION

ISSN 2573-0797

ISBN 978-0-358-69012-2

22 23 24 25 26   LSCC   10 9 8 7 6 5 4 3 2 1

Contents

Foreword

WELCOME TO YEAR eight of *The Best American Science Fiction and Fantasy*! This volume presents the best science fiction and fantasy (SF/F) short stories published during the 2021 calendar year as selected by me and guest editor Rebecca Roanhorse.

About This Year's Guest Editor

Rebecca Roanhorse is a *New York Times* bestselling author who burst onto the scene in 2017 with her short story "Welcome to Your Authentic Indian Experience™," which won both the Hugo and Nebula Awards, and was a finalist for the World Fantasy Award, the Theodore Sturgeon Memorial Award, and the Locus Award. Additionally, on the strength of that story alone, she also won the Astounding Award (for best new writer). All of which is, well, pretty *astounding* for a writer's first published work of fiction.

She went on to publish her first novel, *Trail of Lightning*, the following year, and that work, too, generated critical acclaim: It won the Locus Award for best first novel and was a finalist for the Hugo, Nebula, World Fantasy, Compton Crook, and Crawford Awards—and it should be noted that books that are nominated for the Hugo, Nebula, *and* World Fantasy Awards are incredibly rare indeed. And—no big deal—*Time* called it one of the 100 Best Fantasy Books of All Time.

From there, she published *Storm of Locusts* (a sequel to *Trail*), wrote a middle-grade novel called *Race to the Sun* for the Rick Riordan Presents imprint, and *Star Wars: Resistance Reborn*. Her latest books are *Black Sun*—which won the Ignyte and Alex Awards and again garnered her Hugo, Nebula, and Locus Award nominations—and its sequel, *Fevered Star*, which came out in April 2022. A new novella, *Tread of Angels*, is due out November 15.

Outside of prose fiction, she's also written multiple one-shots for *Marvel Voices* and is the writer of the 2021 Marvel series PhoenixSong. The protagonist of that comic, Echo, is starring in an eponymous Disney+ series due out in 2022, and Rebecca had the pleasure of working in its writers' room. She's been pretty busy in TV and film otherwise, too, with her work being optioned by Amazon, Paramount TV, and Netflix, and along with *Walking Dead*'s Angela Kang, she is adapting and executive producing a *Black Sun* TV series for AMC Studios.

But getting back to where this began, in addition to "Indian Experience" (which first appeared in *Apex*), she's published more than a dozen stories in anthologies such as *New Suns, The Mythic Dream, A Phoenix First Must Burn, Star Wars: Clone Wars, New Voices of Science Fiction, Rick Riordan Presents: The Cursed Carnival and Other Calamities, Sunspot Jungle*, and others. Her story "A Brief Lesson in Native American Astronomy" was selected for inclusion in our 2020 volume. Her short fiction has also been featured several times on the *LeVar Burton Reads* podcast.

Which is all to say: It's hard to imagine someone better to wade through the best of 2021's short fiction with me. I can't wait to see what you readers think of the selections!

Selection Criteria and Process

The stories chosen for this anthology were originally published between January 1, 2021, and December 31, 2021. The technical criteria for consideration are (1) original publication in a nationally distributed North American publication (that is, periodicals, collections, or anthologies, in print, online, or ebook); (2) publication in English by writers who are North American, or who have made North America their home; (3) publication as text (audiobook, podcast, dramatized, interactive, and other forms of fiction are not considered); (4) original publication as short fiction (excerpts of novels are not knowingly considered); (5) story length of 17,499 words or fewer; (6) at least loosely categorized as science fiction or fantasy; (7) publication by someone other than the author (that is, self-published works are not eligible); and (8) publication as an original work of the author (in other words, not part of a media tie-in/licensed fiction program).

As series editor, I attempted to read everything I could find that meets the above selection criteria. After doing all of my reading, I created a list of what I felt were the top eighty stories (forty science fiction and forty fantasy) published in the genre. Those eighty stories—hereinafter referred to as the "Top 80"—were sent to the guest editor, who read them and then chose the best twenty (ten science fiction, ten fantasy) for inclusion in the anthology. The guest editor reads all of the stories anonymously—with no bylines attached to them, nor any information about where the story originally appeared.

The guest editor's top twenty selections appear in this volume; the remaining sixty stories that did not make it into the anthology are listed in the back of this book as "Other Notable Stories of 2021."

2021 Summation

In order to select the Top 80 stories published in the SF/F genres in 2021, I considered several thousand stories from a wide array of anthologies, collections, and magazines. As always, because of the vast wealth of excellent material being published every year, it was, in many cases, difficult to decide which stories would make it into my Top 80 that I present to the guest editor; the difference between a story that made the cut and a story that *got* cut was sometimes razor thin. Outside of my Top 80, I had around fifty additional stories this year that were in the running.

The Top 80 this year was drawn from thirty-two different publications: twenty-four periodicals, six anthologies, one single-author collection, and one standalone digital chapbook. The final table of contents draws from fourteen different sources: twelve periodicals and two anthologies. *Tor.com* had the most selections (4), followed by *Uncanny* (3), and *The Magazine of Fantasy & Science Fiction* (2); every other outlet represented in the table of contents had one story each.

We had a lot of repeat offenders this year; eight authors selected for this volume previously appeared in *BASFF*: Caroline M.

Yoachim (4 times, now tied for most-ever with Sofia Samatar);
Catherynne M. Valente (3); Elizabeth Bear (3); Karen Russell (2);
Kelly Link (3); Meg Elison (2); P. Djèlí Clark (2); and Sam J. Miller
(3). The remaining authors are thus appearing for the first time.

Two periodicals appear in *BASFF* for the first time this year: *Dark
Matter* and *khōréō*; of course, they didn't *exist* before last year, so if
they'd managed to appear in *BASFF* before they even existed, well,
that sounds like the subject matter of a *BASFF*-eligible story. Those
magazines were then, obviously, included in our Top 80 for the
first time this year, and joining them as first-timers are *Catapult*,
Constelación, *Gulf Coast*, *Mermaids Monthly*, and *Oprah Daily*.

New writer Justin C. Key had the most stories in the Top 80
this year, with three; several authors were tied for the second-most,
with two each: A. T. Greenblatt, Catherynne M. Valente, Karen
Russell, Nalo Hopkinson, Rich Larson, Sam J. Miller, Seanan Mc-
Guire, and Stephen Graham Jones. Overall, sixty-nine different
authors are represented in the Top 80.

Several of our selections this year are finalists for some of the field's
awards: "Colors of the Immortal Palette" by Caroline M. Yoachim
(Hugo, Nebula, Ignyte); "Proof by Induction" by José Pablo Iriarte
(Hugo, Nebula, Locus); "Broad Dutty Water" by Nalo Hopkinson
(Locus); "The Future Library" by Peng Shepherd (Ignyte); "Skinder's
Veil" by Kelly Link (Locus); "Delete Your First Memory for Free" by Kel
Coleman (Ignyte); "L'Esprit de L'Escalier" by Catherynne M. Valente
(Hugo, Locus); "Let All the Children Boogie" by Sam J. Miller (Neb-
ula, Locus); "The Red Mother" by Elizabeth Bear (Locus); and "If the
Martians Have Magic" by P. Djèlí Clark (Ignyte, Locus).

Likewise, a number of Notable Stories were so honored: "Small
Monsters" by E. Lily Yu (Locus); "Bots of the Lost Ark" by Suzanne
Palmer (Hugo); "(emet)" by Lauren Ring (Nebula); "The Badger's
Digestion; or The First First-Hand Description of Deneskan Beast-
craft by an Aouwan Researcher" by Malka Older (Ignyte); "The
Music of the Siphorophenes" by C. L. Polk (Ignyte); "The Black
Pages" by Nnedi Okorafor (Locus); and "The Sin of America" by
Catherynne M. Valente (Hugo, Locus).

Note: Several of the other genre awards had not yet announced
their lists of finalists, such as the World Fantasy, Shirley Jackson,
and Sturgeon Awards, and the final results of some of the awards
mentioned above won't be known until after this text is locked for
production, but will be known by the time the book is published.

Anthologies

The anthologies *Vital: The Future of Healthcare*, edited by R. M. Ambrose, and *When Things Get Dark*, edited by Ellen Datlow, had stories selected for inclusion in this year's volume.

Several other anthologies had stories in the Top 80: *Black Stars: A Galaxy of New Worlds*, presented by Amazon Original Stories; *Cities of Light: A Collection of Solar Futures*, presented by the ASU Center for Science and the Imagination; *Speculative Fiction for Dreamers: A Latinx Anthology*, edited by Alex Hernandez, Matthew David Goodwin, and Sarah Rafael García; and *Sword Stone Table*, edited by Swapna Krishna and Jenn Northington.

The anthologies with the most stories in the Top 80 were *When Things Get Dark* (3) and *Black Stars: A Galaxy of New Worlds* (3).

Plenty of anthologies published quality material in 2021 but didn't quite manage to end up with a story in the Top 80. Here's a partial list: *Imagine 2200: A Climate-Fiction Project*, presented by the Fix; *It Gets Even Better: Stories of Queer Possibility*, edited by Isabela Oliveira and Jed Sabin; *Make Shift: Dispatches from the Post-Pandemic Future*, edited by Gideon Lichfield; *Seasons Between Us: Tales of Identities and Memories*, edited by Susan Forest and Lucas K. Law; *Shadow Atlas: Dark Landscapes of the Americas*, edited by Carina Bissett, Hillary Dodge, and Joshua Viola; *Unfettered Hexes: Queer Tales of Insatiable Darkness*, edited by dave ring; *Unmasked: Tales of Risk and Revelation*, edited by Kevin J. Anderson; and *Whether Change*, edited by Scott Gable and C. Dombrowski.

Collections

Only one collection had a story in the Top 80 this year: *Never Have I Ever* by Isabel Yap, but there were several other fine collections published in 2021—some of which contained only reprints and thus had no eligible material, but I'm going to acknowledge them here anyway in order to highlight them as books to check out: *A Few Last Words for the Late Immortals* by Michael Bishop; *Among the Lilies: Stories* by Daniel Mills; *Beneath a Pale Sky* by Phillip Fracassi; *Big Dark Hole* by Jeffrey Ford; *Empty Graveyards* by Jonathan Maberry; *Everything in All the Wrong Order* by Chaz Brenchley; *Fantastic Americana* by Josh Rountree; *Fit for Consumption* by Steve Berman; *How to Get to Apocalypse and Other Disasters* by Erica L. Satifka; *Reconstruction: Stories* by Alaya Dawn Johnson; *Robot Artists and Black Swans* by Bruce Sterling; *Shoggoths in Traffic* by Tobias S. Buckell; *Thanatrauma* by Steve Rasnic Tem; *The Burning Day* by Charles Payseur; *The Ghost Sequences* by A. C. Wise; and *The Tangleroot Palace* by Marjorie M. Liu.

Periodicals

The following magazines had work in the Top 80 this year: *Apex* (4), *Asimov's* (3), *Beneath Ceaseless Skies* (2), *Clarkesworld* (4), *Conjunctions* (2), *Fantasy Magazine* (3), *FIYAH* (4), *Lightspeed* (10), *The Magazine of Fantasy & Science Fiction* (7), *Mermaids Monthly* (3), *The New Yorker* (2), *Nightmare* (2), *Tor.com* (7), and *Uncanny* (5). The following periodicals had one story each: *Analog, Catapult, Constelación, Dark Matter, Escape Pod, Fireside, Gulf Coast, khōréō, Oprah Daily,* and *Strange Horizons.*

The following magazines didn't have any material in the Top 80 this year but did publish stories that I had under serious consideration: *Apparition Lit, Baffling Magazine, Cast of Wonders, Daily Science Fiction, The Dark, The Deadlands, Diabolical Plots, Fusion Fragment, Future Tense, LampLight, Nature Futures, PodCastle, Tales from the Magician's Skull,* and *Underland Arcana.*

Last year in this space, I mentioned the impending launch of several new magazines: *Constelación, Dark Matter, Mermaids Monthly,* and *The Deadlands.* And indeed those all did launch, as did several other periodicals: *Baffling Magazine, Fusion Fragment, Hexagon, LampLight, khōréō,* and *Underland Arcana.*

As was the case last year, there was a surprising lack of periodical deaths, though, sadly, newcomer *Constelación* appears to be on life support. *Terraform, VICE's* SF magazine, didn't publish any new content since March 2020, and so seemed as if it were dead—but as I was finishing this foreword, a new story appeared on their site, so perhaps it's not dead after all . . . to be continued!

As always, I implore you to support the short-fiction publishers you love. If you can, subscribe (even if they offer content for free!), review, spread the word. Every little bit helps.

Acknowledgments

Here, I offer a tremendous thanks to my stalwart assistant series editor, Christopher Cevasco, who helped me pan for gold in the streams of SF/F.

I'd also like to thank Nicole Angeloro, who is now doing the *BASFF*-related wrangling in-house at Mariner Books.

Thanks too to David Steffen, who runs the Submission Grinder writer's market database, for his assistance in helping me do some oversight on my list of new and extinct markets mentioned above. Speaking of people who help with oversight, I wanted to give a big shout-out to all of the short-fiction reviewers out there—y'all make it a *lot* easier to keep up with everything throughout the year . . . and make it harder for me to miss smaller (or newer) periodicals, anthologies, or collections. This goes double to the people at *Locus,* who not only cover short fiction throughout the year but also do the colossal work of assembling the *Locus* Recommended Reading List.

And, finally, a big thanks to all the authors who take the time to let me know when they have eligible works, either by just letting me know or else by submitting them via my *BASFF* online submissions portal. I'm also grateful to publishers and editors who proactively send me review copies of anthologies, collections, and periodicals—especially the ones who do so unprompted and don't wait until December to send a year's worth of material. If you're an author, please do consider asking your publisher if they send review copies to best-of-the-year anthologies such as this, because even after eight volumes I still receive very few anthologies or collections unsolicited—I have to find out about them of my own accord and then specifically request them (and even then sometimes I have to follow up several times!).

Submissions for Next Year's Volume

Editors, writers, and publishers who would like their work considered for next year's edition (the best of 2022), please visit johnjosephadams.com/best-american for instructions on how to submit material for consideration.

—JOHN JOSEPH ADAMS

Introduction

MY CHILDHOOD WAS defined by a mighty need to escape. I grew up a Black and Native kid in Texas in the 1970s and '80s. To complicate matters (and that's putting it lightly), I was adopted into a white family. As much love as my adopted family tried to give me, there was only so much comfort they could provide in the face of an outside world that had other plans. Those plans often centered on making sure I knew how much I didn't belong. Childhood, and children, can be cruel like that. But I survived, and even flourished in large part due to my imagination. An imagination fueled by story. Because the one thing I did have, thanks in part to my mother, who was a high school English teacher, was a love of books.

I cannot remember a time when I wasn't planted in the stacks of my local library. Books offered me that escape I so craved—worlds of magic, heroes and villains, wonder and possibility opened before me. Worlds so unlike my own. I would hole up with Susan Cooper's *The Dark Is Rising* and, later, Hickman and Weis's Dragonlance Chronicles and David Eddings's *The Belgariad*, and lose myself in the worlds and the characters they had constructed. It was a balm, and it served me well until I finally left Texas to attend college in New England—truly, Connecticut might well have been Middle Earth compared to Fort Worth.

Later, I discovered something else besides refuge in my beloved books. I found conscience. It turned out that these imaginary worlds I so loved were not so different from my own after all. There were populated by bad men with too much power who often oppressed those weaker than they were. The stories they told were of people who struggled with difference and identity, the weight of duty versus love, the pull of ambition over family, and the trials of simply trying to survive in a world dead-set on their destruction. I read *Dune* by Frank Herbert when I was in sixth grade, and while much of the story likely went over my head at that age, I keenly felt the injustice of the oppression of the Fremen and Paul's well-meaning but often disastrous attempts to help the indigenous population of Arrakis. Later, I would discover Ursula K. Le Guin's *The Left Hand of Darkness* and Octavia Butler's *Dawn*, and a whole new level of awareness opened to me, powerful and radical and revolutionary. I knew then that I loved these stories, this genre, more than any other. I still do. It has made me who I am today as a writer and a purveyor of the imaginary.

The twenty stories I picked for this collection are exemplary pieces of imagination. Some are escapes into other worlds (as if escape were simple) offering a refuge in these times of pandemic, war, and the worldwide rise of fascism. Some simmer with radical revolution quite loudly, and others subvert our cultural mores more quietly, for what could be more revolutionary than (re) claiming one's humanity, one's capacity for love, one's need for self. And they all—no matter how dark they might twist and turn—offer a glimmer of hope within.

I remember speaking on a panel at Worldcon in San Jose in 2019, and someone in the audience asked the panel participants what big ideas their stories engaged. Many great answers were given, the kind that were expected from science-fiction and fantasy authors, but when it came time for me to speak, I found myself troubled by the question. Yes, as an author of speculative fiction, I often wrangle with big questions, but my writing is more often obsessed with the smaller questions—who are we, to ourselves and to others? How do we define and navigate the tricky waters of human relationship, identity, individuality, and community? What does it mean to reject or conform to what is expected of us, how do we counter the Western narrative that holds individual achievement above everything but also appreciates a good self-sacrifice? Who are we beneath the labels and factions, and is there anything uniquely human that binds us together? These are the ideas that engage me, and that engaged many of the authors of the stories in this collection as well—in various ways, offering answers as diverse as the authors and the stories themselves.

> Wanna ride together?
> —"Delete Your First Memory for Free"

Perhaps in this time of COVID and isolation, it is no surprise to find so many stories about human connection. If there is a trend to be found within these stories, this was certainly the dominant one.

In Kel Coleman's deceptively simple "Delete Your First Memory for Free" we find a protagonist beset by social anxiety who feels they are alone in the world. When offered the chance to delete a memory, they must decide whether it is worth the risk. It is a common trope in science fiction, this idea of mind manipulation, but it is often played to the protagonist's detriment. What could be more terrifying than loss of mental control? Unless, of course, our mind is the very problem. The story is ultimately one of hope, suggesting that if we could let go of the things that emotionally diminish us, perhaps we would find we are not so alone after all.

Sam J. Miller's poignant "Let All the Children Boogie" is about two kindred souls brought together by music and a mystery to be solved in a world of late-night radio and the sticky mess of adolescence. It is about friendship and acceptance and the kind of fierce love that is all too rare in this world.

> All those lives I'd hyperspaced through, they were ways Rance could be out there dying—*would* be out there dying. Unless I kept him alive.
> —"I Was a Teenage Space Jockey"

The loss of a loved one and how to move on without them haunt both José Pablo Iriarte's "Proof by Induction" and Stephen Graham Jones's "I Was a Teenage Space Jockey." In Iriarte's story, an adult son tries to fix his relationship with his father, only his father is dead and a "coda" of him can only be reached within a machine. It is mathematics that binds the pair together, but it is the desire to be seen, to be understood in a way that is impossible once our loved one is gone, that will break them apart.

Likewise, the protagonist in Jones's story has lost a loved one, a brother who has disappeared and left nothing behind for his little sibling except the high score on an arcade video game. But it is enough to fuel the younger brother's imagination as he strives to connect with what he has lost, and who they both could have been if things were different.

> Sometimes, we owe it to the world to help bear the grief of another.
> —"The Frankly Impossible Weight of Han"

Grief fuels the stories of Maria Dong and Fargo Tbakhi, as well. In "The Frankly Impossible Weight of Han," Dong envisions grief as a contagion, passed among people by a machine running unchecked. It takes a mother's invocation of ancient spirits to stop it, but the lesson is learned—we should not have to bear our grief alone.

Loneliness is the driving force behind the protagonist's fate in Tbakhi's "Root Rot," an absolutely shattering tale of a man who has lost himself even as he finds himself colonizing a distant planet. It is a failure to connect that sets the protagonist on his dark path, but even this story ultimately offers the reader hope—if not for this generation, then for the next.

Hope, connection, grief, and love. These are COVID-times stories, all moving us through the darkness of emotional isolation, loss, and grief into a place of connection and hope.

> Alone, what difference can one human being make? More than you think.
> —"The Cold Calculations"

And then there are stories that I loved that reminded me of why I fell in love with the genre to begin with.

> The skalds and the seers tell us we ought to love war. And somebody must. There's enough of it.
> —"The Red Mother"

"The Red Mother" by Elizabeth Bear is one such story, a deft take on what would normally be an epic fantasy trope—a man, a dragon, an impossible quest—rendered in full, colorful detail in only twelve thousand words. A remarkable feat and a delightful escape that left me wanting more.

Catherynne M. Valente's "L'Esprit de L'Escalier" also treads more familiar mythic ground, but this retelling of Orpheus and Eurydice is anything but traditional. A story of domesticity gone sour and marital strife that absolutely dazzles. I would be remiss if I didn't mention Valente's excellent "The Sin of America," which I did not choose to include simply because there was no more room, but brims with visceral prose and is worth the read.

Karen Russell's "The Cloud Lake Unicorn" is a tale that marvels at the wonder still possible in our world, a reminder that no matter the darkness in our mundane day-to-day, miracles are still possible if we choose to live in extraordinary times.

> Mom? I'm back to the future, or whatever . . . You okay?
> —"Tripping Through Time"

No science fiction and fantasy collection would be complete without a look into the future, and while some of the stories I have already mentioned are clearly set in future worlds or on distant planets, there are a handful that squarely offer us a vision of what our future may look like, and how it may serve or harm us.

Both "The Algorithm Will See You Now" by Justin C. Key and "Tripping Through Time" by Rich Larson talk about the future of healthcare, one from a practitioner's perspective, and the other from the perspective of someone caught up in the frustration and neglect of a system meant to benefit only the very few. Each story raises provocative questions about who we are and what kind of future we want, and neither provides easy answers. Larson imagines a dark and all-too-imaginable future in the healthcare wealth disparity, but Key's disassociation of the practitioner with the pain of living a realized life is no less dark.

Sadly, I was allowed to choose only twenty stories, and there are a few from the eighty presented for consideration that were excellent and are among my favorites, but on a particular day at that particular time, I chose differently. They were certainly worthy, and I want to mention them in hopes that readers seek them out. "Saint Simon of 9th and Oblivion" by Sabrina Vourvoulias; "The Badger's Digestion; or The First First-Hand Description of Deneskan Beastcraft by an Aouwan Researcher" by Malka Older; and "We Travel the Spaceways" by Victor LaValle.

In the end, my guiding principle in story selection was inspired by the incomparable storyteller LeVar Burton, who, in his introduction to his reading podcast, proclaims that he picked the stories therein based on a single principle: He liked them. So it was with me. I picked these stories first and foremost because they were my favorites. But the reason they were my favorites was that they possessed something of the joy and comfort and thrill that the very best science fiction and fantasy has always elicited from me. I have no doubt they will offer you something as well.

Enjoy!

—REBECCA ROANHORSE

TONYA LIBURD

10 Steps to a Whole New You

FROM *Fantasy*

(1) Be unaware that the wolf was presenting itself to you in sheep's clothing.

It began, as most things do, simply enough. In a simple neighborhood, on the edge of a town. Too urban to be rural, too rural to be urban.

Women grew old. Some women aged with their children, grandchildren, family around them. Some grew old alone, isolated, bitter. Others might grow old and die sick, in pain.

Then there was you.

You was the woman who manage to live on she own, but who not quite there, harmless, the madwoman on the street. It was a ordinary life you live; a couple of men, you work jobs until your illness start up. You wouldn't be able to live by yourself sometime, but right now, you tried to enjoy your life. And not embarrass the neighbors.

Down at the end of the street was this new neighbor, Francine, one who keep to sheself ever since she husband gone and dead almost half a year ago. No one knew how he die; she ain't saying.

The both of you had evening get-togethers, you and your achy hips, and you cyah walk how you used to, but she walking spright.

That's how she start she trickery on you.

(2) Allow yourself to be seduced.

One evening, when Francine was over, you busy trying to crochet a doily; you use to enjoy it before, but now you having trouble focusing.

She start by acting as if she talking about she old folklore studies . . .

She tell yuh she studied some Liberal Arts at UWI, but the folklore that interest she the most is the one about the soucouyant.

She quote to you, "If the soucouyant draws out too much blood from her victim, it is believed that the victim will die and become a soucouyant herself, or else perish entirely, leaving her killer to assume her skin."

She ask you if you believe in the supernatural.

You say you ain't know; the older one get, the more one know, and questions start coming to mind . . .

She say if the supernatural is real, then other things can be true, you know . . . ?

You say like what, eyeing she.

She say like cures for diseases and . . .

You say and?

She say imagine if there were ways to fix what ails you; what would you do if you were able to fix your mind?

You pretending to have a thicker skin than you do right then. So you say to she, cool and calm, it would be nice.

You ask she if she would have kids.

If eyes were windows to the soul, you seeing she own. Pain. Longing. And something else, deeper, curious, you shoulda take it as a warning. But even in your best days, yuh mind not completely sound, and the clearest sight is hindsight. It have only so much you could get from them honey-toned eyes.

(3) Don't resist the carrot that's dangled enticingly before you.

The next time she see you she say to you, Azelice, I have something to tell you.

What, you say.

She say she a soucouyant.

What, you say. Then you laugh; no, haha. Good one Franc—

She finger start to glow, and she burn a circle into the wood at the edge of the arm of she chair.

All the hairs all over you stood on edge, boy. You find yourself standing up.

She calm calm. All she do was tilt she head, gesture with she other hand, and say to you, don't worry. Come on. Take a seat.

She say how she mean to help you. How the discussion allyuh had the other day could be as true for you as it was already for her. She say how she ain't have no aching joints and she mind clear clear. She say how allyuh could talk more but it have to be at her place, how the old folktales have it wrong.

You still in shock. You think you say okay, sure.

She get up to go and say allyuh would talk tomorrow.

She say see you tomorrow, Azelice, from your gate.

You shoulda run then but your poor brain not only still processing what it just see, it was also buzzing with possibilities.

(4) See the truth and wonder . . .

The power went out.

Neighbors come out on their porch and start telling each other hello over their walls.

If you live with a grandmother, or your parent wanted to, you could get to hear some "Nancy stories" about Anansi, the spider-man, or ghost stories.

Children trying hard hard to do homework with a kerosene lamp, although they could tell the teacher that it was too dark to do anything.

But not you. You eying Francine's house at the end of the road. You damn well know this sudden darkness, people getting catch off-guard and everything, was perfect cover for a soucouyant.

And you see, inside she house, a light that was too bright, too huge to be caused by candlelight. It start soft, then it grow brighter and brighter, it move from the bedroom window to the back of the house, then out a window, past she backyard plants and fly up into the night, disappearing quick-quick.

Your breath catch quick in your throat. You leave your poorch and go back into your house.

(5) Take the challenge like a fool.

The next night you close the gate to your house behind you, and go down to Francine's. You walk through the gate up to the door and knock on it.

You wondering if the supernatural real as you wait for Francine to open she door. She welcome you barefoot, and she ask you to remove your slippers at the door.

She place was all light wood to almost match she honey complexion. It was neat, in all the nooks and crannies, where yours wasn't.

There was stew chicken, with rice and peas and coleslaw, and a glass jug of sorrel sweating and ready for drinking. It make you feel thirsty and you had to try to not smack your lips.

She say to have a seat and allyuh start talking about the weather, and because it was Carnival time, your favorite calypsonians—"Singing Francine's my favorite calypsonian," she say to you—and who might win Road March, and who was your favorite mas band, and if you going to go to Port-of-Spain to see the Carnival Parade or watch it on TV . . .

She live better than you, but she want you for a friend. And it look like she just on the verge of making an offer. An offer you just might take.

(6) See the truth, but go because you're lonely and want a friend.

The next time you visit she, you tell yourself you going for the promise of companionship, for friendship bonding, for camaraderie.

You were being drawn towards the promise of freedom, of renewal.

You two had a nice dinner, allyuh drink some of the passionfruit that growing in she backyard.

Allyuh talking nice nice.

Then, at one point, Francine's voice go deep; you getting mesmerize, and you feeling like you going to go unconscious. You fight it.

The air seem to turn into some kind of tapestry of flames in the wake of her fingers. You not sure what you seeing is real.

You see she tongue flick outta she mouth. It was thick and black and all of a sudden you smelling wet ashes.

You feeling the heat radiating from she body through your shirt and she . . . she put she violent breath into you. Your body go limp . . . what was happening . . .

You hearing, "Lay back. On the floor. That's right . . ." and ". . . Oh, yes . . ." and "yuh feel so good, Azelice . . . !" but you could do nothing.

Then, you couldn't fight unconsciousness no more.

Everything just go black.

(7) Be the living embodiment that hindsight is 20/20.

These are the things that you remembered from when you rose from the dead, having been laid to rest at home:

That you had a new strength, and agile hips, and all your old creaks and pains were gone gone.

That now you had clarity, because the fog lift, that gone too. None of them scatter feelings or thoughts.

That you now know that the folktales were true, and that Francine knew it. Down to every last detail.

That Francine's words, when she was satisfying sheself on you, they like hungry, fat mosquitoes in your mind now, buzzing, buzzing in your ears.

That you feeling unclean remembering.

The rush of your new body, the mightiness of you as you going to she house.

Splinters sprayed all over the floor, some jooking your hand after you smash she door down, and she wreck of a smile when she trying to make nice-nice with you. That she try to use the bond between you, but the advantage she had at manipulating you done gone.

That you could smell she fear. That you decide to call she *Sucking* Francine from then on, because she had like the calypsonian Singing Francine so much.

Baring your fangs when she still trying; "But I make you! I give you a new *life*!" All your strength and power . . .

That she thought she could fool you by saying, "Don't you see, the change has been good! I knew it would be good for you!"

That you damn well know she couldn't have known because she gambled on you.

That you still new to these things, and you didn't recognize bloodlust yet, and that you were confused about how far to go.

How simple it was to just break she bones, to twist she body parts in ways they shouldn't . . . to satisfy a new hunger when you draining she blood.

That, after all of that, you still didn't feel clean even though you left she for dead.

(8) Think that vengeance is done.

You could hear the talk starting, and you know the neighbors spreading the word about what happen to your maker. Somebody come home and see the mash-up door to Sucking Francine's house. You didn't exactly do a quiet exit.

In the depths of your own house, you chuckle. You preparing to move.

You know Sucking Francine would heal supernaturally in front of all them doctors and nurses. She would become whole. And then questions would start up. She would have to move too. Even disappear. But you, you could still blend in, melt away, get out of sight. No one would really look for you.

Your maker was one of them people with "bad mind," people who put their smarts to sinister use. Like preying on the vulnerable—people like you—for their own ends. In a way, what you did to she was better than just killing her. Sucking Francine would have to explain, to hide.

You, you just packing your things quiet-quiet, and making your own plans to move on.

(9) Realize that you can't exactly go back to your old life.

It hit you when you home alone. You didn't know what to expect. Your humanity had not completely sloughed off yet, like oil off water.

But something . . . *something* had started to build, like a slow burn. You dunno know what it was, deep inside.

It come to your attention when you lick your lips when you at a window. There was a late-night breeze.

You needed something, but the food and drink you try earlier feel almost like . . . sand on the tongue . . .

You grip the windowsill tight, tight. The moon did not call to you, but the night air did. You . . . wanted to revel in it, bathe in it, view the world from above . . .

You look behind you into your house. You staring at your bedroom with a some sort of new clarity. You make up your mind right then that you going to straighten the clothes hanging about, fix the bed, dust your dressing table, the entire place.

Routine did not ease the slow burn that was starting to burn bright, hot, fast.

You turn back to your bedroom window. You swallowing hard. You needed something, and you starting to realize what it was. You need it soon.

(10) Embrace the new you, taking to it like a hand to a glove.

You could feel this new need pressing down on you; you were half drowning in it.

You thought back to all the old tales of what a soucouyant covets in the night. You imagined feeding on blood, on life, and your heart beat so hard that your chest thrummed.

And it didn't disturb you. Not one bit.

The thirst, the pain, the desire; each moment was like undiluted pleasure.

To be honest, the old you felt like your skin, which right now was a cold tightness around you.

The pain of your need was . . . unbearable. You fell to the ground and hugged your knees. You tried to shut it out. But you . . . couldn't.

Resisting caused pain. The pain washed over you, drowning you.

The thought of blood flowing down your throat made you moan. You were ready to bite into your own arm to get blood.

You raised your head to the sky and *screamed*. It felt so good to let it out, as if it had been trapped in your chest for too long.

With your scream, you and your skin parted in a rush of release. Your heart was a song, at one with the slow burn within you gone white-hot and bright.

You don't recall leaving your house, but you do recall being one with the sky.

Beyond your skin the whole world was yours, yours for the taking. Beyond this skin you were fire, you were light. Beyond this skin you must take life, you must take blood, you held life and death.

The people on this street were too close to you to take, not enough anonymity, and so you looked further.

You would feed, you would take, and you would revel in it.

But for right now, you would fly.

MEG ELISON

The Pizza Boy

FROM *The Magazine of Fantasy & Science Fiction*

MY FATHER WAS a pizza boy too. His father had gone off to fight in the Garates cluster and left him in charge of the family ship, since he was the oldest of the children. He was only fifteen, but his mother was a surgeon and there was no one else to do it. He taught me everything I know.

It's forty-two deliveries tonight. The first dozen went to the same big medical transport, received by an orderly in their scooter bay. Those were the hottest, and he immediately pulled the lid up on the top pod.

"No mushrooms?"

I shake my head. "Not today."

His face falls considerably and he nods. I'm sure that'll come out of my tip.

The next three go to a troop transport, and I know the guy who meets me in the bay is from comms because of his ear implant. He does the same thing, pulling the seal on the top pod and letting the hot scent puff out all around us. "No mushrooms tonight, huh?"

"They're getting harder to find," I tell him. "I'm going to a spot I know tomorrow. Hopefully I'll have mushrooms again when your creds come in."

He nods and goes back to work, carrying pizzas to his comrades like a hero.

The fleet is stretched out over half a sector, but my scooter is fast and my pods are well engineered to keep pizzas hot.

The Imperial marines do not ask about mushrooms. They also don't tip. And I scoot back home.

My ship, the *Mehetabel*, has to grow its own tomatoes for sauce. Dad had a source for them—some hippies running a hydroponics outfit on some barely terraformed asteroid back in '67. But he returned to the ship one day and told me they were wiped out in a skirmish between the Queen's Armada and the Kralian rebels. He was crying. I don't know if they were friends or it was just the tomatoes. Either way, my dad couldn't stand it.

Dad recultured the cell lines himself when the clones started to fail. He created a diverse set of offspring from that one singed plant we had left. He and Mom worked together, applying the best of her organic chemistry and his exobotany and horticulture. The *Mehetabel* didn't really have the space to spare, and tomatoes apparently need gravity as well as hydroponics. Without synth G, they bash against each other in flight, their shapes are lumpy, and their flesh is mealy. So there's one corridor now that's always too wet and too warm, and the tomatoes hang down from a trellis they built into the ceiling. It's made of struts from a Queen's Armada dinghy they pulled apart when they salvaged the battlefield after the Klut Offensive. Every time I pick tomatoes for a pot of sauce, I try to remember what Dad told me, about how every little piece of the cycle is important.

Mom was drafted by the QA right after I was weaned. I barely remember her. Dad went out after mushrooms one day last year and never came back. I hope he got his wish and was buried in some actual dirt. That's their place in the cycle. I don't know mine yet.

Our sauce recipe hasn't changed in a couple hundred years, and it came from someplace called Sammerazo, system unknown. Dad had it written on actual paper, pressed in borosilicate and bonded to the wall in the galley. We lost it during a secondary-hull decompression when I was a kid; I remember Dad holding an iron pan to the seam in the wall and welding it in place to stop the air leak. He stood there, tears in his eyes, staring after it. That pan is still there. I still oil its surface.

Dad wiped his eyes and said he knew the recipe by heart anyway. The tomatoes have to be stewed and crushed in the pan, after you sauté Axarb garlic in with a little shaved Lirap onion (not too much, they're sharp!). He usually shaved the fat off some preserved sausages to get it all going, some spicy thing he picked up at the space station market in the DMZ. Who knows what was in it? Grubs, frogs, men. Sausage can be anything at all.

We'd talk while he showed me how to do it, told me about how sausage was made somewhere else.

"Why does it matter, Dad?"

"What?" He looked up at me from the sizzling pan, frowning.

"Why does it matter, all the steps and the specifications? The secret sauce matters. And the mushrooms matter. Why the rest of it?"

He put down his spatula and looked at me hard. The sauce was as red as blood. "The effort proves you're a pizza boy," he said. "The effort is what keeps you safe. Any idiot rebel can create a fake delivery to relay a message, and they'll always get caught. This pizza has to be good so that someone who receives it who has no idea what we're doing would never guess it had any other reason to exist. You understand? If the pizza is good, the pizza boy is safe. Never forget that."

I don't forget anything.

The batches of blood-red sauce are a hundred liters apiece and I freeze some to use for the following week. They bounce around in the zero-G deep freeze that just sucks in the cold from outside the ship. The *Mehetabel* was built for efficiency. The ovens siphon the heat directly off the engines, and so do the sleep pods. Never waste heat, Dad said.

I never waste anything. And I do everything the way he did it.

Cheese is the big problem, and I can't make it myself. There are four dairy ships that follow the QA, and they used to sell clabber that they couldn't use. Then one of them figured out their own efficiency and found a way to put it to use. Dad was devastated. We had just made contact with a planetary orbit market when he disappeared.

There are a handful of planets in this system that produce cheese, but my favorite is the one with thousands of little islands in a planet of seas—Benibeni. The dairymen there don't say much, but they use the same code with me that they established with Dad. Their sea cows produce green milk after eating kelp all day. The cheese those farmers make is milky green like jade and rich, salty as hell. It comes in round plugs of varying weights, and they weigh them in front of me every time I pick up. They look at me intently, their horizontal pupils unknowable. We don't speak, but I get the message.

I had to pull all the salt out of the sauce recipe to compensate for this cheese, and the kelp adds umami like you wouldn't believe. But it bubbles and it stretches, and people always rave about it on our review system. That keeps them coming back. If I deliver to a troop transport once, I know that the following week I'll be trundling along in their wake, taking orders from soldiers who saw it or smelled it, but didn't get any.

Always, the question about mushrooms. Sometimes from someone I didn't expect to ask. Sometimes I have to look them over, to figure out whether they mean it as a matter of taste or something else.

The thing is, I went for gray mushrooms two weeks ago, when I knew I'd need them. There's only one place left for them now. I went back to the spot Dad visited last, but he wasn't there and neither were our mushrooms. It was illegal for him—for any of us—to be on a planet. When the QA moved on, it wouldn't be one anymore. Atmosphere burnt off and nothing left.

The spot I go to now, Dad discovered it. He didn't tell me he seeded the spores himself, but he was so proud and protective of it that I have to believe it was his work. Or someone he knew. It's on the dark side of LU5, a tidally locked celestial dwarf that's almost uninhabitable after the QA used ikon torpedoes on it back in '69. They say the radiation is deadly, but there are people living there. I've seen them.

The spore farm is on the underside of a downed Litor ship, its spars cracked and resting upside down, like an animal with its legs in the air. It's dark and warm and drippy down there. Dad always said the first spore drop there was like hitting a temperate planetoid with ice meteors seeded with tardigrades: instant life. This place is temperate enough, but the surface is solid bismuth. No soil. They grow slowly, if they grow at all.

When I was there a few weeks ago, the mushrooms were just coming back. I knew that soon, their broad purple heads would jut out at every angle, growing up and down and sideways from every surface and rock. Back in the deep, where it's almost a cave, I saw the white bone of one of the corpses that feeds the spores. He was old when I was a kid; I can't imagine how he's still recognizable back there. The conditions are perfect for rot, but he doesn't seem to change much. I can see the curve of one of his eyeholes, as if he's always winking at me.

I've got my gather kit and I'm reaching up for a little cluster with long stalks and small caps; those have the best flavor. But then

I feel the muzzle of a blaster nestle into the dimple over my right kidney, just one layer below in my good piron suit. I freeze at once.

"I'm a noncombatant," I say as I have a thousand times before. "I have no planet."

I turn around and face the blacked-out dome visor of an Imperial marine of the Queen's Armada.

"Identify yourself."

"Giuseppe Yang Verdi, 879.5. Spacer. I was born on the *Mehetabel,* and I am her captain."

Two other marines close in behind the one holding the gun on me. I clamp down on the impulse to lose this morning's water ration.

"Verdi? He's the pizza boy," one of the marines says over their comms link. They're open to me; they're not trying to keep me from hearing anything.

"What are you doing here, pizza boy?"

I gesture slowly, one-handed, at the mushrooms growing above my head. "Gathering ingredients. That's all." They can see my face through my visor—it's just shield-yellow, not opaque. I'm trying to smile.

"You deliver to everyone," one of them says, almost spitting with anger. "The Lido. The Kluti. Anyone with creds."

"I'm a noncombatant," I say again. "I don't take a side. I just make pizza."

"Well, not today." One of the other two steps forward and gestures around my mushroom cave. "We're commandeering this site in the name of the Queen."

"Come on, guys." I say it without thinking. They'd kill me for less.

They just watch me. I can't see their expressions change. I don't know if they're amused by me, or totally deadpanning and waiting for the order to kill me. I could feed this place for the next fifty years. I could grow mushrooms. It's not dirt, but it's not bad. What do I know about dirt, anyway? I'd like to be mushrooms. They may not look like much, but they've lived a noble life.

"This planet was forfeit after the battle was won. There are rebel encampments here and it isn't safe. You know it's illegal for you to be planetside." The marine's comms are clean; no buzz and no static.

"LU5 was declassified as a planet. It's a celestial dwarf now, according to your Queen." I try to keep it steady, act like I'm just a punk kid with an attitude. Nothing more.

The one closest to me smacks my helmet with their armored glove, hard. My head rocks and I smash my teeth and lips against the visor. I see blood there before I taste it. I struggle not to fall.

"She's *your* Queen, too, you fucking spacerat. Show me your tag."

I produce my identification tag and hold my breath while they scan it. It's correct; I've never tried to falsify my ID. I have to do this in plain sight, Dad told me over and over again.

I always think this will be the moment. They've figured me out and there's a warrant in the system for me. They found Dad's body somewhere and he had something incriminating on him. Seconds tick by. The winds on LU5 never die down.

The marine reads the results to the others, rather than to me. "Verdi. *Mehetabel.* Clean." To me, he says, "You belong in your can, never touching the surface of any rock. You're not like us. We are earning our homeworld."

The other helmets nod; this is their catechism.

"We were born in space, but we will die on the ground, with honor. We will watch the suns nurture our crops and feed our grandbabies. Rebels and traitors and nobodies like you deserve nothing but synth G and endless darkness. You hear me?"

I'm nodding. If I try to talk, I'll cry. I think for just a moment about telling them how old I am. About how old I was when Dad taught me the secret of the sauce recipe, before the paper was sucked into space. I'm the only one who knows now; it's not recorded anywhere. It can't be. I think about my tomatoes, back on the *Mehetabel.* The UV lights that are my suns. I swallow and stand up straighter for my adopted mushrooms. My babied, nurtured sourdough starter. I have to go home to them. Someone does. I am the only one who can do this work.

"I understand." My voice sounds better than I thought it would.

Silence for a few beats. "We don't want to see you here again."

There's nowhere else to get mushrooms. Nowhere at all. I put my hands down and nod. I spit blood inside my helmet. "Of course. With your permission, I'll return to my ship."

"We'd never hear the end of it if we hurt the pizza boy," one of them says mockingly.

"He might be the last one. How long's it been since you saw another?"

The last one they knew was my father. I'm certain of it.

"Shit, sectors ago. I was a little girl. Not even shaving yet."

"You barely shave now, XKE."

"Eat shit."

The one with the blaster gestures at my trove of purple mushrooms. "If you eat these, you pretty much already do."

Their conversation has nothing to do with me. I return and clip myself to the ribbon that will pull me back up to my scooter.

I wish I knew their ship. I wish they had to print their registry on their suits, or identify themselves at all. XKE. Like that's useful. I never want to deliver to those marines. But I guess they're all the same. And I can't call attention to myself.

Back on the *Mehetabel*, it's easier to be busy than to be mad or scared. I drop my kit and my suit in the tomato corridor and go to the galley in just my underthings.

The starter has to be fed every day. I've used flour from every grain in the galaxy; tough, rough-milled brown stuff and fine, pale rich-people silt. I've used flour they said was made from grass that grew on a turtle's back and yeast I cultivated in a bag from dried fruit and wine I salvaged after a party cruiser collided with a fuel freighter. The whole time I thought the fuel might ignite, but I saw floating bags of yellow fruit leather, bound together in a cargo net. It was worth it. If I go out in the instant of a blue-white-hot fuel explosion with exotic fruits in my hands, what's better than that?

Nothing is better than this moment. My hands punch down and roll the dough, just like Dad taught me. The microbes that grow on my hands are his and my mother's. Some of them have been with me since our last cat, Nedjeb, died. Microbes carry everything. They don't speak, but they swallow all of history. They're like mushrooms that way. Like me.

The dough is stretched and oiled and I have crusts for tonight and tomorrow. The starter has grown and bubbled, and I put it lovingly back into the bowl it has always lived in, since before my grandfather. It's crazed, whitish old polymer-made trash. Ancient. The markings on the bottom are in a script I can't read, including a strange symbol of a triangle made out of arrows. To me, it means that the starter that makes the bread makes the starter. The dead who plant the spores that feed the mushrooms that make the spores. Everything is a cycle like that.

Delivering pizza is a cycle. The orders come in over the comm and I tell them I'm out of mushrooms tonight. I have a good dry salami and the means to shave it thinner than a hair. I'll make it last, and the engines' heat will make it crisp. This batch of sauce turned out great. I'll deliver to them, even the marines. I'll take their creds and I'll drink shitty grain alcohol in some illicit asteroid bar, listening to hear if someone knows a mycologist. Or a cave-diver. Somewhere else in this system there are mushrooms. I know it.

Rebellion is a cycle, too. Imperial power creates its own enemies, which will bring it down one day. It leaves behind its own forgotten arsenals, ready to be reclaimed. It puts out the spores of the mushrooms that will one day flourish on its corpse. There's no receiver in the scooter, so I just sing to myself.

After nearly twelve hours, I can return to the *Mehetabel*. It's tiring, and I am so weary of identifying myself to docking clerks while my best work gets cold, even in the insulated delivery pods. Dad used to tell stories about delivering planetside, right to portals and gates, seeing the person who took their pizza smile and look right at him. Maybe one day the QA will leave this system and I'll be able to do that again. Maybe I'll touch dirt and see what Dad was so excited about.

I made enough sauce for a few slow days, so I don't have to bother the tomatoes for a while. That's fine—they like to be left alone. They grow best when I keep the UV dial about halfway up and let them do their thing. I think about the coordinates encoded in their DNA, how important it is to the rebels inside the QA. Dad said there was no other way to get it to them that hadn't been figured out. This one was safe because we kept it secret. It was my job to keep it now.

Walking down the short corridor to where they grow, I thought hard about the mushrooms. There had to be another way to get some. Mushrooms on a pizza means the praetor is retreating from the resistance front, being driven back. When they ask me how I can be out of mushrooms, how could I forget, I know what they're asking. They want better news. The sea cheese dealers who received the last signal told me that he was in retreat again. They tell me this by the weight of their cheese plugs. More than a kilo each and the praetor is being pushed back. We have never said this out loud. We don't share a language. This was all I inherited. I read the number on the scale and I sigh, good news or bad. We never know who's watching.

And tonight, the pizzas must have mushrooms. They just have to. I've saved a few dried ones for emergencies. That will have to do for now.

In the wet and warm of my grow-room, my eyes adjust to the light. I forgot that I dropped my kit in here, after I lost the mushrooms on LU5. The bag is made from skin; something my dad killed or bought from a butcher, who knows. Probably soaked in my old sweat, and his. I guess it's as good as a corpse. And I guess some spores found their way into it in those few seconds when we were close. I can see the tiny pink spots that prefigure the growth of purple mushrooms.

I go to the kitchen and get some scraps. Any organics will do, right? I open the mouth of the bag and nestle something that will rot into the folds. I put an old pod over it to shield it from the tomatoes' UV.

I stand up in the light of my own little suns and I smile at the battered pod that gives shade to my mushroom spores. I find my vacuum-sealed bag of dried mushrooms that will do for tonight. Even if it's just one per pie, that will be enough to carry the message.

These spores will grow into purple mushrooms and give off spores of their own. That's their place in the cycle.

Being the pizza boy is mine.

P. DJÈLÍ CLARK

If the Martians Have Magic

FROM *Uncanny*

The first Martian War was won not by man, but microbes. The second we fought with Martian weapons that nearly broke the world. The third invasion we stopped by our own hands, using magic.
　　—Wei-Yin Sun, Imperial Historian in the Court of the Empress Dowager, Restoration Period

MARRAKESH'S STREETS WERE a dizzying affair at any time. But at midday they were unbearable, a churning morass that moved to their own rhyme and reason. And though Minette called the city a second home, navigating its roads was a feat of skill, luck, and perhaps, she was willing to admit, sheer stupidity. She dodged a rider on a high-wheeled electric velocipede and rounded about a diesel trolley—only to be brought up short by a young woman who stood in the middle of the busy thoroughfare, beseeching a stubborn goat to follow. Yet no matter how hard she pulled the taut leash, it would not move. The girl yelled, then begged. But the goat only bleated its obstinacy, having decided to start its revolution here and now. Minette slowed to watch, momentarily lost in the goat's stubborn cries—and was nearly run over by a rickshaw. A tall dromedary pulling the two-wheeled hooded vehicle of gilded iron pulled up short, jostling its two occupants. Both gasped, their sculpted eyebrows rising above long overlapping rose-colored veils. But it was the camel that turned an irritated glare Minette's way.

"Mind where you're going!" it brayed, making a gesture with its split upper lip she knew for a curse. Minette frowned at the discourteous display, and with a suck of her teeth shot back a curse in Kreyòl. The camel's eyes widened at the unfamiliar words and it might have said something in return, but she had already moved on.

Of all the creatures gifted sentience with the return of magic, the good God Bondye alone knew why those rude beasts were chosen. But that was the way of magic, unpredictable in its movements, its choices and ceaseless permutations. That's what all of this was about—why she'd canceled morning classes and now rushed to a meeting to which she wasn't invited. Because someone had to speak for the unknowable in magic, the nonlinear, the indefinable.

Someone had to save her Martians.

She stopped out of breath, just across from the Flying Citadel. The stone fortification sat atop a jagged rock that floated like an unmoored mountain peak high in Marrakesh's skyline. Its ivory walls and gold domes looked stolen out of time—or perhaps beyond it—spreading a shadow on the streets below where hawkers sold magic rope and enchanted rugs to gullible tourists along with more useful thaumaturgical devices. A fleet of lavish vehicles were parked nearby: wheeled automobiles driven by golden metal men; air balloons of giant puffer fish that pulled at their anchors; and gilded carriages drawn by fantastic beasts. One of them, a spotted ocelot large as a horse, lapped a blue tongue against its fur and held up a snow-white wing like a canopy beneath Marrakesh's glaring sun. The vehicles bore insignia from over a dozen nations, evidence that the Council was indeed meeting.

Minette swore. Looking around she caught sight of a few taxis, ferrying tourists up to the citadel by way of flying carpets. Absurd. Fortunately, she had other methods. Closing her eyes, she composed a quick prayer.

The loa could be persuaded to answer the call of a Mambo in need—as drawn up in the new understandings (they bristled at mention of the word *contract*) that now administered interactions with their priests. All part of bringing them more devotees in this modern world, where spirits and gods walked unbidden, ever competing for the attention of mortals. Of course, the loa acted in their peculiar time, and followed their own interests—new understandings or no.

After two attempts, she was set to call again when the image of a man in a broad-brimmed hat flashed across her thoughts. He held a mahogany smoking pipe precariously between pursed lips, and his leisurely gait resembled a dance. Legba, the Keeper of Roads, opening the Door. A flaming ram followed. Bade's sign, who she truly wanted. His presence stirred against her with the weight of a feather and the pressure of a mountain all at once. She hashed out a quick agreement—some offerings to perform, a drapo to commission—and was fast swept up in gusts of air. An accompanying rumble of thunder startled those below. Bade's twin, Sobo. The two were inseparable and you didn't get one without the other.

Bade kept to the pact, sending Minette soaring up to the Flying Citadel. Looking down she saw the winged ocelot had paused its cleaning and now stared up at her with four red sapphire eyes. She shook her head. The powerful and their toys. On a draft of wind accompanied by peals of thunder like drums she rose higher still, above rounded minarets, to reach the citadel's upper levels.

Her feet struck stone and she stumbled once before breaking into a run along a lengthy parapet, holding the ends of her white dress up so as not to trip. She moved into a passageway, easily slipping through a set of wards meant to deter interlopers. Aziz's work, and predictable as always. Well, wasn't he in for a surprise. She stopped at reaching a red door inscribed with repeating calligraphy. Taking a breath to collect herself—it did no good to look hurried—she tightened the white cloth that wrapped her hair, adjusted her spectacles, and (remembering to release the grip on her dress) stepped inside.

The Council on Magical Equilibrium was a rare gathering. And, as it was, featured an impressive who's who, and what's what, from across the world. Some faces Minette recognized. Some she couldn't see, and others she didn't know at all. Each however turned from where they were seated about a curving table to stare at her entrance. Aziz, who sat at its center, broke off his words entirely.

"Minette?" His call came too familiar for colleagues. He must have realized as much because he coughed into a waxed mustache before starting again. "Please excuse the interruption. May I introduce Professor Francis. She teaches here at the Academy and comes to us from Port-au-Prince—"

"Port-au-Prince!" a small slender woman in a crimson gown repeated in a throaty slur. A veil of swirling gray mist obscured her face, all but her eyes—black on black pools, deep as a fathomless sea. "Aziz, you did not tell us the Academy held a Mambo in res-

idence. I see no distinct loa hovering about you. One of the Un-
bound then?" She craned her neck and inhaled deeply. "Oh! But
the magic in you is no less for that." Those black eyes narrowed
hungrily, and Minette fought the urge to step back. It was unwise
to show weakness to their kind. They remembered that.

"Professor Francis is one of our most *valued* researchers," Aziz
interjected, seeming to sense the danger. "She has done wonders
with Martian-human interactions. She was the one who first made
the—ah—discovery."

Minette raised an eyebrow. Were they so afraid to just come out
and say it?

Another woman at the table gave a derisive snort. She looked
older than Minette by a decade or more. But the body beneath her
burgundy military uniform was solid, and the dark hands folded
before her thick and scarred. If the number of medals decorating
her breast was anything to go by, she knew how to use those hands
too. She pinned Minette with the one eye not covered by a black
patch—an owl examining a mouse—and flared her generous nostrils.

"And," Aziz went on, "though the professor is one of our finest
faculty, I don't recall her being summoned to this meeting." That
last part was said with an unspoken *and you should leave now*. But
Minette hadn't come this far to be scolded. She tried to ignore the
gazes of the two women and stepped forward.

"Apologies, Director Aziz. And to this Council," she began, re-
citing what she'd hastily rehearsed on the run here. "I only learned
you were meeting this morning and thought my expertise might
be valuable. I'm certain my absence was an oversight." She met
Aziz's gaze squarely at that. It was petty of him not to invite her.
But rather than taking up the challenge, his eyes creased with concern. That only annoyed her further.

"Well, she certainly is direct," the mist-faced woman slurred. "I
for one would like to hear what the Mambo has to share. I say
she stays. Any objections?" None around the table gave a reply—
though the one-eyed woman shrugged indifferently. Aziz put on a
resigned look, beckoning Minette to sit.

"Come, Mambo, whose scent of magic is sweet enough to taste,"
the mist-faced woman purred. "You may sit near me." She patted
an empty chair with a long-fingered hand, pale as alabaster. Those
depthless eyes looked even hungrier.

Minette politely declined the offer three times (any less was just inviting trouble) and took a chair several seats down—feeling peculiarly conscious of her smallness between a broad giant in a blue turban and a fiery djinn encased inside a towering body of translucent glass.

"We were discussing," Aziz began anew, "what we are to do with the three entities following the recent revelations."

Minette's heart drummed. There it was. "There's only one," she spoke up. Heads—and other things much like heads—swiveled back to regard her. "You're calling Them three, but there's actually only the One."

Aziz blinked but then nodded at the correction. "Yes, of course. Professor Francis is referring to how the Martians see themselves. Three are required to form their collective consciousness, and then They become One. The professor is one of the few non-Martians to successfully join a triumvirate."

"Join?" It was the one-eyed woman. She now glared incredulous. "So you allow the beasties into your head?"

Minette paused, trying to place that English accent. "They aren't beasts," she replied. "They're sentient beings, like us."

The one-eyed woman's laugh was brusque. "So you say, Professor. But I've grappled with them face-to-face, not all tame like in your lab." She tapped a finger at her missing eye. "And they're damn beasts if I ever seen one."

Aziz coughed again. "Professor Francis, this is General Koorang. She's here representing the Nations League Defense Forces."

Minette's eyes widened. *The* General Koorang? Who had broken the Martians at Kathmandu? So, that accent was Australian then. No wonder the woman was so hardline.

"In my time in the triumvirate," she tried diplomatically, "I've found Them to be capable of many emotions. They have been kind, even gentle."

General Koorang sputtered. "Kind? Gentle? Is that why they set about invading us *three* times?"

"Not every Martian was a soldier," Minette reminded, speaking as much to the others gathered. "The One I joined with were worker drones. They never even saw fighting. That's why it was so easy for the Central Intellect to abandon Them in the retreat."

"And what did they *work* on?" the general asked, unmoved. "Was it their stalking dreadnoughts? Their infernal weapons what almost blew us to hell? Come visit the Archipelago sometime, Professor, and I'll show you Martian gentleness."

Minette bit her lip to keep from replying. That was unfair. The Archipelago was all that was left of what used to be Australia. The waters of the South Sea were mostly off-limits now: teeming with monsters that wandered in through torn rifts between worlds. That it was humans playing with Martian weapons who had brought on the disaster seemed to matter little to the general.

"Perhaps we should get back to the heart of the matter," Aziz suggested, breaking the tense silence. "We must decide what is to be done with the entities, um, Them, in light of Professor Francis's discovery."

Minette felt a flurry of annoyance. Were they going to dance around this all morning? "By discovery, you mean that Martians can perform magic," she blurted out. Her words sent up murmurs through the Council. Aziz gave her an exasperated look. The general cursed. And the mist-faced woman's eyes creased with a hidden smile.

Minette took the moment to press on. "What we should do with them is clear. They are a conscious soul, protected within the Nations League Charter on Magical Practitioners drawn up over a decade ago in 1919. They should be encouraged to develop those talents."

"Outrageous!" General Koorang roared, her face a thunderhead. "The Charter wasn't made to protect bloody Martians!"

"But it does not exclude them," the mist-faced woman interjected. "The Charter was made quite broad in its application—as evidenced by the makeup of this very Council."

"Precisely," Minette said, seizing on the opportunity. "We already accept a diverse world of spirits, gods, and no end of magical beings. The previous head of this Council was a minotaur, and she served with distinction. How is this any different?"

"A point of clarification," a squat shaman at the far end of the table called, raising a hand that rattled with ivory bracelets. "The Charter the professor references was created to protect unique magical abilities in their nascency. Have these Martians exhibited some magical talent indigenous to their . . . kind?"

"Not yet," Minette admitted. "But I believe it's only a matter of time," she followed quickly. "The triumvirate I share, They claim Mars once had magic. But it's been lost, much as humanity lost it once, too concerned with our factories and industry. Through the rituals to the loa, they've shown that they can understand and practice magic—something we once thought impossible. They're on the verge of self-discovery. We should allow them that right."

"Martians don't have any rights as citizens," General Koorang countered. "They're not even from this world. Just because the Academy lets you keep a few as pets, doesn't change the fact that these creatures are prisoners of war."

Minette clenched her fists to keep calm. "We aren't at war, general."

The older woman leaned forward, imposing in her size. "Oh? Did we sign some peace treaty that I'm unaware of? Is there a Martian consulate? A Martian ambassador?"

Minette pressed on, counting in her head to keep calm and trying to forget she was arguing with a living legend. "The Martians invaded three times, precisely three years apart, on the exact same day. The last war was in 1903. It's been more than thirty years, and we've seen no sign of another invasion."

The general smacked the table heavily and Minette was proud that she didn't jump. "Damn right! Because we beat the hell out of them last time! And we did it with magic. That's our greatest defense, the one thing their calculating overgrown minds can't understand. And you just go ahead and give it to them." She shook her head, that single eye glowering. "I expected more, from a Haitian."

Minette felt her face flush at the insult. The houngan Papa Christophe had been the first to use magic in the Third War, halting the Martian dreadnoughts and sending their armies into disarray. The rout at Cap-Haïtien set an example for the world. She was fiercely proud of that fact and didn't need reminding—not like this.

"I didn't give them magic," she said tersely. "They were drawn to the loa and the loa to them. None of us have the right to stop this development." She turned her appeal to the wider Council, moderating her tone. "I'm not just being an idle academic here. I'm not insensitive to all of your concerns. I understand the suffering the Martians caused this world. But I believe there's a practical side to all of this."

The general folded her arms and struck the posture of someone politely suffering a fool, but Minette continued. "The rediscovery of Martian magic could be a new step for all of us. A new magic system built on Martian ingenuity. Think of all the possibilities! The Martians here on Earth could become valued citizens, sharing what they know. If Mars invades again, as the general believes, we would have a valuable Fifth Column ready to come to our defense. What if this curtails their appetite for conquest? What if it helps them find themselves again, the way we have? We should seize this opportunity to integrate them into society, not shun it."

"Or we should be frightened," General Koorang grumbled. She spared a glance for Minette before turning to the Council. "The professor's determined, I'll give her that. But let's say she's right, and there's some old Martian magic waiting to be tapped. What happens when they rediscover it? Can we trust they won't give it up to protect their own kind? The last three invasions decimated the old powers of this world. Europe's a blasted-out hellhole that might never recover. We're barely managing that refugee crisis as it is. I for one have seen enough of Martian *ingenuity*. When the fourth invasion comes—and it *will* come—do we want to look up to see new Martian dreadnoughts powered by magic marching across Cairo, New Èkó, or Delhi?" She let her one eye latch on to every gaze before continuing. "I'm a soldier, not a diplomat. Thinking about peace isn't my job, and I'll admit I'm no good at it. But I know how to keep us safe. First rule of military defense: deny your enemy any chance of mounting a challenge. The professor's admitted these Martians haven't found their lost magic yet. She says we should give them time. Well I say we use that *time* to stop this threat in its tracks. Now—before it goes any further. Because allowing these Martians to have magic is a risk we can't afford."

Minette felt the weight of those words, settling down with the force of a hammer. So, it seemed, did the rest of the Council. Fear, it turned out, was a potent weapon of its own. And General Koorang was as skilled in persuasion as she was on the battlefield. When the motion was made to declare the prospect of Martian magic "a threat to global security and magical equilibrium," not one voice rose in dissent.

The beat of drums guided Minette's movements. About the room, the loa that had been invited into the Hounfour danced along. Others like Papa Loko only sat watching. The First Houngan had been convinced by his wife to accept the Rada rites of this new world. Now he kept strict governance to see they were properly followed. He was especially taken with the Martians.

With their bulbous heads, it was easy to at first mistake them for giant octopuses. But where an octopus was reduced to flimsy sacks of flesh out of water, Martian bodies were quite sturdy. Their skin was pale, verging on a dull violet that extended the length of sixteen thick tentacles, the latter of which were remarkably malleable. At the moment, they intertwined like roots to form the semblance of a man beneath each head—with arms, legs, and even a torso.

Two of the triumvirate moved gracefully to the song, swaying in hypnotic undulations. A third used myriad tentacles to beat a steady rhythm on a batterie of conical drums, matching the rattling shells of Minette's asson. On the ground, Papa Damballah's veve lay etched in white. He sat as a white serpent, coiled about his shrine and the feast prepared for him: an egg on a mound of flour, bordered by white candles, white flowers, and white rice. His red eyes watched the writhing limbs of the Martians and swayed with them. A current filled the room, and it felt as if they were no longer within this plane, but some other realm of existence where every star in the cosmos danced.

Then it was done, and she was back in the room at the Academy she'd transformed into her own Hounfour. She let herself fall, weakened after housing the loa. Martian arms caught her, strong but gentle, leading her to sit. They sat in turn about her, keeping their semi-human forms and regarding her with round, silver eyes that never blinked. A tentacle extended to wrap warm and sinuous about her wrist: an invitation to join the triumvirate. Still flush from the loa, she accepted.

"That was . . . nice," came the harmonious voices in her head. They layered each other: the three that were One.

"Wi," she answered back, also in her head. The Martians had mouths, sharp beaks like birds. But their speech was beyond human ears. This was much easier.

"Nou danse kont danse nou," They remarked, switching between English and Kreyòl much as she did. "I am very fond of Papa Damballah."

Minette didn't find that surprising. Damballah was the Great Creator of all life, peace, and harmony. He was also the protector of those who were different. It made sense that the Martians would be drawn to him, and he to Them.

"You are quiet," the voices noted. "Sa ou genyen?"

"Mwen regret sa," she apologized. "My mind is elsewhere."

"On your meeting with the Council."

Minette frowned at her lapse, building up her mental guards. In the triumvirate, your mind was an open book if you weren't careful.

"Aziz was there," They said, catching a stray thought. "Was it difficult seeing him again? Much time has passed since the two of you last coupled. But your feelings for him remain disordered. Perhaps the two of you should couple again?"

Minette flushed, absently pulling her dress more tightly about her. An open book indeed. "Non. I won't be coup—intimate, with Aziz again. I explained before, nou te mal. We let things get out of hand." He was married, for one. And they'd collected too many gray hairs between them to be getting on like schoolchildren.

"I have made you uncomfortable," They said contritely. "Mwen regret sa. I am not always aware."

"It's not your fault. I just . . ." She sighed. There was no easy way to say this. So instead she let down her guard. Her memories of the past morning flowed to the triumvirate at the speed of thought. The Council meeting. The debate. The final decision. They examined each recollection and in the silence that followed, Minette waited.

"Your Council is frightened," the voices said finally.

"Wi," she replied in frustration. "It's disappointing they give in to their fears."

"Their reasoning is not unsound."

Minette's alarm reflected back to her in six silver eyes. "How can you say that? It's preemptive nonsense. They're punishing you for something you might do—not what you've done. It's wrong!"

There was a pause as three heads cocked as one, considering her statement. "I do not say I welcome their verdict. But the fear is understandable. My people have not been kind to your world. Even you were frightened of my kind once."

Minette's memories intruded without invitation. She had been a girl of thirteen during the Third Martian War. She remembered hiding in the shelters of Gonaïves with Grann Louise, who whispered assurances that Papa Toussaint and Papa Dessalines would not allow the island to be invaded again. She had grown up with all the fears about Martians, until attending university and becoming fascinated with courses on them. She'd jumped at the chance to study with the three housed here at the Academy, even if in faraway Marrakesh. It had taken her a while to see them as more than "specimens," and even longer to see them as less than monsters. But it was difficult to convince others to understand Them as she did.

"You've read my thoughts," she said. "You know what they plan to do."

"Separation," the voices whispered.

The word struck Minette as hard as the first time she'd heard it. General Koorang had called for euthanasia. But the Council balked. What they proposed, however, was little different, and perhaps crueler. Martians abhorred individualism. Separated, They would lose their single consciousness: effectively cease to be. Like cutting a human brain into three separate parts. It was a murder of the soul, if not the flesh.

Her guilt pulsed through the bond. "If I hadn't introduced you to the loa none of this might have happened. Li se fòt mwen."

"Non!" The sharpness of the voices startled her. "This isn't your fault. You have given my time in captivity meaning. I would not undo this, even at the rescue of my life." There was a pause. "I have something to show you. Es'ke ou ta vle promnen?"

Minette frowned at the question. Go for a walk? But she gave a tentative mental nod of acceptance. She barely had time to brace herself before their combined consciousness enveloped her whole. The world broke apart, shattered, then reduced to a pinpoint of light before expanding everywhere at once—taking her with it. When she found her bearings again, she stood on the edge of a calm moss-green sea. Strange plants tall as trees rooted in the russet soil, with wide blue petals opened to a sky blanketed by clouds.

"Do you like it?" They asked. The three that were One stood about her, their human forms abandoned, and tentacles gliding freely just atop a field of mustard-colored grass. The air here was thick, almost viscous, so that she could feel it hugging her skin. Above them, a flock of featherless creatures soared on broad flat wings that looked more like flippers.

"Se bèl!" she breathed. "What is this place?"

"Home," They answered, with longing in their voices.

Minette gaped. Mars? But how? They had shown her their world in similar mental visions before, taken her to the sprawling subterranean mechanical cities, to the magma fields beneath the birthing catacombs and to the hanging megaliths that housed the technocratic Central Intellect. But the surface of that Mars was lifeless, scoured sterile by the relentless march of Martian industry.

"This is how it was before," They explained, hearing her unspoken thoughts. "The memory lay within me, passed on by forebears millions of years dead, for no consciousness truly dies. The loa awakened it again. And awakened this."

There was a wave of tentacles, and from them flowed a ripple through the air.

Minette gasped. They were symbols and patterns of a multihued cascade, with dimensions that defied description. She reached to touch one with a finger, and the sound of hundreds of chimes trembled the world. In a rush, it all vanished and she was back at the Academy.

"Was that . . . ?" She couldn't even finish.

"The magic of my people," They replied.

"You've recovered it?"

"That is difficult to say," They answered. "I have been trying. But it is not easy working with something from which I have been so long separated. It is alien to me and will take time to understand."

Minette sighed wearily. But there was no time. Once the Council moved to separate the Three, the possibility of Martian magic would die before it even had a chance to begin. "Do what you can," she told Them. "And if there's a way I can help, you must let me know." She was set to say more when a tremor shook her. She turned with the triumvirate to look to the door, sharing their preternatural senses.

"Someone has come to see you," They said.

Minette withdrew from the One, returning to her singular consciousness and feeling suddenly very alone—her mind still ringing with what had just been uncovered. She was prepared to tell whoever it was to go away. Between housing the loa and joining the triumvirate, her body was weakened almost to the point of exhaustion. But it was rare they received visitors. Fear lanced through her. Was this the Council? Had they come for her Martians already? Gripped with trepidation, she forced herself up on wobbly legs and made her way from the room through the hallway. Reaching a door, she paused to lean against it for strength before pulling it open to reveal a stone courtyard where the Martians were allowed access once a day—and found an unexpected sight.

It was a six-wheeled white carriage, pulled by a giant winged ocelot—the very same she had seen beneath the Flying Citadel. The door to the conveyance opened and the haughty beast turned to regard her with four sets of expectant sapphire eyes. Hesitant, Minette stepped forward and climbed inside. Naturally, the carriage was larger within than without, revealing a room lit by flickering tallow candles. At the far end of a long black lacquered dining table sat a familiar figure in a high-backed red chair.

"Greetings, Mambo," the mist-faced woman slurred. "Please, you will sit?"

Minette remained standing. Such offers had to be thought through.

"You may put away any fears, Mambo. True enough, your delectable magic is like sugar to me. It is why I have placed such distance between us—to avoid temptation."

Minette weighed that. She could walk out now. But curiosity gnawed. What was a council member doing here? "I accept that and no more," she said sitting.

"And no more," the small woman agreed.

"Your visit is unexpected."

"Of course. That is why it is a *secret* visit." She placed a shushing finger to the place where her lips might have been. "I have come to save your Martians."

Minette sat stunned. "But you voted with the others."

The woman waved dismissively. "That cause was lost before it began, Mambo. General Koorang will have her way. But perhaps you can have yours. My sisters would like to take in you and your Martians. We would offer them sanctuary, away from the prying eyes of the Nations League."

For a moment, Minette only stared. Sanctuary? "Where?" she finally managed.

The woman wagged a scolding finger. "A secret, scrumptious scented Mambo, would be less so if I told you. But I am willing to provide passage to this place."

A hundred hopes flared in Minette before she smothered them with doubt, remembering who (and what) this creature was. "Why? Why do you care about Them?"

"Why, for the magic," the mist-faced woman admitted openly. "My sisters and I make no pretenses to our desires. We devour magic, savor its many essences. The possibility of Martian magic is most appealing! So exotic and untried. How we would like to taste it!"

Minette grimaced. There was always a price. "So you just want to eat them—drain them of magic."

The woman sighed. "Our kind are too maligned in your fairy tales, Mambo. Contrary to those stories, we are not like the boy with the goose and the eggs of gold. We would not deplete something so precious as to not see its like again. Think of this as an exchange. We offer sanctuary. In turn, we take only small bits at a time—as one would any delicacy."

Minette's stomach turned. Bon mache koute chè, she thought darkly. Like soucouyant she'd known back home, these vampiresses couldn't be trusted. That was certain. But a secret place, where her Martians could be together, and They could explore their newfound magic. That couldn't be dismissed out of hand. Her mind worked anxiously. There had to be a way. She had negotiated agreements with loa and demigods. She could handle this.

"You will promise by heart, head, and soul that no lasting harm will come to either myself or the Martians in your care," she stated. "We will hash out a binding compact with a fair exchange between us and your sisters, where any offer of their magic is willingly given. Any breach of our agreement and I will have each of your names."

Those black eyes above the misty veil narrowed to slits, and Minette thought she heard a low hiss. A minor gale picked up, bending the flames on the candles. To demand the names of their kind was as good as asking them to offer up their cold, barren souls. The mention alone was offensive. Minette held fast, however, a few choice charms at the ready in case she needed to make a hasty exit. But the gale fast subsided and the woman slurred pleasantly, if also a bit tight: "Heart, head, and soul. Or our names be given." Her eyes creased into a smile. And Minette had the distinct feeling that beneath that misty veil awaited a mouth of grinning fangs. "Now, crafty little Mambo, let us see to that agreement."

It was two days later that Minette walked Marrakesh's night market. The Souq was held beneath a full moon and spread out between alleyways and courtyards covered by colorful tents. Hawkers competed for customers, crying out their wares. Behind her followed three figures, two men and one woman. Some might have noted their odd gait: a glide just above the stone streets more than a walk. But in a city brimming with magic this was hardly worth a second glance. Not that a third or fourth glance would be able to penetrate the glamour now enveloping the three Martians.

They seemed to relish their freedom, casting human eyes in every direction. At the moment, they were taken by a guild of harpy artists whose talons inked henna that bled and slithered across the skin. Under other circumstances Minette might have been sympathetic to their gawping. But as it was, she simply wanted them to move faster.

The mist-faced woman had offered passage and sanctuary, but escaping the university was left to her. There was a dirigible waiting at the dockyards waiting to ferry them off. Minette just had to get them there. So far, that had been a success. Concocting a medsin that left the guards who watched over the Martians standing in an awake-sleeping state was simple. Now they only needed to reach their destination before the ruse was discovered.

As the four stepped from beneath a canopy, the dockyards became visible. And Minette dared to believe they just might make it. Until someone called her name.

"Minette?"

She went still as stone, heart pounding at the familiar voice. Turning, she found herself looking at Aziz. He was striding towards her hurriedly, four Academy guards at his heels. Beside him was another recognizable figure. She cursed. General Koorang.

Panic blossomed in Minette. She thought to shout for her charges to run. She would somehow allow their escape. But as she saw the rifles in the hands of the guards, she faltered. The second the Martians ran they would be cut down. Uncertain of her next move, she resolved to stand her ground as the group reached them.

"Didn't I tell you?" General Koorang declared boldly. "Didn't I say she'd try something like this? Your professor's spent too much time in her Martians' heads. Can't find her way out again. Good thing we had them watched."

Minette glared at Aziz. "You had me watched?"

"And for good reason it seems," he retorted. "Do you know how much trouble you're in?" He ran a hand over his mouth, the way he did when thinking hard, then leaned in close. "We can still fix this. We can say the Martians coerced you, did something to your head. Just get them to return. I'll talk to the general. Maybe your post can be salvaged—"

"I wasn't coerced," she said tightly. The nerve of him to think she was simply the dupe of someone else's machinations. He damn well knew her better than that. "I planned this, Aziz." The disappointment on his face only made her want to punch it.

"Enough for me," the general rumbled. She looked over the Martians still cloaked in their glamour. "Arrest her. Then take these creatures back to their cages. If they give trouble, use whatever force is necessary."

The four guards advanced. Minette glanced back to the dirigible meant for them, wanting to scream in exasperation at the nearness of freedom. So close! So infuriatingly close! Something slender and warm curled about her hand. She turned to one of the Martians, the unspoken request writ plain on that human mask. She consented, joining the triumvirate. The sound of drums flowed through their bond, the rattle of an asson, falling white petals, and the call to the loa of the batterie.

"Open the Door for me," the voices came.

"There's no time for this!" Minette said.

"Open the Door," the voices asked again.

She shook her head. "Now? I don't understand!"

"You asked how you could help. I think I know. The magic. I have been trying to make it work as a Martian. But I'm not a Martian anymore, am I? My magic was born of two worlds. It is that twoness I must embrace. Open the Door. Be our Mambo. And I will show you."

Minette looked into those unblinking human eyes that seemed to plead, and did as they asked. Her spirit moved in time to the music. And though she had no tobacco or fine things to give the doorman, she sang:

Papa Legba ouvre baye pou mwen, Ago eh!
Papa Legba Ouvre baye pou mwen,
Ouvre baye pou mwen, Papa
Pou mwen passe, Le'm tounnen map remesi Lwa yo!

Papa Legba came as called. There was a look in his eyes beneath that wide-brimmed hat that Minette had never seen before. He thumbed his pipe and instead of going his usual way, settled down to watch. In the bond, a mix of Kreyòl and Martian tongues sent a current flowing through Minette. One that she'd only recently felt before. Martian magic, both alien and exhilarating. It blended with the song, played along with the batterie and asson, merging her voice and spirit with the three Martians until all became One.

On the ground a symbol appeared all around them, drawn in ghostly white. Damballah's veve: serpents winding along a pole. The flows of Martian magic superimposed themselves upon it, creating multiple dimensions that folded and bent one on the other, calling on the loa who was their protector.

Papa Damballah appeared. But not like Minette had ever seen.

This Damballah was a being made up of tentacles of light, intertwined to form the body of a great white serpent. And she suddenly understood what she was seeing. The loa met the needs of their children. Papa Damballah had left Africa's shores and changed in the bowels of slave ships. He changed under the harsh toil of sugar and coffee plantations. And when his children wielded machetes and fire to win freedom, he changed then too. Now to protect his newest children, born of two worlds, he changed once again.

Minette opened up to the loa and Martian magic coursed through her, erupting from her fingertips. The guards, General Koorang. and Aziz drew back as the great tentacles of Papa Damballah grew up from her, rising above the market tents as a towering white serpent: a leviathan that burned bright against the night. For a moment brief as a heartbeat—or as long as the burning heart of a star—it seemed to Minette she saw through the loa's eyes. The cosmos danced about her. It trembled and heaved and moved.

And then Damballah was gone.

Minette staggered, so weakened she almost fell.

Once again Martian hands caught her, lifted her, supporting their Mambo. She caught a glimpse of Legba and her thoughts reached out to him. *Had she seen another face of Papa Damballah? Or was this the birth of a loa? Something old, yet new and different?* But the Keeper of Roads didn't answer. He only smiled—as if to a child asking at the color of the sky. With a flick to the brim of his hat, he vanished.

Minette returned fully to the world to find Aziz staring. His face was rapt, gazing over both her and the Martians—and every now and again glancing skyward. He had seen Damballah. She looked about. All through the Souq, tongues had quieted as eyes watched both she and the Martians—gaping at the phantom glow in the night sky left in the loa's wake. They had all seen.

"Nice show you've put on," General Koorang growled. "Doesn't change anything." Her voice was brusque as usual. But something of it was less sure than before. Oh, she'd seen too. But this woman was too tough—too stubborn—to be quelled by even a passing god.

"Actually, this does change things." Minette turned in surprise to see it was Aziz. His voice tremored, but he turned to address the general. "The Martians have shown that they can create their own magic. You saw it. Felt it. Everyone did." He gestured to the gathered crowd. "That at the least allows them protection under the Nations League Charter."

General Koorang's jaw went tight. To his credit, Aziz didn't back down—though Minette was certain the woman could go through him if need be. The guards at her side looked on nervous and uncertain. Finally, something about the woman eased: an owl deciding perhaps there were too many mice to snare at once. She spared a withering glare for Aziz before eyeing Minette. "Do what you want with your Martians, professor, for now. Just you remember though, laws can be changed." Then turning on her heels she stalked off, shouldering her way through the crowd.

"She's right," Aziz said, releasing a relieved breath. "Things could be different by morning. The world will be different by morning." He nodded towards the waiting dirigible. "Wherever you were going, you should get there. At least until we can sort all this out." There was a pause. "I should have backed you."

"Yes," she told him. "You should have." And then, "Thank you." She thought she even meant it.

Not waiting for things to get awkward, she allowed herself to be helped by the Martians to the dirigible. Once inside, she slumped into a seat just as the craft lurched off the ground and watched their slow ascent into Marrakesh's night and down to where Aziz still stood. He grew smaller as the pulled away, melding into the city. Turning, she looked to the Martians that sat nearby. No longer wrapped in the glamour They regarded their mambo with silver eyes. Expectant eyes. There was more to show her.

When a tentacle extended in invitation, she gladly, eagerly, accepted.

And the Four became One.

Delete Your First Memory for Free

FROM *FIYAH*

THE BUS JERKS to a stop and I tighten my grip on the smooth metal bar. Doors open. More passengers.

Bodies hem me in, which makes me anxious, which makes me bite my nails. I maneuver the shredded bits with my tongue, push them out past my lips, pinch them between my fingers, slither my hand down to my side, flick the moist clippings to the floor.

I feel eyes. I think it's the lady in the beige knee-high boots. She must get on at one of the first stops 'cause she always has a seat. She's looking at her phone now, but she probably saw. White women are always pretending they don't see me.

I make myself stop biting my nails, look at my phone. Pull up Connext and expand my web of friends. Accept a request from Ava. The new link tugs the existing ones with Max and Ye-jun closer. A recommendation pops up. The picture makes my heart race:

Fatima. Sitting on a park bench, looking off to the side, light-brown skin warm in the sunlight. She's almost smiling.

I close out the pop-up, minimize the web, spend the rest of the commute trawling the feed for jokes. Trigger an ad that interrupts my music. A breathy voice, bland as pastel, offers a discount on my first visit.

"You have nothing to lose, Devin. Try what some are calling 'detox for your mind.' Satisfaction guaranteed."

I'm early to work so I can eat breakfast alone in the breakroom.

Someone says, "Hold the elevator!"

FUCK.

I press hold.

Nancy fast-walks over the threshold, smiles. *Ugh.* Every time I see her, I think about that time I joked about smoking pot. I know she remembers. Old people love it when you prove them right and—

Shit. She's saying something. Can't she see my earbuds?

"Sorry," I mutter, press pause, lose my bubble. "Didn't hear you."

Nancy laughs, quiet. "Oh, just good morning."

"Oh, yeah. G'morning." *Not polite enough.* I say, "Going to the karaoke thing later?"

"Yesss," she says, eyes bulging. A snake spotting a nest of eggs. "Are you?"

I would rather down a jigger of pus than hang out with my co-workers. "Can't. Already have plans."

I stopped trying to be New Devin after summer, when everyone was showing off their Cancun pics and telling me, "You just *have* to see Alaska someday," and "You don't know how much you don't know until you've traveled abroad." So I hide in my cubicle and no one invites me to lunch anymore. That's good. And that's bad.

I eat a rushed breakfast at my desk since Nancy is in the breakroom digging through the fridge and tutting about expired food. Brush crumbs off my keyboard, crank up the volume on my earbuds. The music turns to syrup in my brain.

Transferring data from one spreadsheet to another and digging up gold for some blue-blood motherfucker isn't saving the world, but I actually like my job. Minus the meetings.

I find an excuse to work through the first one, but the second one, just before end-of-day, is mandatory. Nancy and a guy whose name I can never remember talk about quarterly goals. I watch myself doodle on a notepad. Monster faces. *F* inside a heart. And *PANIC PANIC PANIC* stacked like bricks in the margin. The meeting finally ends with an enthusiastic reminder, "Everyone gets two free drinks at karaoke!"

On my way out, I tear the page from my notebook, ball it up, toss it in the trash, then pretend I need something I wrote on there, pluck it back out, pocket it to throw away at home.

I wanna bail on my plans. They're my friends so they'll understand, but since they're my friends it's good to spend time with them, right? And Fatima will be there . . .

That could be good. Or bad.

I leave work without saying goodbye to anyone. Bite my nails on the bus, skim the news for conversation starters, stress about happy hour.

"Hello," the hostess says. "Dining in?"

I nod.

"How many in your party?" She takes out one menu.

"Four. No, five."

She hides her shock, grabs four more menus, leads me to a table.

"Sorry, can we have a booth?" High backs so I can't feel the eyes.

She smiles and pivots to a booth. She'll tell the server I'm difficult.

I sit where I can watch the door and say, "THANK YOU." *Too much.*

She leaves the pile of menus but I ignore them. Checked yesterday when Ye-jun sent the address.

The server appears. I stare at the table, ask her for water and house vodka on the rocks. When the drinks come, I watch the door harder. Maybe they changed the plan and forgot to tell me?

I grimace through the first half of my vodka. Pull up Connext. Get hit with the "clear your mental clutter" ad again. *Am I getting this 'cause I searched for therapy?* Check my messages. He said 5:30. It's 5:30. I should text him but don't want to seem desperate.

I know Ye-jun from high school. We weren't friends or anything, but we had that part-of-the-minority awareness of each other. Me and a few other black kids even let him in on "the nod." We went to different colleges but linked through Connext. We both moved here around spring. Random. He invited me to a hangout at his place. I was trying to reinvent myself, so I accepted. All that's left of New Devin is an updated wardrobe, but Ye-jun keeps inviting me out and I don't want to fuck it up.

I finish the vodka. Chug the water. Play a puzzle game on my phone till 5:55. Time to text him.

Hi!—No. *Hola*—NO. *Hey. I'm here and*—backspace. *Hey, I've been here since*—backspace, don't be that person. *Hey, I'm at the restarant, but I haven't seen y'all come in. Did I get the time wrong or something?*

Reread. Nonchalant enough? Yeah. Hit send. See the typo and my heart does its favorite wiggle-out-of-my-chest dance. It blossoms, blooms, sends tendrils to steal my breath like that guy who grew a tree in his lungs. My worries are oak trees. Or maybe one of those paper trees with the peeling—

"Devin?"

I look up. Ye-jun is staring down at me, puzzled.

I can't find words.

"We're in the back." He points unnecessarily.

"Oh." I scramble to my feet. "I didn't . . ." 'Course I didn't.

I follow Ye-jun, cross paths with my server. She makes eye contact, but, again, I can't find words. I gesture at Ye-jun's back like "ain't this the darndest?"

She nods, says she'll tell the other server. I should tip extra.

My friends have a six-seater, and of course Ava and Max left a seat between them, and of course Fatima is across from them but in the corner and Ye-jun has the seat next to her so *ahhhhhhhhhh*. I take the seat next to Ye-jun. The note from work is a rock in my pocket.

I'm outside of myself. Maybe I should've eaten before the vodka.

I say, "Hi. Hi," to Max and Ava, who look like a department store ad for his-and-hers knit sweaters. Lean forward to look past Ye-jun. Fatima's staring into her water like it's doing something fascinating.

I give her a tiny wave even though she isn't looking. "Hey, Fatima."

She glances up, says a quick, quiet, "Hey, Devin," then goes back to her water. A lock of shiny dark-brown hair falls into her face.

I made a terrible joke the first time I met her. I don't remember the lead-up, but the punch line was "*naan*-sense." Fatima gave me that almost-smile, but I have a feeling she was offended. It's been four or five hangouts since then. She doesn't say much to me.

"You didn't see us, huh?" asks Max. Lieutenant Obvious. Give the man a medal.

I shake my head. "Yeah, no."

Ava makes a sound like a laugh got stuck in her throat. "Glad we found you! I told Ye-jun to message you. You're never late. Didn't I say that?"

Ye-jun shrugs. "We got off work early. I figured you would spot us."

"He should've messaged you."

"Ava . . ." says Max.

I mumble, "'S okay." *Please drop it.*

They do. Thank God. But all four of them work in education, so I'm stuck doing my spectating thing while they talk shop. Every so often Ye-jun tries to steer the conversation to a different topic, but it always circles back around.

I don't fight it. It's just nice to be around people. Sometimes. And I notice things.

Max looks at Ye-jun like he's candy. Or a sunset. Meanwhile, Ava looks at Max the same way *he* looks at Ye-jun. Max is bi, so she's not totally off-track, but his eye twitches whenever she spatters us with giggles. Ye-jun acts like he doesn't see any of this. I think he knows he's the center, doesn't want to throw the group off balance. And Fatima . . . well, I can't look at her without being too obvious, but she's quiet. Makes me feel less alone.

The food comes. Max blows on a steaming french fry while Ye-jun and Ava talk about video games. Every time they mention one I'm familiar with, my mouth opens, I suck in air, but nothing comes out. By the time my words are right, they've switched topics.

Eventually, Max catches my eye. "Have you ever gotten one of those?"

I frown. "Huh?"

"Fatima and I were talking about Connext ads. You know, the ones that are obnoxiously targeted?"

I blurt, "I keep getting ads for memory deletion." I should stop drinking.

"That's weird," Ava says.

Fatima speaks low, but my ears are tuned to her frequency. "I've seen those too."

Ye-jun asks, "What is this?"

"It's like a brain spa," says Max. "They attach wires to your head, you think of a bad memory, and they delete it."

"What?" Ava asks. "That can't be good for you."

Max rolls his eyes. "It would be illegal if it was dangerous."

I want to ask him if he's heard of cigarettes or alcohol.

"Guys," Ye-jun says, looking at his phone, "there's one not too far from here. Does anybody want to check it out?"

Ava gasps. "No."

Max makes an affirmative sound around a mouthful of fries.

"Y'all have fun with that," I say. "Gotta fold laundry." Don't wanna prove those ads right.

Then Fatima says, "I'd like to go."

Ye-jun leans forward to show Max something on his phone and suddenly I can see her. A thought escapes before I can finish it.

"So, you're uh . . . this is your kinda thing?"

Fatima shrugs. "It might be fun, to go as a group." Pause. "Are you sure your laundry can't wait?"

Health In Mind has a punch-you-in-the-face modern storefront. It's all gleaming silver and white granite and fuzzy chairs that hang from the ceiling like spider sacs.

"You guys sure about this?" Ava asks, eyes skittering over the window displaying posters of grinning, presumably satisfied, customers and the "menu" of options. I wish she'd chill. Her nervousness is making me itchy.

Max puts his arm around her shoulders and I watch her thoughts scatter. "You don't have to do it, Ava." He sounds sincere.

"No, I said I would. It's weird, but I'll do it." Then, more mumbly, "I just wish we were getting tattoos like normal drunk people."

As we all enter the "brain spa," me and Fatima exchange a glance. Her mouth is a tiny O as she takes in the decor. I ask her, "Ever done this before?"

"No," she says, "but I've thought about it."

I start to ask what memories she wants to get rid of, but it's my turn to check in. I sign a waiver that amounts to "this procedure is totally safe, but it's not our fault if you break your brain," then show the coupon from the Connext ad and leave a credit card for my tab. Even with the discount, I can only afford to delete three memories. I'll have to live with the rest.

A woman in gray scrubs, who I'd bet good money is not a medical professional, leads me to a private room with soft, blue overhead lighting. She puts a swim cap on my head—it's not really a swim cap, but it fits like one—and has me lie down in a white, oval pod that's basically an oversized tanning bed. She tells me I can get out or ring for help at any time, then closes the lid.

It's surprisingly roomy in the pod. Cushy too. Feels like I'm resting on a stack of pancakes.

The screen built into the dome lid comes to life, and a pleasant voice runs through the rules with accompanying animations:

Stay relaxed. You'll be asked twice before anything is deleted. It's basically impossible to delete anything vital but if you're worried you might have, call for assistance. Brains are tricky, so we can't promise results will last forever. If you know what's fucking good for you, you'll stay relaxed.

I spend a few minutes fidgeting. Tell myself to relax. Fidget. Shove open the lid. Get out. Pace around the room. How do people relax? Should've kept drinking. *Why isn't there a fucking chair?* Sit on the floor, cross-legged. I need to clear my mind. Close my eyes. Fatima's face. *"Naan-sense."* Open my eyes. Get back in the pod. Close the lid.

Fatima? High school? No. Smaller. Press "Ready." Think of Nancy and the Pot Incident. Wouldn't miss that one.

The pleasant voice says, "Please repeat memory." The words appear on the screen too.

I think about that day in the breakroom again.

"Verification."

The memory rushes through my mind, unprompted.

"4/20 should be a holiday if you ask me."

Nancy's pinched expression. She looks up from her tablet and says, "Hm?"

I take a bite of my sandwich.

I try to think about something else, but it clobbers its way to the front.

"4/20 should be a holiday if you ask me."

Nancy frowns, looks up from her tablet. "Hm?"

I bite into my sandwich, pretend I didn't say anything.

How is it—

"4/20 should be—"

"Yes!" I tell the pod. "That's it! Jesus . . ."

"Would you like to delete this memory?"

"Please."

"Yes or No?"

"Yes."

"Are you sure?"

"Yes."

A pause. A quick, almost painful shudder in my skull. The pleasant voice says, "Memory deleted."

My heart does its dance and my hands search for something to grip, slipping along the sides of the pod with a streaking sound.

"Would you like to delete another memory?"

The pod is too small, the dance is frenetic. This feels like when I wake up and expect the object I was holding in a dream to still be in my hand. I squeeze and grasp and grieve for the empty space.

"Would you like to—"

"Stop—"

"—recall the last memory you deleted?"

"Oh. Yes!"

"Are you sure?"

"Yes."

"There will be no additional cost should you choose to delete this memory again."

My brain gives a shiver and the memory rushes back. Nancy, the 4/20 joke. I break the surface of my panic and gulp the pod's filtered air. As if it knows I need a minute, the voice says nothing. The joke plays over and over in my mind. I wish I'd let it go, let it stay gone.

I say, "Hello?"

"Would you like to delete another memory?"

Now that I know what to expect . . . "Yes."

I take a deep breath. Press "Ready." Think of tenth grade.

I see the freshman I have a crush on. Maddy. Smart, funny. Pretty too. There's a five-minute break between periods so I pop into her classroom. She smiles at me, indulgent.

"Hey, D."

"Hi."

We chat. I'm awkward, but she laughs at the right moments.

Another freshman comes over, steps between us. I know him as Smug Prick. He cocks his head, gets in my face. "Why are you always coming in here?"

I can't find a witty response. "Why do you care?"

"Because you're always in here being weird. You're not even in our grade. What kind of loser doesn't have friends their own age?"

It goes unspoken that kids from his and Maddy's demographics don't typically socialize with kids from mine.

"I-I do." Glance at Maddy. She bites her lip.

Smug Prick steps closer, "Yeah? Then go hang out with your 'friends.'" He air quotes the last word.

I look at Maddy again. Thought we were friends. She finally puts a hand on Smug Prick's arm. "Come on. Stop it."

But my eyes are hot and I can't cry here. I say, "Whatever," and leave.
"Please repeat memory."

I run through it again, then tense up, waiting for the computer's intrusive repetitions.

Instead, there's an animation of a corkboard. Reminds me of my Connext web when it's all zoomed out, except the hundreds of links are colorful pins attached by thin yarn. Some of the pins have only one or two threads, others a handful. The green pin labeled "Your Memory" has more threads than I can count.

The pleasant voice says, "Our patented system works by blocking pathways leading to and from the targeted memory. I apologize, but this memory is too interconnected to be safely or effectively deleted. May I email you a list of Deep Memory Removal clinical trials that are currently enrolling subjects in your area?"

"Jesus."

"Yes or No?"

"Uh . . . no."

The animation fades out. "Would you like to delete another memory?"

A stubby fingernail finds its way to my lips, but I decide to try the Pot Incident again. At least I know that one works.

When the voice says, "Memory deleted," there's a hole but I don't panic. I recall the first time and I have to believe I got rid of something I didn't need or want. Feels like right after throwing up. I'm shaky, but it's a relief.

"Would you like to delete another memory?"

Back outside of Health In Mind, the five of us compare notes.

I deleted three memories, Ye-jun and Max two, Ava one. Fatima tops us all with six. That sounds intense, but if I had the money I would probably delete dozens.

For real, I should get serious about finding a therapist. I've been scared they'd tell me I was hopeless, but . . . maybe there's a chance. I'm feeling calm. At least, calmer than usual, and when I listen for it, the hum of my worries is so low it almost freaks me out.

Max reminds us that, as a test, we all agreed to forget his full name. I'm not surprised when he says the computer wouldn't let him do it. Identity is everything.

Ava punches his shoulder. "So what is it?"

"No way I'm telling *now*," says Max, laughing louder than usual. We're all louder than usual, even Fatima.

"Come on," says Ye-jun. "You have to tell us. For science."

Max groans but he can't resist Ye-jun, so he tells us. The name doesn't ring a bell for me, but Ava says, "Oh yeah. That time I stole your wallet."

And just like that, I can find it again. Not just the name, but the memory and agreeing to forget it.

Ye-jun's apartment. Ava playing keep-away with Max's license, shimmying and giggling and shrieking, "Maximillian Keene?" The rest of us laughing our asses off.

I should be disappointed—so many things I'd like to forget forever—plus something about the memory tingles like a sleeping limb, but now the hum is stronger, familiar. Though it's still quiet enough I can smile at Fatima. She gives a little smile back. I convince myself she means it.

I say, "You live east of the city, right? Does the 32 go your way?"

She nods.

"Wanna ride together?"

Me and Fatima pick inward-facing seats near the front of the empty bus. We leave a seat between us, and Fatima—who's not so quiet now—finishes telling me a story about college and an ex of hers.

"I don't have any exes," I say. "Only been on a few dates." *Fuck.* What made me say that?

"Really? But you're so . . ."

I risk meeting her eyes, begging her to keep going.

"Nice. And cute."

"Uh . . . so are you." The hum is SO loud.

She looks down. Mumbles, "Thanks."

Silence. The bus rolls past three empty stops.

Time presses on me. I don't want the night to end like this.

"That was weird, right? The memory place?"

Fatima perks up and we try to share our experiences at Health In Mind. We go over our decision-making processes. Follow thoughts that are like smoke. Conclude that maybe—possibly?—we both deleted something from the first time we met at Ye-jun's. At first we think it's Max's name, but no? No. The tingle's still there. I'm half-scared, half-excited to remember 'cause what if we deleted the same thing?

"I probably did somethin' foolish," I tell her.

"It could've been me," she says, shrugging. "I have a serious case of Foot-in-Mouth disease."

I bark a laugh, which startles her. "Sorry, it's just . . . I get that."

Fatima smiles. There's nothing *almost* about it. "Then let's forget it."

We ride in silence for a while. Whenever I look up, I see her reflected against the dark city beyond the window. A few times, I catch her peeking at me. I start to bite my nails but make myself stop. I put my other hand, palm up, a few inches into the space between us.

ELIZABETH BEAR

The Red Mother

FROM *Tor.com*

A PALL OF ash turned my red horse roan as he and I ambled between tuffs of old lava. Basalt fields spread on either side, dotted with burnt-orange or gray-green lichen. Flat flakes of ash drifted past the brim of my hat.

We were crossing a big flow near the Ormsfjoll, and the reek of sulfur in the air left both Magni and me over-eager to complete our trip. It couldn't be too much farther to the village. Magni's ears were pricked. His walk tended to rush into a tolt. I knew he had scented or heard other livestock that was still too far away for me to detect.

He knew that where there was livestock, there was fodder. He was thinking of grain and grass and company, and I couldn't blame him. It had been a long ride, and a lone horse is never comfortable. They're meant to be in the company of their own kind.

Some would snipe that this makes my horse the opposite of me.

Fair enough. I felt no need for company. I *did* need supplies, however, and—if it were to be had—information to complete my quest.

My journey was for kin-duty. I had an obligation to find my brother and give him the news that his name was cleared, his honor restored, and his exile ended. To that end, I had spun the threads of his fate by sorcery and was following them.

This was where they led.

The first sign of my return to civilization was a graveyard. The road passed through it, flanked on both sides by neat cairns. Some were marked with runestones; some stood uncommemorated. The li-

chen had grown over a few. But lichen grows slowly and most of
the graves stood barren, sad heaps of brown-black rock with the
sea in the distance behind.

Not long after, I came within sight of the village.

It wasn't a big village, Ormsfjolltharp, and I was in among it
almost as soon as I noticed it. Men and women working outdoors
turned to watch me as I rode past the two dozen or so houses. Turf
houses, some with goats or sheep grazing on roofs that looked
more like low hillocks than dwelling-places. I had been corrupted
by too much time spent in southern lands where exotic building
materials like wood existed. Any trees that grew here would be for
boats and bows and axe-hafts, not for houses.

A group of men stood around an open-fronted cattle shed not
too far from the well, the baker and the blacksmith. They were doing what folk generally do in such circumstances: passing the time
of day and pretending to work a little, in case their wives should
check on them.

I fingered the ebony-and-bone spindle in my coat pocket. The
thread on it was wound tight, and I was almost to the end of the
roving. I'd followed the thread all the way here, woven my path
along Arnulfr's fate-thread. I'd soon need a new thread to follow.
It would raise questions for a solitary man to buy carded wool in
such a place, however.

I rode Magni to the hitching rail—not too far from the cluster
of gossipers, but not too close either. There were five men: one
black, one red, one dun, and two as nondescript in color as I had
been before my hair and beard went to pewter.

They looked up as I swung down from the saddle. Magni stood
placidly except for turning his head to glance over his shoulder,
hopeful of a treat. He got a scratch instead and sighed in compan-
ionable disappointment when I didn't loosen his girth. You never
know when you might need to leave in a hurry.

"I know," I said under my breath. "I'm a grave disappointment
to you."

I seemed to be a grave disappointment to the cattle-shed
malingerers as well, judging by the scowls they turned on me. I
forced my own face into a friendlier expression than I was feeling,
stopped a healthy few paces back, and said, "I'm looking for a man
called Arnulfr Augusson. Or his wife, Bryngertha Thorrsdaughter.
It's possible they passed this way."

"Be you a kinsman?" the black-haired one asked. His cheeks were sun-creased above a thicket of beard.

I nodded. That sharpened their gazes.

One of the nondescript ones asked, "Would that make you the one they call Hacksilver?"

I tipped my head to let the question slide off one side. A weight shifted along the broad brim of my hat, but it was just all the ash piled there. We go viking or we starve; we send our sons off to settle the coasts and rivers of Avalon and the Moonwise Isles; we build our trade towns and send our mercenary bands almost to the heart of the Steppe. And *still* there aren't so many Northfolk that a man can escape his reputation—or a lawsuit—with ease.

"Some sort of sorcerer, I heard," said the black one.

"Right," said the red. "They say he laid warfetter on a whole castle full of sentries. A double dozen of them, out in Avalon. Across the poisoned sea."

"Little renown to be won in such work," I remarked conversationally. "Who'd sing a man's name for butchering the blinded and limb-bound?"

"Womanish work, spell-weaving," said the black-haired man. "Don't they usually keep camp whores for that?"

He watched me with narrowed eyes.

I made myself sound as if I were not disagreeing. "A curious tale. From whom did you hear it?"

My voice gets a little more precise when I'm being Not Angry. I pulled my hand out of my pocket so I wouldn't finger my spindle, and I didn't place it on the hilt of my knife.

"There's an old Viking up the cinder trail," the red man said. "A Karlson. Supposed to have been a sea-king in his youth. Nobody here calls him naught but Half-Hand."

A chill lifted the hairs on my neck. Behind me, Magni snorted and shifted, making the saddle creak. I knew a man with half a hand once, a man whose father's name was Karl. A Viking, a sea-king, a giver of arm-rings. Yes, he had been those things.

I said, "I never heard of a sorcerer who could lay warfetter on as much as a hand of men all at once. The strain of more would kill the wizard . . . so they say."

The skalds and the seers tell us we ought to love war. And somebody must. There's enough of it.

Maybe Ragnar Karlson, called Half-Hand, called Wound-Rain, was still that man. Men get old—even sea-kings—and I hadn't seen him in ten years or more. So I couldn't be sure. He certainly wasn't a skald or a seer.

I might have passed for a seer, but as for the man who loves war . . . I didn't think that was me. I was the man who didn't know what else to do with himself if he wasn't fighting a war that he hated.

Farming's harder work and at least as uncertain as raiding. Because the world is not a fair place, farming doesn't win renown. Extorting towns and ransoming priestlings and chieftains, that is where the glory lies.

Magni was less than pleased with me when I dusted the ash off his saddle and climbed back on. He'd hoped our walking was over for the day, and there might be hot mash and cool water before long. But after a longing look and a little drunken swerve toward a paddock across the square populated by a half dozen other horses, he cooperated.

Ragnar's homestead was not too much farther. We crossed another finger of the basalt flow and came down into a second grassy valley. From experience, I knew that turf lay over soil no more than a finger length deep, comprised of dust, sand, and loess that had collected in this valley that was little more than a crevice between tuffs. Ragnar would have worked himself and his thralls hard to enrich it with dung and fish guts and make it bear the rich green grass that now poked forlornly through drifts of ash.

Cattle would starve this winter if the hay were lost. And if cattle starved, men starved as well.

Viking *was* an easier way to make a living. Until you weakened.

Ragnar's homestead was more than a turf house in the village, and less than a sea-king's hall. I saw its long shape against the hillsides that would have been green with the flush of summer grass. It was built of thatched basalt, not sod and turf, and it seemed to have been built over a stable dug into the slope behind it. The beam over the door was wood, carved with dragon-heads on the ends like a ship's prow.

Ragnar was cutting dried turf in the yard. His ropy, scarred back did not suggest that *he* had weakened. I halted Magni well clear of the gate and whistled, then dismounted once he turned. He would have heard the hooves, but it was polite to let a man know you were not a raider.

As I walked up, leading my gelding, Ragnar's eyes flicked from me to Magni and back again. His face went through a couple dozen expressions before settling on incredulity.

"Auga Hacksilver, you old bastard. Making friends already, I imagine?"

I shrugged, and in attempting to brush some ash off Magni's flaxen mane merely ground it in.

Ragnar shook his head at me. "I'd wish I'd known you were coming. I would have laid odds that you'd turn folk against yourself in the first half day, and I would have cleaned up. I've never met a man like you for going to a new town and finding somebody who's already mad at you there. It's almost as if you make enemies on purpose."

"Some would say that those who spread the tales make the enemies," I answered easily.

"A man's earned fame shall never die," Ragnar replied.

I snorted loudly enough that I could have blamed it on Magni. It's a comforting thing to tell ourselves, that the name lives on. And in my experience, it's nonsense.

He continued, "Speaking of death, what are the odds that you're still breathing?"

I laid my fingers on my throat. "Two to one," I offered. "I'll give you a better spread on it this time tomorrow."

"Isn't there some sort of ill-considered decision-making process regarding other people's spouses you could be engaging in right now?"

"Hey, your wife came to me, Ragnar." I waggled my hand non-committally. "She wasn't so great that I'd think it would be hard to keep her at home if you put in a little effort, though."

He cursed like a piked bear, and I wondered if I'd overplayed. I've never had the skill of knowing when to walk away from a flyting.

It was safer to take the punch than to look at him. You had to seem like you didn't care. Like you didn't fear.

Nobody ever won a flyting by seeming a coward.

He surprised me, though. He didn't swing. He glowered, and then he said, "What the hell brings you to the ass end of Ormsfjoll?"

"One thing and then another."

Ragnar's lips worked. "Stay in my hall tonight. Turn your horse

in with mine. The wife won't thank me if I let you pass without
paying your respects."

Does he have a new wife? I wondered.

I did learn a few things from the time I spent with Ragnar. One
was that if you're going to fuck a man, and fuck his wife, it's better
for domestic harmony if you make sure everybody involved is on
board with the plan right from the beginning. Another was that no
one ever got anything out of Ragnar Wound-Rain without paying
for it—one way or another.

I untacked Magni and sent him off to the herd with a pat. Then
I knocked the ash off my hat and followed Ragnar up the steps to
the door.

The fire on the long hearth was banked low, to not overwarm the
house in summer. The food was rye bread and ewe's butter with
stewed fish and onions. Ragnar still had the same wife, Aerndis,
and somehow she'd kept everything from tasting of sulfur and ashfall. I was surprised at how warmly she greeted me. Perhaps Ragnar's irritation was not without basis.

I sat at the trestle and washed my hands in the bowl she brought,
drank her ale, and bantered with Ragnar while Ragnar's tenant
farmers filed in and found their places along the board. There was
plenty of food, and Aerndis served me again before the bondi ate.
Then she sat at Ragnar's right hand, and a couple of women who
might have been wives of the farmers present brought them their
bowls and their ale. All three of us were stretching uncomfortably
to ease our fullness by the time the tenants were fed and filing
back out again for the work of the afternoon.

I watched them go, and watched the women clear the table, and
thought that there should have been children about: grown and
near-grown sons and daughters. I didn't ask after their absence.
It might have been that girls were married into nearby farms. It
might have been that sons were away viking, or trading, or a little
of both, but in that case you'd expect a young wife or two carding
and spinning and tying off leading-strings to keep the babies out
of the fire. You'd expect them in silks with silver brooches to hold
their gowns up—or even gold, like the ones Aerndis wore—and
not like the wives of the bondi with their bronze and pewter.

It might have been that they'd had ill luck conceiving, or ill
luck in keeping children alive. But it's hard on a couple my age to

run a farm all on their own, even with tenants. Tenants have to be supervised, and thralls have to be driven.

Under most circumstances, Ragnar and Aerndis would have taken on a few oath-sons and oath-daughters, to everyone's benefit. They might have elevated the best of their bondi, or they might have taken in the children of dead companions of the war-band.

Curiosity might seem insolent, and I take care never to seem insolent unless I mean to. It might cause grief, and that's another response I do not seek to provoke unintentionally.

Ragnar had, it seemed, no such bounds on his inquisitiveness. He looked at me rubbing my belly and laughed at me. "So. What are you doing up in the bright country, so far between good meals? Running from a weregild yourself?"

"Might be looking for a place to settle," I said noncommittally. My fingertips automatically reached for the spindle in my pocket. I eased them away again.

He'd taken me in and given me guest right. I knew, based on our history, that that probably meant he wanted something. We hadn't parted on such warm terms that I would expect him to put me out in the ashfall. But . . . farm me out to one of the cottages of his bondi, maybe.

His giving me guest right in his own home meant he couldn't take a physical poke at me. Nor could any of his men.

Perhaps it was unkind of me to provoke him with the threat of my continued presence. But kindness has never been a fault that much afflicted me.

"Can you buy land?" he asked.

I shrugged. Ragnar had to know that I had money unless I'd lost it—and he knew that by preference I diced with fate rather than for silver. My years of viking had been several and my needs while traveling were few. A path for my gelding; a mossy rock to lay my head on.

I could buy land. "It remains to be seen if I want to. It seems you've been spreading a great many rumors about me."

"Your rumors spread themselves."

I refrained from provoking him further. It took an effort when he handed me straight lines like that, however.

"I could just kill you for your money. Your brother being absent, there's no one to pay a weregild to, and it's not as if anyone who knows you would complain."

"If I were fool enough to carry my money with me." The money was in a bank twenty days' ride south, or five by boat if the wind were favorable. "If I filled up my saddlebags with gold, Magni would waddle. And it would be bad for his back. And there would be no room for my food."

Aerndis had always been a quiet one, but clever with it. She gave me a sly look. "As I judge from the crumbs in your beard, there's been little enough room for that as there is."

"Your cooking outshines mine, it's true." Especially when I was cooking up boiled soup-cake thickened with shreds of wind-dried fish.

I found myself reluctant to open the bargaining. When you want something from someone that you can't just take, letting them know it exposes your vulnerability.

Still, I had to try.

And maybe Ragnar would be feeling generous with a full belly and his ale-cup to hand.

I said, "You weren't far wrong when you brought up my brother being missing. The real answer to your question of what I am looking for is 'Arnulfr.' Did you hear my brother was exiled for manslaughter?"

"Hm." It sounded like agreement around a mouthful of rye bread. Ragnar had gotten ropy with age rather than thick and I couldn't imagine finding a corner into which to fit another bite of anything, but cutting sod is hard work.

I glanced toward the hearthstone, as if fascinated by its ornate carved and dyed reliefs. "The line of Arnulfr's fate led me here, and it ends here."

Aerndis refilled my cup while Ragnar wiped ale froth from his beard. "What do you want with him?"

"I found the real killer. He can go home."

Ragnar swallowed, washed it down with ale, and snorted. "Who'd you frame?"

"You wound me."

He said, "In that case, you could have kept your father's farm."

"And what about Arnulfr?"

"Your brother's got his patch of ground by now."

I gestured to his rough hands, the whole one and the one the axe had split. "Farming looks like hard work."

"I've half a hundred head of cattle and seven horses. Sheep

and goats. Chickens and geese and a dog. Four bondi look to me for protection. I even managed to keep nearly all of them alive last winter, which wasn't easy." He waved vaguely at the doorway, through which the ashy dooryard was just visible.

So the eruptions had been going on that long. Perhaps that explained the number of new graves along the road. "Not a lot of Vikings this far north."

"It's a long swim to civilization," he agreed. "You really cleared his name?"

I nodded, looking back toward my host, away from the fire.

Ragnar eyed me levelly. His eyes were light, for such a black-haired man. "So, when you say that someone else was to blame. In all seriousness: factually, or conveniently?"

I smiled.

"And if you can find him and tell him, you're delivered of your kin-duty."

"Yes."

The sun had not set, would not brush the horizon for hours yet. Its rays crept through the vents beneath the roof. It lit the underside of the thatch and all the things stored in the rafters sideways, creating a bright and alien relief. The interior walls of the longhouse were plastered white with lime render and lime wash to make the interior bright in daylight, painted with coiling trees and flowers in ochre reds and yellows. I wondered why they hadn't finished a ceiling under the thatch.

Ragnar rattled his fingertips on the trestle. "Why *not* take that land and farm it yourself? It's an easier living down south than up here in the bright country."

"I wasn't lying when I said farming was too much hard work for me." I decided to be generous. "So you don't actually have to worry about me buying the next farm over, and my presence weighing on you the rest of your days."

Ragnar frowned judiciously. "What's news worth to you?"

"Curse you, Half-Hand. This is a kin matter—"

"Sure it is, and so you shouldn't mind running a little errand in return for news of your brother." He smirked. "*And* his wife."

I weighed it. Ragnar always had known me a little too well. "Your word that you know where he is."

Ragnar shrugged. "I know where he was, and where he was going."

If he'd been lying, I thought, wouldn't he have made a bigger promise? "What's the errand?"

"Let's go outside."

He drained his cup and set it down. I did the same, standing as he stood. I nodded to Aerndis, then put my hat on as I followed him into the yard.

If Bryngertha *had* wanted me, I might have been content with the quiet and backbreaking life of a farmer. Might have *made* myself contented, anyway. But Bryngertha had wanted Arnulfr, and all Arnulfr had ever wanted in truth was Bryngertha . . . and that quiet and backbreaking life.

Though my brother's experience showed that even the life of a simple landed farmer was not without its risks.

Ragnar leaned on a stone fence and watched his seven horses and my single one brushing the ash aside to graze. I leaned beside him. I waited a long time, watching his expression from the corner of his eye, before I ventured to ask, "About that errand . . ."

"So," Ragnar said by way of answer. "I don't suppose you're still a witch."

His braids were down to his waist now, befitting a chieftain. If you ignored the bald spot they framed, impressive. He hadn't bothered with a hat.

"Eh," I said. "Are you about to claim I ever was one?"

He snorted. "You were a clever shit, anyway. Clever as Lopt and just as likely to get snagged on your own pretensions. How are you at volcanos?"

"I can ride away from them as well as any man. They say you ought to head upwind and keep to the high ground."

He pointed at the thread of smoke that rose through the smoky sky. It was just discernable through fumes and falling ash. I could imagine the outline of a conical hill poking above the horizon if I squinted.

He said, "What about one with a dragon in it?"

"There's no such things as dragons," I said.

"Should be easy to slay, then."

"No," I said, wondering if it was Arnulfr's fate-thread that ran out here in the bright country, or Auga Augusson's. "What kind of naturalist would I be if I went and slew every strange beast I ever came upon?"

Aerndis sniggered, which was when I realized she had come out behind us. Woman moved like a cat.

Ragnar glared at her but spoke to me. "So now you're a naturalist?"

"I'm not a dragon-slayer."

Aerndis spoke in a tone I recognized as the voice of sweet reason. "If you slay the dragon, you stop the eruption, I warrant. He's been digging around in that volcano with his great black claws. There was nary a rumble until he showed up, this time last year. We were lucky to get enough hay in for winter, and then the sickness came and a lot of us got a late start on planting this year. There isn't much left, and people are going to be hungry when the dark comes again, especially with a dragon picking away at the livestock. Folks would be grateful to the man who saved this harvest. Grateful enough to give him a home. And they say dragons hoard gold . . ."

Ragnar glared at her.

"Darling of you to think of my future, sweet Aerndis, and to want to keep me around," I said.

Ragnar glared at me.

"All right," Ragnar said, when the glare was well out of his system. "Well, getting rid of that dragon is the only way you're getting to your brother."

Aerndis suddenly, abruptly turned and walked away. Too far away to hear us, and then she kept walking. I had seen what her face did before she turned, and a chill lifted my hackles. "What do you mean?"

Ragnar cleared his throat and spat over the rail. "Arnulfr's here."

". . . here."

He tapped the earth underfoot with his toe. "Buried. Dead. His wife too. And my daughter and two sons."

"I don't—"

"They came. And they stayed the winter. And they never left."

Ah, Auga Hacksilver and his famously glib tongue. I was struck as dumb as a stone when the sea washes over it.

"Aerndis understates. There was a great sickness," Ragnar said, taking pity. "It was a hard winter. And the sickness was especially cruel. It fell hardest on the young and those in their prime."

"Oh," I said, because it was what I could think to say. I touched the spindle in my pocket, felt the wisp of roving at the end of the thread.

Ragnar drew a deep breath and shook himself together, turning his bright gaze back to the horses. The horses were calm, and I watched them too. We stood together for a moment. Then he turned and grinned at me, gap-toothed, as I stared. "And that dragon, Hacksilver. That dragon's man-long fangs drip venom. *Eitr.* So if you want to send your brother home, and his wife, you're going to bring me the gall of that dragon, and you're going to help me get my sons back, and my little girl."

Eitr. There was a word I hadn't heard in a while. A complicated word that could mean *anger*, or it could mean *poison*, or it could mean *gall*, in all the senses of gall—the sort that is spoken, and the sort that burns flesh less metaphorically. But *eitr* was also the source and the font of all life in the world.

Life and death are not so far apart, as it happens, and neither are venom and the truth.

"Have you turned into the cowardly sorcerer they call you, then? You'd leave your brother lying in his grave, and Bryngertha beside him, doomed to the meagre afterlife allotted those who die of pestilence?"

Ragnar was trying to get a rise out of me and coming perilously close to an insult I could not with honor ignore. But guest right stood between us. I crossed my arms the other way on the top course of the fence. A few of the horses, including Magni, decided it was a good time to amble over and see if we had carrots.

"Usually, one doesn't have a lot of options, once a man is in the grave. Anyway, people pay more attention to what a man says than to his deeds, and even more than that to whatever lies others tell about him." I pushed a soft, inquisitive horse nose away from my pocket. "It's all spin. Maybe I can buy him a better afterlife if I write a few songs about him. Why don't you go and get your own dragon venom?"

"Most folk are stupid," Ragnar replied. "And I know the truth behind the stories. At least as far as you're concerned. You've got a better chance of walking into a dragon's lair and back out again than I do. Than any man I've ever met."

"Simple. Kill the dragon, collect its gall. Raise a bunch of people from the dead and save the harvest. That's what you want of me."

"I'll feed you breakfast first."

Despite myself, when I met his gaze, I found myself smiling at the audacity in his smirk. That audacity is why I sailed with him. It's why I did other things with him too.

"I'd think—"

He rolled his eyes. "Nobody cares what you think. They only care what you do."

I wished Ragnar to Hel in company with my brother. I stared him in the eyes and said, "Your word that everything you've told me is true."

Without looking, he flicked his knife from its sheath and across the back of his hand. A thin line of blood formed, the wound-rain that was his byname. We'd spilled enough in each other's company.

"My word of honor," he said.

I sighed gustily, from the bottom of my lungs. Ash whispered past my forehead, swirling on my breath. I took my hat off and nodded.

"Sure," I said. "I'll need some jars with stoppers. And for you to give me your fattest horse."

"What's wrong with your horse?"

I stroked Magni's neck. He hated having his face touched. "I'm not going to feed *my* horse to a dragon."

Ragnar pursed his lips, making the mustache jut. Then he nodded, reached out, and gave Magni a scratch under his mane. "All right. But if *you* get eaten he belongs to me."

We went back inside, and when Aerndis brought me more ale I caught her attention and said, "I have agreed."

She brought me seed-cake too.

They gave me a sleeping place on the bench along the wall. Sometime before the brief interlude that passed for sunset, we retired. I slept alone, and better than I had any right to in Ragnar Karlson's house.

The sun was already high in the sky when we awoke, washed, and broke our fast. I followed him outside, still trying to reckon some way to avoid the task he had set me. There wasn't any dragon, I thought—just the living land heaving beneath us. And there was no god I knew to pray to and no spell I knew to weave that could

so much as delay the eruption of a geyser, let alone make a volcano stop smoking. We'd all be lucky if it didn't decide to send
out a tongue of lava to fill up this grassy valley nestled between its
previous flows.

Ragnar grumbled some more, but he brought me the horse.

The dark gelding was fat, all right. He was shaped something
like a mangelwurzel, and his hooves were overgrown, and he
limped in the off hind.

"This horse is lame."

"You said fattest, not soundest. And you'd not expect me to give
you a sound one, to feed to a dragon."

"It's far to walk." I gestured at the smoking hill on the horizon.
"And I can't ride him."

"Why not?" Ragnar cackled like a raven that has spotted an old
enemy. "It's not like riding him is going to impede his healing. His
name is—"

"Don't tell me his name." I gave the horse a withered piece of
carrot. "There's no point in getting attached."

Ragnar didn't have a saddle that fit the gelding, round as he was.
And I wasn't going to hop on a strange horse bareback and try
to get him to take me, all alone, to the den of some monster—or
even to a fiery hole in the ground. So I walked, and led him. The
basalt hurt my feet through my boots; it seemed to hurt his feet,
too, because he minced along like a courtier in heeled shoes. It
didn't help that he tripped on his own overlong hooves with every
third stride and limped on that bad leg. Watching him try to move
was a sad old comedy.

I lured him on with bits of turnip and carrot. He wasn't terribly enthusiastic about the turnip. He grabbed at the carrot, and I
knocked on his teeth. "Manners."

I laughed at myself. Was there any point in civilizing this animal?

A sharp bit of basalt stabbed me in the sole as if my boot leather
didn't even exist. I stopped, leaned on the gelding's neck, and
inspected my foot. No blood, and it hadn't gone through that I
could tell.

I turned and glared at the horse. He put his nose in my face
and blew carrot-scented breath over me. He had braced himself
as if standing on tiptoe, the bad foot cocked off the ground so his

weight wasn't resting on it. I ran my hand down the leg. He didn't like me handling it. But there was no swelling, heat, or sign of a fracture. No bulge of a bowed tendon. No sign of a bruise inside the hoof or any of the other thousand things that could go wrong with a horse's foot.

Which meant the injury was probably a strained ligament, which might heal with a few months of rest, or might be with him for the rest of his life. If he were going to have a life beyond the next few hours.

He wasn't badly made, if you didn't mind the hooves and the fat and the fact that he might have been born dark as night but the long summer days had weathered him the same red-black as the crumbling lava underfoot. He was smaller than Magni but built sturdily enough to carry a grown man. The only marking on him was an ashfall stippling of white hairs on the flat plane of his face, stretching from brow to muzzle but not defined enough to be properly called a blaze.

He had a pretty head with defined cheekbones and a tapered muzzle. Intelligent ears. I had his full attention as I stood back and looked at him.

He nickered at me.

I felt a pang for the basalt-colored horse. There probably wasn't a dragon. But if there *was* a spirit of the volcano, it would want some kind of sacrifice, and if I couldn't trade with a dragon for *eitr* to bring my brother and his wife back, maybe I could trade with the whatever-it-was to end the eruption and save the harvest. But one lame horse still probably wouldn't be enough to fix anything.

. . . the basalt-colored horse.

I'd been going along for such a while without one that the tickle of an idea surprised me. I heard myself whistle.

The gelding's ears pricked and he limped a step toward me.

"Don't get your hopes up," I said. "But if you get really lucky, maybe there *will* be a dragon."

He took another step . . . and tripped again. Those feet were a disgrace. Long as a town woman's pattens, and the pony couldn't walk any better in them.

I pulled my hook knife from my boot. He looked at me suspiciously. I let him sniff it. He obviously considered it something of a disappointment.

"Sorry, boy. It's not a weird carrot." He had to be motivated, to get that fat eating lichen and silage and straw chaff and turnips and wind-dried fish all winter. Ragnar probably would have slaughtered him for horse-meat come the frost.

I bent to lift one foot. He leaned away from me, worried. Ragnar had never been much of a farrier, and I remembered that most of his horses were afraid of having their feet handled. He apparently hadn't improved.

With the aid of carrots and some rye bread sweet with birch syrup, I got the hooves trimmed anyway. He was easier about the last one than the first one. He was still lame after, but at least he stopped tripping.

The trim made him even more footsore on the basalt. After watching him mince for fifteen or twenty steps, I sighed in disgust, pulled my hook knife out again, and cut a wide strip and a narrow strip off the edge of my oiled leather cloak. He fussed at me while I tied the crude boots around his ankles, but when he stepped out again he seemed surprised and pleased at the improvement.

I fingered the spindle in my pocket. *Dammit, Hacksilver. Don't you go getting attached to your bait.*

After several more painful hours of walking, the basalt was replaced by a steep slope of cinders. The air stung my lungs and we both grunted and leaned forward, pushing up the slope, cinders crunching. I started to notice the bones. Not complete skeletons, or scattered limbs. But here the skull of an ox; there the pelvis of a horse. Big bones, with scraps of meat cured on them by the hot, lifeless air.

The horse didn't like the smell.

Unease pricked through me, sourceless and unsettling.

I was not, as I mentioned, *really* expecting a dragon. The basalt-colored horse was apparently smarter than me. He stopped halfway up the cindery slope, ears pricked, head craned, neck tense. A steady fellow: he was spooked and snorting, but he stood his ground and inspected the way ahead instead of skittering or trying to bolt.

I stopped also. Strained every sense, as the horse was straining his. The air reeked of brimstone. My eyes teared; wreaths of smoke obscured what vision I retained. But as I held myself still, my bones and the soles of my boots were shaken by a low sound. One that seemed to emanate up from the burnt ground underfoot as much as propagate through the air. It felt like the rumble of a geyser gathering itself to explode.

I pulled the spindle from my pocket and inspected the thread wound around it. Gray, scratchy, thin as wire and as like to cut you. The measure of a kinsman's life.

I'd spun fine to spin long. Long enough for my purpose, maybe.

It would have been better woven into a net—a net to catch the vision and imagination. But even the long summer days were not long enough for that. So I found a rock about the right height, dusted the ash off it to be certain it wasn't a desiccated pelvis, and sat down. A silver coin from my pocket had already been clipped and shaved a fair bit in its travels. I used my hook knife to shave it a bit more, dulling the edge but collecting a pinch of silver dust in a fold of my trousers. Silver like mirrors and silver like tongues.

I put those tools down and picked up the spindle, dipped my finger in the silver, drew a loop across my open hand, and gave the spindle a twirl. It dropped, and I rubbed metal dust into the chain-ply of my brother's life, making the thread into yarn that could be unwound from the spindle without unraveling.

I supposed it didn't matter, really, if the thread unwound itself—assuming Ragnar was telling the truth and Arnulfr and Bryngertha were dead. A poor omen perhaps for Arnulfr's legend, but Arnulfr's legend was the tale of a quiet man quietly damned for a crime by treachery. There are a lot of sagas about lawsuits. There aren't too many about the losers of lawsuits.

Being born again by dragon venom would be the most songworthy thing that had ever happened to him.

Was Ragnar telling the truth? Well, I had known Ragnar to be sly, to misdirect, like any good warlord. I had not known him to betray his word of honor.

Getting eaten by a dragon was a death worth singing. Maybe that would be enough of a legend to gain me admittance into one of the better heavens. Or maybe the End Storm would blow up while I was plying, and I wouldn't have to worry about legends or kinsmen anymore.

Having thought of songs, I sang to myself as I worked. As the ash fell around me. Songs for the goddesses who measured every man's life, and then measured him for his coffin. Songs for the spinners. Warlock songs, scithr songs. Women's songs, but there was no one to hear me except the basalt-colored gelding, and he was in no position to impugn my masculinity.

At last, I was out of silver dust and all the yarn was plied. Gray, scratchy. Smelling faintly of lanolin and lye. I stretched it between my fingers and let it twirl into a skein. If there had been any sunlight beneath the ash plume, I might have detected a subtle sparkle in the twist.

The basalt-colored horse dozed disconsolately at the end of his lead rope. I'd bored him to sleep.

I hoped it wasn't a comment on my singing.

I let him sniff the skein, which he did with curiosity but no apparent concern. That was a relief. Some animals will not abide the smell of sorcery.

I started by braiding his mane, working the fate-cord into it as I went. I wound the line around his chest and shoulders like a girl binding her wooden horse with thread to make a play-harness. He stood for it, remarkably still and even-tempered. I braided traces back on themselves without cutting the line and let them trail, then bound the whole thing off just as I ran to the end of the thread.

The horse craned his neck around to watch me, ears alert, eyes bright and expression dubious. I wished I had a walking stick or a long bone from which to make a whiffletree, but it would only drag on the ground. And probably spook even *this* horse. So I just draped the traces over his rump and tied them in a little bow.

It was, after all, the symbolism that mattered.

"Well, buddy, I hope this works," I said.

He blew a warm breath over me. We resumed climbing the cone.

The slope leveled as we came close to the top of the volcano. We stopped to drink at a spring that bubbled up from a cluster of stones, clearing some of the ash from our throats. I splashed water on my face. It was lukewarm and fizzed like surf, full of bubbles. It reeked and tasted of brimstone, but at least it wasn't boiling. The horse drank, snorted to clear the fumes from his nostrils, and gave me a look before drinking again as if to say, "Yeah, I've seen worse."

When I lifted my head, I realized we were nearly to the vent. The horse grew increasingly restive as we came up the final slope, and with a couple furlongs to go he planted his feet in their ridiculous leather bags and refused to walk another step.

I chirruped to him and shook the lead. He planted his hind

feet, rocked back, and reared. Not a dramatic, sky-pawing rear, but a clear declaration that he was not moving.

It was honestly surprising we'd made it this far. "Good lad," I told him, and turned him around to face downhill. I wound the fragile-seeming traces around a head-sized piece of pumice and tied them off.

Careful not to loop the lead rope around my hand, I stepped up beside the twitching horse and unfastened his halter. I stroked his sweating, ash-gritted shoulder as I slid the straps off his nose. He stood harnessed in sorcery, fate-threads, and kin-duty, leaning against the yarn-spun traces as if against a plow stopped by thick turf.

I stepped away and tossed the halter onto the cinders before turning back uphill. I cupped my hands to my mouth and used a little twist of luck, a scrap of thread wound 'round my fingers, to shift the wind so that my voice would carry. I took the deepest breath I could, tightened my diaphragm, and bellowed.

"Here, dragon, dragon! Nice fat pony. Lame, too! An easy dinner!"

For a long moment, nothing. The reek of fumes swirling on the breeze I'd conjured up; the steam rising from the cinders. The vast silence of the lifeless mountainside.

Then came a rumble, and a long, hard clatter like a bag of armor bits and chopped-up candelabras dragged over stone. The scraping of stone on stone. I levered my neck back, peering through streaming vapors, blinking away the fume-begotten tears.

A great head that only seemed small because it was on a neck as long as a ship's mast poked over the rim of the crater. The head was hammer-shaped, and scaled, and horned, and fanged. I could have called it red or orange in color and not been wrong, but the rough scales seemed translucent, and refracted rainbows in their depths, like the planes of light struck within an opal. Even under the dim overcast of smoke and the haze of fumes, it dazzled.

The owner of the head—and the neck—sniffed deeply. Once, twice. Then it reared back and struck with surprising speed.

I threw myself to the side, cinders bruising my palms. The horse, being nobody's fool, took off. I winced for his bad foot, because I am a soft, womanish fool of a sorcerer. He galloped down the slope with all the alacrity and focus of a horse running Hel-bent away from a dragon, the boulder bouncing behind him in its traces.

The glamour that I'd spun and sung and knotted around both horse and stone caught on the weave of threads and mirror-bright silver scrapings and made it seem the whole mountainside was collapsing into a vast horseshoe depression. The basalt-colored horse was just one more boulder bouncing along in the midst of the rest.

I was rather proud of the effect, and the way the sound of hoofbeats was lost in the simulated rumble of the rockslide.

I turned my attention back to the dragon as it pulled back again and took a long, slow sniff. Red nostrils flared darker in the fire-faceted muzzle. The upper lip drew back to move air across the palate and a forked tongue flickered.

Steam hissed from its nostrils. My vision swam with acrid tears. The head swung down again, falling toward me like the hammer it resembled.

If I'd been some hero out of sagas I'd have swung up a sword or had a venomed spear at the ready. I just raised my empty hands as if that could somehow fend off an avalanche.

The blow stopped before it fell, the dragon's enormous head so close that the heat of its hide and breath curled my hair. I smelled the ends scorching.

The dragon spoke, and despite the shape of tongue and mouth it surprised me by uttering words I could understand completely. Its phrasing was archaic, its voice as deep and hollow as caverns.

"I smell a horse," it said. "But much closer, I smell a witch. Hello, little witch. That was a clever thing, for a wisp such as you."

Well, I had been hoping to impress it. And I'd lured it out all right.

Now what?

It sniffed again. "Have you come to slay a dragon?"

A bead of saliva gathered along the edge of the dragon's lip. I stepped to the side as it dripped, stretching a long thread behind it. The venom looked like honey glowing in the sun, but when it touched the ground it sizzled on the ash. The spot smoked slightly.

I thought about the jars in my pack and felt as cold as if the blood were draining from my body.

I gulped down the lump in my throat. "I came to bargain with one. You see I carry no spear, no harpoon—"

The rumble of the dragon's words shook my diaphragm. "If you wish gold, I will not give it. If you wish ancient and storied weapons, there is nothing you can give me that I could not take. If you wish to die gloriously and be remembered in song, you should have brought a poet. You reek of sorcery."

"As long as I don't smell like a snack."

"Hmmm." It tilted its head to one side. "You smell pickled and stringy."

The wings rustled as it shrugged.

Perhaps it was not strange that the dragon's verbal jousting made me feel as if I had come from the wilderness into a safe and familiar hall. I was comfortable in an argument. The fear and tension drained away and in their place a manic energy buoyed me.

I crouched and held my hand over the smoking *eitr*. I turned my face up to the dragon. I was gray with ash and streaked with tears.

I felt the warmth of the poison and the warmth of the ashes on which it rested as if I held my hand over gentle coals. "I've come to bargain for this."

The great head tilted and drew back. The lambent eyes with their shattered planes of iridescent scarlet and vermilion blinked lazily. "I could give you more of it than you wished for, little witch."

"Your presence here, your awakening of the volcano—they've brought a blight upon the land. Men and women have died of illness and hunger. The cattle will die as well, if the grass is buried under ash and pumice, or they will choke on the poison fumes of the volcano. I have been asked to win your *eitr* to bring back those who have died."

"Cattle die and kinsmen die, little witch. If they cannot live in a place, then they should go."

"Look," I said bluntly, "what can we give you to leave this place and not return?"

"What can you offer me? A fat horse is all very well, but I can fetch my own when I want one. I have . . . commitments that will keep me in this lair."

"For how long?"

"Not long," said the dragon. To my amazement, it placed first one and then the other enormous talon on the rim of the vent. Having done so, it settled its head between them, bringing its eye level down to mine. I could see the great humped shoulders, the leathery folds stretching back from its forelimbs. Like a bat's, they seemed both wing and foot to walk upon. Unlike a bat's, they shimmered with all the colors of flame.

It tilted its head and rippled the taloned fingers as if counting. "Hmm. Perhaps a hundred seasons more."

Well, twenty-five years of active volcano and dragon occupation would certainly put paid to the village—and all life within miles. I rose to my feet and discovered that the air was slightly better up there. Apparently the fumes were heavy.

"Assume for a moment that I can get you whatever you desire," I said. "If you will only leave this place, and give me some of your venom."

The dragon curved its sinuous neck like a goose and glanced over its shoulder, back down the length of its body into the vent. I wondered if it were assessing a hoard I could not see. I wondered how anything remained unmelted, down in the hot mouth of the earth.

It turned back. With a sigh, it said, "I have no need of human treasures."

"This obligation you mentioned—is there a way I could help you fulfill it?"

If you have never seen a dragon throw its head back and laugh (and I suppose very few have), it is a sight not easily described. I hastily tugged my hat down as a fine mist of caustic venom descended around me. A few invisible drops smarted on the backs of my hands.

"You are not boring, little witch," the dragon said. It looked this way, and then that. To my amazement, it seemed to be making a show of casualness, of reluctance.

"Hmm," it said. Then: "Do you like riddles, little witch?"

I closed my eyes.

I hated riddles.

"I have played at riddles a time or two."

"Well then." The dragon shifted its weight, settling into the mountainside like a great jarl settling into his broad, bearskin-adorned chair. "Come up a little closer, witch, and choose a stone to sit upon, and we can play at riddles for what you wish. But if you win, you must grant me a boon."

How under the Wolf Sun of my fathers did I keep getting myself into situations like this?

But I was a man on kin-business, blood-bound to do what I could. Damn my brother anyway, for being a simple farmer, for being the victim of a brutal scheme, for dying of a dragon's miasma, for getting me into all of this.

I walked up to the smoking crater as if I had not a fear in the world—certainly without *any* cringing as I came under the shadow of the dragon's wings—and while I was selecting a rock of the correct height for sitting, could not resist a peek over the edge into the vent.

I almost fell in.

I had expected the vent to contain . . . shining masses of gold, perhaps. Seething masses of lava.

Not a careful circle of boulders each as big as a cart, and a claw-raked ground of soft ash within, like a giant's campfire ring. Upon that, dead in the center, lay three enormous, mottled eggs like the last remaining embers.

The dragon, it seemed, was not an *it* but a *she*.

"Well," I said. "I see what you mean by 'obligations.'"

Have you ever heard a dragon chortle? I have, and it was in no way rendered less unsettling by the knowledge that this was a female with young. For nothing on the waters and the wide wide world is fiercer than a mother.

I found a rock, as directed, and as directed I seated myself upon it. I swung the pack with the jars down between my knees and set it gently on the stones.

"So, little witch," said the dragon. "Shall we play?"

"You go first," I said. "Best two out of three?"

The dragon stretched and sighed, settling itself. "I believe it is traditional. As for that boon—"

"As long as it's not my stringy hide."

She sniffed. "I dislike the taste of woad, and I see from your forelimbs that you're pricked all over with the stuff."

I glanced down at the old and faded ropes of tattoos. They were meant to be for protection, to ensure the forbearance of the gods.

First time in my life that the damn things actually worked.

"If you get a boon if I win," I said, "I get a boon if I lose."

"It can't be the same as the stakes," she said cagily.

"What forfeit will you have of me if *you* win?" I pushed my hat back as she thought about it.

"Have you a hoard?" she asked finally.

I thought of gold and silver and jewels of great store. The wealth of a lifetime spent riding the whale roads, reaving and trading. The price of my retirement, when I found a place I wanted to retire. All safe in a vault down in Ornyst, where there were bankers and banks.

I thought about kin-duty. I thought about my sister-in-law.

"Not on my person," I said.

"Wager your hoard against my venom, then," the dragon invited.

"Don't you even want to know how much I have?"

She hissed a laugh. "It's enough that it's valuable to you. That's what makes a wager interesting. That, and the story that attaches to it. That someday I may say to my children, yes, this is the gold I won riddling with a sorcerer, while you were yet in the shell."

It was a dragonish way of thinking, and not so alien to anybody who had gone a-viking. I touched my arm-rings, fingering them until I found the one that had been a gift from Ragnar when he was a sea-king and I sailed at his command. When we had been bright and young and too naïve to know any better.

I said, "If you will wager both your venom and your leaving, I will add my adornments to the pot. Those mean more to me than any hoard."

None of it was the richest that I owned, but it was enough— earrings and arm-rings, the brooch that closed my cloak and the clasp that pinned my hair—to lend me dignity. I felt a sentiment for each object. Especially since I had so recently won it all back from a murderer.

At least it wasn't my coat and boots this time.

"Your folk should move on, not me. This land is far more suitable for me than . . ."

There are few things more eloquent than the dismissive flick of a dragon's talon, it turns out.

"That's likely true," I admitted. "But you have to understand that the people of the village have built houses and barns and planted crops. Our lives are short. They won't have time or resources to up stakes and build those houses anew someplace else."

She said, "There are far more suitable places for your sort to live than there are for brooding eggs. I won't be the last to come here, so long as the earth stays hot."

"I can't wager for my folk any more than you can speak for yours." I hoped she wasn't a dragon queen, or something, who did have the power to bargain for the whole. Anyway, the future wasn't my concern. She was right; this was a stupid place for a settlement.

She huffed at the back of her throat, not hard enough to spray venom—but hard enough to cause a mist of it to curl from her nostrils and ignite into a transparent lash of flame. She tilted her head to regard me, and I got the oddest sense that her interest was more in the bargaining and the company and the game than in who lost or won.

Sitting on eggs must be extremely boring for a creature with wings to span the open skies. I'd only had the broad sails and swift rowers of a dragon-boat to carry me, and although now my joints ached even in good weather and my feet hurt every day, I could not bring myself to settle into a farmstead and raise cows. Though I was no youth to harden my muscles on an oar without injury, I could not see myself raising a hall and draping a big throne-chair with wolf-hides and bear-hides to cushion my ass and seem fierce at the same time. No matter how much the saddle galled my behind.

I might have more in common with this dragon than I did with Ragnar or with my brother.

Damn Arnulfr.

"Done," the dragon said. "I shall begin.

"I am the shrill singer
"Who rides a narrow road.
"With two mouths I kiss hard
"The hot and pliant maidens."

I blushed, because I hadn't been expecting racy double meanings from a dragon. But I knew the answer to this one, when I thought about it a little. "Hammer," I said. And then, "Smith's hammer. The road and the maidens are the metal to be forged. The mouths are the two ends of the hammer."

The dragon snorted another curl of fire, slightly larger than the last one. How good was the word of a dragon, anyway? Especially when exposed to a little frustration?

Perhaps I should have been surprised that the dragon knew about hammers—but the dragon knew about treasures, and steel for swords and gold for gauds alike must be refined, then hammered pure.

I hoped there were other human things the dragon knew less about. I said,

"I am the black horse.
"On eight legs I bear my rider.

"He holds no rein.
"At the end of the journey it is he who is left in the stall."

I am not sure dragons frown. Their scaled foreheads are not designed for furrowing. But I could not shake the sense that the dragon was frowning at me.

After a little while, she responded calmly, "A coffin and its bearers." I sighed. "You can't blame me for trying."

The tongue flickered. "Can I not? Here is my next one.

"We are the old women
"Who walk on the beach
"We braid the shells and seaweed
"In our white hair."

"Damn," I said.

"Do you forfeit?" The dragon leaned forward eagerly. Its talons tensed as if already imagining raking through treasure.

"Not so fast!" I held up a hand and tried to ignore the warmth of the dragon's breath ruffling my hair. Unless that was just the wind off the volcano. *What walks on a beach . . . ? Crabs. Birds.*

"Waves!" I said suddenly, as it came to me. The word burst from my lips before I could second-guess myself. "It's waves!"

"It's waves," the dragon agreed, sounding slightly disappointed.

"My next." Of course, because I was looking at a dragon, I could only think of one riddle.

Hoping she wouldn't be offended, I said,

"I am a dragon with only one wing.
"But of limbs I have a score.
"I fly to battle.
"I grow more fearful when I shed my scales."

"Really?" the dragon said.

I spread my hands. The rock was making my backside ache. I tried not to fidget. It would only make me seem nervous.

Of course, I *was* nervous.

"A long-boat," the dragon said. She yawned before she continued. "The limbs are oars. The scales are the shields hung over the gunwales and retrieved when the men go to fight."

"You've seen that?"

"I've destroyed a few. Sometimes they're full of livestock. Or treasure."

If dragons didn't frown, did they smile? Or had she always been as toothy as she seemed now.

"What do we do if it's a draw?" I asked.

She chuckled. "A sudden-death round? By which I mean, then I eat you."

I couldn't tell if she was joking and I didn't want to ask. It might be better to let myself lose. I could always find more treasure, after all. Never mind that it would take a desperate Viking indeed to give a berth to a man as old as me, and those were the sorts of raiders who did not come home with their ships wallowing with gold.

"Last one," the dragon said cheerfully. Did they play with their prey, like cats?

"A stone on the road.
"I saw water become bone."

How on earth did that happen? It was a metaphor, of course—riddles always were—but what was water a metaphor for? Blood that clots? A stone was hard, and so was a sword . . . brigands? Something that could stop a journey?

No. No, of course not. The water wasn't the metaphor. The *road* was the metaphor. The whale-road, the ship-road. The sea. What was a stone on the sea?

"An iceberg," I said.

"Brave little witch," the dragon remarked. She lifted one talon and waved idly. Her opalescent eyes seemed to enlarge until I felt as if I were falling upward into them.

I'm not sure how long I gaped at her, but I was startled abruptly back into my skin when she said, "Hurry up, then. Let's see this done."

My mind went blank.

My wit ran dry.

I could think of not a single riddle.

No, not true. I could think of a riddle. But it was a children's riddle, and not one worthy of a dragon. I needed something better. Something clever. Something I stood a chance of stumping her with.

She sighed a slow trickle of flame.
Dammit.
I said,

"Fat and full-bellied
"Welcome and warm
"I rise with joy
"Though my bed is hard."

A loaf, of course. A loaf, puffing up and baking on a flat hearth-stone before the fire.

No sooner had the words left my mouth than I thought of half a dozen better ones. The onion riddle with all the dick jokes in it . . . anything. Anything at all would have been better . . .

There was the end of my chance to save my kinfolk. There was the end of my chance to put this obligation to rest—

I was so engaged in flyting myself that I thought I must have missed the dragon's answer. And indeed, when I lifted my eyes again, she was staring at me quizzically.

"I'm sorry," I said. "I didn't hear you."

She snorted rather a lot of fire this time. "I said, I don't know. I don't know the answer."

"What?" I said foolishly.

"Little witch, tell me the answer."

"Bread," I said. "A loaf of bread. It rises when you cook it on a hot stone."

"Fascinating." The tip of her tail twitched like a hunting cat's. "*Fascinating.* Is that where bread comes from?"

She sounded genuinely excited.

Dragons, it seemed, knew about death and war. But not so much about baking.

Her wings folded more tightly against her sides. "Well, you've won. That's the end of the riddles, then."

"I have another one for you," I cried, struck by inspiration now when it was too late. "As a gift. No wager."

The dragon definitely had facial expressions, and this one was definitely suspicion. "No wager?"

"None."

"What do you want if you win?"

"Just the joy of winning," I said. "Here.

"Alone I dwell
"In a stone cell
"With a gray roof.
"Though kept captive
"None holds the key.
"I am not soaring above the halls of dawn.
"I do not see the sun rise.
"What creature am I?"

She stared, tongue flickering. Moments passed, and I worried I had misunderstood her—or worse, offended her.

When she burst out, "Me!" she nearly incinerated me with the spray of her venom. "It's *me*! Oh, sorry . . ."

"I'm fine. It's fine." I remained standing, so I could dodge faster if there were more outbursts. And to get away from the eyewatering, sinus-stinging smoke curling from the cinders where the *eitr* had fallen. "Unscathed." I held out my hands to demonstrate.

"Good," she said. "How odd it is that a small, frail, temporary person like yourself should make me feel so clearly seen."

Well, from her point of view, I supposed I was all of those things.

She had been lying along the edge of the vent, just her head and forequarters poking over. Now, with a motion that was half slither and half chinning herself, she crawled up to the rim and stretched out. "Did you bring vessels?"

"Jars," I said, lifting the pack.

"Cheeky," she said.

"What's worse?" I asked. "Preparing too much and not using everything, or needing a thing and not having it to hand?"

"You swore to grant me a boon."

She had me there. "I did."

"I'll give you the *eitr*. You won the wager honorably. And I will leave this place and take with me my two children. We shall make our nest further from human habitations, though I must complain that there are more and more of you with every passing season. If you cover the whole damn landscape and keep breeding even when you encroach on other people's nesting grounds, I don't see how you can complain about a little volcano." She sighed. "And here I am helping resurrect your whelps, who will probably just make more of you."

They weren't my whelps, but I was more concerned with

something else she'd said. I snuck a sideways glance over the rim of the vent. Yes, three eggs. "Wait. You and your *two* children?"

"Yes," she said. "That's the boon. Don't worry, I'll leave you plenty of *eitr* for feeding the whelp on. And I will come back every season or so to be certain the whelp is well-taken-care-of and replenish your supplies."

That sounded less like reassurance and more like a threat.

"You want to raise a brood of your own."

"Not I," I said. "A friend."

"Well, if I save his children, let him care for one of mine. But you, little witch—you must see that the care is good. Yourself."

"Why me?"

"Because," she said. "Because I have tested your word and your mettle. And because I'm giving *you* the foster of my whelp. I have seen what you will do for the bonds of kinship. And because you understood me and gave me a gift, so I know you understand how bound to this boring rock I am."

"But I . . . I don't want to stay here either."

"Once a turning should suffice," she said, relentless. "As I said, it's only another hundred seasons or so. The egg will hatch in . . . twelve more seasons. Make sure your folk know that if they don't take care of my little one, though, I *will* come back and eat them."

I imagined the little whelp—perhaps only as large as the horse—looking up at the giant creature before me with wide, adorable eyes and begging, "Mama, can I eat him?"

"What about the volcano?" I asked. "My people cannot survive it. Doesn't the egg need its heat to incubate?"

"Oh, a lone egg will do well enough if they bury it in dry ground near a hot spring," she said.

"Like baking a loaf of bread," I mused.

"You," she said, "and your baking."

The dragon said she would give me time to return to Ragnar's farmstead before she flew the egg down and delivered it. My backpack sloshed with jars of *eitr* as I walked, the downhill steep and full of rocks that stubbed my toes through my boot leather. I'd be lucky not to lose a nail or two.

I was lucky that was all I seemed to be in danger of losing. Unless I tripped and fell and broke the jars, in which case the venom within would saturate my clothes, melt my flesh, and then probably catch on fire for good measure.

I walked very carefully and kept my eyes where my feet should be going.

It was a good thing, too, because the glamour I had cast on the little horse was strong enough that it even fooled me until I tripped over one of the spell-spun traces.

I had been singing to myself as I walked, songs more fitting for a warrior this time, and I had not been fingering my spindle. My hands, being free of my pockets, flung out and smacked into the horse's warm flank.

The glamour fell away in the face of concrete evidence, and I could see that the boulder he was dragging had gotten jammed into a crevice and was stuck there.

I slipped off my extremely caustic load and set the pack down carefully before going to unwind the string from around the boulder. Then I had some extra string and a horse that was already wearing a conjure-ish harness, so it only seemed fair that the horse carry the pack. That was what horses were for, after all, among other things.

I lashed it on over his withers. He was a convenient size, not so tall I had to reach up to tie things across his back. While I worked, I thought about getting back to town and explaining to Ragnar that he could have his children back, and all it would cost him was to spend his dotage babysitting a dragon.

I would get out of town before my brother and his wife woke up, I decided. It would be preferable to watching their teary reunion. Or having to endure either their thanks or their lack thereof.

I finished my harnessing and patted the horse on the shoulder. He nickered at me under his breath, friendly. Or hoping for carrots.

I draped an arm over his withers. He was a good height for leaning on. I made up my mind that I was taking him with me when I went, in addition to Magni. I would have to find someplace easy for him to recuperate, assuming the leg could—and would—get better. That would mean a winter off the road, which was probably wise for a man my age anyway, even if it griped me.

Anyway, if I left him here, Ragnar would probably eat him. I felt after using him to bait a dragon, I owed him better.

I scratched under his mane. He leaned into me, lip twitching in pleasure.

"Good lad," I said. "I think I'll call you Ormr."

AIMEE OGDEN

The Cold Calculations

FROM *Clarkesworld*

Once upon a time, a little girl had to die. It's just math. Wrong place, wrong time. Bad luck; too bad, so sad.

We've all heard such stories, told them, shared them, collected them. Not in the way that we collect trinkets; more like how a sock collects holes. We're submerged in such stories, we breathe them in like carbon dioxide— poisonous, in the long term, but a fact of life, nonetheless.

But stories have authors, from the gauziest fantasy to grim autobiography. And when once upon a time becomes so many, many times, surely someone must think to ask: had to die? On whose authority?

It's simple physics, of course. Natural law.

Unless, of course, someone's been fudging the numbers.

Álvarez is standing beside the airlock as it cycles, pretending not to hear the girl cry.

If he acts like he can't see her, can't hear her, then at least he's leaving her some dignity. Right?

As if there's any dignity to be had in this godforsaken mess. As if it's *dignified* to jump out of an airlock in nothing but a jumpsuit and your stockinged feet. As if anyone could have a reason to hold her head up high after she's been told her dumbass little stowaway life is worth less than the razor-thin fuel margin that will safely decelerate this drop ship when it reaches its destination.

The math is nauseatingly simple. There's no other ship with a possible intercept course. There's no other drop ship that can get the dying colonists at August Minor the nanotherapy antivirals they need. There's no give in the physics of it all—only in the squishy human parts of the equation.

There's still something wrong here. Or, if not *wrong*, then at least *not right*. Álvarez just can't put his finger on what, yet.

The airlock clanks; it's fully dilated on this side, now. The kid blows her nose on her sleeve. Sharra. Her name is Sharra. She deserves the dignity of a name, at least. "Thank you," she says. Her voice doesn't break. God, how does her voice not *break*? "For trying."

She's walking to her death to save him, a man twice her age, and a bunch of colonists she'll never meet, and she's thanking him? This isn't the *big* wrongness, the one that's underlined every moment since he pulled her out of the nanotherapy storage capsule, but it's a damned big one anyway. When she lets go of the loop and floats up toward the airlock, he grabs her by the sleeve— too hard—so that she bounces lightly against the inside hull of the drop ship. "No," he says, into her too-close face. "No, fuck this. We'll figure something out. We *will*."

That's when she starts crying for real: not when she thinks she's about to die, but when God sends something down the mountain and there's still a chance it might be a ram. When the tears get too big, they float up from her face and pelt him, like rain in reverse. He grabs her and crushes her against him, and she cries like he thinks babies must cry before they get taught that pain is something to hide.

"It's not right," he says, into the top of her head. He never had kids—a drop ship pilot's life is not exactly conducive to parenthood—but for a moment, this one, little dumbass stowaway that she is, is his kid, is every kid. "We never should have had to make the—"

"—choice." Mollie Maggia's sisters talk in whispers. In the back room of the little tenement apartment, Mollie is sleeping; Mollie is *dying*. "Money or health. Money or your life. The bastards. What else were we supposed to *do*?"

Their mother is at the stove, stirring the sauce for supper. Every now and then, she puts a hand in her pocket and fingers the pitted black tooth that lies at the bottom, the latest one collected from Mollie's mouth. When she closes her eyes, she remembers the first time Mollie came home from the watch factory with a gleaming greenish smile. How they'd all exclaimed, how they'd laughed. *My pretty girl*, she'd said. So proud. Such a good living, such a good girl. *My beauty.*

She would take this pain away from her daughter and make it her own, if she could. She digs harder with her wooden spoon, scraping the bottom of the pot, and doesn't wipe away the sweat that rolls into her eyes. This is her daughter—and even if she wasn't, even if she were someone else's, good God, she's only twenty-four, still a *child*. The spoon clatters to the floor and Mrs. Maggia leans against the kitchen wall. Who are they, the factory owners and foremen and faceless scientists in their white coats, to put this on her? Some man at a desk, totting up columns in his ledger: profit on this side, little girls' lives on the other. Who gave them the *right*?

No one gave them the right. It's something that they took. And it's not something one woman can snatch back all on her own, not even when the little girl who had to die upon that *time was her very own.*

Armed only with the cheap-ass screwdrivers from the ship's repair kit, Álvarez and the kid do their best to tear the drop ship apart. The ship wasn't outfitted with the proper tools to be strip-mined from the inside out; hindsight is, as ever, a bitch. Together they chuck anything they can get out the airlock: cleaning supplies, every last scrap of food, Álvarez's spare uniform and all of his bedding that can be torn loose from the wall. They even manage to rip up one of the metal panels lining the ship's interior, one that hadn't been screwed in squarely. The rest are flush and refuse to budge. The lone panel goes out the airlock anyway, one more piece of space junk. Hopefully it doesn't become another drop ship's urgent problem someday—but space is big, and the inside of the drop ship is small.

They do the math, with each piece of mass that goes flying off on a new career as interstellar jetsam. They crunch the numbers—and the numbers crunch back. It's not enough. Not enough to add up to a single scrawny kid with her whole damn life ahead of her.

If he could flush the whole water system and run dry all the way into August Minor, that would be more than enough. But he can't find a manual release, not on the hardware itself and not in the emergency handbook in his handheld, and there's an emergency rationing shutoff if he tries to draw too much at once. Water water everywhere, and not a drop to sink.

"I'll do it," Sharra says as he curses out the plumbing. Her tone is leaden; too bad he can't throw *that* out the airlock. "It's my fault anyway. I wanted to see my mom and dad. They'll die along with everyone else if these supplies don't get there in time. It's fine."

"It's *not* fine!" He punches the water filtration unit, which does no harm other than sending him rebounding across the ship. "Just let me think. There's something I'm missing, I know it." There must be a way out. No one had to—"

"—die." Russayev mops his brow with a handkerchief as he and Yuri trudge together up the cement-block stairwell. They keep moving, their voices buried beneath the echo of their footfalls. It's not safe to stop; every ear is always listening. It's not safe to return to Russayev's apartment; if the Party hasn't bugged it yet, that's due only to incompetence, not will.

"No one *had* to die." Yuri Gagarin is only thirty-four, and he moves heavily, like an old man. Guilt lays extra weight across his shoulders. When a man lays down his life for yours, that's a weight you'll carry the rest of your days. Vladimir Komarov knew what he was doing, who he was saving, when he stepped aboard the Soyuz-1. "But he did anyway. We all knew the flight was doomed. *They* knew it too."

His lips barely move around the word *they*. Best not to say aloud who *they* are, to name a thing gives it power, and Yuri holds too little power already to surrender more. He keeps folders full of well-creased papers inscribed with pleas for his help: dear Comrade Gagarin, Esteemed Hero of the USSR; can he not pull the strings to secure an officer's commission for this excellent young man, can he not see that this good daughter of the Fatherland be admitted to university despite her father's Jewish heritage? Can he not snap his fingers and make medicine, food, housing rain down upon the comrades who esteem him so?

He cannot. He cannot, could not even when he had friends in the Politburo, and he has only enemies there now. Komarov died to save a hero of the Soviet Union who has never really existed.

He fumbles for a cigarette, but his pocket is empty. Russayev produces a pair, and they smoke in silence, finally still, as the air grays around them.

"I should have done something else to keep him grounded," Yuri says, the words floating out of him on his smoky breath. Dangerous words, and the smoke does nothing to obscure the truth of them.

Russayev shakes his head, holding the smoke in. "They had already made up their minds." The nebulous *they* again, an all-hearing hobgoblin invoked if his name is spoken thrice. "No evidence could have changed that. There was nothing to be done." He claps Yuri's shoulder firmly, briefly. Yuri has forgotten his jacket and Russayev's hand is cold through his shirt. "I should go."

He should. Yuri stays, sitting alone on the stairs, smoking until only ash remains. Ash, and doubt. Like guilt, doubt is a cruel master to bear for the rest of one's life. But, Yuri knows, even then, he has not so much life left ahead of him that he cannot bear it, for a little while. His knuckles tap restlessly against the battered aluminum tread on the step.

Guilt is often all that's left when what we should be feeling—anger—is an inconvenience to the people with blood on their hands and fingers on the scale.

The data refuse to make sense. Fucking rude, if you ask Álvarez.

He queries and re-queries his interface station, poring over the numbers, until his anxiously firing neurons finally strike a connection. The naughty data resolves into one vicious big picture. He knows what it is he's been missing. Oh god, does he know what it is.

His jolt of hysterical laughter brings the kid's head up. "What?" she demands. She bobs over his shoulder, almost hitting her head on the bulkhead, to peer at the interface. As if she can make heads or tails of the techno-jumble on the screen. "What is it?"

"The launch," he says. "Christ. The *launch*." He highlights one particular figure in red. "It's not just the deceleration. There was extra mass on board when we were accelerating too." Her blank, frightened face wakes an obscure anger in him. He swipes one arm hard, wiping away the calculation display. "Even if I did push you out the airlock—fuck, I'm not going to do that, I said '*even if I did*'—there's still not enough fuel left for me all on my own." The margin was razor-thin; the kind of margin you could cut yourself open on. He rides another wave of hysterical laughter into dissociation, into the euphoria of perfect understanding. "We've been fucked since the get-go."

She stares at him. Her eyes are huge and dark in the big gray moon of her stupid sixteen-year-old face. "I killed you," she says. "I killed you. I killed you I killed you I—"

She's beating her own head and chest and shoulders with her fists, and Christ, Álvarez has never done zero-g wrestling before, let alone with somebody half his size whose dumbass head he would just as soon not split on the bulkhead, because if they're both going to die out here, and they are, why the fuck should they have to do it *alone?*

When she's calmer (which is certainly not to say *calm*), he produces a small plastic pouch from inside his flight suit. Her lips curls at the sight of it. "That's extra mass." It sounds like a curse word, the way she says it.

"I know. I was planning to piss it out the airlock pretty soon here." He opens the outside lid and squeezes some of the liquid inside into his mouth, then offers it to her. She takes a tiny sip and gags, sending tiny spheres of whiskey into orbit around Álvarez. She shoves the flask back at him; he takes it with a shrug. Plastic-flavored liquor is better than none. It's not really enough to take the edge off. It was meant to be a victory toast upon a successful touchdown, not an opportunity for self-medication. But it seems a damn shame to waste it.

"I hate physics," she says as he takes another pull.

He wipes his mouth with the back of his hand. Gone already. The caramel flavor lingers on the back of his tongue. "No, you don't."

"I'm allowed to hate the thing that's killing me."

"It's not physics that's killing us." He throws the empty pouch at the inside of the airlock door. It bounces off and spins lazily across the inside of the drop ship. "It's some accountant in Winnipeg who fucked us over to save the company some cash." Whose cold calculation was it? How much did it save? Twenty, thirty thousand bucks. A single externality: one small human life. Cheap as hell, all things considered. "Money's all that counts. Who cares what happens to the likes of—"

"—us?" Ha Wan shouts into the railroad foreman's face, so that his spittle flecks the man's brown beard. Perhaps he would take a swing at the foreman too; but with what? One of his arms terminates just below the elbow, the other at the narrow point of a wrist. Sweat crowns his forehead, and the sour stench of sickness clings to him, to the stained bandages on the stumps of his arms. There is a list, on the foreman's table, of employees to be paid for their time. Ha Wan's name is not on it. "My family depends on me!"

The foreman doesn't speak Cantonese, and the fever has curtained off whatever part of Ha Wan the English words occupy. Would it matter, if the foreman understood him? What would that change? His countrymen pull him away from the table before the foreman's bully boys can intervene. They try to lead him back to his cot, but he pulls away before they can stuff him back inside the hot, half-dark tent. They do not follow as he stumbles out into the scrubby highlands. Each of them is exhausted, too, spirits hammered flat with every blow of their iron mallets, every blast of dynamite. And how far can he go, they ask themselves, alone, on foot?

Not far. Dizziness catches him first, then exhaustion, and he crashes knees-first into the side of a boxcar laden with lumber for the new line. Bright new lines of pain crawl up through the dull, enveloping ache, and the morphine haze; he has scraped his back on the rough metal. Two drops of blood strike the sandy soil. In the dust-scratched sunlight, they already look faded and brown. Ha Wan is only surprised that he has blood left to lose.

Alone, what difference can one human being make? More than you think. Change comes incrementally. This is a symphony—not a solo.

Álvarez is supposed to be sleeping. Instead, he and the girl drift in silence, separately. Less than sixteen hours out from August Minor now.

He thinks the kid's asleep, her breathing uninterrupted by hitches and starts. A polyp of snot hangs by a thread from her upper lip, and her face looks sunken, dehydrated.

Grief is exhausting. But Álvarez isn't tired. There's an artery beating a staccato fringecore rhythm in his neck and an acid burn at the back of his throat. Periodically, he reminds himself that he *absolutely* cannot throw up right now.

He and the kid have fallen into opposing patterns, her spinning in place roughly clockwise, him counterclockwise. They've only known each other a little while, but there's a strange sense of belonging here, this person inextricably tied to him over the course of hours in a way that feels like DNA, or more than that, like she's sprung fully formed from the bulkhead of his own ship. A fractal spider web of veins spreads at her temples, maps to places that have never existed and never will.

For another few rotations, Álvarez studies these subtle geometries, seeking the kind of organic understanding that doesn't come from math anyway. Then he uses one hand to quietly push himself toward the computer. One more set of numbers to crunch, between her and oblivion.

The math doesn't cooperate willingly. But Álvarez doesn't ask nicely. He smashes the physics wide open like his own personal piñata, bashing it with calculations on fuel reserves and trajectories and human gravitational tolerance. There should have been fail-safes and backups, extra reserves. There should have been possibilities—possibilities other than the company literally nickel-and-diming two people to their deaths. There should have been a world where this story has a happy ending.

No, fuck that: there should be a world where this story has an ending *at all*. Because as Álvarez sees it, staring down the sawed-off barrel of the ugly math, staring down the long line of failures and accidents and miscalculations just like this one, it's never actually gotten around to ending before. It's the same goddamn story, told over and over in a Möbius loop of tragedy. Once upon a time, the people in charge told some peons they had to die, so they did. Rinse and repeat.

He pauses, eyes unfocused, staring into his screen until the numbers blur and run. How much pain has he already poured into this job? The backaches, the solitude, the exoskeleton he has to cram himself into whenever he gets to spend a hot minute on the ground somewhere. Pain is the only truly renewable resource, and it's the only asset the corporation has never stinted with.

He swipes away his calculation and keys in a simple message. Then he pushes off and glides silently across the capsule, to the airlock control. His hands aren't shaking. He thought he'd be more nervous, but his neurological system can't work up to a proper panic: dulled by the booze or short-circuited by the recent excess of adrenaline.

The cover flips up. He flexes his hands; he'll have to move fast, before the kid realizes what's happening. He keys in the control sequence.

The first door cycles open. He moves.

A wiry hand latches on to the back of his suit. "No!" the girl screams, as they flip end over end away from the airlock, a graceless ballet. "No! No! Don't!"

"Let go! Shit—" He struggles to free himself, but her grip is strong, and she clings to his back like a strangling vine. "I wasn't going to push you!"

"I know what you were going to do!" Her shriek in his ear makes him wince and they rebound together off the far bulkhead. "You can't!"

"I *can*." He doesn't want to hurt her, is the problem. It's like wrestling a lizard, one of those tiny little wall-climbers that were always all over the house where he grew up in Iowa, fast and sneaky but so small and fragile. He tries to pull her up and over his head. "Let go!"

She's less concerned about hurting him. Her fingers snag tight in his jumpsuit, and she draws blood through the cheap fabric. "Dammit!" he hisses, but the jolt of pain is enough for him to tear her loose. He pushes her away and the momentum sends him flying toward the airlock, her away from it.

She scrambles to reorient herself—too slow. He keys the code on the other side and the airlock seals itself shut between them. "It's okay!" he shouts through the metal door. She bangs on the other side, swearing viciously. "The ground crew at August Minor will talk you through deceleration. You don't have to land a ship; they'll be able to send a local shuttle up for you."

"This isn't fair!" she screams, which is a stupid-ass thing to say, but she's young, so he lets it go. "Stop it! Stop it! You can't do this!"

"Again, I think you'll find I can." He grins crookedly, then remembers she can't see him. "I've made my decision. It's okay. In fact, I've never been more sure in—"

"—my life!" Humasha's fingernails have splintered against the brown-stained stone of the garment factory wall. It's already ninety degrees in Savar Upazila, and the dust and humidity make her feel as if she's breathing mud. "Child, there are still people alive under there, I swear it. Help me dig!"

She doesn't know the young woman standing beside her;

she doesn't work on Humasha's line. A cut in her forehead has masked half her face in dust-caked blood; a careless hand has painted bruising all around the wound too. "Auntie, no!" Either she's younger than Humasha guessed, or fear throws her voice high and small. "Come away from there. It's not stable!"

Humasha does not come away. The building wasn't stable when they walked in to work that morning, either, or any other day that week. Some accountant, perhaps on the other side of the world, had decided that a sturdier factory wasn't worth cutting into the profit margin on cheap T-shirts. "Didn't you hear me, girl?" One lump of rubble comes away, under her weight; there are so many, many more that remain, and the voices of the trapped are small and far and frightened. Lost in a man-made underworld. Somewhere, above ground or below, someone is weeping. "They are still alive down there."

The girl shuffles back. Blood drips from the point of her chin onto her pink shari: one spot, two, three. A constellation in miniature. "And I don't want to join them, auntie!"

Humasha is not young, but age has not made her weak. Her ankles and knees pop as she forces herself upright and grabs the girl by the wrist. "You think you're better than them?" she snaps. "*You* are spared? Special?" She shakes the girl by the arm. "It's luck that we're up here and they aren't. That's all. You hear? It could always be you, next time. You know that? You want someone else to dig—when it's you at the bottom of the heap?"

The girl yanks her arm, twisting it out of Humasha's grasp. They both stumble; the girl catches herself first and sets her feet. She does not look at Humasha's face, but she kneels and forces her fingers into the crack between two broken fragments of what used to be a wall. "There shouldn't be a next time," she mutters, and winces as she leans back against the rock's recalcitrant mass.

"Shouldn't," says Humasha, leaving ten tracks of her own blood on the opposite side of the stone. She pushes, the girl pulls, the rock tumbles free. "Fill your belly with *shouldn't* and see how long till you're hungry again."

There is another stone, beneath the first, and they set their strength against that too. There is always another stone.

Have you been following along closely? We're coming to the hands-on portion of the exercise.

Don't feel guilty. Find your anger.
You're going to need it.

The girl pounds on the closed airlock; she smashes the keypad, but she doesn't know the magical password to reveal the secret passage.

The astronaut reaches for the internal keypad. It's cold in the airlock, and his fingers shake; he mistypes the code the first time. He puts his hands in his armpits to snatch a last moment's warmth. Perhaps he should have recorded a message, for his sister and her family. Too late now. Too late. But this is the only thing left for him. This is the *right* thing, because all the other options that remain are too ugly to choose.

The girl hasn't stopped screaming. She's so loud they must be able to hear her on August Minor, he thinks, and his lips fail to fit themselves into a smile. Loud enough to wake the dead.

"It's not fair!" she howls again. "*Someone do something!*"

But there isn't anyone left who could, or would.

Is there?

Somewhere, sometime, a man sits behind his desk, killing a girl with the stroke of his pen. Not because he hates her; he feels nothing for her at all. To him she is a simple tool, an externality. An inconvenient hunk of mass. It's never his fault that she dies, of course, even as he damns her over and over again. He's just doing his job. We must, the men at desks insist, chalk her death up to the cold, uncaring universe in which we live.

That's the point, of course. Pay no attention to the man behind the curtain.

Physics are impersonal, the fabric of reality, the canvas onto which we paint our lives. Physics existed before us. Math was created by human beings; and that is why math knows how to be cruel.

Other things than cruelty can still be taught, given time. Given opportunity.

If one man can kill a girl with the stroke of a pen, what can the rest of us do?

It's easy to decry his callousness, to raise our voices and shout over him. But this girl is not Tinker Bell, and a show of hands and a little noise will not be enough to bring her back. It's not enough, it never was, just to point at the evil and name it for what it is (though that is the starting place).

Feel your feet on the floor, or the line where your back meets your chair.

You're stronger than you think. There are some desks that need to be flipped, and they need you to flip them.

Some of them are heavy, but don't worry: you won't be expected to set your shoulder to them alone. Some of those desks will have men behind them, clutching pens and indignation. Some people will be very upset at the very notion of a desk that's the wrong side up.

But there's a girl out there whose life is hanging in the balance. She's going to need you to get out in front and push.

Yes, you.

All of you.

So push *already.*

It's not fair!

Mollie Maggia's mother pounds her fists against the kitchen wall: one, then the other. Then both. Again. It's not fair, it's *not* fair, her little girl, her angel, rotting alive in her own bed. She leans into the wall with all her weight, driving her grief into the cheap plaster, and when her other daughters run into the kitchen to see what's wrong, she slaps them away and slams her whole body against the wall so that the little apartment trembles in its foundations. "Not one more girl," she sobs, and she shouldn't be crying, not in front of her daughters, grown women themselves, but there is a blackened tooth in her pocket, and it weighs a thousand pounds, and she pushes her whole being into the door under that terrible weight. "Not someone else's baby."

Someone do something!

Yuri's knuckles twist harder into the aluminum strip on the stair. He grinds his fist down, though the rough pattern scrapes off a layer of skin and the blood squeezes between his clenched fingers. He could have stepped in. It could have been him instead. It should never have to be anyone else, not again. He pushes his hand into the stair until the bones in his wrists grind together.

It's not fair!

There can be, under the weight of injustice, a certain terrible strength, and it weaves itself into Ha Wan's muscle and bone. His legs flex and the air drives out of his body as he puts his back against the boxcar. His foot almost slips on the gravel, but he centers his weight and pushes again. There is a soft wail, like the call of a far-off locomotive, and it is coming from his throat. One more great thrust, the scrapes in his back tearing anew, and the front wheel of the boxcar squeals its dismay. It does not tip over, though he would like it to, for the railroad runs on suffering as much as coal. But he pushes anyway.

Someone do something!
   Humasha and the girl aren't alone. The emergency responders, the neighborhood, they dig together. They keep digging. There are people in the rubble. There are lives that might yet be saved, rock by rock, pebble by pebble, every last one worth the price in blood and toil to bring it into the light of the sun. "Push!" a medic yells, and six men and women set their shoulders against a fallen-in wall. They strain, someone curses, another groans. The wall shifts, and the wall moves. Daylight crawls over the cracked table that had been hidden underneath. A hand emerges, stretching, trembling. More hands reach down to meet it.

You, too. It might not feel like much, your little body fighting the terrible gravity of that cold arithmetic.
   But it is so much. It's everything. It's all there is.
   So push!

"It's not—"
   The entire drop ship decelerates as if slapped by the careless hand of God. Álvarez is thrown against the side of the airlock under the unexpected arrival of g-forces; the girl's cry is cut off as she, too, is flung aside.
   Shit. Shit. What the shit *was* that? He mashes in the code to open up the internal airlock again, even though it's going to be a hundred times harder to get past the kid this time, he has to make sure she's not concussed or hemorrhaging or otherwise a waste of a goddamn sacrifice.
   She's got a bloody nose, which has made a nightmarish three-dimensional abstract painting of the drop ship's interior but seems otherwise mostly unharmed. "What was that?" she asks, voice thick with blood and confusion. "Did we hit something?"
   "Couldn't have. We wouldn't be here to have this conversation at all." He nudges her aside to check his screens. Nothing out of the ordinary, all systems green. Except—

If a man at a desk can kill a girl with a little bit of ink, then we can save her in exactly the same way. There are more of us than there are of him. Break his pen, throw it out the window, and send the desk after it.

"This can't be right." He checks the readout again, double-checks it; does a quick-and-dirty visual verification against the star field visible through the porthole over his head. It can't be right. And yet, it is.

"What's wrong?"

Too much for him to sum up, too much to explain away, except in one little word: "Nothing." He bobs aside and shows her the screen that projects their trajectory toward August Minor. Everything is, impossibly, green. "We'll make planetfall just ahead of schedule. Six hundred twelve, local planetary time."

She doesn't blink, as if closing her eyes on the display will wipe it from existence. "That's impossible."

"Yup."

"How could that have happened?"

"Couldn't have."

She clings to the pilot's seat, adrift, still fixed on the readout. The glow of the screen paints her over with a pale green glow, and when she smiles slowly, her teeth shine in the dark drop ship. "Now what?"

Álvarez doesn't have an easy answer for her. When a miracle hands your life back to you, what do you do with that? How can you ever pay it back?

"I guess . . . I guess now I'll go home. Back to Earth, I mean." *Home* can mean a lot of different things to a drop-ship pilot. The ship hums gently around them, anthropomorphically innocent, as if it didn't nearly become their mutual coffin.

"Home." She's staring at the screens, as if not blinking for a solid minute will make the readouts comprehensible to her. For her, home is the people waiting on August Minor. "Why Earth?"

"Well, that's where Company HQ is. Thought I'd pay them a visit." He keys in the deceleration sequence and smiles, his lips pulling tight over his dry teeth. Miracles are hungry things. He'll feed this one by living long enough to be a pain in the company's ass. "There's a few desks there that I'd like to flip."

Pain is a renewable resource.
Time to see how well it burns.

C. L. CLARK

The Captain and the Quartermaster

FROM *Beneath Ceaseless Skies*

COMMANDER MAEB LEN knows that, more than anything, an army needs hope in order to struggle onward. They need a vision to fight for and faith that the future will be better than the past. Better than the present.

The People's Army itself is one such hope. The fall of the Tyrant is one such vision.

Commander Len also knows that people find hope in other, smaller things.

In the laughter that replaces the moaning of the wounded after a quiet winter of healing and souls put to rest.

In the green shoots of grass, wildflowers blooming in the untrampled fields around the Army's camp.

In the unwavering dedication of Commander Len and Quartermaster Omopria to each other, and to the People's Army. Their teasing romance. The brilliance of their successes. Together, they can do anything.

Anything to remind the Army that the world will go on, and that perhaps, they will too.

Commander Len clasps arms and grips shoulders with the other officers as they gather in the command tent one last time before the final campaign against the Tyrant begins. (No one has said out loud that it is the final campaign. No one would dare.)

Captain Dhissik, the new leader of Len's old company, gives her a fierce hug. High Commander Aulia does not. She nods gravely, warily. Lately, Len has been keeping her distance from her old sparring partner.

The new season brings new promotions, and it will take time to see how they fit.

Once they are all seated on the circle of blankets, High Commander Aulia raises a hand for quiet.

"Officers of the People's Army." Aulia looks at them each in turn, and Len feels the strength in Aulia's certainty spread from officer to officer, commander and captain alike. "We've been fighting against the Tyrant for six years. He's stolen our youth. He's stolen our good looks." She smiles, and the scar that splits from below her right eye to the left side of her sharp chin stretches. She sobers immediately, though. "He's stolen the happier lives we might have lived, and the loved ones we might have spent them with."

Solemn nods from all. Len isn't the only one whose grip tightens around a sword hilt or into a fist. Here in this stuffy tent, they are the same. The People's Fist. The Hand That Would Open the Cage.

"It's time we steal from him." The officers cheer Aulia's words. "This spring, when the flowers bloom and the trees fruit, so do we." They cheer again.

But as the high commander details the plan for the campaign, Len's heart sinks. They will need the best quartermaster in the world for such a risky campaign. The Army's standing supply caches had been targeted early in the war. Their quartermaster had worked without sleep to decentralize what remained. From then on, each unit became responsible for carrying a portion of the Army's stores so the Tyrant couldn't destroy them with a single blow. It is a delicate balance; one overlooked shortage or faulty supply line, and the entire Army risks slaughter or starvation.

And unlike everyone else in the room, Len knows in her bones that the best quartermaster in the world wants to leave the People's Army and go home. She doesn't think Quartermaster Omopria will last another full campaign.

The worst part about it is that Len can't blame her, won't blame her, if she leaves.

While the other officers leave the command tent feeling determined, Len finds herself drifting. Instead of convening with her captains, she stands outside of the tent and watches the camp shake off winter's slumber. There, in the eastern corner, is the sparring square, bright with the clack of wood, the grunts of effort and laughter.

There, toward the center of the camp, the supply wagons, where Quartermaster Omopria and her staff would be, counting and loading, loading and counting. Someone is cooking the beans for lunch.

Then she looks to the north, toward the city where the Tyrant waits, not knowing he has rats in his larder, stealing hope for the People.

"Is everything all right?"

Len jumps at High Commander Aulia's soft voice beside her. "Fifth," Len greets her with her old company's name.

Len knows that the smile she gives doesn't pass muster. Aulia's expression softens with understanding. Somehow, the scar on her face only makes the expression more tender.

"I know it's none of my business, but the soldiers talk and—"

Len walls up her expression, and she looks balefully at the high commander of the People's Army.

Aulia crosses her hands awkwardly behind her back, leather armor creaking. "Just. If you need anything, I'm here. I was married once too."

"Oh?" Len turns sharply, hungry for someone else's answers. Someone else's sorrow to show her what to do with her own. "What happened?"

"A little thing called a civil war." A complicated grief crosses Aulia's face.

Cold fills Len's belly as realization dawns. "We're fighting them."

Aulia nods solemnly. "We're fighting them."

"I'm so sorry."

"So am I."

A long time ago, when the People's Army was first born from the spark of rebellion against the Tyrant, Captain Maeb Len of the Third Company trudged back into camp on her own sore feet. Agno, her horse, had fallen, stabbed behind one of his legs, and she'd jumped from the saddle, praying for mercy and so much blind luck. She hadn't even had time to cut his poor throat before she had to face the onslaught of the enemy. Maybe the very ones who'd brought down Agno.

The rage of the battle gone, her company limped into the marching camp after her, their faces drawn in pain or shame or exhaustion—likely a combination of it all. Truth to tell, Len felt more than a twist of shame herself. And not just because she hadn't given Agno the mercy he deserved after faithfully carrying her for so long. But the battle was done, and ahead of her was a meal and her first bath in weeks, if she could make the walk to the stream. A dry scrub if she could not. But first, she would ki— No, she wasn't sure that was true, that she would kill for a decent meal. Not right now. The memory of running her bloodied sword through another thick body, scraping it back out of a bone-caged heart, coating her hands in sticking blood—it made her want to bring up food instead of shovel it down. Luckily, she'd lost all the food she had to spare on the field amid the corpses. Many of her soldiers had. The sick still tasted sour in her mouth.

Water. A drink of water first.

She lined up at the officers' soup queue, among other young captains and senior captains without the colors of distinction on their coats. Well—no color of distinction but the deep arterial red of close combat.

A woman, the quartermaster's assistant, doled out the soup in carefully measured ladles, making sure each was equal. So careful, even here with the officers, to make sure that precious goods lasted. The sergeant wore her hair in a tight braid, but curls sprang free at her wide brow; some of them clung in sweat there. She looked thin, as if she should have her own rations doubled.

"Come on, missy, you cannot give me more than that?" A senior captain shook his bowl expectantly at the woman, stalling the entire line of weary and aching soldiers. The soup's scent reached Len. Beans. Again. Thank the gods. Better than nothing at all, and though beans could wreak havoc in the communal tents, they would hold to your guts and keep you full. At that moment, Len could not have stomached meat.

"No, *sir*, I can't." And when he refused to move on, the quartermaster's assistant shoved past him to the next officer with the next carefully measured bowl. That officer had the sense to move along quickly.

The senior captain did not. He pushed his way back in front of the assistant. "Excuse me? Do you not think you're out of line?"

The quartermaster's assistant met his glare with hers. "No, I do not, but I would be *most* glad if you were out of this one." Then she beckoned the next person to the pot.

Captain Len stifled a smile as she watched the woman pour, watched the irritation creep into the set of her jaw. This close, the captain saw a streak of gray climbing through her hair. Surprising, as she didn't look a day out of her second decade, cheeks round, skin unlined. Likewise, Len could smell the blood on the senior captain's coat. Could trace the tension in his shoulders through the fabric, the bunching before a blow.

Captain Len reached up and placed a hand on his shoulder. "Sir! Sir, you were brilliant on the field today. I hope I'm half as good as you before I'm promoted. You'll have a high commander's cloak before we're done here."

The senior captain looked at her, disdain in his gaze for the interruption but courtesy toward a fellow winning out over it. The higher-ups looked on mentoring as favorable for promotions.

"Thank you, Captain . . . ?"

"Len. Maeb Len. Do you want to share a drink?" She leaned close to his ear. "I've been hiding a stash of 798, if that interests you."

His mood perked up instantly. "Now, that I cannot turn down." And Len led him away, past the other cookpots with other men and women on the quartermaster's staff and around to where her company would pitch her tent.

Later, when the senior captain had gone, a slight stagger in his step, Len lay under the stars, stomach growling, still dirty and unwilling to sully her tent with her own filth. That was where the quartermaster's assistant found her.

"You forgot your dinner." The woman smiled, with a bowl of soup in each hand, and lowered herself down.

"Thank you." Len sat up, taking the offered bowl. "I'm sorry he was an ass."

The quartermaster's assistant waved the apology away. "It comes with the post. The People's Army welcomes all people, and so on. Thank *you* for getting rid of him."

"It took almost an entire 798. Well worth it, I'd say." Len waved the squat-bottomed bottle by its short neck, but the stars spun and her soup sloshed at the bowl's rim.

"Steady on," the quartermaster's assistant said with a chuckle, easing the bottle from Len's hand. "I'm Jissia Omopria."

"Maeb Len."

From the beginning, Jissia had taken care of Len.

Four years later, Captain Maeb Len knelt by Quartermaster Jissia Omopria's side in her own tent. It was bigger than the quartermaster's tent, and Len didn't have to share it with subordinates like Jissia did. Still, it smelled sour with sweat and sick.

Jissia burned with fever. Her hand was clammy in Len's, and she muttered to no one, delirious and barely conscious. Half the camp was.

The People's Army had been fucked for four years, but this day had been an exceptionally bad day.

"Captain!"

Her lieutenant's voice was frantic outside the door. She startled upright, out of her almost-doze.

"What now, Balissen?" Len tried to shout it, but her voice was too hoarse. She'd been screaming retreat after retreat for weeks. The Tyrant wasn't letting her people rest. That was the point. Harry them, and when they stopped to catch their breath, harry them again, until they collapsed from exhaustion. If Len let herself go to sleep now, she would never wake up, and she would be glad for it.

It wasn't Balissen who came in. Len blinked blearily in the dim candles lighting the tent. Oh. Right. Balissen had taken an arrow through the throat three months ago. She hadn't been the one to find his body or she would never have forgotten. So she told herself.

"What is it?" she croaked.

This new lieutenant's name was Dhissik. Lieutenant Dhissik first handed her a small cup of what Len already knew was dirty water masquerading as coffee. Jissia had stretched the rations as far as she could so that the soldiers could keep moving, over and over again, but now the officers were hoarding it jealously. Jissia hadn't approved, but how was Len supposed to make the decisions that would save their lives if she was more than half-asleep?

Len sipped, to make the cup last.

"Captain Aulia found out what's wrong." The lieutenant swayed with exhaustion, but fear made her eyes wide. "It's the water. They're dumping corpses upriver. It's running straight to us."

Len's eyes went down to her coffee. "Shit."

"Not that water."

The lieutenant didn't leave.

"What else?"

"The Tyrant's moving again. Not to chase us," Dhissik said quickly, to forestall Len, "but something else. The Fourth and Fifth just arrived. They want to speak with you."

Len turned back to Jissia. The fever hadn't broken, but the murmuring had stopped. She didn't once think of sending Dhissik in her place. Dhissik had been a corporal three months ago. She wouldn't even have sent Balissen, who had been her lieutenant for three of the five years.

Four years. She turned Jissia's right forearm over. The inked marriage mark matched the one on Len's, so that when they clasped forearms the images made a whole.

There was duty, and then there was *duty*. Len heaved herself clumsily to her feet. Though the young lieutenant had to grab her by the arm to steady her, Len didn't spill the coffee.

"Tell me where they're meeting," Len said. "You stay here with her."

"Sir," Dhissik said with a sigh. Her voice cracked. "I can't. I have messages to run to the other two captains."

"Why do they have my lieutenant doing everyone else's job?" Len growled as she pulled her leather armor back on and buckled her sword belt.

But she knew the answer. Everyone else was dead.

And the People's quartermaster lay alone in her sickbed.

How different that was from the beginning.

With her hand in Deputy Quartermaster Omopria's, sneaking away from the Army's camp, Captain Len felt like she could climb the clouds. But the sky was clear and blue, and the quartermaster's smile was bright and warm, and the captain was sinking hopelessly into it.

Back when the war was new and hope was sweet on the tongue. Freedom from the Tyrant. Rule by the People.

Len tugged Jissia's hand again, smiling slyly. "They'll be fine without us for ten minutes."

"Ten minutes?" Jissia raised an arched eyebrow. "Is that all?"

Len blushed but, even so, pulled Jissia close. "I'm happy to draw this out longer if you are."

Jissia's body melted into hers as they kissed, delighting in the sensation of eyelashes on cheeks, noses nuzzling, hands holding tight at the wonder of it all. Len wanted it to last forever.

And so she asked, after they peeled apart and lay in the soft grass of the clearing they had claimed. Amid their strewn clothing there was even someone else's jacket—neither of theirs but another lover, perhaps, who had forgotten it because they were too flush with the warmth of their own kindling. Len would bring it back to camp and tease the owner mercilessly, knowing she would be teased in return. But that, too, was the joy of it.

"What are you doing in a few months' time?" Len rolled over to walk her fingers gently up Jissia's sternum before tracing the lower curve of her right breast. "When this is all over?"

Jissia rolled over, tangling her boots with Len's. She'd pulled her uniform trousers back up but they were still unlaced, and Len gave them a playful tug. "You think this will be over that soon?"

"No civil war on the entire continent has lasted longer than two years! We're close. Look how easily we've routed them." She met Jissia's gaze and held it earnestly. "We have the people on our side. The Tyrant can't stand against his own nation."

Jissia raised both of her eyebrows this time and snorted. "The folly of youth."

"You weren't complaining about my youth a few minutes ago." Len used their tangled legs as a lever to roll back on top of Jissia and kiss her deeply. But when Jissia sank her hands into Len's long braids, Len stopped. She stroked the thin streak of gray in Jissia's dark hair. "Would you make a life with me, when it's all done?"

Jissia's face softened in surprise and then tenderness. "Are you sure you'd be happy? You're a fighter. Even off the field."

"I've had enough of trouble." Squads of soldiers lost, the roughness of sleeping in cold tents, waking up knowing so clearly that the day could be her last. Len could walk away happily and never look back. "Let's have something simple and easy."

"And when you get bored, Maeb?"

Len bent down and kissed her on the forehead, then the nose, then the lips. "No one can fight forever."

Much later, Captain Maeb Len will remember that day with the fever as the day it all broke because it was the day many things broke. It was the day that she learned she would fail again and again and again. It was the day she learned that she never wanted to fail those she loved but she loved too many.

It was the day she truly felt in her bones that war is not kind to love. She had loved Lieutenant Balissen like a brother and had not even looked for his body after the report came in. She had tried not to let the deaths become rote, to force herself to feel disgust instead of numbness at bloody leathers, because that, too, was a failure of love.

Love was the only thing that held any of them together. The People's Army went to fight for love of their neighbor, who the Tyrant would have let starve in the street. For love of the mothers, who died in childbirth rather than give birth in the fine hospitals that became debtors' prisons. For love of the teachers, who starved rather than let their students go hungry.

War brought the captain and the quartermaster together, because they believed in love over the Tyrant. They had to love each other more than the war would have torn them apart.

It would not be one crack but many, and still Len would always try again.

After six years of civil war, Len sits at her travel desk to draft a letter to a potential ally recently freed from their own queen. That is the first task High Commander Aulia has given her. The words don't come out right. If she sounds too desperate, they might balk; what use in sending troops to fight for a lost cause, no matter how just?

But the People's Army *is* desperate. Six years. Even Len can see that there won't be a year after this. Not with this army. Not these leaders.

Len looks down at the embroidered crimson fist on the breast of her jacket. She is a commander now. Aulia is counting on Len's intelligence for the new campaign.

She feels a warm hand on her shoulder. Jissia hands her a cup of coffee that smells strong, black as pitch. Len's eyes watered. It smells like hope.

"Where did you—"

Jissia shakes her head and kisses Len gently on the cheek.

"This is it, isn't it?" Jissia asks softly. "Either we win or . . ."

Or. They both know the other would finish that sentence differently.

Len takes Jissia's hand and kisses the knuckles gently.

*

Len also remembers a time, in the middle of the war, the third year, maybe the fourth? They had already been fighting longer than the People's Army had prepared for. Longer than Len had prepared for. Still, Len thought they had turned a corner in the war. She'd had an idea for a new, more devastating munition.

"Jissia!" she called happily when she found the quartermaster in her domain. The unit's supply wagons were nestled within the camp so that they couldn't be easily picked off by the Tyrant's raiders. Even though the ground around them had been trampled, green grass had begun to shoot up in tufts between the wheels.

Jissia pecked Len on the cheek, and Len caught one of the junior quartermasters hiding a smile. Len smiled tentatively at Jissia in turn.

"Yes?" Jissia said suspiciously.

"We've had an idea," Len said, now almost shy. "We need to melt all of our extra iron into some kind of heavy-impact projectile."

Jissia's face darkened immediately. "*Extra* iron? We don't have any iron left."

"Wait. What do you mean we're out of iron?" Len pursued Jissia around the supply wagons while Jissia checked this thing and that thing in her inventory ledger. "Jiss, we've been doing shit-all for a whole season! What do you mean we're out of iron?"

Jissia pressed the ledger to her forehead before enunciating slowly, as if Len were stupid. "I mean that between the reinforced shields, the re-shod horses, and the new wagon axles that you'll need to start moving your army again—we're left a bit short." Jissia lowered her voice so the underlings couldn't hear. "Besides, we don't have the facilities for casting iron. If you stopped playing games and paid attention to the actual war, you'd know this."

"Playing games?" Len was almost tempted to throw her sword into Jissia's arms, to make her swing it. It would show her just how easy these games were. "This is why we *have* you. You help us make this possible. *My* job is to coordinate the ground strategy within the army. That includes knowing my soldiers and training them too."

She didn't understand why Jissia begrudged her the time in the sparring square even though it brought Len some of the only peace she ever felt.

Jissia's own outlet had soured. At first, she had painted, carrying small scraps of canvas and painting until she tired of the same dull colors, the same dull scenes. Len wondered if Jissia saw the same things she did, over and over again. Brown mud, gray-brown corpses, red-brown dried blood.

"I saw you with the captain of the Fifth." Jissia didn't look at Len when she said it.

Len didn't look at her either. She felt the need to protect something small inside of herself. She dug the toe of her boot into the dirt.

"That wasn't the vow we made."

"She understands me. That's all."

"Good for her. I'm glad someone does."

And the silence. Cold, lonely silence.

Len had also struggled to find her place, though Jissia perhaps hadn't realized it. By the third year, Len finally understood the cycle of war: the wintering camps, the spring thaw into movement. When spring came, the fighting would start over again without care for those who needed time to catch their breath or whose legs and back had become too weak to carry the weight. She was still not used to the death, not exactly; she would regret the day the dead were nothing to her. Her body, however, could learn to tolerate the exhaustion.

(And yet, she no longer thinks of Balissen. There are the living to think of.)

One day that third winter, the sparring square was full of soldiers trying to keep themselves sharp. And by sharpening herself here, Captain Len thought that, perhaps, she could forge herself into something better for Jissia.

Len pulled a practice blade and arced it across her body. Already she was able to replace thoughts of Jissia with the natural flow of her own body.

"Third!" A cheerful voice interrupted the flow. Captain Rix Aulia, of the Fifth. She was tall and narrow, with sharp eyes and a sharper chin. Her face was smooth and unlined despite a few sporadic gray hairs amid her cropped black curls.

"Fifth!" Len tapped Aulia's bare blade with her own in an invitation.

They crashed together in a joy of panting. Each near miss, a curse tinged with laughter. In the end, Len slipped within Aulia's longer reach to disarm her. They fell to the ground. She ended up weaponless beneath Aulia, whose forearm rested on her throat.

Aulia of the Fifth smiled, showing crooked eyeteeth.

Len left the sparring square with the flutter of finding cherished jewelry that she thought she'd lost.

Four months before High Commander Aulia gave the army its commands for the final campaign, Len and Jissia lay awake in the pitch-black tent. The candles were snuffed. Outside, the early winter wind howled like the hungry coyotes dogging the supply train. The Tyrant was pulling back for the season.

Len felt the hands-breadth of space between them like a wall. The effort it took to keep themselves distinct. And still, she could have drawn the shape of Jissia's body beside her.

"I want you to go," Len whispered. "I can't do this anymore."

Saying it felt like siphoning poison from her blood.

"What?" Jissia's voice cut through the quiet.

"I know you want to leave. Go. There's still time to live the life you dreamed of. I won't steal it from you, like the Tyrant."

"You have no idea what I've dreamed of. What I've given up for this war. Do you?"

"The same things we've all given up."

"No. You've found glory. You've found friends. People who think and act like you. I've grown more and more isolated, with each passing year."

"Your assistants—"

"They're not my friends any more than an unranked soldier is yours."

"Some of them are my friends."

"Then I'm not like you. It's not easy for me."

"You're right. And it doesn't have to be. You can go."

"I stayed here for you. I'm not leaving now. We'll see this through to the end. Together. Like we promised."

Silence stretched, full of Len's doubts. Jissia's hand snuck over, hesitant. Len remembered times that the two of them had been as tightly laced as fingers, able to support more together than apart.

"You're sure?"

"Of course."

During that autumn campaign season, the captain and the quartermaster worked miracles together, even when they thought they couldn't.

"There's no way to get an extra two weeks' worth of food all the way to a company you've stationed on the ass-end side of the world." Jissia ran her hand through the snarl of her curls, a riot of gray and brown. She rounded on Len. "You've stationed them too far from us."

"I know. I'm sorry. We didn't mean to let it get like this, but it was our only option. They knew the risks and—"

"An army marches on its stomach. And its gear. You've stripped away my ability to provide for either. That is my *job*." Jissia about-faced and strode away, leaving Len to trail, limping, after her.

"I know. Of course, I know." Len searched for the words to soothe her quartermaster, but, as happened more and more often these days, she found herself at a loss. No matter how much she explained, it was never quite enough—or perhaps, never quite right. When they ducked into their tent, she added, "It's my job to make sure this war is won."

"And then we can stop, yes? Isn't that what you said four years ago?" Jissia didn't bother to light a candle. They were running low, and she limited them to strategy meetings only now. The officers needed to read missives and see the maps. Letters from home—such that they were—could be read by daylight or moonlight or not at all.

Len didn't need a candle's flickering flame to see the severe set of Jissia's mouth.

"Part of me feels like you'd be fine for this to keep going forever," Jissia said. "You thrive on this. I don't."

The remark stung. "No? You don't thrive on the satisfaction of keeping our soldiers alive?" Len snorted. "I know the way you get when you solve a problem we couldn't figure out." Smug and beautiful with the sheer brilliance of her mind. Jissia had saved them more times than Len could count. The two of them could do it again, but only together.

Len could see Jissia gathering breath, like a snake coiling for a strike. As if granted a vision of the future, Len knew what could happen: they would strike and parry until there was nothing but silence between them. Tonight of all nights, she didn't want that.

Len held up her hands in surrender. "I'm sorry." She reached out to clasp Jissia's forearm. Though their clothing covered it, their marriage marks lined up and reminded Len why they had bound themselves together.

Jissia clasped back, tentatively at first, as if she wasn't sure she was allowed. "Me too."

They slept together that night for the first time in many months, but it wasn't until after Jissia rolled away that Len admitted to herself what she couldn't during the act. Jissia had either forgotten how to touch her, or didn't want to. The captain turned her back to the quartermaster. Her core felt hollowed out.

Two days after receiving High Commander Aulia's orders and one day before the People's Army marches, Quartermaster Jissia Omopria requisitions all of the sugar in the army. She calls it hope.

With her help and the People's cooks, every soldier has one sweetened biscuit to eat.

It shouldn't be enough to cry over, or enough to set a field army to carousing happily through the rows of tents as if at festival.

But it is. Jissia is right. Sugar is hope, and that's what the People's Army needs after six years of attrition. That's what they need for one last push.

Commander Len and Quartermaster Omopria eat their biscuits with their closest friends. Captain Dhissik of the Third. The First. High Commander Aulia and the new captain of the Fifth. Deputy Quartermaster Chessian.

Len's knee bumps Jissia's, and when Jissia cups Len's knee with her hand, Chessian giggles. He has a sweet laugh and dark doe eyes, and he idolizes Jissia. Len feels Aulia's eyes on them.

"How long *have* you two been together?" Chessian asks. "Longer than the war?"

Jissia tears up a clod of dirt and tosses it at him as she laughs. It sounds as forced as Len's own strained smile.

They share a knowing look before answering.

"We're as old as the war."

"We started because of the war."

Chessian mock swoons, but when he recovers, he looks at them with a sugar-shine in his eyes. "It's nice to know that something good can come out of this, after all."

And behind the forced smiles, the silence still; now scalding to the touch and swollen, like a blister.

But a blister must be lanced before a march.

*

And in the morning, the People's Army is on the move again.

Len helps Jissia saddle her placid horse and kneels to offer her a vaulting step onto its back. It is the horse least tempered for war that Len has ever seen. Jissia strokes its neck from the saddle.

High Commander Aulia rides over. She looks anxiously at the sky, judging the position of the sun, which has not even crested the horizon. The deep black of night is only just turning gray. It's time to go.

Aulia sees Jissia's saddlebags. They don't have the familiar waxed ledger cases to keep the inventory books safe from rain and blood and whatever war would throw at them. "What's going on, Commander?" Her eyes flick between Len on the ground and Jissia, on her horse. "Quartermaster?"

"Quartermaster Chessian has his orders," Jissia said. "He's more than up to the task."

"We have a plan in place," Len added.

And though something inside Len is asking, *Are you sure are you sure are you sure that you will not break without each other*, Len knows that she has never been more sure of anything.

She sees the same certainty in Jissia's face.

She expects Aulia to balk at losing the best quartermaster in the world; expects her to try and convince Jissia to stay.

Instead, Aulia turns her horse. She nods to Jissia in farewell and says to Len, "We move out in ten." She leaves them their privacy.

"I always knew—"

"You know, I thought—"

They stop. They laugh. It feels as if they should weep.

Len holds her arm up one more time, and Jissia clasps her elbow. Len's bare arm, her sleeve rolled up, shows one half of the marriage mark, tattooed in black.

"You're my best friend."

"We'll be okay."

There is nothing else to say, and their efforts to find the right words, the right *last* words, feel futile.

Nothing else to say but: "Thank you, Jissia."

As Len looks up at Jissia, her face finds it hard to smile, even though it is all she wants to do, for Jissia's sake.

Jissia squeezes Len's arm. "Thank you, Maeb."

They stay like that, arms linked, for eight more minutes, even though Jissia's back must be straining and Len's shoulder aches.

Then, when the former quartermaster is gone, the commander reaches for the reins of her own horse, pulls herself up, and rides after the high commander.

The night before, after the celebrations, they sat on their shared blanket amid their shared pillows. Years of words unspoken sat with them.

"That was well done, Jissia," Len said. "Genius."

Jissia smiled. "An army marches on its—"

Len rolled her eyes and gave the quartermaster a playful shove. "Len?"

Len looked into Jissia's eyes, startled to see them shining. Outside, the revel continued. Firelight and starlight crept in through the cracks of the tent.

Suddenly, it was as if there wasn't enough air in the tent. Len could only say, "Mm?"

"Chessian is ready to take over." Jissia let the weight of her words sink in.

"What happened?" By which Len meant, *Why now, how did you change your mind,* are you sure?

"We've been the captain and the quartermaster for so long. I thought we couldn't be anything else." Jissia shrugged. "Tonight . . . I realized that may not be true. But if I stay, I won't find out."

And instead of pain and fear, Len felt the salt tears of relief.

For the first time in too long, the air felt truly easy between them.

"Here." Jissia smiled through her own tears as she pulled out a tiny paper parcel.

Len knew what it was the moment she held it in her hand. She laughed. She pulled out her own small package for Jissia, this one wrapped in admittedly dingy cloth.

They opened them at the same time. Each parcel held the slightly crumbled half of a sweetened biscuit.

When the quartermaster and the commander go separate ways, no one will understand why. Commander Len will assure everyone that Jissia is still a dear friend; they will exchange letters—when the war ends, when Jissia opens a school, when Len takes a seat on the People's Council.

They will both remember things that they had forgotten, like how to walk on two legs instead of four, or how to take enough food just for one, not two. They will both love again; other people, other ways.

Len doesn't weep until the People's Army is riding away from their winter camp and her quartermaster is just a speck on the road, heading the other direction.

Life goes on. In their own corners of the world, they will go on too.

NALO HOPKINSON

Broad Dutty Water:
A Sunken Story

FROM *The Magazine of Fantasy & Science Fiction*

"GET IN, LICKCHOP." Jacquee lifted her pig into the main cabin of Uncle Silvis's ultralight she'd borrowed from home.

Lickchop merely grunted, *Chow* aloud via the vocoder illegally implanted in his scalp. Jacquee didn't know who'd done that to him; is so she'd found him last year, a half-dead lump of throwweh, unconscious and sinking fast in the center of a medical waste trash vortex about seventy nmi offshore of the Grande Soufrière false atoll that loomed over sunken Guadeloupe. No one back home could figure out why the vocoder had a ring of tiny rods, each a couple millimeters long, sticking out the top of Lickchop's skull. Jacquee called it his tiara. Lickchop didn't much use the vocoder, except to demand chow. At the moment, he was eagerly paddling his stubby legs in the air.

"I know, sweetness," Jacquee said to him. "I'm impatient too." She was mad to try out her brand-new wetware. Dr. Lin had said she should wait a week, but he always exaggerated that bullshit. He was an old boyfriend of Uncle Silvis's. As hospitals became too overwhelmed with flood, plague, and starvation victims to function adequately, he'd moved his surgery practice to his home. Five years now Jacquee had been going to him. He'd replaced her left elbow after she splintered it on a dive in a dead coral reef. He kept her taz supplied with antibiotics he mixed up in his kitchen. She regularly brought him gifts of food her taz bred. Some of those were illegal to have, but he'd never turned her in to the World Bioheritage enforcers.

As soon as Jacquee put Lickchop down on the floor of the ultralight's tiny cabin, he trotted click-click over to the spongiform food puzzle she'd bolted to the floor in one corner. He stuck his snout into it and began happily rooting for the algae pellets she'd made and tucked inside it.

Activity on the post-Inundation dock bustled all around them: people with their belongings on their backs hustling from the mainland to the water along the rocky wooden boards of the makeshift bridge over the new wetlands; boats and catamarans docking and getting underway; people shouting orders; the air-filling duppy moans of ships' horns; the oily fishswamp stink of water polluted by gas engines. The original land was somewhere below them, swallowed by the polluted black waters of the risen ocean. Nobody was really sure what Florida town or city they were floating above; catastrophic flooding and the resulting seismic activity had changed shorelines too much and were still doing so.

Jacquee clambered behind Lickchop into the small cabin of her ultralight. Her knapsack dragged at her shoulders, though it really wasn't plenty heavy. She was just a little tired from the surgery. She straightened up, and her world spun backward. Vertigo. She clutched for one of the hand-straps in the ceiling. She was a bit unsteady on her pins after the slicendice Dr. Lin had performed on her the day before. She should have stayed in his spare bedroom one more day, to recover from the laparoscopic surgery and get a bit more training in how to use the wetware he'd just implanted in her brain. But a whole two days a-landlock? Enough. She and Lickchop needed to get home, back to the sea and their taz massive—them in the Jamdown Ark. The floating platform on which her community lived had been traveling for weeks to get to the next berth on its annual route, the one east of the Caribbean crescent. Now it was time to reestablish their vertical farm. This week, Jacquee would be helping to lay out the floating grid of plastic pipes with the newest kelp seedlings sprouted along their lengths. Then there'd be mussel socks to attach to the grid and lower into the water, plus the cages stocked with clam and oyster seeds. She liked this part of the endless round of tasks it took to keep the taz functioning. She got to free-dive amongst the hanging fronds of kelp, swerving around the vertical cooling rods that chilled the ocean water passing through them to keep the kelp at optimum temperature. She was up to five minutes of being able to hold her breath.

Uncle Silvis could do seven; Plaidy, who lived with her children and her man five habitats over on the taz, was the current record-holder—almost nine minutes under the water before she would faint and have to be yanked out.

Jacquee pulled the ultralight's cabin door shut and looked through the porthole. So much waste being spat out all around her; a treasure trove. "Lickchop," she said as she went to top up the pig's water dispenser, "give our taz two days here, and yuh would see how much we could salvage!"

The pig, busy filling his belly, ignored her. She got to work locking the lid on his stale litter box, opening a fresh one and dampening the peristaltic pad. A-pure truth she was talking. It would be easy for them to strain oil and microplastics out of the sludgy dockside water. Scoop up the dead birds and fish floating stink on the surface, render them into fat and ash. Sell all of that back to the factory suppliers, fund ongoing taz maintenance for weeks.

She swung open the door of Lickchop's well-padded crate and locked it in that position. The crate was made from a large grocery shopping cart she'd traded for a few months ago with one youth in a passing taz called Travelers' Green. She'd given him an empty lard tub of dried coconut meal and a handful of freeze-dried chiton meat for it. And though the youth kept asking her, she hadn't told him where she'd found the forlorn piece of rock sticking up out of the sea that still had chitons living on it. Not that it mattered; next time she went back, there weren't any, just scum floating around the base of the rock. Saltwater was so acid these days that it was removing the calcium carbonate so many now near-extinct sea creatures relied on to build their shells. How long since she'd tasted lobster or crab?

She did a quick check of the repair patches bolted onto the ultralight. Uncle Silvis had printed the body of the aircraft in pieces from biopolymers her taz cultured from marine algae. The assembled ultralight had held up well for the past few years, but it would soon be time to feed it back to the algae. Uncle Silvis kept joking that it had been mended so much that it was more patch than plane. By now, Uncle Silvis had probably realized that she'd taken it for a ride. There would be some music to face when she got back home.

She was a little bit light-headed after her flight prep, but never mind; time to go. She patted Lickchop, went forward to the flight deck, and closed the cabin door behind her. No control tower to radio to, no one to register a flight path with, or to broadcast an "all-clear" for takeoff. Everyone used visual flight rules this near to a port; keep your eyes peeled like johncrow head and don't get too close to any other craft.

Pretty soon, she was kiting near-soundlessly 1,200 feet above sea level. World Bioheritage couldn't come after her once she reached her taz. Not legally, anyway. Land-liberated micro-nations were a protected category. Though now that the open oceans had been declared a heritage site, Worldbio porkpies sometimes got over-eager and took the chance of invading tazes, hoping they could make an arrest under the claim of defacing an international heritage.

The ultralight console began an insistent beeping. Jacquee opened her eyes, checked the readout, corrected the ultralight's flight so that its right wing was no longer dipping downward.

The intercom clicked on. "Yes, Lickchop?" Jacquee responded.

She should never have taught the pig how to use the intercom, much less have rewired the controls to low enough on the wall for him to reach. But he got lonely back there in the cabin on long trips. She couldn't have him in the cockpit. He'd be a menace.

"*Columbus considered it to be the fairest isle that eyes have beheld,*" said Lickchop.

The skin on Jacquee's arms sprang out in goose bumps. She stared at the receiver in her hand. That hadn't come from Lickchop's limited vocabulary range. "Is who back there?" she barked into the receiver.

No answer.

"Assata," she said, "automatic pilot, current course heading."

"*Yes, pilot,*" replied the ultralight's AI.

Jacquee leapt out of her seat and snatched up the cricket bat she kept behind the door. She threw the door open and stepped into the cabin.

Lickchop was dozing in his crate. He didn't even have the TV on. And the intercom hadn't been activated. "Wah gwan?" Jacquee muttered to herself. Frowning, she returned to the cockpit. True, she was feeling not quite herself. Dr. Lin had said a few people developed mild sensory hallucinations as this kind of wetware established its pathways in the brain. Looked like she was one of them. Cho.

But Dr. Lin had said they were temporary. Push come to shove, she could have Assata fly them home. Uncle Silvis had grumbled when she'd installed it—he thought Jacquee's love of bootleg tech was an addiction—but now he used Assata too. He kept threatening to change its name, "ascording to how the real Assata never took a rassclaat order from nobody." But he hadn't done so yet. The list of things Uncle Silvis planned to get to someday was everchanging and never-ending.

Her headphones crackled to life, causing a pain-pulse to start throbbing along the top of her skull. "Jaks! A-you that?"

Oi. Time to face the music with Uncle Silvis. "Come in, Tayzone 67," she replied. "A-who this?"

"Is Kobe." It usually was, if it was a matter of telecommunications. "Yuh business conclude?" he asked.

"Ee-hee." No need to tell him about her worrisome symptoms. She'd be all right. She basked in the familiar sound leaking from Kobe's side; children yelling as they played all through the complex.

Kobe said, "You enjoyed your visit to landlock?"

"So you know is there I went?"

"Cho. Is who you think you talking to? Of course I know!"

"The whole rahtid place don't move!" This she knew how to do, to cover her doubts with humor. "They pretend they do, everything rushing all around you, cars and trains and people. Everybody trying to keep things going fast just so them don't haffe realize that them NAH GO NOWHERE!"

Kobe laughed. "Well, yuh know what dem seh: If yuh worl' nah rock, it a-'tan 'till."

"My legs couldn't adjust, even after three days. No water jostling beneath my feet. I was walking like I was drunk. How people live like that, Kobe?"

"After you barely been living ten years at sea," he teased. "I know you didn't forget so soon. Listen, we picking up a light breeze. We gwine ride it, gie de sea under we some time to freshen herself up. Change your course heading minus twenty degrees, so you could catch up."

"Seen. And I coming home with a new toy in my head." She glanced at her console. "Twenty minutes."

From her headphones came the sound of a familiar voice: "Kobe, hand me that blasted microphone. Jacquee? A-you that?"

Jacquee sighed. "Yes, Uncle Silvis."

"Jimmy text me to say you leave his surgery too soon. You all right, Jacquee? Why you went to Dr. Lin? Something happen to you?"

So worried the old man sounded. He wasn't even her real uncle. That's just what everyone called him. Didn't he know by now she could look after herself? She replied, "Yeah, man. Just a little mod. Help me see better in muh—murky water." Even just saying the phrase made her belly twist, every time.

"More bootleg tech?" said Uncle Silvis. "And in your head this time? What the rass Jimmy was thinking, letting you talk him into doing something like that?"

Jacquee tried for a light tone. "Better him than some backawall operator with no training, nah true?"

"Jacquee, this is foolishness! When you going to start acting like you have a brain in your head?"

The pounding in her skull increased. "Jesus Christ," she barked, "if you going to carry on like that, maybe I won't come home at all! Maybe I gwine right back to landlock, where I belong!" She cut off the connection before he could reply, and sat stewing—kissing her teeth and muttering under her breath about interfering, overprotective . . .

There was the thunderhead Kobe had talked about, looming up ahead. It would bring a storm surge. No problem for Jamdown Ark. Its large, flexible base—a neural matrix of algal polymers extruded in a ring shape—would just rise and fall with the swells. The sway would make it a bit wobbly underfoot for a few hours, is all.

A decade ago when Jacquee was still living a-landlock, rainy season might mean some flooding. Nowadays, every downpour was a tropical storm, and every storm saw the waters rise more and destroy more land. At least there were no hurricanes due for another few months. The old-time stories talked about the devastation of Category 5s. But the classifications had had to be revised. In these days Category 5 was common, and the new Category 6 was a banshee-shrieking horror that could tear away coastlines permanently, eat small countries whole.

Uncle Silvis insisted that the aftermath of storm surges was the best time to go collecting. Worldbio porkpies didn't patrol during storms, and the storm waters churned interesting stuff up from the depths. That's how Jacquee had stumbled upon the chitons; she'd been clambering on a slippery thumb of rock jutting out of the ocean. The storm that had just washed over it had deposited caches of glass jetsam, weathered and rounded over decades into gleaming lumps by being tumbled along the ocean floor. She would keep the prettiest, most beadlike pieces to make jewelry with for market. The rest could be sold to recyclers. Prying the barnacles out of the rock had broken a good hunting knife, but Uncle Silvis had been delighted to find that Jacquee's haul included twenty-three of them she'd kept alive in a little tub of seawater. "Viable gametes probably still dey inside," he'd said. "Good for you." He'd extracted some sperm and ova from a few of the chitons and cryopreserved the gametes in DMSO, cooled then stored in a liquid nitrogen flask. Maybe they could find a way to add chitons to the vertical marine farm suspended underwater in the doughnut-hole center of Jamdown Ark. They might be good for chowder.

Blasted man. She wasn't going to let him spoil her fun with her new mod. "Assata," she said, "take the helm. Maintain course."

Yes, pilot, said Assata.

Jacquee flicked on the intercom. She needed some company. Lickchop was singing along with some TV show contestant. Jacquee could hear the show in the background, but the loudest sound was Lickchop. He was making excited squeal/grunts that his vocoder was struggling to render into some approximation of human speech; Jacquee's best guess was *Shake that t'ing, Miss / Oonuh betta shake . . . * An oldie but a goodie. Wasn't helping her aching head, though. "Lickchop!" she barked.

The "singing" stopped. *What Jah-kay want?* he responded.

"Turn down the TV for a second, nuh man?"

He did. Then he was silent, waiting for her to answer his question. She didn't even self know what she wanted from the pig. Just his attention. Ongle that. Lickchop didn't pass judgment. She rummaged in her knapsack for the bootleg addy she'd been carrying around for months. "He think I so foolish," she muttered to Lickchop. "Like I can't think for myself. Gwine show him."

Don't think you foolish.

"Not you, Lickchop; Uncle Silvis." She hadn't been sure she was going to try it. But she was a hard-back woman who could make her own decisions. So now she was going to see if the bootleg addy would pair with her new mod.

The woman she'd bought the addy from in the mainland market had said, "Medically non-intrusive for sure, darling." Then she'd tapped the side of her head. "You already have wetware installed, right? Maybe to correct myopia? Just piggyback it onto that. So easy, it's sleazy."

Well, she hadn't had any wetware back then. But she'd been thinking to get some. So she had. The mod was well natty on its own; enhanced vision would help direct her through murky, particulate-heavy water and sharpen her proprioception. Accomplished via some process she didn't really understand. Something about ninety percent modifications to her DNA and ten percent implanted hardware. Didn't matter.

A pop song cover came pouring out through Jacquee's headphones. Lickchop had clearly decided the conversation was over. She grimaced and turned the sound off.

She got the addy out of her knapsack. It was matchbox-sized, plastic, standard 3-D print white, and near featureless but for a readout window and a couple of buttons. She unfolded the piece of paper with the instructions written on it in fading umpteenth-generation print; they were easy enough to follow. In a few seconds, the readout was flashing "ready" in squared-off green letters. Addy successfully onboarded! Her brain felt a little . . . itchy. That was the only way to describe it.

The headache scoured the inside of her skull, making her wince. She should be lying in Dr. Lin's lavender-scented guest bedroom with a soft mask over her eyes, wearing a cooled gel skullcap and gently putting her aching brain through the exercises that would, in about a week, fine-tune her skill with the mod. She closed her eyes for some relief.

The discomfort receded. She took a breath. Focused her mind the way Dr. Lin had shown her. She was supposed to wait a couple more days before trying out the commands, but she summoned the wetware anyway. Gave it the "standby" command, then squinched her lower-left eyelid. That was the action she'd chosen to activate the addy. The headache became a shout of pain. She did her best to ignore it. She felt/heard the internal click as the addy connected with the ultralight's controls. Success! Now she could pilot the ultralight hands-free. Assata was great for uneventful flight paths, but not for the myriad split-second decisions required in more challenging conditions.

So often Jacquee had wished she could do that without having
to lay her hands on the controls all the time. "Assata, give me manual control."

Yes, pilot.

Jacquee called up the addy's display. Telemetry danced across
the upper-left-hand corner of her mind's eye. Red, yellow, and
green images on a black background. She felt/saw the ultralight's
controls. Tasted them too. Like goat-head soup mixed with pineapple and toothpaste. She gagged as she fought to do the mental
twitch that turned the gain down. The ultralight swung dizzyingly
to the left. Carefully, Jacquee got it back on track. She experi-
mented for a while with pitch, yaw, speed. Pretty soon, she felt
comfortable enough to climb to 2,000 feet to get above the storm.
Grinning, she frolicked the aircraft amongst the clouds.

Oh, shit. The telemetry was signaling that she'd dipped too low.
She was tipping them into the thunderhead. With the sickly swan-
ning motion of a piece of paper drifting down from a height, they
sank into the storm cloud. Like a truck on a quarry road, they
dugga-duggaed through turbulence. A buffet of wind jerked the
ultralight sideways. Rain beat fists against the window screen, hammered the ultralight with a roar that made bile rise in her throat.
She spat it down the front of her sweatshirt, kept trying for the
right combo of commands to decouple the addy from the ultralight's controls. A storm like this could literally tear the ultralight
in two. Automatically, she reached for the controls just as the craft
hit an air pocket and dropped so fast that Jacquee's butt lifted out
of the chair. The heel of her hand hit multiple buttons and levers.
She didn't know which ones. Panicked, she tried to use the mental
commands instead, succeeded only in jamming the whole system
up. "Assata!" she yelled. "Take the con!"

Not possible, pilot, the plane replied calmly. *Please disengage
override.*

"I can't!"

The rain had become hail, slamming like fastballs against the
hull.

The ultralight's nose dipped at a vomitous pitch and exited the
cloud layer. There was a mountaintop floating in the dark swells of
the ocean below her, like a meringue in wine. For a brief second,
she thought she'd pulled the ultralight out of its dive, but it just.
kept. falling. She fought to stay conscious during the plummet,

tried pushing one combo after another of buttons that now made no sense to her confused brain. She could hear Lickchop's fear squeal from the cabin behind her. G-forces pressed her into her chair like a ripe mango beneath a boot. Dirty-blue water getting closer and closer. "Assata," Jacquee yelled, "controlled descent! Parallel to the shoreline ahead!"

Please disengage override.

"I still fucking can't figure it out!"

Then suggest you deploy your parachute. Ditch at 1,000 feet.

The ultralight continued its dizzying descent. The silence was eerie, except for the tinny music of Lickchop's TV show coming from her discarded headphones. *Shake that thing, Miss. . . .*

Jacquee scrabbled for the life jacket with its attached chute. She pulled the package out from beneath the seat, mentally rehearsing how to put it on.

She only had one on board. And the ultralight had two passengers. "Pussyclaat, batty-hole . . ." she swore.

She undid her seat belt, stood against the steep downward angle of the ultralight, and clawed her way through the door into the main cabin. She rushed to Lickchop's crate, yanked its door open. He was crouched inside, his eyes rolling in terror. *Fallingfalling,* said his vocoder. He tunneled his way into her arms. He was shivering. He had shit inside his crate; she could smell it. And sympathize.

"You gonna be okay," she lied. She had no way of knowing that. She clutched Lickchop against her chest and struggled into the life vest, wrapping it around both of them.

Nonono, said Lickchop. He fought and kicked. *No leash.*

"Is not a leash. Shut up."

In his struggling, Lickchop slashed her forearm open with a back trotter.

"Ow! Fuck!" Blood was seeping through the sleeve of her jacket. But still she held Lickchop tightly.

1,200 feet, said Assata. *The aircraft is losing altitude too quickly. It will break up on the coral formation at crash site. On my mark, release the hatch, open the door, and jump.*

Jacquee stood near the hatch, her hand on the handle. She knew what she had to do. Open the hatch outward. Leap out. Open the first chute once she was clear of the plane. Steer herself and Lickchop down, hopefully onto the dry land of the little island below them. She didn't even know what country it used to be.

1,000 feet, said Assata. *Mark. Exit the aircraft now. Exit the aircraft now. Exit the aircraft now.*

Jacquee felt her kidneys clench, her gut knot. Everything about her body was telling her this was a bad idea. But she pushed down on the handle, leaned against the door to shove it open.

Mistake. A buffeting wind slammed the door open to bang against the ultralight's carriage. She didn't have to jump; the force of the wind sucked her out of the ultralight, into a heels-over-head somersault. She saw the bottom edge of the open hatch but couldn't avoid it. Her head crashed against it, then she was out.

The day the waters had swept over the house in the valley where teenaged Jacquee lived with her parents, she'd been in the living room, dozing her way through her history homework in the big Berbice lounge chair. She woke when water swarmed to her chin, carrying the chair along in the surge. Coughing, she struggled to her knees in the chair. The back half of the house was gone, open to an iron-colored sky and an avalanche of angry brown water where neighbors' houses had been. The roar of wind and water had been like a train coming through. She'd yelled for her mummy and daddy. They had been in the backyard, bringing in the lawn chairs and picnic umbrella so they wouldn't blow away in the storm. There was no sign of them. The river maelstrom had claimed the yard, and the rest of the house was crumbling into it, fast. Her mind couldn't take it in. She waded from room to room, splashing and coughing in the gritty, bitter water, calling and calling for her parents. No answer. Something long and snaky, concealed in the torrent, went whipping along the front of her, wrapped itself around her ankle, and held her fast. Then the water had fountained over her, filling her mouth. It felt like a long, pounding forever of terror before she'd been able to bend and unsnarl the thing from her ankle. Its hard metal nose told her that it was their garden hose. Her parents had probably brought it indoors.

With a nail-bending screech, the roof of the house tore away. The house was disintegrating. She had to go. The garage was higher than the house, a bit farther along the uphill grade. The structure itself was gone, but the waters hadn't reached the car yet. She gave thanks her parents had recently keyed the car lock to her fingerprints. By the time she'd fought her way snotting and sobbing to the car, the sewage-tainted water was up to its tyre tops and she had lost her sweatpants and one shoe. Crouched on the car's bonnet was their cat Smarty Pants. She was bone-dry as God's sense of humor, her lemon eyes wide in terror.

By some miracle, the car started. Jacquee headed for even higher ground. She picked up six more shell-shocked survivors on the way. They made it to the stadium, which had been converted into an emergency center. She spent two weeks there, being drip-fed antibiotics and shitting bloody E. coli flux. That's where the man she would come to know as Uncle Silvis found her and a handful of other people willing to form a taz and take to sea with him. Yes, he'd already ordered a taz platform. It would be grown and ready in a couple of weeks. Yes, he knew how to manage himself on the water and could teach them. Yes, she could bring Smarty Pants.

The first month at sea she huddled in her bunk while others were busy setting up the habitats of the newly grown taz. She fought seasickness while grief raged through her. Wha' mek Mummy and Daddy dead, but she still alive? And every night of the decade since, she would dream of struggling in rushing, murky water as snakes wrapped around her ankles and pulled her down to drown.

She was . . . dizzy. Spinning along every axis possible. A keening shriek filled her thoughts. She told herself she had to open her eyes. Herself disagreed.

The keening was her. She was screaming. She closed her mouth. The screaming stopped. That slight bit of control made room for her to take more. She opened her eyes, and nearly began screaming again. The world was whipping around edge over edge, twisting; sky to sea to mountains, whup whup whip. She craned her neck upward, looking for the parachute. It hadn't inflated. It was flapping in circles above her, flaccid as a used rubber, dragging behind her and Lickchop as they plummeted.

She was still holding Lickchop.

Her thoughts were going so slow!

What had Kobe said in his flight training?

"If you can't pilot it, ditch it to rass."

Ditch . . . how? Yes. There should be a lever at the front of the jacket. She had to squeeze Lickchop even tighter to reach it. If the pig protested, she couldn't hear it above the wind whooshing in her ears. She found the lever. Grasped it. Pulled downward. She felt the tug of the first parachute releasing her, then the sharp yank upward as the second chute deployed. It was smaller, round rather than the rectangle shape of the first one. It began rapidly filling with air. But would it be enough? She was coming in hot. The second parachute was only half-full and couldn't be steered like the first. The vista surrounding her had zoomed in dizzyingly from a wide glimpse of the Earth's curvature, sky above and sea below with patches of brown terrain barely poking like noses above the water, to sea with a scrim of land too far out of reach in front of her, to just sea, then waves became apparent, and then she hit the surface of the water, feet first. But she hadn't kept her feet properly together. She felt her right ankle wrench as she plunged into the drink.

Lickchop couldn't hold his breath!

He could swim, though. Loved it, in fact. She pulled him out of the life jacket and let him go, knowing his rotund, pot-bellied self would pop up to the surface.

And still she cannonballed downward, despite the life vest. She could do this. She had practiced holding her breath. Her vision tunneled and her head felt light and airless as the space between stars. She could barely restrain the instinct to take a big gasp. The second she slowed enough to make it possible, she began frantically frog-swimming back up to the life-giving air. Adrenaline rush kept the pain of her ankle at bay.

Her head broke the surface. She sucked in air. She was alive. "Lickchop!" she yelled, spinning in a circle. No pig. The rope-tentacled mass of the second parachute was floating nearby, dragging her along. Lickchop didn't appear to be on it. She pressed the button on her vest that disengaged the parachute from her. It obediently began shrinking and rolling itself up for transport. Jacquee swam around a few strokes, calling Lickchop's name. She dove briefly, but couldn't see him beneath the surface, either. He was gone.

Reaction to her close call was setting in, and she wasn't safe yet. She could drown or be attacked by sharks or stung by some of the nastier jellyfish before getting to safety. Was that going to happen to Lickchop? Had it already? Sobbing, exhausted, she turned and began swimming for the beach, towing the parachute roll awkwardly. About a half mile farther along the shore were the smoking pieces of the wreckage of her ultralight. She couldn't business with that now. Out of the water first. See to that ankle. Maybe rig up a canoe and go looking for Lickchop.

She had reached the breakers. They were big today, in the wake of the passing storm. A good ten, twelve feet. She swam and body-surfed her way through them, diving beneath them when necessary. It was a mercy the water was cool enough to numb her ankle likkle bit.

She didn't deserve mercy.

One more crashing wave shoved her closer to the shore. Jacquee's feet hit the bottom with a thud. She shouted at the jarring of her injured ankle. She staggered the rest of the way through a porridge of roiled-up, mealy sand and suspicious solids that banged against her legs and twice knocked her off her feet to splash into the nasty water. She hated being in water she couldn't see through. The second time, a big branch scraped painfully across her body and snagged in her vest. She had to yank frantically at the branch. It tore free, dragging her life vest off with it, and sped into the undertow, heading out to sea. Great. The survival kit and tracking device had been packed into that vest. Home didn't know she was down. Would the tracker even still be broadcasting by the time they figured it out?

Once she was out of the surf, Jacquee half hopped onto shore, groaning. When she could no longer hop, she got down on hands and knees and crawled like any baby, dragging the wadded-up parachute behind her. Saltwater stung inside her nose, driven into her sinuses by the speed with which she'd plunged into the water. Never mind. Her own snot would flush them soon enough. She was bawling and coughing at the same time. Lickchop had been in her care. How she could go and do him so? Uncle Silvis was forever telling her not to take him on her trips. But she hadn't listened. Losing beings she loved to the water; that was what she did best.

Tainted sand and pieces of sodden, rotted branches gave way to rockstones and tangles of stinking seaweed harried by sandflies. The beach was lined with what were probably sea grape bushes. Frayed and bent, their slimy stems dragged on the sand, their broad, heart-shaped leaves yellowed. A handful of the usual coconut trees arched over the beach, but their fronds drooped wetly. Which meant that, now the Earth's waters were rising higher than most had predicted, this beach was regularly completely covered by the sea. Jacquee had to get to higher ground. And she couldn't crawl the whole way.

She rolled to a sitting position. Her ankle was already puffy. Wincing, she palpated the area. It didn't feel broken.

A patch of sand in her peripheral vision writhed. But when she looked good at it, it wasn't moving. Jacquee scooted backward away from it. Since that day with the garden hose, she couldn't abide anything snakelike.

Out of her eye-corner, another patch of sand squirmed. Again, it was still when she looked at it. She thought she heard someone say, *It's all good / Just turn.* . . . She snapped her head around in the direction of the voice. No one.

Although she was dripping wet, heat flushed over her, like being splashed with warm water. The world started to wobble on its axis. Her ears were suddenly ringing, the tinny sound occasionally resolving into a whisper of not-words as her brain tried to make sense of the racket. And she was shivering. Bloody hell. There were no snakes in the sand. Leaving Dr. Lin's before she had healed, landing-up in unsterile water . . . she'd picked up some kind of bug, and now she was delirious. And her mouth was dry. All that saltwater had her dehydrated.

She took stock as best she could, while her head rang like Sunday-go-to-meeting and the world got further and further away . . . Pocket knife still in her front jeans pocket. Cut a piece from her parachute to make a solar still, throw the rest of the parachute over a branch to make a tent. She was a thikk gyal, wouldn't need food for weeks. Felt like her fever was rising, though. She needed clean water now, but the still would take hours to generate it. And what about predatory animals on this island?

Seawater splashed her feet. The tide was rising. She had to get above the shoreline, quick.

Give it up to me . . .

She found a sea grape bush with a branch long and thick enough. She tore it off to use as a crutch. Last minute, she thought to grab up a discarded PET bottle from the jetsam tumbling in the incoming water. She began the trek to drier ground.

Hot day. Jacquee was used to sea breezes playing over and through Jamdown Ark. Landlock felt stifling to her nowadays. Especially today. Is fever that? She didn't know. Her jeans and sweatshirt were mostly dry. Scratchy sea salt powdered her face and hands. Her clothes were stiff with it. It weighed down the parachute roll. She limped along, leaning on the stick. The pain in her ankle first went numb, then came back shrieking with each step. Flashes of light at her eye corners. Smarty Pants on the deck of the taz outside the habitat they shared with Uncle Silvis, purring and chowing down on algae protein pellets. But her cat was long gone, dead peacefully in her sleep at a ripe old age.

Voiceless voices. A ghost of Lickchop's demodulated vocoder demanding, **Chow, Jacquee. Chow.** Jacquee kissed her teeth. Lickchop couldn't say her name smooth so. Always hesitated between one syllable and the next.

So of course the next thing was that she felt he was trotting beside her in the screaming-hot sun, berating her for letting him die. She started arguing with him. *The calculus of dampness*, she said, *eating along the rimrock*. She briefly came back to herself, half remembering the words she'd just muttered, vaguely aware they were nonsense. Then she was back in the fever-dream. *Lickchop floated in the air, on his back, gnawing at a snake with brass fangs. It hissed and spit and tried to wrap itself around Lickchop, who calmly sucked it up like a strand of sea grass.*

She caromed off a knee-high rock, hissed as she jammed her injured foot into the sand to prevent a fall. Two-handed, tilted forward from the waist, she hung on to the branch she was using to help herself walk. Bone-tired. She straightened up. One foot forward, then the other. Repeat.

There was a water-trickle sound, different from the rhythmic roar of the seashore. She tried to focus, to see ahead of her, but it was all delusion, her afflicted brain telling itself gigo stories; garbage in, garbage out. Through it all, the one constant was the tuneless piano-plink of water. She stumbled in the direction of the sound. Throat parched. Fever rising. Even as she swam through imaginary kelp fronds, ate a bat sandwich, won a not-game of dominoes with a not-Silvis who was chanting the wrong words from the Book of Revelation while he silently slapped the tiles down onto the rickety wooden table between them, she knew she had to hydrate, soon.

Jacquee's eyes opened briefly on . . . a river? Weeds around its edges
Lilies at the brink
Even some seagulls wheel-and-turning above it
Odorous indeed must be the mead
Some struggling but living sea grape bushes
And sugar-sweet their sap
Hush, she told her dreaming brain. You can't drink that. You don't know what kinda parasites inna it. You should dig a solar still. Wait till some clean water condenses into it.

Her gritty, obstinate throat impelled her forward. She dimly knew she was on her belly, face nearly in the water. Then she was scooping brackish liquid up with the PET bottle, bringing it to her mouth, and drinking deep.

Uncle Silvis had told her his dream often enough. Of the smog levels gradually falling. Of the Earth's climates returning to cooler levels. Of the land reappearing.

But the world had lost so much. The Gulf Coast. The Eastern Seaboard. The Amazon River Basin. Most of Southeast Asia had dived beneath the waves. And the Pacific Island nations. Refugees, misery, sickness everywhere. And the grief. A whole planet keening, mourning.

Jacquee slapped the side of her neck, hard. She woke to find it was pitch-night. She was scraping away the mosquito she'd squashed against her neck in her sleep. She was sprawled by the waterside, curled around the plastic bottle. Her head was pillowed on the still-damp parachute roll, which was already rank with stale saltwater.

She sat up. She couldn't see a rass. And it was so quiet! She remembered nights like this on dry land when the peeping of thousands of frogs was deafening. No more frogs. Indicator species were dying out the world over.

There was a lightning flash, far out at sea. A few seconds later, a grumble of thunder. The storm. Was it coming this way? She hadn't made a shelter yet. And she had drunk untreated water. She resigned herself to the belly-griping that was sure to follow.

The quiet pressed in on her ears, insistent as a pressure wave. The darkness had its hands over her eyes.

Something rustled along the ground, a little way behind her. Jacquee swung to her knees and spun around. "Uncle?" she called out, her voice quavery. "Lickchop?" No answer.

At least her knife was still in her front jeans pocket. She retrieved it, snicked it open and held it low, near her thigh. She tried to calm her breathing so she could hear better. Finally, she remembered she could see in the dark now, if she chose. If it was working. If she hadn't gone and infected her brain in her eagerness.

She breathed in. Then, slowly, out. She—is what Dr. Lin had called it?—engaged her mindfulness. Then did the little twitch of lower eyelid, a half wink that should turn on the infrared. And gasped as the world blossomed into glowing blues and greens on a black velvet background. The rustling was coming from breadfruit tree leaves, big as dinner plates, that were being blown along the ground by the freshening breeze. The tree branched out above her. It was stunted, only about fifteen feet high. But there were one or two green cannonballs of breadfruit amongst its branches. She hadn't even seen the tree when she made her way here in the daytime. Too feverish. Was it really there, or was she still delirious? No. Her head felt clear, and she was no longer shivering. The fugue seemed to be over.

There was a manicou on the tree's trunk, climbing higher. It was no bigger than Lickchop. It gripped a branch with its prehensile tail and turned to stare down at her. Its eyes glowed. It resumed its climb.

The tinkling sound of water drew her eyes to examine the place where she'd drunk from in her delirium. Not a river; a lagoon. Partly fed by the ocean. That's why it tasted brackish. The water shifted back and forth. Her altered vision showed it black as tar, the plants around its edge a pale green.

Another mosquito bit her neck, and one whined in her ear. She looked down at her body. If she switched to heat-signature vision, she would be able to see her warmth that was attracting them.

But first she had to make some shelter, since it seemed she was going to spend the night there. Stringing the parachute from a low branch of the breadfruit tree and digging a shallow pit in the ground nearby for a solar still would have been easy with her new mod, except her ankle sang with each step. By the time she got set up for the night, she was sweating, drawing mosquitoes in a cloud around her.

She couldn't bear the stinging any longer. Plus, she had to wash the sea salt out of her clothes and put them to dry. And relatively fresh water was right there, steps away. . . .

She promised herself she wouldn't drink any more of it, just use it to clean herself and her clothes. Swim for a bit, escape the mosquitos.

She removed her boots and socks, then stripped off the rest of her clothing. The night air hardened her nipples. She limped to the water's edge and eased herself in, shivering in the chillier water. She trod water for a bit until she'd warmed up. Then she took in a breath and let herself sink into the blue-green-black world below.

When Jacquee was little, maybe eleven years old, and living on land, she once had a homeroom teacher who'd made them read a poem about some old-time Britishy town that slid into a lake because the townspeople had been too stingy to give bread to a starving beggar. She could be looking 'pon that town now, settled onto the lagoon bottom. Because there was a nighttime city block down there. One quite a bit worse for having been battered by the water. Rusted cars and lengths of copper pipe. Broken bricks and chunks of cement. Waterlogged tree trunks. Whole pieces of buildings, drowned for the world's original sin; a human-triggered, human-stoked runaway train of climate change.

Moonlight beamed down through the water, making motes suspended within it twinkle: microorganisms; microplastics. The town was lit by fairy lights. Jacquee explored for a bit, wiping algae off street signs and peering in through slimy windows at sodden, broken computers and furniture, tossed every which way. Through one window she spied an armchair, upside-down and semi-buoyant. She pulled away from that window quickly.

She dove down to street level. Tumbling through the diffuse beams were translucent blobs, rounded by wave action, each about the size of a soccer ball. They streamed along with the current. Filaments of blob-stuff, like tresses, trailed from them. She could see where in some cases, strands of filaments were caught in rock cracks, anchoring them. What the rass were those? She swam down toward the shimmering globules.

One of them had encased a whole shrimp; another, a small fish. She recoiled. Were they being digested? But no, both fish and shrimp were swimming calmly, going about their business. They didn't look engulfed. It was more as though they had sprung multiple antennae, all over their bodies.

Jacquee went up for air and dove back down a few times, trying to understand what she was seeing. The more she did, the more lagoon creatures she saw, apparently in symbiosis with the small clouds of who-knows-what. Phosphorescent, an oddly fuzzy turtle flippered lazily past her nose, seemingly unbothered by being coated with the strange organism. She spied three more. All looked plump and healthy. Turtles were dying everywhere else, weakened by their softening shells.

Entranced, Jacquee dug a fist-sized lump of the matter out of a crevice in a rock. It was attached to the rock by a fleshy string.

It looked as though swiping a finger through it would disperse it. But no; it was membranous, pale green with darker green filaments threaded through it. She rubbed it gently between thumb and middle finger. Slightly slippery. It didn't look or feel like a colony of tubifex worms, which is what she would have expected in a lagoon.

The blob began to glow more brightly, perhaps in response to her touch. The picky threads inside it began to undulate. Minuscule lightning-forks inside a tiny green cloud. She found herself smiling. The thing was beautiful. She brought it closer to her face to better inspect it.

Her action broke the umbilical connecting the blob to its rockstone. It convulsed and snapped toward her, flattening clammy against the side of her face and half covering one eye. Jacquee clawed at it as she kicked for the air above. Her head broke the surface of the lagoon while she was still trying to scrape the thing off her face. It came away in strips, thin and flexible as skin. Fuck! Had she gotten all of it? She dunked her head back into the water and scrubbed her cheek and eye with one hand. Too late considered that it was the same hand with which she'd been holding the blob. She was probably just depositing more of it onto her face. She switched to the other hand and rubbed away all the remaining bits she could feel. She lifted her head for air again and kicked as quickly as she could for the edge of the lagoon. Once on land, she squatted and surgeon-washed her two hands in the water. Glowing motes flowed away from her fingers, going dull again as she watched; remainders of the blob.

She put her clothes back on. They would dry more quickly against her skin. Then she sat at the waterside, knees clasped to her chest, and shuddered. Stupid. Stupid. To go and put her hands on some unknown organism.

With her night vision on, the retreating thunderhead was a light show. She watched the funnel of it move slowly away, lit up every few seconds by lightning flashes. She rocked and tried not to think of what would happen if no one found her. When the storm had disappeared over the horizon, she crawled into her shelter. She wadded her sweatshirt for a pillow. To keep the worst of the mosquitoes away, she cocooned herself in a trailing edge of the parachute. She turned her night vision off, leaving herself in the uncertain dark. Eventually, she sank into a slurry of disturbed sleep.

She woke ravenous the next morning. A sickly sunrise tinted the clouds with tainted orange-browns and greens, painterly and poisonous. Jacquee busied herself with the business of survival: drinking the cup of sterile water she'd gotten from the solar still; using her stick to knock a breadfruit out of the tree; the forever it took with two twigs and a guy line from the parachute to make a fire for roasting the breadfruit. While she ate, she tried to raise the ultralight's onboard computer with her addy. Only the crackle of static, which suddenly, alarmingly increased till it was like having ants crawling around inside her skull. She yelped, then mentally deactivated the addy.

Careful of her ankle, she slowly made her way a little higher up the elevation till she could see the beach where she'd come ashore. Or at least, where it had been. High tide had completely covered it, and the wreck of the ultralight was nowhere to be seen. The water had taken it, had probably already swept it miles away out to sea.

Jacquee sat down hard on a rock. Things were bad. She had really messed up this time. How to let her taz know where she was? She didn't know how far away they were, or in what direction.

She scratched her forearm, and only then realized she'd been doing that all day. The forearm tingled, so gently she could have been imagining it. So did the side of her face. It was happening on the side of her body where the organism had tried to latch on to her.

Fuck, fuck, fuck. Jacquee tore up a handful of scrub grass and used that to scour her arm and face. All she got for the effort was dirt ground into the scrapes she was giving herself with the scrub grass; scrapes she wouldn't be able to wash clean until she'd collected more sterile water. That wouldn't be until next morning. And she needed to conserve the clean water for drinking, not bathing. The calculus of dampness, to rass. Jacquee swore and slammed her stick against the ground. She'd infected herself with a parasite, and she was injured. Her taz could probably fix both, but she was stranded with no way to contact them. She was fucked.

And if she wasn't careful, she was going to give herself sunburn into the bargain. She made her painful way back to the shade of the broad-leaved breadfruit tree. She sat morosely beneath it, pelting rockstones into the lagoon and cycling her vision through its different spectra. She was sweaty and lonely and her pig was gone. She wanted so badly to be where she usually went when she was in need of comfort: the water. She glared at the lagoon, lying there all spread out and tempting, making beckoning little wavelet sounds. She needed to survive, but for how long? Suppose rescue never came?

Surviving. That was all she was doing. Surviving and waiting. That was all the world was doing. Taz communities were self-sufficient and did better than much of the rest of humanity. But really, they were doing the same as everyone else, making do with fewer and fewer natural resources as time went on. Treading water and praying in vain for rescue.

Did it have to go so?

Not quite sure what she was doing, Jacquee levered herself to her feet. She eased herself into the warmish lagoon water—because fuck it—and waded across to a patch of mangroves she'd noticed at the far side of its lip. Seagulls wheeled and quarreled overhead as she swam. Her new vision showed her that the mangrove roots, where they entered the water, were as filamentous as any living thing in that water. And at first, she thought the roots had somehow trapped rockstones between them, till a jolt of recognition told her what she was seeing. Oysters! In the wild! Her belly rumbled joyfully. She fell to her knees in the mud, dug out a bunch of them, and shucked them open right there-so. She looked at the glistening meat in the shells. She made her decision. She slurped down the oysters and their salty liquor, every last one.

Then she beat around the mangrove roots and the shore of the lagoon until she found another plastic bottle with no cracks in it. Blasted things were everywhere. She dove to the lagoon bed and collected a few of the smaller globules in her bottle. She returned to her campsite with it and wedged the bottle upright in the mud near the water's edge to keep it cool. She had no idea what was going to become of her, but for now, her belly was full and her mind occupied. She crawled into her makeshift tent and dozed, dreaming big dreams. What would come, would come.

The sound of an air horn rousted Jacquee from under the parachute. She looked out over the water. Two dots on the water, heading her way. Porkpies, or . . . ? She stayed up there, hidden by the trees, till she could see for sure. They were coming quickly. Pretty soon, she could make them out. Two electric speedboats. From her taz! She recognized the colorful patterns painted on their hulls. Kobe's on the left, green circuits painted on a black background. The red, green, and gold stripy one on the right was Uncle Silvis's.

Jacquee's heart was slamming in her chest. She nearly sprained the other ankle hurrying down to the beach. She drew off her sweatshirt and waved it in the air. "Hey!" she shouted. "Over here!" The ocean breeze blew the sound off in another direction. Did they see her? Please. They had to see her.

They must have, because the boats started angling her way, bouncing through the swells. A small, black form clambered from inside Uncle Silvis's boat, plopped into the water, and started making for shore. Uncle Silvis had to stop and circle back. He plucked the wriggling body out of the water. *Lickchop?* Joy surged like storm seas. How was he alive?

Little more, the boats were close enough to shore that the two men were able to jump out onto the sand below the surface and begin pulling them from the water. Jacquee waded to meet them, ignoring the ache of the waves yanking her injured ankle. Lickchop was out of the boat again, trotting to meet her. His coder was trumpeting, **JA-KAY!** over and over. Who the rass knew it could be so loud?

The men had their backs to her, concentrating on getting their boats safely out of the water. Kobe looked over his shoulder at her. He was grinning. Uncle Silvis never turned around. Uh-oh. She was in big trouble.

A low wave lifted Lickchop, bringing him to thump against her shin. Luckily, on her good leg. He was squealing and snorting, his snout turned comically upward to keep it out of the water. **Ja-kay!** said his 'coder. **Ja-kay good!**

Hanging on to her crutch for balance, Jacquee bent and, one-handed, scooped the little pig's bristly, squirming body up into a hug. "Yes," she whispered against his shoulder, "I good." She blinked away the salt tears she was adding to the sea.

Lickchop was wriggling to get down. Kobe took him from Jacquee and lowered him into the ankle-deep water to splash happily around their feet. Jacquee supported herself with one hand on the gunwale of Kobe's boat as she followed them onto the beach. "How you find me?" she asked the two men.

Kobe replied, "Nearly didn't. We lost the signal from the ultralight. Thought you went down with it. Uncle Silvis was frantic. Everyone was."

Uncle Silvis only grunted and pulled his boat on ahead of Kobe's.

"But," Kobe continued, "we kept getting interference on our channels, first one, then the next. And then the message came through clear—SOS from Lickchop. Found him swimming in open water, belting out EM pulses to keep the sharks away. Bet you didn't know his head rig could do that."

She hadn't. "But how that helped you know where I was?"

Uncle Silvis, his boat now well clear of the water, was leaning against its side, arms folded and scowling at Jacquee. "Rahtid little trenton kept saying him could hear you," he ground out. "We had to wait till low tide, but all the way here, that sintin on him head been calling out coordinates."

Maybe that explained the tickling between her ears, the ghost snippets of Lickchop's voice. That old Sean Paul song he loved. "Hmm. I think maybe I could hear him, too."

That got Kobe's attention. "Tell me more about that."

"Later. Uncle, I sorry about your ultralight. If you show me how, I will print out a replacement. You gwine haffe help me with the wiring, though."

Silvis's expression was unreadable. He rushed toward Jacquee and pulled her into his wiry, iron-cable arms. He smelled of sweat and ocean salt and good sinsemilla. "Wha mek a pig be your salvation, ee Jacquee? A haraam?"

Jacquee chuckled. "Promise I never going to put him on the supper table."

Uncle Silvis held her away at arm's length, a reluctant smile quirking his lips. "Never mind. Gwine treat the little so-and-so like a king from now on. He bring daughter Jacquee back to us. To me. You ready to come home?"

"Too ready. I haffe get some things first, though."

"Ee-hee? Like what?"

The parachute. They could mend it. And the bottle of lagoon

water with the green globs in it. Jacquee smiled at Uncle Silvis. "I find something in a lagoon over there. A living thing. I think is new."

Uncle Silvis put an arm around her waist, started helping her limp in the direction she had pointed. Kobe and Lickchop followed. "A-whoa. And what you think it good for?"

"Me nah know. We should preserve a sample of it. Because I have an idea. Jamdown Ark, we could become a databank of gametes to reseed the waters with when the time come. Maybe we could even breed stronger strains. And then we could—"

Laughing, Kobe shook his head. "Lord Jesus, not another Jacquee idea for saving the world."

Uncle Silvis was smiling, though. "Tell it to me when we get back."

Lickchop butted her calf. Second time he had avoided touching the injured leg. Jacquee wondered what the sensors that were apparently in his rig let him perceive. *Chow* he said.

As Uncle Silvis's boat bounced on the swells, racing Kobe back to Jamdown Ark, Jacquee studied Lickchop. She asked him, for the first time, "Is what you are?"

Lickchop stopped rooting around under the gunwale to gaze 'pon her, his black-in-black eyes inscrutable. *Are pig mind* his 'coder stated.

Is "pig mind" he was saying? Or "big mind"?

Lickchop continued, *Is what Ja-kay are?*

Maybe "are" was the right word. Lickchop apparently knew what it was to be a neurolinked creature, after all. Maybe it didn't matter if the link was with an artificial network or an organic one. Maybe he was referring to her in the plural because like recognized like.

A seaweed-green tracery, barely visible under the skin of her forearm, had crept up toward her elbow. It itched. She couldn't be sure, but she suspected it was responsible for the interference patterns in her wetware display. They were almost beginning to make sense. The world was looking a little bit different, in ways she couldn't yet articulate. She was changing. She should have been worried, but she wasn't.

She was cradling the bottle containing the lagoon creatures between her knees. She leaned over and with her free hand scratched

Lickchop under his chin. He grunted happily, angled his head so she could reach the best place. She echoed back his question: "What are I and I? We don't know, darling. Time will tell."

She leaned back to enjoy the salt spray the speedboat was kicking up onto her face as it hurried them home.

I Was a Teenage Space Jockey

FROM *Lightspeed*

TWO DAYS AFTER my brother turned seventeen, he was gone, just like he'd guaranteed my dad. No sad goodbyes, no notes, no taking a knee in the hall before dawn to give me any good advice for high school when I got there. My mom's story when anybody asked was that he'd moved out, he was old enough, he needed room, it was completely natural. My dad, if asked, would just shrug, knock back the rest of his can of beer, and say he hoped Rance was in the military, where someone else could tell him to get up, face the day.

Just to piss my dad off, I secretly hoped Rance had gone military as well: Air Force, so that one morning bright and early he could buzz the house in his fighter jet, waggle his wings to announce it was really him, and then burst through the sound barrier, breaking every window on the block. If he did that, then I would know for sure there was some way out. That there was something else.

This was sixth grade for me, fall semester, ramping up to Halloween. Homeroom was all pumpkins and skeletons with brass rivets at their joints, so whoever was first to class could tack those white cardboard hands and feet up in lewder and lewder positions.

My best friend that year, and for the rest of the years we'd have together, was Marten French. Me and him were the only Indians for two grades in either direction, and since he'd been held back one year, we were even in the same class now. His dad made him keep his hair long, not buzzed short like in my house, but Marten hated all the attention his braids drew in the halls, in PE, in every bathroom we had no choice but to eventually brave. Yes, we knew it was the boys' room, not the girls'. Thank you, ha ha. That one never gets old.

Just because he had to have his hair in twin braids when he left for school, though, that didn't mean they wouldn't be down by the time he got to his locker before class—down and puffing out all crinkly and metal, which meant he was always glaring out of a frizzy shroud of black, just the way he liked it.

You'd think all the attention of being the only two red kids would turn us into scrappers, just out of necessity, out of survival, but neither of us had any size yet. We'd gloved up with his mom's oven mitts and tried fighting each other for practice once, but we had to admit that, at best, we were just slapfighters, that our main and best defense would be to curl up like pill bugs, wait this next thrashing out.

To try to avoid that, we hid—surprise—and the main place we hid was the arcade down at the mall. It had started out as our place because, for the two years before he left, Rance had been the longtime *Galaga* champ. He would strut in every other week or so to leave his initials at the top of the high-score reel. His quarters lasted forever, and, my mom said, so long as he was there, I could be too. Not that Rance watched me in the scratchy reflection of that plastic screen or even knew I was alive and breathing the same air as him, but I guess the idea was that if my big brother was around, nobody would try anything with me.

While Rance was doing his thing on *Galaga*, Marten and me— Coach was already calling him "Frenchie," a name that would stick—would tag-team the games on the other side of the arcade: *Zaxxon, Defender, Tempest*. They were all too complicated, were pretty much just quarter-donation machines, but they were ours, pretty much. And everybody would be crowded around Rance's *Galaga* machine anyway, his eyes glassy, his right hand on that fire button an absolute blur, his forearms ridged with veins, his feet set one ahead and one back, the front knee bent like he was leaning against some great wind blasting out of the machine, and all he could hold on to was that joystick.

If he really was piloting a fighter jet somewhere out there now? He'd shoot faster than anybody, and he'd never say die, would just keep taking on wave after wave of alien.

Just—Marten and me talked about this—would he really cut his hair for the government? While Marten's hair just put a bull's-eye on his back, Rance's shaggy mane had always been hair-sprayed what my dad, when he'd even acknowledge Rance, would call "six ways from Sunday and halfway to an ass kicking."

I thought Rance's hair was the most amazing thing ever. Put him in a pair of tights, give him a mic, and he'd own any stage, would have the whole arena in the palm of his hand. My hair was a sandy throwback to some trapper or Indian agent or fallen Jesuit nobody in my family even remembered. We don't all come out looking full-blood. Either that, or the way to explain the difference between Rance and me had to do with whose eye my mom might have caught nine months before I cried my way into the world, which I guess would explain the way my dad always watched me, growing up, like he was looking for a trait he recognized, that could confirm his suspicions.

Anyway, with Rance gone, Marten and me figured it was my job to continue the family tradition. He stole all the quarters from his mom's ceremony jar, the one she saved to get them back to South Dakota every year, or at least pay for half a tank of gas, and we shrugged our way down to the mall, to the Gold Mine Arcade.

Trick was, though, we were the only ones who knew this was my night to carry on Rance's *Galaga* ritual. The place was packed, I mean. It was Friday night, right? We should have known. Except . . . at first I thought this wasn't the usual crowd, but maybe it was—everybody was already wearing their Halloween masks. The sign at the door said you'd get two free plays if you were in costume.

Marten pinched my sleeve, pulled me deeper into the mall.

What we needed were masks, or at least makeup, and we knew that the velvet ropes at the movie theater had metal balls at the top of their heavy little poles that screwed on and off. But we didn't need the balls, or the ratty ropes. What we needed was the grease rubbed onto the threads.

Marten covered while I rubbed as much into the crook of my index finger as I could, then I covered for him, and in the long bathroom hall by the Orange Julius we applied our makeup: Marten got shiny warpaint over the top of his face, including his eyelids, which was a pretty cool look, but then we ran out of grease partway through my *Star Trek* "half a black face" plan, so I ended up having to smudge it around, try to pull off a black eye. Because that wasn't any kind of costume, just meant I hadn't mowed the lawn or something, we scrounged some lipstick from under the payphone, drew blood coming down from my nose and my mouth and my other eye, and, in a flash of inspiration, Marten traced a drippy line of red across the top of my forehead.

Fifty cents is fifty cents.

Jess, the Gold Mine's attendant, looked back and forth from Marten to me. My belt was looped around my neck, its long tongue in Marten's hand because I, the sandy-haired buzzcut of the two of us, was this Indian's prisoner.

"He nearly scalped me," I explained, tilting my head back to show off my bloody hairline.

"Good job," Jess said, extending one spindly hand to tug Marten's left braid, though he knew it was real.

"*How,*" Marten said in his deepest voice, like this was a movie.

Jess thumbed a dollar in quarters from the dispenser at his hip, passed them over.

"Where's your brother?" he said to me then. "He needs to defend his title."

"He's shooting commies," Marten said for me about Rance, and mimed like he was Rambo with a Gatling gun, Arnold against the Predator.

"What game is that?" Jess asked, looking over his shoulder like a new one had been delivered without his knowing.

"*I'm* getting the new high score," I said, and shouldered past, leading Marten by the leash he was still holding.

Our idea had been to get me better and better at *Galaga* until I could fire as fast as Rance, until I knew all the patterns, could wipe out whole armadas of aliens. As it turned out, Janet Reilly, a senior from the smoking circle, was already at the *Galaga* machine, and drawing a crowd.

Since she and Rance has been trading top slot on the high-score list for the past year, I'd always kind of known they were going to have to start going out, like that was the rule. Unlike Rance's Silent Indian routine, though, she was vocal, always chirping and screeching in retreat, snarling and growling when caught in a corner, then screaming when she shot her way out again, as if the aliens could hear her, be intimidated by her. Rance was more reserved, had a steadier game, knew the dive patterns, the levels, and he never made any real sound, would just thin his lips about this next challenge, but he'd had to respect Janet's game, I knew, especially the way her reflexes seemed to come alive best when the game was tilting against her.

We tried watching for a couple of minutes but the crowd was too thick, and a short skeleton right beside Janet kept inserting its index finger into its mask to pick its nose, so we took our quarters elsewhere.

Centipede was open, but that was a panic attack waiting to happen.

Joust would have been fun, but it was taken by the stoners, as usual.

"*Track and Field?*" Marten said, trying to make it sound better than it was.

We patted our back pockets for the Ace combs we'd need to pump that runner's legs fast enough. No luck.

Counting the dollar Jess had given us for playing Cowboy and Indian at the door, we had eight dollars total. We were *in* the Gold Mine and we *had* a gold mine, yeah.

"So?" I said.

"Hyperspace?" Marten said with a shrug.

It was what he called *Defender*, because when it got you back on your heels, you could push that hyperspace button, go to whatever random spacescape the game kicked up. Usually it meant instant death, just death in a different place, but you were dying anyway, right? Might as well blip across the galaxy.

We ended up dropping three dollars on *Asteroids*, even though Marten had it on Atari at his house. His brother always hid the controllers, though, or else he'd reach his hand down the front of his pants for a long scratch session, then rub that hand all over the joystick, hand it across.

Like every time in *Asteroids*'s field of space rocks, and in spite of our standing-in-place gymnastics—it was like we were really *in* the cockpit of that fragile little ship—we shattered into glowing lines that had just enough inertia to spin insultingly, like going down some cosmic drain.

When we turned around, thoroughly beaten and breathing hard from it, three of the stoners were shaking their heads at our theatrics, at our wimpiness, at our make-do costumes.

"Jess," I said, my head on a swivel for the arcade's lifeguard.

"He's talking to that redhead at the hot-dog stand again," the lead stoner said, his eyes still gliding on ostriches from platform to platform of *Joust*. He wasn't smoking, but he still smelled like a train.

"It's Rance's tagalong," the second stoner said, stepping in to get this started.

"Baby Red," the third of them said.

Rance's initials should have been RATB, for Rance Allen Two Bulls, but video game high-score reels aren't made for Indians. So, on *Galaga*, and in spite of his black hair, he'd always been *RED*, like claiming that top spot for all Indians everywhere.

Since I was his little brother, I was "Baby Red," I guess. This wasn't the first time they'd cornered us in their wall of grimy denim to claim all our quarters, but, *because* it wasn't, I juked left, went right, shouting "*Run!*" to Marten while already doing it, picturing myself vaulting over *1942*, diving through the cockpit of one of the racing games, tearing out into the food court.

It all went pretty great in my head, I mean.

They were older, though we were slower, Jess was AWOL, Rance was gone, and—and it was Friday night, it was nearly Halloween, which isn't when sixth graders have their best luck.

We made it maybe three steps.

What they took from me was my pocketful of quarters, which one of them hefted while watching me, as if judging this weight against my soul, or trying to gauge how many eggs this would be worth on *Joust*.

What they took from Marten, with a yellow pocketknife sawed back and forth, was his right braid.

"Shit, that was real!" the second of them said, holding Marten's hair up, covering his own mouth with his other hand, which just made his laugh louder, somehow.

Marten's chest was heaving, his eyes welling up. Not because he'd ever wanted that braid, but because his dad and brother were going to kick his ass when he came home lopsided, and then they were going to pile into the family car and find whoever had done this.

It had happened before. Marten's dad had had to serve three months of weekends in county because someone had left a red handprint on the flank of their light-blue Buick, so it could be a real war pony, ha ha. This time it wouldn't just be weekends, though, we knew. And there was no way Marten could hide what had happened.

Because there was always the chance of Jess stepping back in, the hot-dog girl in tow, the stoners crowded us into the back corner by the kiddie games and then pushed us behind them, into that dusty space of cables and cigarette butts and sticky bottles and gum and the one rubber everybody knew about.

They were locking us up, making sure we wouldn't run tell, get them busted, maybe banned from the Gold Mine. To be sure the walls of our little prison cell held, they took our pants. To guarantee we wouldn't forget this anytime soon, they forced our faces down into the grossest stickiest spaces they could find behind the machines, then told us to count to one hundred before we lifted our heads. If we didn't, they'd do it all over, and take our underwear this time, how would we like that?

We laid there crying.

Okay, Marten was maybe crying harder, I guess—he had reason. Me, I was staring ahead, under the broken *Ms. Pac-Man* machine, waiting for this to be over. When I got up into the eighties with my count, I saw it: there in the dust-bunny coated sludge under *Ms. Pac-Man* was a glint of silver.

We didn't go all the way to one hundred, wouldn't give the stoners that. We just listened to our heartbeats drum down slower and slower. Listened to each other's sobs become normal breathing. Normal enough. Our bare thighs were touching. Our faces were hardening into the floor.

"Yet?" I finally said.

"Yet," Marten agreed, and I could hear his cheek peeling up.

I wasn't stuck as hard, I didn't think, and still had one thing to do anyway: reach forward, pinch into that sludge for that glint of silver.

What I came back with was one quarter.

"What year?" Marten said, because his luck system was that if the quarter was the same age as him, it was lucky, he could win with it.

"Rance's age," I said, trying to clean the gunk off it.

"Mail it to him," Marten said in defeat, and we sat there like that, making useless quiet jokes and detailing grand, never-to-be-enacted revenge plans until Jess turned the lights off, ran his vacuum cleaner over the more obvious parts of the arcade.

Then the cage door came down. We were officially in jail.

"I'm going to cut the other one off," Marten said, holding his left braid out. "I'm going to tell my dad I did it on my own."

"He'll kick your ass for it," I told him.

"Cops don't care about that," Marten said.

He was right. It was a solid plan.

We stood, no pants, and crept out among the machines, all of them still cycling through their holding screens—Jess hadn't pulled the plug, had probably been making a horny beeline for that hot-dog girl. Marten was still in his black warpaint. I was still some white dude who'd almost got himself justly scalped. Still, walking through the arcade all alone, half-naked, bathed in what felt like neon, it was kind of magic.

Marten was the first to smile, but I caught it soon enough.

We pushed our faces against the cage, looked out at the darkened mall.

"We can erase them from *Joust* anyway, right?" Marten said at last.

Like that we were behind the machines again, hungrily tracing out cables.

"This one," I said, and pulled it.

We ran around, but *Joust* was still blinking.

"*This* one," Marten said, pulling another, and we ran around again, had only killed *Galaxian*.

"Close," I said, and then touched my brother's initials on the *Galaga* screen, balled my hand fast around that, promised to never let it go.

"What are you doing?" Marten asked.

"This one," I said, sure this time, but when I pulled it, the whole junction-thing it was plugged into yanked from the wall. The whole bank of machines behind us went dark.

"Think you got it," Marten said with a thrilled chuckle, and we crept around. I had definitely gotten it, yeah.

But then I realized what else I had got: *Galaga*.

"Shit," I said, my face going cold.

I'd erased Rance's last game, the high score he'd left behind for all of us to wonder at. Janet hadn't beaten him earlier, nobody had beaten him, but now nobody would ever know.

Marten's dad was going to kick his ass, yeah, but I was going to be kicking my own ass for twice as long.

"I'll get it back for him," I said, holding that magic quarter up.

Dutifully, we plugged *Galaga* back in, and, after holding the quarter up between us, honoring its power, its promise, its birth year, I kissed it, thumbed it into the slot.

It fell through to the change return.

"What the hell?" Marten said.

I inserted it again, and again it rattled down to that metal flap.

Marten tried, same thing. We tried shooting it through harder, we tried rubbing all the quarter's edge-grooves clean on the carpet, we breathed on it to make it hot—nothing.

"Cursed quarter," Marten said, shrugging.

"Jess should give us a new one," I said, and looked around as if the ghost-version of Jess might be skulking around, talking up the eighth graders.

Because we knew we could make it last, we dropped the quarter in *Pac-Man*, just to prove it was a real and actual quarter, but it hit the change return again.

Every machine we tried, even the kiddie ones.

"Hyperspace," Marten said, lifting his chin to *Defender*.

"Like it'll—" I said, thumbing the quarter in, but the machine *took* it before I could finish.

I pushed back from the controls, giving them to Marten, but he stepped back as well, said, "It was Rance's year, he'd want you to."

I dove in, grabbed the joystick right as the game went live, and did my usual thing I did with *Defender:* held on, shot at complete random, stars streaking past at ridiculous speeds.

"Hyperspace! Hyperspace!" Marten yelled when I was about to die, but I shook my head no, was in what felt like a Rance-trance, was one with this game for once.

I pulled up at every last moment, shot past, lived through. Maybe my problem all along at the arcade had been that I'd been trying to play like Rance, when I was really a Janet-player: I only came alive in a corner.

Marten was breathing hard beside me, his hand on my shoulder, the grease sweating down his face like he was crying black.

Maybe this *was* my game, I thought. Rance had *Galaga*, but me, I was *Defender*, right?

I sure wasn't anything else.

I fired, fired faster, felt one foot creeping forward into my version of a power stance. It felt weird enough that I looked down, even, and what I saw on the way was light bleeding out from the quarter slot.

"*What?*" I said, and then Marten was lunging forward to jerk the joystick to the side, save my life.

"Thanks!" I yelled to him, taking control again.

The light from the quarter slot was a hot spot on my bare thigh. I shifted away from it, felt the heat smear across to my other leg.

"What was that quarter *made* of?" I said, and Marten nodded hard with this, because this was my best game ever, was the best we'd ever seen.

Still, *Defender* being what it was, I finally had to scream and panic, slap the hyperspace button, because any point in space was better than where I was now.

Like always, everything jumbled on the screen, and—and when I leaned over for a different angle, like I could get a bead on whatever forces I was about to blip down in front of, what I saw kind of in the reflection wasn't the game at all. I was—I was behind the windshield of an eighteen-wheeler at night? I could tell it was a big rig from the height, and from the monster of a steering wheel in my lap. And then I was nudging that wheel to the right just enough to edge my truck over into the ditch, to tag the Indian walking on the shoulder, just turning around to hike his thumb up.

That hitchhiker was Rance.

I slapped hyperspace again, to get away from this, keep it from having to happen.

Now I was watching from behind a chain-link fence in Denver, watching Rance and three white dudes brush past each other on the sidewalk, Rance not giving room, their shoulders hitting, tempers flaring, brake lights stopping in the street to help these three guys with this Indian, who I knew could have taken on two of them, maybe even three. But not a whole carload.

I hit that button deeper to stop this from happening either and I held it down this time, cycling through Rance dying this way, that way, all the ways an Indian can die in America—shot on a porch, sleeping under a bridge, caught in a car rolling through a fence, throwing up in his sleep—and when I finally, timidly, let the button come back up, I was in the arcade again.

My ship was blasting across the alien landscape, each orange mountain peak the leading edge of a massive lurking asteroid, the ship so fragile, and Marten was yelling my name, telling me *up, up!*

"No," I said, using my whole body to move the joystick just the littlest bit. Marten moved with me, and then—he told me later, so I know it's true—he saw what I was seeing: my little ship in *De-*

fender was a dull gray fighter plane now, blasting faster and faster, its background a blur.

"Rance," I said, almost smiling.

I'd blipped to a *good* version at last, a *good* outcome.

"This isn't—what game *is* this?" Marten said, checking the side of the machine, like that could tell him anything.

But it wasn't broke.

"I can do it, I can do it," I said, zoning in, the skin of my face going cold, my eyes speeding up to see everything at once, my hands hardly even connected to me anymore they were so fast, so right, so true, and no one but Marten was there to see my game that night, the night I beat *Defender*, the unbeatable game, but I wasn't playing for them.

All those lives I'd hyperspaced through, they were ways Rance could be out there dying—*would* be out there dying.

Unless I kept him alive.

The stars blurred, my fingertip on that hyperspace button was both numb and more alive than it had ever been, and I fired, and I fired, and I fired deeper into the heart of whatever this was, clearing a path for him, one farther than our dad could ever reach, one that would get him away and safe and let him live the life he should have, that he deserved.

"What the hell, what the hell, man!" Marten said beside me, his left hand worrying his left braid, his whole body bouncing on the balls of his feet, and if anybody would have looked through the cage they would have seen two twelve-year-olds not yet ready for life, so unready that they didn't even have pants, their faces streaked black from tears, their eyes blasted wide for every alien, every way to die.

In the morning when Jess opened up we were sitting on the counter, still breathing hard, telling ourselves the story of this, and we were different now, we knew. We'd won.

"Real funny, losers," Jess said, stepping to the side so we could leave. "You didn't break anything did you?"

"Just the high score!" Marten yelled on the way past him, and then we ran without pants through the morning, without pants and with sandy hair, with one braid, one black eye, and in the alley behind Marten's house I cut his braid off to keep his dad out of jail, and we shook hands in the gangster way we'd seen in a music video, pointed at each other to end it, and I didn't mean to, it wasn't on purpose, but I took a mental snapshot of Marten anyway, leaned against his back fence, his hair so stupid, his eyes so nervous, his chest raised so he could fake like he was tough enough to walk inside, and I want to lie and say that when I was walking home that bright Halloween morning, a fighter plane cracked thunder over my street, punched through the sound barrier like it was nothing, but, though I closed my eyes to wait for just that, it didn't come, and didn't come. There was just me rushing from bush to bush, car to car, and, somewhere far behind me, and also in my heart, a video game blinking RED, RED, RED.

Let All the Children Boogie

FROM *Tor.com*

RADIO WAS WHERE we met. Our bodies first occupied the same space on a Friday afternoon, but our minds had already connected Thursday night. Coming up on twelve o'clock, awake when we shouldn't be, both of us in our separate narrow beds, miles and miles apart, tuning in to Ms. Jackson's *Graveyard Shift*, spirits linked up in the gruff, cigarette-damaged sound of her voice.

She'd played "The Passenger," by Iggy Pop. I'd never heard it before, and it changed my life.

Understand: there was no internet then. No way to look up the lyrics online. No way to snap my fingers and find the song on You-Tube or iTunes. I was crying by the time it was over, knowing it might be months or years before I found it again. Maybe I never would. Strawberries, Hudson's only record store, almost certainly wouldn't have it. Those four guitar chords were seared indelibly into my mind, the lonesome sound of Iggy's voice certain to linger there for as long as I lived, but the song itself was already out of my reach as it faded down to nothing.

And then: a squall of distortion interrupted, stuttering into staticky words, saying what might have been "*Are you out there?*" before vanishing again.

Eerie, but no more eerie than the tingly feeling I still had from Iggy Pop's voice. And the sadness of losing the song forever.

But then, the next day, at the Salvation Army, thumbing through hundreds of dresses I hated, what did I hear but—

"*I am the passenger . . . and I ride and I ride—*"

Not from the shitty in-store speakers, which blasted Fly-92 pop drivel all the time. Someone was singing. Someone magnificent. Like pawn-shop royalty, in an indigo velvet blazer with three handkerchiefs tied around one forearm, and brown corduroy bell-bottoms.

"*I see things from under glass—*"

The singer must have sensed me staring, because they turned to look in my direction. Shorter than me, hair buzzed to the scalp except for a spiked stripe down the center.

"*The Graveyard Shift,*" I said, trembling. "You were listening last night?"

"Yeah," they said, and their smile was summer, was weekends, was Ms. Jackson's raspy-sweet voice. The whole place smelled like mothballs, and the scent had never been so wonderful. "You too?"

My mind had no need for pronouns. Or words at all for that matter. This person filled me up from the very first moment.

I said: "What a great song, right? I never heard it before. Do you have it?"

"No," they said, "but I was gonna drive down to Woodstock this weekend to see if I could find it there. Wanna come?"

Just like that. *Wanna come?* Everything I did was a long and agonizing decision, and every human on the planet terrified me, and this person had invited me on a private day trip on a moment's impulse. What epic intimacy to offer a total stranger—hours in a car together, a journey to a strange and distant town. What if I was a psychopath, or a die-hard Christian evangelist bent on saving their soul? The only thing more surprising to me than this easy offer was how swiftly and happily my mouth made the words: *That sounds amazing.*

"Great! I'm Fell."

"Laurie," I said. We shook. Fell's hand was smaller than mine, and a thousand times stronger.

Only then did I realize: I didn't know what gender they were. And, just like that, with the silent effortless clarity of every life-changing epiphany, I saw that gender was just a set of clothes we put on when we went out into the world.

And even though I hated myself for it, I couldn't help but look around. To see if anybody else had seen. If word might spread, about me and this magnificently unsettling oddball.

Numbers were exchanged. Addresses. A pickup time was set. Everything was so easy. Fell's smile held a whole world inside it, a way of life I never thought I could live. A world where I wasn't afraid.

I wanted to believe in it. I really did. But I didn't.

"What did you think that was?" Fell asked in the parking lot, parting. "That weird voice, at the end of the song?"

I shrugged. I hadn't thought much about it.

"At first I thought it was part of the song," Fell said. "But then the DJ was freaked out."

"Figured it was just . . . interference, like from another station."

"It's a big deal," Fell said. "To interrupt a commercial radio broadcast like that. You need some crazy hardware."

"Must be the Russians," I said solemnly, and Fell laughed, and I felt the world lighten.

And that night, tuning in to Ms. Jackson, "This song goes out to Fell, my number one fan. Wouldn't be a weeknight if Fell didn't call asking for some Bowie. So here's 'Life on Mars?' which goes out to Laurie, the girl with the mousy hair."

More evidence of Fell's miraculous gift. A thousand times I'd wanted to call Ms. Jackson, and each time I'd been too intimidated to pick up the phone. What if she was mean to me? What if I had to speak to a station producer first, who decided I wasn't worthy of talking to their resident empress? And who was I to ask for a song?

Also, I loved "Life on Mars?" I wondered if Fell knew it, had read it on my face or smelled it on my clothes with another of their superhuman abilities, or if they had just been hoping.

I shut my eyes. I had never been so conscious of my body before. David Bowie's voice rippled through it, making me shiver, sounding like Fell's fingertips must feel.

I wondered how many times I'd been touched by Fell, listening late at night, trembling at the songs they requested.

I remembered Fell's smile, and stars bloomed in the darkness.

But before the song was over, a sound like something sizzling rose up in my headphones, and the music faded, and a kind of high distortion bubbled up, and then began to stutter—and then become words. Unintelligible at first, like they'd been sped up, and then:

"*. . . mission is so unclear. I could warn about that plane crash, try to stop the spiderwebbing epidemic. But how much difference would those things make? I'm only here for a short—*"

Then the mechanical voice was gone. David Bowie came back. And just as swiftly was switched out.

"Sorry about that, children," Ms. Jackson said, chuckling. An old sound. How long had she been doing this show? She always called her listeners children, like she was older than absolutely everyone in earshot. I heard a cigarette snuffed out in the background. "Getting some interference, sounds like. Maybe from the Air Force base. They're forever messing with my signals. Some lost pilot, maybe, circling up in the clouds. Looking for the light. Good time to cut to a commercial, I'd say."

Someone sang, *"Friendly Honda, we're not on Route Nine,"* the inane omnipresent jingle that seemed to support every television and radio program in the Hudson Valley. I thought of Fell, somewhere in the dark. Our bodies separate. Our minds united.

"Welcome back to the *Graveyard Shift*," she said. "This is Ms. Jackson, playing music for freaks and oddballs, redheaded stepchildren and ugly ducklings—songs by us and for us, suicide queens and flaming fireflies—"

Fell's car smelled like apples. Like spilled cider, and cinnamon. Twine held one rear headlight in place. When we went past fifty miles an hour, it shook so hard my teeth chattered together. Tractor trailers screamed past like missiles. It was autumn, 1991. We were sixteen. We could die at any moment.

The way to Woodstock was long and complicated. Taking the thruway would have been faster, but that meant paying the toll, and Fell knew there had to be another way.

"No way in hell that was a lost pilot," Fell said. "That interruption last night. That was someone with some insane machinery."

"How do you know so much about radio signals?"

"I like machines," Fell said. "They make so much sense. Does your school have a computer? Mine doesn't. We're too poor." Fell went to Catskill High, across the river. "It sucks, because I really want to be learning how they work. They can do computations a million times faster than people can, and they're getting faster all the time. Can you imagine? How many problems we'll be able to solve? How quickly we'll get the right answer, once we can make a billion mistakes in an instant? All the things that seem impossible now, we'll figure out how to do eventually."

I lay there, basking in the warmth of Fell's excitement. After a while, I said: "I still think it was the Soviets. Planning an invasion."

"No Russian accent," Fell said. "And anyway I'm pretty sure the Cold War is over. Didn't that wall come down?"

I shrugged, and then said, "Thanks for the song, by the way."

Instead of answering, Fell held out one hand. I took it instantly, fearlessly, like a fraction of Fell's courage could already have rubbed off on me.

In that car I felt invincible. I could let Fell's lack of fear take me over.

But later, in Woodstock, a weird crooked little town that smelled like burning leaves and peppermint soap, Fell reached for my hand again, and I was too frightened to take it. What if someone saw? In my mind I could hear the whole town stopping with a sound like a record scratching. Everyone turning, pointing. Shouting. Pitchforks produced from nowhere. Torches. Nooses.

Space grew between us, without my wanting it to. Fell taking a tiny step away from me.

We went to Cutler's Record Shop. We found a battered old Iggy Pop cassette, which contained "The Passenger." Fell bought it. We went to Taco Juan's and then had ice cream. Rocky Road was both of our favorite.

Twilight when we left. Thin blue light filled the streets. I dreamed of grabbing Fell's hand and never letting go. I dreamed of being someone better than who I was.

As soon as the doors slammed, we switched on the radio.

"Responding to this morning's tragic crash of Continental Express Flight 2574, transport officials are stating that it's impossible to rule out an act of terrorism at this—"

"No *shit*," Fell said, switching it off.

"What?"

"The voice. They said *I could warn about the plane crash*."

I laughed. "What, you think the voice in the night is part of a terrorist cell?"

"No," Fell said. "I think they're from the future."

Just like Fell to make the impossible sound easy, obvious. I laughed some more. And then I stopped laughing.

"Could be a coincidence," I said.

Fell pushed the tape in, pressed play. After our third trip through "The Passenger," rewinding the tape yet again, they looked over and saw the tears streaming down my face.

"It's such a sad song," I said. "So lonesome."

"Sort of," Fell said. "But it's also about finding someone who shares your loneliness. Who negates it. Cancels it out. Listen: *Get into the car. We'll be the passenger.* Two people, one thing. Plural singular."

"Plural singular," I said.

I'm sorry, I started to say, a hundred times, and told myself I would, soon, in just a second, until Fell looked over and said: "Hey. Can I come over? I don't feel like mixing it up with my mother tonight."

And that was the first time I ever saw fear on Fell's face.

My parents were almost certainly baffled by my new friend, but their inability to identify whether Fell was a boy or a girl meant they couldn't decide for sure if they were a sexual menace, so they couldn't object to Fell coming upstairs with me.

Three songs into the *Graveyard Shift,* Fell asked, "Can I spend the night?"

I laughed.

"I'm serious."

"Your mom wouldn't mind?"

"Probably she'd barely notice," Fell said. "And even if she did, it'd be like number nine on the list of things she'd want to scream at me about the next time she saw me."

"Fine by me," I said, and went downstairs to ask Mom and Dad. *Big smile. Confident posture. Think this through.* "Cool if Fell spends the night here?" And then, without thinking about it, because if I'd spent a single nanosecond on it I would have known better, stopped myself, I added: "She already called her mom, and she said it was okay."

They smiled, relieved. They'd both been sitting there stewing, wondering whether what was happening upstairs needed to be policed. Whether a sex-crazed-menace male was upstairs seducing their daughter. But no. I'd said *she.* This was just some harmless, tomboyish girl.

"Yes, of course," Mom said, but I couldn't hear her, just went by the smile, the nod, and I thanked her and turned to go, nausea making the room spin and the blood pound in my ears.

I felt sick. Somehow naming Fell like that was worse than a lie. Worse than an insult. It was a negation of who Fell was.

Cowardice. Betrayal. What was it, in me, that made me so afraid? That had stopped me from taking Fell's hand? That made me frightened of other people seeing what they were, what we were? Something so small that could somehow make me so miserable.

I was afraid that Fell might have heard, but Ms. Jackson was playing when I got back to my room, and Fell was on the floor be-side the speaker, so that our hero's raspy voice drowned out every shred of weakness and horror that the world held in store for us.

We lay on the bare wooden floor like that for the next two hours. The window was open. Freezing wind made every song sweeter. Woodsmoke seeped into our clothes. Our hands held tight.

Six minutes before midnight, approaching the end of the *Graveyard Shift*, it came again. The sizzle; the static; the chugging machine noise that slowly took the shape of a human voice. We caught it mid-sentence, like the intervening twenty-four hours hadn't happened, like it blinked and was now carrying on the same conversation.

"—out there. I don't know if this is the right . . . place. Time. If you're out there. If it's too late. If it's too early."

"Definitely definitely from the future," Fell whispered.

"You're so stupid," I said, giggling, so drunk on Fell that what they said no longer seemed so absurd.

"Or what you need to hear. What I should say. What I shouldn't."

The voice flanged on the final sentence, dropping several oc-taves, sounding demonic, mechanical. Slowing down. The *t* sound on the last word went on and on. The static in the background slowed down, too, so that I could hear that it wasn't static at all, but rather many separate sounds resolving into sonic chaos. An endless line of melodic sequences playing simultaneously.

The voice flanged back, and said one word before subsiding into the ether again:

"—worthwhile—"

Control of the radio waves was relinquished. The final chords of "Blue Moon" resurfaced.

"There's our star man again," Ms. Jackson said with a chuckle. Evidently she'd had time to rethink her Air Force pilot theory. "Still lost, still lonely. I wonder—who do you think he's looking for? Call me with your wildest outer-space invader theories."

"Want to call?" Fell whispered.

"No," I said, too fast, too frightened. "My parents are right across the hall. We'd wake them."

Fell shrugged. The gesture was such strange perfection. Their whole being was expressed in it. The confidence and the charm and the fearlessness and the power to roll with absolutely anything that came along.

I grabbed Fell's hand. Prayed that some of what they were would seep into me.

Fell touched my mousy hair. Sang softly: "*Is there life on Mars?*"

"We'll find out," I said. "Right? Machines will solve all our problems?"

At school, two days later, during lunch, I marched myself to the library and enrolled in computer classes.

"Shit," Fell said, pointing out the window, driving us home through snowy blue twilight.

Massive green Air Force trucks lined a long stretch of Route 9. Flatbeds where giant satellite dishes stood. Racks of cylindrical transformers. Men pacing back and forth with machines in their hands. None of it had been there the day before.

"What the hell?" I said.

"They're hunting for the voice in the night too," Fell said.

"Because it's part of a terrorist cell and knew about a plane crash before it happened."

"Or because it's using bafflingly complex technology that could only have come from the future," Fell said.

Then they switched on the radio, shrieked at what they found there. Sang-screamed: "*Maybe I'm just like my mother, she's never satisfied.*"

"*Why do we scream at each other?*" I said, and then we launched into the chorus with one wobbly crooked magnificent voice.

My first view of Fell's house was also my first view of Fell's mother. She sat on the front porch wearing several scarves, smoking.

"Fuck," Fell said. "Fuck me, times ten thousand. I thought for sure she'd still be at work."

"We can go," I said. I'd been excited to see the house, for that insight into who Fell was and what had helped make them, but now panic was pulling hard at my hair. Fell's fear of the woman was contagious.

"No," Fell said. "If I act like she can't hurt me, sooner or later she really won't be able to."

She laughed when she saw me. "Of course it's a girl."

"Mrs. Tanzillo, I'm Laurie," I said, holding out my hand. "I'm pleased to meet you."

My good manners threw her off. She shook my hand with a raised eyebrow, like she was waiting to see what kind of trick I was trying to pull. I smelled alcohol. Old, baked-in alcohol, the kind that seeps from the pores of aging drunks. Which I guess she was.

"Don't you two turn my home into a den of obscenity," she called after us as we headed in.

Fell let the door slam, and then exhaled: "God, she is such an asshole."

The house was sadder than I'd been expecting. Smaller; smellier; heaped with strange piles. Newspapers, flattened plastic bags, ancient water-stained unopened envelopes. A litter box, badly in need of emptying, and then probably burning. My parents were poor, but not poor like this.

"You're shaking," I said, and pulled Fell into a hug.

They stiffened. Wriggled free. "Not here."

"Of course," I said. "Sorry."

The TV was on. Squabbling among the former Soviet states. A bad divorce, except with sixteen partners instead of two, and with thermonuclear warheads instead of children. I watched it, because looking around the room—or looking at Fell looking at me—made me nauseous. A talking head grinned, said: "*It's naïve to think our children will get to grow up without the threat of nuclear war. There's no putting this genie back in the bottle.*"

Fell talked fast, the shaking audible in every word. "This was a terrible idea. I felt good about us, like, it wouldn't matter what this place looked like or what you thought of it, because you know I'm not this, it's just the place where I am until I can be somewhere else, but now, I'm not so sure, I think I should probably take you home."

So Fell wasn't fearless. Wasn't superhuman.

So it was in Fell too. Whatever was in me. Something so small, that could chain down someone so magnificent.

Of course I should have put up more of a fight. Said how it didn't matter. But I hated seeing Fell like this. If Fell was afraid, what hope was there for me? Fell, who welcomed every awful thing the world had to show us. Fell was my only hope, but not this Fell. So I shrugged and said, "Whatever you want," feeling awful about it already, and we turned around and went right back outside, and Mrs. Tanzillo thought that was the funniest thing she'd ever seen, and we didn't talk the whole ride home.

"That *is* what it sounds like when doves cry," Ms. Jackson said, as the spiraling keyboard riff faded out, as the drum machine loop wound down.

I'd called the song in. I wondered if Fell was listening, if they knew what it meant. How hard it had been for me to dial that number. How bare the floor beside me was. How cold. How much my chest hurt.

"This extended block of uninterrupted songs is brought to you by Friendly Honda," she said. "They're not on Route Nine. Let's stick with Prince, shall we? Dig a little deeper. A B-side. 'Erotic City.'" Her laugh here was raw and throaty, barely a laugh at all, closer to a grumble of remembered pleasure. Some erotic city she'd taken someone to, ages ago.

The song started. A keyboard and a bass doing dirty, dirty things together. Strutting, strolling. Becoming one thing, one lewd gorgeous sound that made me shiver.

I imagined Fell listening. Our minds entwined inside the song. An intimacy unencumbered by flawed bodies, troubled minds, or the fear of what could go wrong when we put them together. Small voices inside our heads that made us miserable.

What a magnificent thing we would be. If Fell ever spoke to me again. If we could make whatever our weird thing was work.

Just when things were getting good, as Prince was shifting to the chorus, the static sizzle:

"There are a million ways I could have done this. But anything else, something more straightforward, well, I thought it might just blow your minds. Cause panic. Do the opposite thing, from what I wanted to accomplish."

Prince and the star man struggled for dominance, dirty talk giving way to flanged static only to steal back center stage. I only heard one more intelligible phrase before the intruder cut out altogether, even though I stayed up until three in the morning to see if they'd return:

"—know it's all worthwhile—"

"I want to find her," Fell said, the next day, when I walked out the front door and there they were, sitting on my front steps.

I hid my shock, my happiness. My shame. My guilt. "Find who?"

"The voice in the night. The one Ms. Jackson keeps calling the star man."

I sat down. "You think it's a she?"

Fell shrugged. I had been imagining the voice belonged to a male, but now that I thought about it I heard how sexless it was, how mechanical. Could be anything, in the ear of the beholder.

Cold wind swung tree branches against the side of my house, sounding like someone awful knocking at the door. I could not unhunch my shoulders. The magnitude of my awfulness was such that I didn't know where to start. What to apologize for first.

"How would we even begin to do something like that?" I asked instead.

Fell picked up something I hadn't seen before. The size of three record album sleeves laid out in a row. Four horizontal lines of thin metal, with a single vertical line down the middle.

"A directional antenna," they said. "It picks up radio signals, but it's sensitive to the direction of the origin signal. Point it directly at the source and you get a strong signal; point it away and you'll get a faint one. Plug it into this receiver"—Fell held up a hefty army-green box—"and we can take measurements in multiple directions until we find the right one."

They talked like everything was fine, but their face was so tight that I knew nothing was.

"Where did you get that?" I asked, making my voice laugh. "And how do you know how to use it?"

"I told you, machines are kind of my thing."

"So, wait, we just turn it around until we find the signal, and then go in that direction?"

"Not necessarily," Fell said. "It tells direction, but not distance. So the signal could be three miles away, or three thousand, depending on how strong it is. With just one measurement, we could be driving into the wilderness for days." Fell produced a map from the inner workings of the complex blazer they wore. "So the best way to do it is to take a measurement from one place, draw a line on the map that corresponds precisely to the signal, and then go to another location and take another measurement, and draw another precise line on the map—"

"And the point where they meet is the probable location!" I said, excited.

"It's called triangulation," Fell said.

"Amazing. But for real. How do you know all this?"

"My uncle, he learned this from my grandfather, who did it in the war. Transmitter hunting is kind of a nerd game, for amateur radio operators. They call it foxtailing."

"Your uncle as in your mother's brother?"

Fell nodded. And there it was, the subject I'd been trying to avoid.

"He was the closest thing to a dad that I had," Fell said. "We used to have so much fun together. Didn't give a shit about sports or any of that standard dude shit. He was into weird shit like directional antennas and science fiction. Then he met this girl and moved to Omaha with her. Fucking *Omaha.* I'm sorry about the other day, at my mom's. I acted like an idiot."

"*You* acted like an idiot? Don't be dumb, Fell—that was all me. I'm the one who should be apologizing. I didn't know how to react when I saw how upset you were. I should have stayed. I wanted to stay."

Fell grabbed my hand. I had so much more to say, and I imagine so did Fell, but we did not need a word of it.

Mom might be watching out the window, I thought, but did not let go of Fell's hand.

"What if the source of the signal is moving?"

Fell nodded. "I thought about that. I don't have a good solution. We just have to hope that's not the case, or we'll be triangulating bullshit."

"It's not the end of the world, if we end up standing in some empty field together."

We drove to the top of Mount Merino to take our first measurement. And then we waited. Kept the car running, blasting the *Graveyard Shift* from shitty speakers. Across the street was a guardrail, and then a sheer drop to the river beneath us. The train tracks alongside it. We lay on the hood and looked at stars.

"You won't run out of gas like this?"

"The average car can idle for ninety-two hours—that's just under four days—on a full tank of gas, which is what we have," Fell said. "The battery will die long before we run out of gas."

I marveled at the intricacies of Fell's mechanical knowledge, but I had some knowledge of my own to share. I told Fell about my computer classes, and how, yeah, computers were incredible, they could do anything. Fell was as impressed as I'd hoped they'd be, but they kept asking me questions about the hardware that I couldn't answer. All I knew was software. Fell looked at programming the way I looked at machines: probably fascinating, but way over my head.

Fell told me about transistors, and how processing power was increasing exponentially; had been for decades. How eventually

computers would be able to store as much information and process as many simultaneous operations as swiftly as a human brain.
Then Fell showed me how to work the antenna, read the receiver,
detect signal strength. We practiced on other radio stations, pen-
ciled lines on the map.

Then three hours passed. We were way past my curfew, and the
star man hadn't shown.

"Fuck it," Fell said, at the end of Ms. Jackson's program. "Star
person stood us up. We should go for a long drive. Charge the
battery backup."

"Okay," I said, just assuming Fell was right and that was how
those worked.

"Your parents won't mind?"

"Nah," I said, although they absolutely would, if they caught
me sneaking back in, and there was a very good chance that they
would because I am extremely clumsy, but that was the future and
I didn't care about that, I only cared about the here and the now
with Fell in Fell's car on this freezing night on this weird planet in
this mediocre galaxy.

The radio show after *Graveyard Shift* was significantly less awesome, but we had to stick with it. Who knew whether star person
would stumble onto any other stations. I had my portable radio
and my headphones, so that I could periodically coast back and
forth across the radio dial in search of our elusive visitor, but somehow I knew that this would be fruitless. For whatever reason, the
signal was pegged to this specific station.

The new DJ talked too much between songs, and he had the
voice of a gym teacher. The opening notes of "Where Is My Mind?"
came on and we both started screaming, but this asshole kept rambling on about a concert in Albany coming up next weekend, and
he only stopped when the singer started singing.

"Goddamn him," Fell said, and then—static—then—

*"—that's why I'm doing this, I guess. To tell you the future can be more
magnificent, and more terrifying, than what you have in your head right
now. And the one you embrace will be the one you end up with."*

As soon as the voice began, Fell raised the antenna, held it out
like a pistol. Turned slowly. We watched the receiver respond to
the signal's varying strength, and hastily drew a bold thick line on
the map when we found it. Cheered. Watched our breath billow.

"Told you he or she was a time traveler!" Fell said.

"That's *not* what that means."

"What does it mean, then?"

"We're picking up lines of dialogue from a movie, maybe. Or love letters from a lunatic. We should keep driving, wait for another one."

"It's late," Fell said. "My mom's not doing so well lately."

The temperature dropped twenty degrees. The final notes of "Where Is My Mind?" faded away.

"You can talk to me about it," I said, gulping down air as the ground opened up beneath me. "Whatever you're going through, I have your back. You know I love you, right?"

"I love you too, Laurie," but I could hear the unspoken rest of the sentence—like our minds had linked up already—like Fell knew, in a way I never would, how little love mattered.

"We'll go hunting tomorrow night," I said.

Fell nodded.

At school the next day, alone with the computer, I saw why Fell loved machines so much. Not because they were simple, but because the rules were clear. And when something went wrong, there was a way to fix it.

And the next night, hands clasped on the hood of Fell's car again, listening to Ms. Jackson with the directional antenna balanced across our thighs, I thought—if only *we* were machines. The sturdiness of hardware; the clarity of software. Not these awful meat puppets, in this awful world. Heads full of awful voices holding us back.

"I feel so good, when it's just us," Fell said, tapping into my thoughts with that eerie precision. "Our minds linked up inside the music. I want to stay there, forever."

"Maybe someday," I said, nonsensically, and Fell had the kindness not to point out that it was nonsense. We were what we were. Damaged minds alone in dying bodies.

Ms. Jackson exhaled smoke. "This one goes out to our friend the star man. Hope you get where you're going, buddy."

I groaned at the opening chords. "Starman," by David Bowie. "This song always makes me cry," I whispered, the lump already emerging in my throat.

Fell said, "I knew you were a Bowie girl."

We listened. The chorus hurt.

Fell heard me sniffle. "Hear the way his voice rises, between 'star' and 'man'?" they asked. "That's the same octave jump as in the chorus of 'Somewhere Over the Rainbow.' You hear it? Star-*man;* Some-*where?*"

Fell was right. I'd listened to the song a million times before, and never noticed. And now for as long as I lived I'd never hear it without noticing. And now I was crying. Because the song was so beautiful; because Fell was so incredible; because the world was too awful for love like ours to last.

The final chorus wound down:

> *Let the children lose it*
> *Let the children use it*
> *Let all the children boogie*

And the guitar cranked up, and the background singers crooned, and we were doomed, Fell and me, I felt it as heavy as the skin on my bones, how impossible we were, how soon we'd be shattered, and then—there the voice was again:

"The future is written, you might say. What will be will be. What's the point of this? But so many futures are written. An infinite number, in fact. A billion trillion ways your story could end. I want to make sure you end up with the right future."

Fell raised the antenna. Turned slowly, searching for the signal. Found it. We drew a line on the map. We circled the spot where our two lines met.

Both of us were crying, but Fell's tears were happy ones.

Fell didn't call me the next day, the way they say they would. Nor did they come by the house. And there was no answering machine at the Tanzillo household, and no one picked up, no matter how many times I called.

I told myself this was something sacred, something practically supernatural, to go to the spot on the map where our lines crossed, where the star person's signal came from. So of course Fell was scared.

I told myself that's all it was.

I told myself that, the whole long bike ride to Fell's front door, where I knocked three times. The pounding echoed. How had I found the courage to come at all? What was I becoming?

"Quit calling my house," said Fell's mom when she opened the door. I'd only seen her sitting down before. She was taller than I'd imagined. Her long, loose gray hair would have been glamorous on anyone else. "Christ, I feel like I spend half my time watching the phone ring, waiting for you to give the hell up."

"You could pick it up, actually talk to me."

She shrugged. The gesture was the same as Fell's, heavier on the left shoulder than the right, but this version oozed with cynicism and inertia instead of energy and exuberance. The news was on in the background, turned up too loud, more talking heads talking nuclear annihilation. On the way in, I'd passed more military trucks. Trailers getting set up along the Hudson River. Satellite dishes blooming like steel flowers.

"Where's Fell?"

"Not here."

"Do you know where?"

"Sometimes they go to sleep at their grandpa's place." Except Mrs. Tanzillo used the wrong gender pronouns, and clearly took great pleasure in doing so. "Old trailer, been abandoned since the man died ten years ago. Full of raccoon shit, and wasps in summer. I'll tell Fell you dropped by though." Her sweet smile made it clear she'd do no such thing, and then she shut the door in my face.

I got on my bike.

This pain, it was Fell's. It wasn't mine, and I couldn't do anything to diminish it. I could ride away and never feel it again.

I said that, but I didn't believe it. I remembered what the star person had said. About how we could have a future that was magnificent or one that was terrifying, depending on which one we embraced.

I got off the bike.

Fell couldn't see it, what a sad little creature their mother was. How absurd it was, that someone as magnificent as Fell could be made miserable by someone so weak.

Someone so small.

I knocked again.

She said nothing when she opened the door. Just smiled, like, *Come on, little girl, hit me with your best shot.* And I had nothing. No practiced, witty wise one-liners. Fell would have, for anyone but her.

"You're only hurting yourself, you know."

Her eyebrows rose. Her smile deepened.

"You might have the power to hurt Fell now, but that power won't last long. As soon as Fell realizes what a useless angry pitiful person you are, you'll lose that power." I wanted my words to be better. But I was done letting wishing I was better stop me from being what I was. "And Fell will leave you here, drowning in cat shit and bills, while they go conquer the world."

She said something. I didn't hear what it was.

That night I heard the star man again. Somehow I knew it was just me this time. Like our minds were already beginning to overlap, and I could see Fell lying in silence in that dirty trailer, shivering under a blanket, no radio, listening to pine trees shush overhead while I heard the star man whisper:

"... *Two soldiers trapped behind enemy lines* ... "

I stayed late after school, in the computer lab. In the library. Reading the science and the science fiction Fell had rhapsodized about. All the impossible things that could save us from ourselves. Solar power; a post-petroleum future; superfoods. Cold fusion. Brain uploading. Digital immortality. Transcending the limits of the human.

Each time I shut a book, it was the pain of waking up from blissful dream to wretched reality.

But then, blissful dream: Fell was on my front steps when I got home. Alone in the deep black-blue of late twilight. Snow fell in halfhearted flurries.

"Sorry," they said when I ran straight at them. My hug took all the air out of them.

"Never disappear again," I whispered.

Fell nodded. A crumpled map in one raised fist. "Are we gonna do this?"

"We are."

A cassette blasted when Fell started up the car. David Bowie. We drove, heading for where our lines crossed. The gulf between us was still so wide. Maybe I believed, now—that we could work, that what we added up to could survive in this world—but Fell did not. Fell still believed what Mrs. Tanzillo believed: that Fell was hellbound, disgusting, deserving of nothing good. The miles inched past my window, closing in on the X on the map, and I had no words, no weapons to breach the wall between us.

And then: Fell did.

"Whatever you said to my mom? It really pissed her the fuck off."

"I am so sorry," I said. "It was selfish. I didn't think it through. What it might mean for you."

"No," Fell said, and turned onto Route 9. "I never saw her like that before. I went home and she didn't say a word to me. Like, at all. Except to say you stopped by. That never, ever happens. I don't know how, but what you said messed her up really bad."

"She—"

"No fucking way," Fell said, turning off the main road. "This can't be it."

We'd reached the spot on the map. We were stopped outside the Salvation Army. Where we'd met, a mere two weeks before.

"Nobody's broadcasting from here," they said.

We rolled down our windows. Snow fell harder now. Science-fiction scenarios blurred in my brain. Time travel. Brain uploading.

"They'd need so much equipment," Fell said. "If we heard it on the other side of the river? They'd need a massive antenna, but there's nothing. And—"

Fell trailed off.

I looked up at the sky. Snow tap-tap-tapped at my forehead. I remembered what the star man said, the night before, to me and me alone. *Two soldiers trapped behind enemy lines.*

It was talking to me and Fell.

"The equipment's not here," I said. "Or, it's *here*, but it's not *now*."

Fell got out of the car. I turned up the radio and got out after them.

"I get it," I said, laughing, crying, comprehending. One wobbly crooked magnificent voice. "You were right, Fell. It's coming from the future."

We stood. Snow slowly outlined us.

"It's us," I said. Fell had finally infected me. The audacious, the impossible, was not only easy—it was our only way forward. "That machine voice? That's . . . you and me. Our two voices together, somehow. A consciousness made up of both of our minds."

Fell turned their head, hard, like they weren't listening, or were listening and not understanding, or understanding and not believing.

"Plural singular," I said. "We are the passenger."

"Plural singular," Fell said, snow falling into their perfect face, while David Bowie told us *let all the children boogie.*

They still didn't see, but that was okay. There would be time to tell Fell all of it. To say that there was so much to be afraid of— nuclear winter, ecological devastation, the death spasms of patriarchy. That the next fifty years would see unspeakable suffering. But we could survive it. Overcome it. Surmount the limits of our flesh and our mortality and our separateness. Combine into some new kind of thing, some wobbly magnificent machine who could crack the very fabric of time and space. We could send a signal back, into the past, a lonely sad staticky voice in the night, to tell the beautiful damaged kids we had been that the future would be as good as they had the courage to be.

Skinder's Veil

FROM *When Things Get Dark*

ONCE UPON A time there was a graduate student in the summer of his fourth year who had not finished his dissertation. What was his field? Not important to this story, really, but let's say that the title of this putative dissertation was "An Exploratory Analysis of Item Parameters and Characteristics That Influence Response Time."

By the middle of June, Andy Sims had, at best, six usable pages. According to the schedule he had so carefully worked out last year, when a finished dissertation still seemed not only possible but the lowest of the fruit upon the branches of the first of many trees along the beautiful path he had chosen for himself, by this date he should have had a complete draft upon which his advisors' feedback had already been thoughtfully provided. June was to have been given over to leisurely revision in the shade of those graceful and beckoning trees.

There were reasons why he had not managed to get this work done, but Andy would have been the first to admit they were not *good* reasons. The most pressing was Lester and Bronwen.

Lester, Andy's roommate, was also ABD. Lester was Education and Human Sciences. He and Andy were not on the best terms, though Lester did not appear to have noticed this. Lester was having too much sex to notice much of anything at all. He'd met a physiotherapist named Bronwen at a Wawa two months ago on a beverage run, and they'd been fucking ever since, the kind of fucking that suggested some kind of apocalypse was around the corner but only Lester and Bronwen knew that so far. The reek of sex so thoroughly permeated the apartment in Center City that Andy began to have a notion he was fermenting in it, like a pickle in brine. There were the sounds too. Andy wore noise-canceling headphones while doing the dishes, while eating dinner, on his way to the bathroom where, twice, he'd found sex toys whose purpose he could not guess. He was currently in the best shape of his life: whenever Bronwen came over, Andy headed for the gym and lifted weights until he could lift no more. He went for long runs along the Schuylkill River Trail and still, when he came home, Lester and Bronwen would be holed up inside Lester's room (if Andy was lucky) either fucking or else resting for a short interval before they resumed fucking again.

Andy did not begrudge any person's happiness, but was it possible that there could be such a thing as too much happiness? Too much sex? He resented, too, knowing the variety of sounds that Lester made in extremis. He resented Bronwen, whose roommates apparently had better boundaries than Andy.

No doubt she was a lovely person. Andy found it hard to look her in the eyes. There were questions he would have liked to ask her. Had it been love at first sight? In the fateful moment that day, standing in the refrigerated section of the Wawa, had Lester's soul spoken wordlessly to hers? Did she always love this deeply, this swiftly, with this much noise and heat and abandon? Because Andy had been Lester's roommate for four years now, and aside from a few unremarkable and drunken hookups, Lester had been single and seemed okay with that. Not to mention, whenever Andy brought up Lester's own dissertation, Lester claimed to be making great progress. Could that be true? In his heart of hearts, Andy feared it was true. He mentioned all of this over the phone to his old friend, Hannah. It all came spilling out of him when she called to ask her favor.

"So that's a yes," Hannah said. "You'll do it."

"Yes," Andy said. Then, "Unless you're pranking me. Please don't be pranking me, though. I have to get out of here."

"Not a prank," Hannah said. "Swear to God. This is you saving my ass."

The last time they'd seen each other was at least two years ago, the morning before she left Boston for an adjunct position in the sociology department at some agricultural college in Indiana. "Adjuncts of the corn," she said, and had done three shots in succession. She'd been the first of their cohort to defend, and what had it gotten her? A three-year contract at a school no one had ever heard of. Andy had felt superior about that for a while.

Yesterday, Hannah said, her recently divorced sister in California had broken her back falling off the roof of her house. She was in the hospital. Hannah was flying out tomorrow to take care of her two young nieces. All of her sisters' friends were unreliable assholes or too overwhelmed with their own catastrophes. Her sister's ex was in Australia. What Hannah needed was for someone to take over her housesitting gig in Vermont for the next three weeks. That was what she said.

"It's in the middle of nowhere. It's outside of town, and the nearest town really isn't a town anyway, you know? There's not even a traffic light," Hannah said. "There's no grocery store, no library. There's a place down the road where you can get beer and lightbulbs and breakfast sandwiches, but I don't recommend those."

"I don't have a car," Andy said.

"I don't have one either!" Hannah said. "You won't need one. There's a standing grocery order, so you won't need a car for that. I get a delivery every Tuesday from the Hannaford in St. Albans. If you want to make changes, you just send them an email. And I'm leaving a bunch of stuff in the fridge. Eggs, milk, sandwich stuff. There's plenty of coffee. I have an Uber coming tomorrow at five p.m. Can you get here around three? I went ahead and mapped it; it should take you about seven hours to get here. I'll send directions. Show up at three, we can catch up and I can go over stuff you need to know. But don't worry! There isn't a lot of stuff. Really, it's just a couple of things."

"You're not giving me a lot of advance notice," Andy said.

"What's your Venmo?" Hannah said. "I'll send you nine hundred bucks right now. That's half of what I'm getting paid for three months."

Andy gave her his Venmo. The most he'd ever been venmoed was, what, around forty bucks? But here it was immediately, nine hundred dollars, just like that.

"So," Hannah said. "You'll be here. Tomorrow, by three p.m. Because promise I will hunt you down and remove the bones from both legs if you don't come through. I'm counting on you, asshole."

*

He was googling one-way car rentals when Bronwen wandered into the kitchen. She had Lester's old acapella T-shirt on (Quaker Notes) and a pair of Lester's even older boxer shorts. She got a Yuengling out of the fridge and popped it open, then stood behind Andy, looking at his screen.

"Going on a trip?" she said. She sounded wistful. "Cool."

"Yeah," Andy said. "Kind of? I agreed to take over a housesitting gig in Vermont for the rest of the month and it starts tomorrow afternoon. It's out in the middle of nowhere, and even if I took a bus I'd still be over an hour away, so I guess I'm renting a car."

"That's a terrible idea," Bronwen said. "Car rental places will just rip you off, especially in summer. I've got a car and I'm off work the next couple of days. Lester and I'll drive you."

"No," Andy said. He had spent most of the month trying to avoid being in the same room with Bronwen and Lester. Hadn't she noticed? "Why? Why would you even offer to do that?"

"I've been trying to get Lester to get off his ass and go somewhere all summer," Bronwen said. "Just say yes, and I'll tell him it's a done deal. Then he can't weasel out. Okay? We'll drop you off and then camp somewhere on the way home. A lake, maybe. Lots of lakes in Vermont, right?"

"Let me think about it," Andy said.

"Why?" Bronwen said.

There really wasn't anything to think about. "Sure," Andy said. "Okay. If you're okay with it and Lester is okay with it."

"Great!" Bronwen said. She seemed truly delighted by the prospect of doing Andy this favor. "I'm going to go home and get my tent."

He spent the rest of the afternoon avoiding Lester—who despite Bronwen's reassurances was clearly sulking—and going through his piles of reading and research material. In the end he had a backpack and three canvas bags. He stuck his laptop and printer and a ream of paper in his gym bag, wrapped up in underwear and socks, a sweatshirt, his last two clean T-shirts, running shorts, and a spare pair of jeans. A waterproof jacket and a pair of Timberlands and his weights. There was a guy down the street who made regular trips up to various weed dispensaries in Massachusetts to buy merchandise, which he then sold on locally at a healthy profit, and after perusing what was on offer, Andy spent a hundred dollars of Hannah's money on supplies. After some thought he also purchased a pouch of Betty's Eddies Tango for a Peachy Mango gummies for Bronwen as a thank-you.

Because, really, it was Lester that Andy bore a reasonable grudge against. There was, for example, the time Lester had been complaining about Andy at top volume to Bronwen, not realizing Andy had come home and was right there, next door in his bedroom. "It isn't that he's a terrible person. He's so fucking smug. Has to map every single thing out, but only because he won't let himself think about whether or not he wants any of it. What does he want? Who knows? Definitely not Andy. No interior life at all. You know how people talk about the unconscious and the id? The attic and the basement? The places you don't go? If you drew a picture of Andy's psyche it would be Andy, standing outside of the house where he lives. He won't go inside. He won't even knock on the door."

Which was rich, coming from Lester. That's what Andy thought. And anyway, Lester wasn't a psychologist. That wasn't his area at all.

He texted a couple of friends he hadn't seen in a while and went out, leaving Lester and Bronwen to fight about Vermont or fuck or watch Netflix in peace. It was good to be out in the world, or maybe it just felt good to know that tomorrow he was going to be in Vermont with all the time and space he could possibly need to get some real work done. To all of the questions about the house and its owner, he just kept saying, "No idea! I don't know anything at all!" And how good that felt, too, to be on the threshold of a mysterious adventure. It wouldn't be terrible, either, to see Hannah again.

As if this thought had summoned her, his phone buzzed with an incoming text. *You're still coming right?*

All packed, he wrote back. *So I guess I am.*

You're going to love it here. Promise. See you tomorrow. BE HERE BY 3!!!!

The plan had been to leave no later than six a.m. They got a late start, because Lester needed to find his spare inhaler, then bug spray, then a can opener, and then he wanted to make a second pot of coffee and take out the recycling and trash and check email. By the time they were in the car it was eight a.m., and of course they hit traffic before they were even on the 676 ramp. Lester fell asleep as soon as they were in the car.

Bronwen, checking the rearview mirror, said, "We'll make up the time once we're on 87."

"Yeah," Andy said. "Okay, sure." He texted Hannah, *on my way hooray*, put his AirPods in and closed his eyes. When he opened them again, they were stopping in New Jersey. It was ten thirty. According to his phone, they were now five hours away.

Andy paid for gas. "I could drive," he said.

"Nah, buddy," Lester said. "I got it." But he took the wrong exit out of the rest stop, south instead of north, and it was five miles back before they were going in the right direction again.

Bronwen, in the passenger seat, turned around to inspect Andy. "One time I missed an exit on 95 going down past D.C. and so I just went all the way around again. It's a big ring, you know? Turns out it was a lot bigger than I thought it was."

There were a lot of trucks on 87, all of them going faster than Lester. No cops.

Bronwen said, "You got any brothers or sisters?"

"No," Andy said.

"Where you from?"

"Nevada," Andy said.

"Never been there," Bronwen said. "You go back much?"

"Once in a while," Andy said. "My parents are retired professors. Classics and Romance Languages. So now they spend a lot of time going on these cruises, the educational kind. They give lectures and seminars in exchange for getting a cabin and some cash. They're cruising down the Rhine right now." No, that had been December. He had no idea where they were now. Greece? Sardinia?

"That sounds awesome," Bronwen said.

"They've had norovirus twice," Andy said.

"Still," Bronwen said, "I'd like to go on a cruise. And once you've had norovirus, you're immune to it for like a year."

"That's what they told me," Andy said. "They were actually kind of psyched after they had norovirus the first time."

"This friend," Bronwen said, "the one in Vermont, what's her name?"

"Hannah," Andy said.

"Did you ever date?"

"No," Andy said.

"Yes," Lester said.

"It wasn't really dating," Andy said. "We just kind of had a thing for a while."

"And then Hannah went off to teach at some cow college," Lester said. "And Andy hasn't gotten laid since."

"I'm just really, really trying to concentrate on my dissertation," Andy said. Sometimes, avoiding Lester, he forgot exactly why he ought to avoid Lester. It wasn't just Bronwen, and sex. It had a lot more to do with just Lester.

"Yeah," Bronwen said. "That makes so much sense. Sometimes you have to keep your head down and focus."

She really was very, very nice. Unlike Lester. "You have any brothers or sisters?"

"Nope," Bronwen said. "Just me. My parents are over in Fishtown."

"Fancy," Andy said. Fishtown was where all the nice coffee shops and fixed-up rowhouses were.

"Yeah," Bronwen said. "My mom's mom's house. But they're saying they're gonna put it on the market. The real estate tax is insane. But, you know, I think my mom is afraid if they sell the house they'll end up getting divorced, and then she'll have no husband and no house."

"I'm sorry," Andy said.

"No," Bronwen said. "I mean, my dad's kind of a dickhead?"

"I can vouch for that," Lester said.

"Shut up," Bronwen said. "I can say it but it doesn't mean you can."

"Whatever," Lester said. "You love me. It was love at first sight. *Coup de foudre.*"

"I like you a lot," Bronwen said.

"She doesn't believe in love," Lester said to Andy. "She's only with me because I'm ghost repellent."

"Believe it or not, he isn't my usual type," Bronwen said. "I'm actually more into girls."

"Go back a minute," Andy said. "To the thing about ghost repellent."

Lester said, "So we met at the Wawa, remember? There was only one six-pack of Yuengling in the cooler and I got it. And Bronwen came up while I was at the counter to ask the guy if there was more, and there was, but it wasn't cold. So I invited her over and we hooked up and she ended up spending the night, but she said that at some point she'd probably have to split because everywhere she goes eventually this presence, this ghost, shows up, and unless she's at work or something and can't leave, she'll just take off again. But the ghost never showed up. It never shows up when she's with me. So, you know, we started hanging out a lot."

"What do you mean a ghost shows up?" Andy said.

"It's just something that happens," Bronwen said. "Ever since I was a kid. Just after my fourteenth birthday. I don't know why it happens, or why it started. It doesn't bother anyone else. No one else sees it. I don't even see it! I don't even really know if it's a ghost or not. It's just, you know, this presence. I'll be somewhere and then it will be there too. It doesn't do anything. It's just there. My mom used to tell me that it was a good thing, like a guardian spirit. But it isn't. It's kind of awful. If I leave a room, or if I go somewhere else, it doesn't come with me right away, but eventually it's with me again. If I stay in one place long enough, like if I'm asleep long enough, then when I wake up it's there. So, yeah. I'm a terrible sleeper. But I went home with Lester and I fell asleep in his bed and then I woke up and it wasn't there."

"Ghost repellent," Lester said smugly. There was a car in front of them that wasn't even doing sixty-five. Lester just stayed there behind it.

"I thought maybe it was gone for good," Bronwen said. "But I went home and took a shower and it showed right up. So, not gone. But anytime I'm with Lester it stays away. So, yay."

"Incredible," Andy said.

Bronwen was facing forward again. "You probably don't even believe me," she said. "But, you know. There are more things than are dreamt of."

"I don't *not* believe you," Andy said, equivocating.

But this didn't appear to satisfy Bronwen. She said, "Well, whatever. I bet you've had weird shit happen that you can't explain. Weird shit happens to everyone."

"Except me," Lester said.

"But that's your weird thing," Bronwen said, patting him on the arm. "If nothing weird ever happens to you, then that's pretty weird."

Andy said, "Once a kid knocked on our door, and when I went to answer it, he didn't have a head."

"Right," Lester said. "Last Halloween. We gave him some Tootsie Rolls."

"Both of you are utter and complete assholes," Bronwen said. She put Ariana Grande on the stereo, tilted her head back, and closed her eyes. Apparently she found it easier to ignore assholes than a ghost.

They stopped at a McDonald's just off the highway around three p.m. The map function now said they'd get to the house around 4:15. Andy sat at a table outside and texted Hannah. She called him back immediately. "Cutting it close, asshole," she said.

"Sorry," Andy said. "But it isn't my car, so there isn't much I can do."

"Whatever, I owe you for agreeing to do this at all. It sucks, you know? Having to take off like this. This is such a sweet job. Please don't fuck it up for me, okay?"

"How's your sister?" Andy said.

"She's okay, sort of? Doesn't want to take the good painkillers, because she has a history with that stuff. So that's going to be fun for everyone. Oh, hey. She's calling. See you soon."

Bronwen came outside and sat down on top of the picnic table. She was dipping french fries into the remains of her chocolate milkshake.

Andy said, "I can't tell you how much I appreciate you guys driving me."

"Not a big deal," Bronwen said, tilting her head up and back toward the sun. She was a tawny golden brown all over, hair and skin. There were little golden hairs all over her forearms and legs. Andy could almost understand why a ghost followed her everywhere. Hannah was long and pale and freckled and sort of mean, even when she liked you. She was funny, though. She changed her hair color when the mood struck her. In her last Instagram post her hair was brown with two red pink streaks, like a Porterhouse steak.

"Oh," Bronwen said. "Oh, that was quick. Much quicker than usual."

She'd dropped her milkshake. Andy picked it up before much could spill, but when he tried to give it back to her, Bronwen ignored it. She was watching a space on the sidewalk a few feet away.

"What?" he said. "What is it?"

Bronwen said, "I'll go see if Lester's done." She jumped off the table and went back inside the McDonald's.

Did Andy feel anything? Some kind of presence? He went over

to stand, as far as he could gauge, in the place Bronwen had been staring at. There was nothing there, which probably meant that Bronwen had some kind of mental health issue, but also she'd just driven him most of the way to Vermont. "I don't actually think you're real," he said, "but if you are, maybe you could go away and stop bothering Bronwen. She's a nice person. She doesn't deserve to be haunted."

Saying this seemed the least he could do. When he went inside to check on the situation, Bronwen was in a booth, slouched down with her face in her arms and Lester rubbing her back. Andy went and got her ice water.

Eventually, she sat up and took a sip. "Sorry," she said.

"No worries," Andy said. "But we'd better hit the road. I need to get there before Hannah's ride shows up. I don't want to cut it too close."

"Dude," Lester said. "Give her a minute." He actually seemed to be irritated with Andy and did that mean he believed Bronwen? That there was a ghost?

"Yeah," Andy said. "Of course." He went and used the bathroom and when he came out again, Lester and Bronwen weren't in the booth. They weren't at the car, and eventually he realized they had to be in the family restroom because there was no one else in the McDonald's and the lock was engaged. It was another good twenty minutes before they emerged, and apparently the ghost had gotten tired of waiting and left, because Bronwen seemed much more cheerful getting back in the car. Lester too, for that matter.

Shortly after that, Andy's phone lost all reception, which was probably for the best, because although Bronwen drove at least ten miles above the speed limit the rest of the way, they didn't reach the address Hannah had given him until well after five.

The place Hannah had been housesitting was off a two-lane highway, the kind they'd been following for the past two hours. There were two stone pedestals on either side of the dirt drive, but nothing on top of them. There were a lot of trees. Andy didn't really know a lot about trees. He wouldn't have minded if there were fewer. It was the first turnoff in maybe half a dozen miles, which was what Hannah's directions had said. If you kept going, you got to the store where you could get sandwiches and gasoline. That would have meant they'd gone too far. But Hannah's directions had been clear, and they hadn't gotten lost once. Nevertheless, they were late and Hannah was long gone.

You couldn't see anything from the turnoff because of all of the trees. It was like going into a tunnel, the way the trees made a curving roof and walls over the narrow lane of white gravel, but then suddenly there was the house in a little clearing, very picturesque, three wide gray flagstone steps leading up to a green door between two white pillars, a pointed gable above. The house itself was a sunny yellow color, two-story with many windows. Behind the house, more trees.

"Nice place," Bronwen said. "Cheerful."

Andy's phone still had no reception. It seemed to him that there were several possible scenarios about to play out. In one, Hannah's Uber had been delayed. The green door opened and Hannah came out. In another, this all turned out to be a substandard prank, and the door would open and a stranger would be standing there. But what happened is that he got out of the car and went up the steps and saw that there was a note on the door. It said:

CAN'T WAIT ANY LONGER. WILL CALL FROM AIRPORT.
WROTE UP INSTRUCTIONS FOR YOU AND LEFT THEM ON
COUNTER. FOLLOW ALL OF THEM.

Andy tried the door. It was unlocked. Bronwen and Lester got out of the car and began to unload the trunk.

"We must have missed her by, what? A half hour?"

Andy said, "I guess she waited around a little while."

"It always takes longer than you think it will," Bronwen said. This seemed accurate to Andy, but not representative of the whole picture.

Lester said, "Come on. Let's get Andy's stuff in and hit the road. There's a sugar shack near the campground we booked that does a maple IPA, and today's Tuesday so it closes at six thirty."

"Or you could stay here," Andy said. "Why camp when you can sleep in a bed?"

"Oh, Andy," Bronwen said. "That's so nice of you. But the whole point of this is camping. You can sleep in a bed anytime, you know?"

"Sure," Andy said. "I guess. You want a quick tour before you go? Or to use the bathroom?"

"Here," Lester said. He passed Andy's backpack over and then went back to the car to get the gym bag and the rest. Something about his body language suggested that perhaps Lester was as weary of sharing an apartment with Andy as Andy was of sharing one with him.

Bronwen and Andy remained on the porch. You could see, through the door, an open-plan living room with furniture arranged around a central fireplace and chimney of stacked gray stone. Even though it was summer, there was a stack of firewood piled up beside the fireplace. Everything looked comfortable and a little shabby. There was no reason not to go inside.

"At least come get a glass of water," Andy said.

"No," Bronwen said. She sounded very certain. "I'm good."

"What?" Andy said. "Are you getting a bad vibe or something? Is it haunted?" He was joking. He was kind of not joking.

"No," Bronwen said. "No vibe at all. Promise. It's just I don't think I want to go inside, if that's okay. That's all."

"Oh," Andy said. He mostly believed her, he thought. "Okay, good." On the whole, however, he had liked Bronwen better before he knew she was an authority on the supernatural. He decided he would keep the gummies for himself.

"That's everything!" Lester said. "Have fun, buddy. Get lots of work done. See you in a couple of weeks."

"Will do," Andy said. "Enjoy sleeping on the ground. Bye."

They got back in Bronwen's car, Lester driving again, and turned around, disappearing back into the trees. You could see how the lower branches were practically scraping the top of the car. It was cooler here than it had been in Philly, which wasn't exactly a surprise. The coolness must collect in the trees, little pockets under each leaf. There was no breeze, but the leaves were not still. They flexed and turned, green to silver to black in a shivering cascade as if Lester were catching a glimpse of the scaled flank of some living, crouching thing, too enormous to be seen in its entirety.

Andy picked up the carrier bags and went inside the house. It was a very nice house, very welcoming. He was lucky Hannah had thought of him. He went in search of the instructions she'd left.

Your phone won't get reception here, she'd written, *unless you're online. Then it should be okay downstairs. Upstairs not so great. You'll see the network. Skinder's Veil. No password. Get on and send me a text, please, so I know you've arrived. If you don't, I'm going to have to turn around and come back.*

Sleep in whatever bedroom you want. The one at the back of the upstairs on the left has the most comfortable bed. Also the biggest. The bathroom upstairs is a little finicky. Don't flush if you're about to take a shower.

Don't forget groceries come on Fridays. Driver comes around ten a.m. and leaves everything on the porch. The delivery list and all the info is on the fridge if you need to add anything.

If there's a storm the power will probably go out, but there's a generator. You have to fill it every twelve hours when it's running. It's in the little shed out behind the kitchen. Internet is mostly good if slow.

Help yourself to whatever you find in the cabinets. Laundry is upstairs next to the bathroom.

This house belongs to Skinder. I don't know if that's his first name or his last name. He's eccentric but this is a sweet gig so whatever. He only has two rules for the housesitter, but please take them very seriously. Like, Moses coming down with the stone tablets level serious. All of this was going to be much simpler to explain in person, but you've already fucked that up, so let me hammer this home. TWO RULES. DON'T BREAK THEM.

RULE ONE! IMPORTANT! If any friends of Skinder's show up, let them in no matter what time it is. No matter what or who they are. Don't worry about taking care of them. Just let them in and do whatever and leave when they're ready. Some of them may be weird, but they're harmless. Some of them are actually pretty cool. Hang out if you want to and they want to. Or don't. It's totally up to you! You've got your dissertation to finish, right? Anyway, it's entirely possible nobody will show up. Some summers a bunch of Skinder's friends show up and some summers I don't see anyone at all. No one so far this year.

RULE TWO! THIS ONE IS EVEN MORE IMPORTANT!!! Skinder may show up. If he does, DO NOT LET HIM IN. This is HIS OWN RULE. Why? I have no idea, but for the duration of the time during which he pays me to stay here, Skinder may not enter his own house. No matter what he says, he is not allowed to come in. I know how bizarre this sounds. But, fingers crossed, this will be a non-issue and you won't see Skinder at all. If you do, then all you have to do is not let him in. It's that simple.

ANDY: This is my favorite place in the world and the easiest job in the world and you had better not fuck it up for me. If you're thinking of fucking it up, then also start thinking about how I'm going to murder you one inch at a time.

Love, Hannah.

P.S. If you look outside at night and there's mist coming up from the ground all over, don't freak out! There are a lot of natural springs around this area, a lot of water underground on the property. The mist is a natural phenomenon. It's called Skinder's Veil which is also the name of the house, which has belonged to the Skinder family for a long, long time. Also, the water here comes from a well. It's spring fed so it tastes funny but apparently it's good for you. It's supposed to, and I quote, "open your inner eye." So, basically, free drugs! There's plenty of bottled water in case you don't like the taste but I always just drink the water from the tap.

P.P.S. Seriously, if Skinder shows up, do not let him in the house no matter what he says.

Andy put the note in his pocket. "Much to think about," he said out loud. This was a thing that one of their TAs had liked to say at the end of every class, back in undergrad. There'd been a certain intonation, and it had cracked Hannah and Andy up all semester. They'd said it to each other all the time. It had been the working title of Hannah's dissertation. Andy couldn't even remember the guy's name.

He found the network on his phone, waited until he had a few bars back. And here were Hannah's texts, increasingly frantic, then terse. Three voicemails. He went back to his bags at the front door and dug through the backpack until he'd found the pouch of gummies. Ate one and then texted Hannah back. *Here! Just missed you, I'm guessing. So so sorry. Call me when you can. I have some questions.*

He investigated his new living situation while he waited for Hannah to call. The kitchen and the living room he'd seen. There was a farmhouse table off to one side of the open-plan space, set in front of a big window overlooking a small area of flagstones, furred with moss. There was an Adirondack chair in case you wanted to sit outside, which Andy was not sure he did. Everything was very green: the mossy flagstones, the chair, the slumped, ferny ground, and trees, trees, trees crowding in close around it all. It had taken Andy some time to get used to the East Coast, the way there were trees growing everywhere, but this was another order of magnitude. Here there was nothing but trees and this house and whatever lived in and among trees.

There was the start of a path, too, heading off into those trees. Maybe it went somewhere interesting. More likely it was just going to be more trees.

There was a flat-screen TV, though, on the wall opposite the fireplace. And there had been a satellite dish on the roof. That seemed promising. They didn't have a TV back in the apartment in Philly. There was a bookshelf with a blue ceramic bowl of small pinecones, a perfectly ordinary and unremarkable piece of granite, and some paperback books, mostly Stephen King and Michael Connelly. No family pictures, nothing sentimental or which might indicate the kind of person who lived here.

Andy set up his printer and his research material on the table. Then he took his small assortment of clothes and toiletries upstairs. There were four bedrooms. The two at the front of the house were smaller, the beds and curtains made up in cheerful floral fabrics, one red and white, the other green and blue. In the green and blue bedroom there was an amateurish painting of some sort of creature standing on two legs beside a river. So, a bear, perhaps? Were there other animals that stood on two legs? But then again, bears didn't have long and luxuriant tails, did they. In the red and white bedroom, instead of a painting there was a framed cross-stitch that said: "WEST EAST HOME IS THE BEAST." He would have to google that.

Above the bed in each room were two dainty bells, mounted just below the crown molding. A wire attached to the canon disappeared into a small hole drilled into the wall. They were called servants' bells, weren't they?

"Much to think about!" Andy said, and went to see the other two bedrooms. These were larger than the front bedrooms and the ceiling sloped down over the headboards of the beds. Here, too, were the bells, but no paintings, no vaguely Satanic cross-stitches. He decided to claim the left-hand bedroom, the one Hannah had suggested. The bed had been stripped; he found the sheets in the dryer.

Andy made himself a grilled cheese for dinner and had what turned out to be pasta salad out of a Tupperware container. There was a half bottle of white wine in the refrigerator. He finished that and was sampling the tap water, which was a little musty but perhaps would get him high, when Hannah finally called.

"You're there," she said.

"Eating your pasta salad," he said. "Not sure about the raisins."

"It's my mom's recipe," Hannah said. "You grow up eating something, it's comfort food."

"Mine is grilled cheese," Andy said. "But it has to be Swiss cheese."

They were both silent for a minute. Finally, Andy said, "Sorry I didn't get here in time to see you."

"Never mind," Hannah said. "At least you're there. I started thinking you weren't going to show at all. What do you think?"

"I think I should have brought some sweaters," Andy said. "So what's with the rules? I'm supposed to let everyone in except for Skinder, who is the one who actually owns the house?"

"That's pretty much it exactly," Hannah said.

"So anyone can just show up and I let them in? But then, what if I accidentally let Skinder in? It's not like I've met him."

"Oh, wait, no," Hannah said. "Shit. This would have been so much easier if I'd been able to explain this in person. Look, Skinder's friends show up at the back door. The kitchen door. So, someone shows up and knocks at the kitchen door, let them in. The only person who will knock at the front door is Skinder. It's actually pretty easy. Don't let anyone in if they knock at the front door."

"Doesn't he have a key?" Andy said. "To his own house?"

"I know," Hannah said. "It's freaky. If it makes it easier, think of it like a game. Like Settlers of Catan. Or Red Rover! Or, whatever. There are rules and everyone has to follow them. If you think about it that way, then you just do what the rules say and you're fine."

"Okay, but what happens if I mess up and I let Skinder in?"

"I don't know," Hannah said. "I lose my summer job? Look, I signed a contract and everything. I'd have to give back what he paid me, which means you'd have to give me back the money I passed on to you. Just don't let him in, okay? If he even shows up, which he probably won't do. I've done this for a while and he only showed up three times, once the first summer, and then twice the summer before last. He knocks on the front door and you don't let him in. I didn't let him in. He asked me to let him in and I didn't and so he went away again. It was a little weird, especially when he came back the second time, but it was fine. You'll be fine. Just don't let him in."

"Okay," Andy said. "So what does he look like?"

"Skinder?" Hannah said. "Oh, boy. You'll know it's him. I'm not going to try to explain it because it will sound crazy, but you'll know. You'll just know. For one thing, he always has a dog with him. It's this little black dog. So if you see the dog, that's him."

"What if he doesn't bring the dog? Or what if the dog's dead? You didn't see him last year. The dog could have died."

"It really doesn't matter," Hannah said. "You don't have to know what he looks like to know it's him. He only comes to the front door. Just don't let anyone through the front door and you'll be fine."

"Don't let anyone in the front door," Andy said. He took another swallow of musty water. Perhaps he would acquire a taste for it. "But if anyone knocks on the back door, then I have to let them in, right?"

"Right," Hannah said.

"I don't really understand any of this," Andy said. "I'm kind of feeling like you've gotten me into something here. Like, I thought this was just a housesitting gig. You didn't mention all of this other stuff on the phone the other day."

"Yeah," Hannah said. "I was pretty sure that if I brought all this up then you'd pass on the golden opportunity I was holding out to you. And I really, really needed you to come up so I could get out to my sister."

"And this is in no way a hilarious prank," Andy said.

"I'm paying you nine hundred dollars to stay in a secluded house in the country where you can finally get some real work done on your dissertation," Hannah said. "Does that seem like a prank?"

"Much to think about," Andy said.

"Much to think about, asshole," Hannah said. "I'll call you in a day or two, okay? I have to go catch my flight."

"Safe travels," Andy said. But she had already hung up.

There was a six-pack of some fancy IPA at the back of the fridge, and a jar of Red Vines on the counter beside the sink. He took a couple of those and one of the beers through to the living room and sat at the farm table. He turned on his laptop and put aside thoughts of Hannah and rules and the person who owned this house. He set aside, too, thoughts of Bronwen and the thing she said followed her. Regardless of whatever she felt or thought, it wasn't real. Nothing was following anyone. He had felt nothing. And if there had been something, well then, it wasn't here, was it? It was her ghost, not his, and so it would be wherever Bronwen was, waiting for the moment when Lester wasn't there.

Andy worked for an hour, comparing penalized splines in various studies, until at last the edible kicked in, or perhaps it was the
tap water smoothing down his splines and his thoughts and all
the strangeness of the day. He watched TV and at nine he went
upstairs to bed. He slept soundly through the night and only woke
up because he had forgotten to close the blinds and sunlight was
coming through the windows, turning all of the room to auspi-
cious gold.

For the next two days he did not return to his dissertation, though
he told himself that he would tackle it after breakfast. After lunch.
Before dinner. Instead of doing this, he took naps, got stoned,
played Minecraft, and did his sets and reps. After dinner he
watched old science-fiction movies. He left the television on when
he went to bed. It wasn't that he was lonely. It was just that he was
out of the habit of *being* alone. On the third night, when he looked
out of his bedroom window, threads of mist were rising from the
ground below the trees. As he watched, these threads wove themselves into pallid columns, and then a languorous, uniform cloud,
blotting out the patio. The Adirondack chair shrank away until
only its back and arms remained, floating in whiteness. Andy went
to the red and white bedroom at the front of the house and saw
that the driveway had already vanished. If Hannah hadn't told him
this would happen, he supposed he would have found the phenomenon eerie. But it was perfectly natural. Creepy but natural.
Natural and also quite beautiful. He tried without success to get a
good picture with his phone. No doubt it would be possible to get
better results if he left the house to take a picture at ground level,
but he dismissed this idea when it came to him. He preferred not
to go stand outside knee deep in something called Skinder's Veil,
natural phenomenon or not.

Instead he went to bed and had two hours of sleep before he
woke. One of the bells above his head was ringing, ringing, ringing.

No one was at the front door. The TV was on: he turned it off. The
bell was still ringing and so he went to the kitchen and turned on
the lights. A woman stood at the back door, peering in. She must
have had her finger on the bell and Andy, against his better judgment, did as Hannah had said he must and unlocked the door to
let her in.

"Oh, good," she said, stepping into the kitchen. "Did I wake you up? I'm so sorry."

"No," Andy said. "It's fine. I'm Andy. I'm housesitting here. I mean, my friend Hannah was housesitting, but she had a family emergency and so now I'm filling in."

"I'm Rose White," his visitor said. "Very nice to meet you, Andy." She opened the refrigerator and took out two beers. She handed one to him and then headed into the living room, sitting down on one of the chintz sofas and dropping her leather carry-all on the floor, plopping her muddy boots upon the coffee table.

She couldn't have been much older than Andy. Her hair, longish and dirty blond, looked as if it hadn't seen a hairbrush in several days. Perhaps she had been backpacking. In any case, she was still extremely attractive.

"Have a drink with me," she said, smiling. One of her front teeth was just a little crooked. "Then I'll let you go back to bed."

Andy opened the beer. Sat down in an armchair that faced the fireplace. Hannah had said he didn't have to hang out, but on the other hand, he didn't want to be rude. He said, "Mist's cleared up."

"The veil? It usually does," Rose White said. "Don't recommend going out in it. You can get lost quite quickly. I was quite surprised to find myself right on Skinder's doorstep. I thought I'd been going in another direction entirely."

"You live nearby?" Andy said. It didn't seem polite to ask why she was out so late at night. "Hannah comes and housesits every summer. Maybe you've met her?"

"Phew," Rose White said. "The big questions! Haven't been through in years, actually. Let's see. The last housesitter I met was an Alma. Or Alba. But I see nothing's much changed. Skinder's not much for change."

"I don't really know much about Skinder," Andy said. "Anything, really."

"A complicated fellow," Rose White said. "You know the rules, I suppose."

"I think so?" Andy said. "If he comes to the house, I'm supposed to not let him in. For some reason. I don't really know what he looks like, but he'll come to the front door. That's how I'll know that it's him. But if anyone comes to the back door, then I let them in."

"Good enough to get by," Rose White said. She began to unlace her boots. "Aren't you going to drink your beer?"

Andy set it down. "I might just go back to bed, unless you need me for something. Going to try to get up early and get some work done. I'm working on my dissertation while I'm here, actually."

"A scholar!" Rose White said. "I'll be quiet as a mouse. Leave your beer. I'll drink it for you."

But she was not, in fact, as quiet as a mouse. Andy lay in his bed, listening as she rattled and banged around the kitchen, boiling water in the kettle and pulling out various pans. The smell of frying bacon seeped under his closed door in a delicious cloud. Andy wished he had his noise-canceling headphones. But they were on the table beside his laptop, and he did not want to go downstairs and get them.

He thought, *Tomorrow I really will get some work done, visitor or no visitor. Otherwise all the time will just melt away and in the end I'll have accomplished nothing.*

Without meaning to, he found himself listening for the sound of Rose White coming up the stairs. It must have been after three when, at last, she did. She went into the bathroom beside his bedroom and took a long shower. He wondered which room she would choose, but in the end it was his door she opened. She didn't turn on the lights, but instead got into the bed with him.

He turned on his side and there was enough moonlight in the room that he could see Rose White looking back at him. She had not bothered to put clothes back on post-shower. "Do you have a girlfriend?" she said.

"Not at the moment," Andy said.

"Do you like to fuck women?"

"Yes," Andy said.

"Then here's my last question," she said. "Would you like to fuck me? No strings. Just for fun."

"Yes," Andy said. "Absolutely, yes. But I don't have a condom."

"Not a concern for me," she said. "You?"

Yes, a little. That was the problem with knowing a fair bit about how statistics worked. "No," Andy said. "Not at all."

But afterward, he wasn't quite sure what the etiquette was. Should he try to get to know her a little better? He didn't even know how long she was going to be staying at the house. It would have been easier if he'd been able to fall asleep, but that seemed to be out of the question.

He decided he would pretend to be asleep.

"Not tired?" Rose White said.

"Sorry," Andy said. "A lot to think about. Think I'll go downstairs and watch TV for a while."

"Stay here," Rose White said. "I'll tell you a story."

"A story," Andy said. "You mean like when a kid can't fall asleep. So one of their parents tells them a story? A story like that?" He wasn't a kid. On the other hand, there was a woman in his bed he'd just met, and they'd had sex and now she was offering to tell him a story. Why not say yes? If nothing else, it would be something, later on, that would be an interesting story of his own. "Sure. Tell me a story."

Rose White drew the covers up to her neck. She was lying on her back, and this gave the impression she was telling the story to someone floating on the ceiling. It felt strangely formal, as if Andy were back in a lecture hall, listening to one of his professors. She said, "Once, a very long time ago, there was a woman who wrote books for a living. She made enough from this to keep not only herself in modest comfort but also her sister, who lived with her and was her secretary. She wrote her novels longhand and it was the sister who read the manuscript first, before giving it back to the writer to edit. This sister, who was a romantic with very little outlet for expression, had a peculiar way of marking the parts she liked best. She would prick her finger with a needle and mark the place with her own blood to show how good she thought it was. A little blotch over a well-turned phrase, a little smudge. She would return the manuscript, the writer would do her revisions, sparing the lines and scenes that her sister had loved, and then the sister would type everything up properly and send it along to the writer's agent.

"The writer's books were popular with a certain audience, but never garnered much critical favor. The writer shrugged this off. She told her sister the merit of the books was that they were easy to produce at a rate which kept a roof over their heads, and they served a second purpose, which was to entertain those whose lives were hard enough. But, the writer said, she had in her a book of such beauty and power that anyone who read it would be changed by it forever, and one day she would write it. When her sister asked why she did not write it now, she said that such a book would take more time and thought and effort than she could currently spare.

"As time went on, though, the writer's books became less pop-ular. The checks they brought in were smaller, and their lives be-came little by little less comfortable. The writer determined that she would at last turn her attention to this other book. She labored over it for a year and into the next winter, and slept little and ate less and grew unwell. At night while she worked her sister would hear her groaning and coughing, and then one morning, very early, the writer woke her sister and said, 'I have finished it at last. Now I must rest.'

"The sister put on a robe and lit a fire and sat down to read the manuscript at once, her needle in her pocket. But upon reading the very first sentence, she drew out her needle and pricked her finger to mark it. And the second sentence, too, she marked with her blood. And it went on like that as she read, until at last she had to go down to the kitchen to fetch a peeling knife. First she cut her palm and then she cut her arm and each line and every page was marked with the sister's blood as she read, such was the power and beauty of the narrative and the characters and the writer's language.

"Many days later, friends of the writer and her sister grew con-cerned because no one had heard from them in some time. Upon forcing their way into the house they found the sister exsanguina-ted in her chair, the manuscript in her lap all glued together with her blood. The body of the writer, too, was discovered in her bed. She'd died of an ague she'd caught from overwork and too little rest. As for the book she'd written, it was quite impossible to read even a single word."

"That was really interesting," Andy said, just as awake as he had been at the start, possibly more so. In a minute he would say so, get dressed, and go downstairs. "Thank you."

"You're welcome," Rose White said. "Now go to sleep."

He woke at the table downstairs, his laptop beside his head.

Rose White was on the couch. "I built a fire," she said. "Thought you might catch cold. Vermont weather is unpredictable, summer or not."

She'd done this, Andy realized, because he was entirely naked. His shoulders ached and his ass was unhygienically stuck to the rattan seat of the chair. "What time is it?" he asked her. "How long have I been here?"

"You were gone when I woke up," Rose White said. "Discovered you here when I came down this morning. It's past noon now."

"I must've been sleepwalking," Andy said. His laptop was open, and when he woke the screen, a prompt appeared. *Save changes?*

"Get dressed," Rose White said. "I'll make you a sandwich. Then you can get back to it."

He dressed and ate, reading over what he'd written the night before. It was rough, but it was also a reasonably solid foundation for revision. Moreover, there were four thousand words that had not been there the night before. This seemed like enough work for one day, and so, at Rose White's suggestion, they spent the day in bed and the evening drinking bourbon they procured from a locked liquor cabinet. Rose White knew where to find the key.

The next few days and nights were pleasant ones. Andy took leisurely naps in the afternoon. He shared his stash with Rose White. They took turns cooking, and let the dishes pile up. Rose White had very little interest in his life, and no interest at all in explaining anything about herself. If, after sex, she enjoyed telling him her strange little stories, at least they were mostly very short. Some of them hardly seemed to be stories at all. One went like this: "There once was a man possessed of a great estate who did not wish to marry. At last, beset by his financial advisors, he agreed to be married to the first suitable individual he encountered upon setting into town, and when he came home with his fiancée, his friends and advisors were dismayed to find that he had become engaged to a tortoise. Nevertheless, the man found a priest willing, for a goodly sum of money, to perform the ceremony. They lived together for several years and then the man died. At last a distant relative was found to inherit the estate, and on his first night in his fine new home, he had the tortoise killed and served up as a soup in its own shell. But this is not, by any means, the worst story about marriage that I know."

Another story began, "Once there was a blood sausage and a liver sausage and the blood sausage invited the liver sausage over for dinner." None of Rose White's stories were cheerful. In all of them, someone came to a bad end, but there was nothing to be learned from them. Nevertheless, each time she finished and said to Andy, "Go to sleep," he promptly fell asleep. And, too, each morning he woke up to find that he had, in some dream state, produced more of his dissertation, though after the second time this happened he moved his laptop and his notebooks up to the vanity in the red and white bedroom.

The groceries were left on the porch on the appointed day, and the dissertation progressed, and in the afternoons when it grew warm Rose White sunbathed topless on the patio while Andy did reps. Hannah called to check in, and to report her nieces would eat nothing but sugar cereal and mozzarella sticks, while her sister was camped out on a blow-up mattress in the dining room because she could not get up and down the stairs and needed Hannah's help getting onto the toilet and off again.

"Everything's great here," Andy said.

"Any visitors?" Hannah asked.

"Yeah, some lady named Rose White. I don't know how long she's staying."

"Never met her," Hannah said. "So, what's she like?"

"She's okay," Andy said. He didn't really feel like getting into the details. "I've been really focused on the dissertation. We haven't really hung out or anything. But she's done some of the cooking."

"So, pretty normal, then," Hannah said. "Good. Sometimes the ones who show up are kind of strange."

"How so?" Andy said.

"Oh, you know," Hannah said. "Some of them can be a little strange. I'm gonna go make lunch now for the two small assholes. Call if you need anything. And I'll check in again later. As soon as I know when I can head back, I'll let you know."

"No rush," Andy said, looking out the window to where Rose White lay, splendid and rosy upon a beach towel. This was wonderful, yes, but what if she were developing feelings for him? Did he feel something for her? Yes, possibly. This was very inconvenient. They didn't really know each other at all, and she was, as Hannah had said, kind of strange.

The whole thing made him uncomfortable. Much to think about. He had a gummy and pretended to be working when Rose White came back in. But she'd only come into the house to use the bathroom and put her clothes back on. Then she was off for a hike, not even bothering to ask if he wanted to come along. She came back at dinnertime with a pocketful of mushrooms. "*Psilocybe cubensis*," she said. "I'll make us tea. The water here has some excellent properties of its own, but there's no such thing as too much fun."

"Isn't that dangerous?" Andy said. "I mean, what if you haven't identified the mushroom correctly?"

Rose White gave him a withering look. "Go teach your grandmother to suck eggs," she said. "Are you a man or a chicken, Andy?"

It was, again, the study of statistics that presented the problem. Nevertheless, Andy had some of the tea and in return shared his vape pen. It was the first time he'd ever tried mushrooms, and only pieces of the night that followed were accessible to him later on.

Rose White, sitting astride him, her hands on his biceps, the feeling that her fingers were sinking into his flesh as if either he or she are made of mist.

Rose White saying, "I think my sister must be quite near now." Andy tries to say that he didn't know she had a sister. He doesn't really know anything about her. "I'm Rose White but she is Rose Red." When he looks at her, her hair is full of blood. Rose Red!

The realization that Skinder's house has no walls, no roof, no foundation. The walls are trees, there is no ceiling, only sky. "It's all water underneath," he is explaining. Rose White: "Only the doors are real."

Later, he is seated in front of the vanity in the red and white bedroom. The bell on the wall is ringing. When he leaves one bedroom, Rose White is coming out of another. Andy has to sit down on the staircase and bump down, one step at a time. Rose White helps him stand up at the bottom. His head is floating several feet above his body and he has to walk slowly to make sure he doesn't leave it behind.

Two deer are arranged like statuary upon the flagstone patio. Are they real? Did these deer ring the doorbell? Do they want to come in? He finds this hysterically funny but when he opens the door, the deer approach solemnly on their attenuated, decorative legs. One and then the other comes into the kitchen, stretching their velvet necks out and down to fit through the door. Inside the velvet-lined jewel boxes of their nostrils the warmth of their breath is gold. It dazzles. Andy's head floats up higher, bumping against the ceiling. He stretches out his hand, strokes the flank of an actual fucking deer. A doorbell-ringing deer. A moth has flown into the kitchen, he's left the door open. It blunders through the air, brushing against his cheek, his ear. He opens his mouth to tell Rose White to close the door and the moth flies right in.

*

Rose White says, "Once upon a time there was a real estate agent who made arrangements to show a property. When she arrived at the property, she realized at once that her new client was none other than Death. Suspecting that he was there for her, she pretended she was not the agent at all, but rather another prospective buyer. Claiming she had been told to meet the listing agent around the back, she lured Death around the side of the house and told him to look through the French windows to see if anyone was there to let them in. When he did this, she picked up an ornamental planter and bashed in his head. Then she dragged the body of Death into the full bathroom and cut it into twelve pieces in the bathtub. These she wrapped in Hefty bags and, after cleaning the bathtub thoroughly, she parked her Lexus in the garage and placed these bags in the trunk. Over the next week, she buried each piece deep on the grounds of a different listing, and each of those houses sold quite quickly. Decades went by and the real estate agent began to regret what she had done. She was now in her nineties and weary of life, but Death did not come for her. And so she visited each of the properties where she had disposed of his corpse and dug him up, but perhaps her memory was faulty: she could not find the last two pieces. She is still, in fact, searching for Death's left forearm and his head. The rest of him, badly decomposed, is in a deep freezer in her garage. Some days she wonders if, in fact, it was really Death at all. And what if it really had been Death? What if he had only come to see a house? Isn't it likely that even Death himself must have a house in which to keep himself?"

Andy woke in his own bed with a dry mouth but no other discernable effects from the night before. In the red and white bedroom, his laptop was open. When he looked to see what he'd written, it was only this: *How to work? Deer in house. Not sanitary!!! WTF.* He deleted these.

When he went downstairs, though, there were no deer and no Rose White, either. She'd left a note on the kitchen table. "Headed out. Finished off bacon but did a big clean (badly needed!) so think we're even. Thanks for the hospitality. Left you the rest of the mushrooms. Use sensibly! Take care if I don't see you again. Fondly, Rose White."

"Fondly," Andy said. He wasn't really even sure what that meant.

It was one of those signoffs like "kind regards" or "best wishes." A kiss-off, basically. Well. "Summer loving, had me a blast." Lester's acapella group liked to sing that one. He didn't even have her phone number.

While he was microwaving a bowl of oatmeal, he inspected the tile floor of the kitchen. He actually got down on his hands and knees. What was he looking for? Rose White? Some deer tracks? The rest of his dissertation?

He gave himself the rest of the day off. Texted Hannah: *There are a lot of deer around here, right? Do they ever come up to the house?*

She texted right back: *Lots of deer, yes. Bears too, sometimes.*

Well. He didn't feel like explaining that he'd had shrooms with a houseguest he'd also been having sex with, and that possibly he had let some deer into the house. Or else hallucinated this.

Without Rose White in his bed, he found he did not fall asleep easily. Neither did he work, in his sleep, on his dissertation. He made some progress during the days, but it was much like it had been in the apartment in Philadelphia, except here he had no excuse.

About a week after Rose White had gone, the servants' bell rang again. It wasn't midnight yet, and he was in bed, skipping to the end of a Harlan Coben novel because the middle was very long and all he really wanted was to see how it all came out.

He put a pair of pants on and went downstairs. At the back door was a wild turkey. After deliberating, Andy did as he was supposed to do and let it in. It did not seem at all wary of him, and why should it have been? It was an invited guest. Andy went into the living room and sat on the couch. The turkey investigated all the corners of the room, making little grunting noises, and then defecated neatly on the hearth of the fireplace. Its cheeks were violet, and its neck was bright red. It flew up on top of the cord of stacked wood and puffed out all the formidable armature of its feathers. Andy's phone was on the table: he took a picture. The turkey did not object. It seemed, in fact, to already be sleeping.

Andy, too, went up to bed. In the morning, the turkey was waiting by the back door and he let it out again. He cleaned up the shit on the hearth and two other places. This was when, no doubt, he should have called Hannah. But she was probably waiting for him to do exactly that, and really, she should have been up-front with him. And also, he realized, he was having a good time. It was like being inside an enchantment. Why would he want to break the spell? The next night the bell rang again, though to Andy's disappointment it was neither a beautiful girl nor a creature at the back door. A grayish man of about sixty in Birkenstocks, a Rolling Stones T-shirt, and khaki shorts nodded but did not speak when Andy opened the door. He did not bother to introduce himself. He didn't speak at all. Instead, he went straight upstairs, took a long shower, using all the towels in the bathroom, and then slept for two days in the blue and green bedroom. Andy kept his bedroom door locked while the gray man was in the house. It was a relief, frankly, when he was gone again. After that, it was an opossum, and the night after the opossum, the mist was on the ground again. Skinder's Veil. When the bell began to ring, Andy went down to let his guest in, but no one was at the kitchen door. He went to the front door, but to his relief, no one was there either. The bell continued to ring, and so Andy went to the kitchen door again. When he opened the door, the mist came swiftly seeping in, covering the tile floor and the feet of the kitchen table and the kitchen chairs. Andy closed the door and at once the bell began to ring again. He opened the door and left it open. The guest was, perhaps, Skinder's Veil itself, or perhaps it was something which preferred to remain hidden inside the Veil. Andy, thinking of Bronwen's ghost, went up to his bedroom and shut the door and locked it. He rolled up his pants and wedged them against the bottom of the door. He left his lights on and did not sleep at all that night, but in the morning he was the only one in the house and the day was very sunny and bright. The door was shut tight again.

The last human guest while Andy was in Skinder's house was Rose White's sister, Rose Red.

When Andy opened the kitchen door, it was Rose White who stood there. Except, perhaps it was not. This person had the same features—eyes, nose, mouth—only their arrangement was somehow unfamiliar. Sharper, as if this version of Rose White would never think of anyone fondly. Now her hair was exuberantly, unnaturally purple-red, and there was a metal stud in one nostril.

"Rose Red," she said. "May I come in?"

This was the sister, then. Only, as she spoke Andy saw a familiar crooked tooth. This must be Rose White, hair colored and newly styled. And would he even have noticed her nose was pierced previously? Not if she'd not had her stud in. Well. He would play along.

"Come in," he said. "I'm Andy. Filling in for the original house-sitter. Your sister was here about a week ago."

"My sister?" she said.

"Rose White," Andy said. It was like being in a play where you'd never seen the script. He had to give Rose White this: she wasn't boring.

"We don't even have the same last name," Rose Red said. She looked very prim as she said this. She was, it was true, a little taller than he remembered Rose White being, but then he saw her ankle boots had two-inch heels. Had she really come up the path wearing those? Mystery upon mystery.

He said, "My mistake. Sorry." After all, who was he to talk? He'd managed not even one complete paragraph in two days. Maybe he'd do better now that she was here again.

Rose Red (or Rose White) went rummaging through the kitchen cabinets. "Help yourself," he said. "I was just about to make dinner."

Rose Red was regarding the plate beside the sink where Rose White's mushrooms were drying out. "Yours?" she said.

Andy said, "Happy to share. You going to make tea?"

"What if I made some risotto?" she said.

And so Andy set the table and poured them both a glass of wine, while Rose Red made dinner. The risotto was quite tasty and, Andy saw, she had used all of the mushrooms. Once again, he tried to discover more about the owner of the house, but like Rose White, Rose Red was an expert at deflection. Had he hiked any of the paths, she wanted to know. What did he think of the area?

"I've been kind of busy," Andy said. "Trying to finish my dissertation. It's why I'm here, actually. I needed to be able to focus."

"And when you're finished?" Rose Red said.

"Then I'll defend and go on the job market," Andy said. "And hopefully get a teaching job somewhere. Tenure track, ideally."

"That's what you'll do," Rose Red said. "But what do you want?"

"To do a good job," Andy said. "And then, I suppose, to be good at teaching."

Rose Red appeared satisfied by this. "Have you been on the trails at all? Gone hiking? So much to explore up here."

"Well," Andy said. "Like I said, I've been busy. And I don't actually like trees that much. But the Veil is pretty interesting. And people keep showing up. That's been interesting too. Rose White, the one I mentioned before, she had all these weird stories." He wasn't sure whether or not he should bring up all the sex.

After dinner they had more wine and Rose Red found a puzzle. Andy didn't much care for puzzles, but he sat down to help her with it. The longer they worked on it, the harder it grew to fit the pieces together. Eventually, he gave up and sat, watching how his fingers elongated, wriggling like narrow fish.

Upstairs, one of the bells began to ring again. "I'll get that," Andy said, excusing himself from the puzzle of the puzzle. In the kitchen he could perceive, once again, that it was not a kitchen at all. Really, it was all just part of the forest. All just trees. The puzzle, too, had been trees, chopped into little bits that needed arranging into a path. It was fine. It was fine, too, that a brown bear stood on its hind legs at the door, depressing the bell.

"Come in, good sir, come in," Andy said.

The bear dropped down onto all fours, squeezing its bulk into the kitchen. It brought with it a wild, loamy reek. Andy followed the bear back into the living space where Rose Whatever Her Name Was sat, finishing the puzzle. You could see the little fleas jumping in the bear's fur like sequins.

Rose Red jumped up and got the serving bowl with the remains of the pasta. She placed it before the bear, who stuck its whole snout in. Andy lay down on the floor and observed. When the bear was done, it leant back against the couch. Rose Red scratched its head, digging her fingers deep into its fur. They stayed like that for a while, Rose Red scratching, the bear drowsing, Andy content to lie on the floor and watch them and think about nothing.

"This one," Rose Red said to the bear. "He's going to be a great teacher."

"Well," Andy said. "First there's the dissertation. Defend. Then. Go on the job market. Be offered something somewhere. Get tenure. There's a whole path. You have to go along it. Through all the fucking trees. Like Little Red. Little Red Riding Hood. You know that story?"

"I don't care much for stories," Rose Red said.

"Oh, come on," Andy said. "Tell me one. Make it up. Tell me one about this place."

"Once upon a time there was a girl whose mother died when

she was very young." It wasn't Rose Red, though, who was speaking. It was the bear. Andy was fairly sure that it was the bear, which he felt should have troubled him more than it did. Perhaps, though, it was all ventriloquism. Or the mushrooms. He closed his eyes and the bear, or Rose Red, went on with the story.

"Once there was a girl whose mother died when she was very young. They lived on a street where almost every house had a swimming pool in the backyard. Not the girl's house, but the house on either side did. There was an incident, the girl never knew exactly what, and the mother drowned in the swimming pool that belonged to the house on the left. It was a mystery why she was in it. It was late at night, and no one knew when or why she had come over. Everyone else had been asleep: her body wasn't discovered until morning.

"When she wasn't much older, the girl's father remarried a woman with a daughter of her own. Don't worry, though, this isn't a story about a wicked stepmother. The girl and her stepmother and the stepsister all got along quite well, much better, in fact, than the girl got along with her own father. But all through her adolescence, there were stories about the pool next door; that it was haunted. The family who had lived there when the mother drowned moved away—the new family loved their house and their pool, but it was said that they never went swimming after midnight. Anyone who went swimming after midnight ran the risk of seeing the ghost down in the deep end, long hair floating around her face, her bathing suit losing its elasticity, her mouth open and full of water.

"The girl sometimes swam in the neighbor's pool, hoping she would see her mother's ghost, and also afraid that she would see her mother's ghost. All the girls in the neighborhood liked to swim in that pool best. They would dare each other to swim after midnight, and the rest would take turns sitting on the edge of the pool, facing away, in case the ghost was too shy to appear in front of them all. Sometimes one of the girls even saw the ghost—a thrill, a ghost of their very own!—but the girl whose mother had drowned never saw anything at all.

"Eventually, she grew up and moved away and made a life of her own. She had a husband and two children and thought that she was quite happy on the whole. The path of her life seemed straightforward and she moved along it. Her father died, and she grieved, but her stepmother was the one who had been her true parent. Her mother she hardly remembered at all. Life went on, and if the path grew a little rockier, her prospects a little less rosy, what of it? Life can't always be easy. Then, one day, her stepsister called to say that her stepmother, too, was dead.

"The daughter left her children with her husband and flew down for the funeral. Afterward, she and her stepsister would sort out their childhood home so it could be put on the market. The economy was in a downturn, and the daughter was not sure she would have her job for much longer, so half the proceeds from the sale of the house seemed fortuitous. But the real estate market was not good, and she saw that over half of the houses on her old street were for sale, including both houses on either side. Several others were vacant, or seemed so. It seemed to her possible the house would not sell at all, but she and her stepsister gamely went on for three days, making piles for Goodwill, piles for the trash, and piles that were things they might sell or keep for themselves.

"They reminisced about their childhood, and looked through old photos, and confided in each other their fears about the future. They wept for the loss of the two mothers and drank three bottles of wine.

"Now, the house on the left was vacant, and so was the house on the right. The swimming pool of the house on the left had been emptied, and the swimming pool on the right had not. Twice, in the middle of the day, they climbed over the chain-link fence and went swimming when they needed a break from sorting. The last night, tipsy and wide awake, the daughter left the childhood house where her stepsister lay sleeping in the bottom bunk of their childhood room, putting on one of the old-fashioned bathing suits from the pile they were taking to Goodwill. But instead of climbing over the fence to the right, she climbed the fence to the left.

"She found that the pool, which should have been empty, was instead full of clear blue water. The lights along the edge of the pool had been turned on and she could smell the chlorine from where she stood as if it had just been freshly cleaned. Little bugs, drawn to the lights, flew just above the water. Some of them had already tipped in and struggled. They would drown unless someone scooped them out.

"The daughter walked down the steps at the shallow end of the pool until she was waist deep. The water was pleasantly cool. The elastic of the suit had long ago crumbled, and so the pleasant and impossible water came creeping up the skin of her thighs.

"For a while she floated on her back, looking up at the stars and trying not to think about the future or why the pool was full of water. One was uncertain and the other was a gift. She floated until she grew, at last, cool and tired enough that she thought she might be able to sleep. Then she turned on her front, to wet her face, and down at the bottom of the pool she saw her mother at last. Here was the face she barely remembered. So young! The long, waving hair. It even seemed to her that her mother wore the twin of the suit she was wearing now. It seemed to the daughter that she could stay here in the pool, that she could stay here and be happy. Step painlessly off the path as her mother had done. It seemed the woman in the pool wanted for her to stay. They would never grow old. They would have each other.

"She could have stayed. She was very tired and there was still so much of her life ahead of her. There were so many things she needed to do. But in this story, she got out of the pool. She went back to the house of her childhood and she woke up her stepsister and told her what she had seen. The stepsister, at first, did not believe her. Wasn't the pool empty? Perhaps, intoxicated as she was, she'd gone to the other pool, the one that was full, and hallucinated seeing her mother.

The daughter argued with her. Her mother had been wearing the bathing suit that she'd drowned in, the very same one the daughter was wearing now. Couldn't the stepsister see how her bathing suit was wet? She was dripping on the tile floor.

"The daughter insisted she'd gone swimming in an empty pool. She had finally seen the ghost. Okay, her stepsister said, what if you did? But you didn't see your mother. There is no ghost. Your mother wasn't even wearing a bathing suit. She had a cocktail dress on. That's what my mother told me. And even if she had been wearing a bathing suit, it wouldn't be that one. No one would have kept the bathing suit your mother drowned in.

"No, the daughter said. I saw her. She was so young! She looked exactly like me!

"Come on, said the stepsister. She brought the daughter down to the room where they'd been sorting keepsakes. She spread out photographs until they found one of the mother. It was dated on

the back, the date of the mother's death. Is that who you saw? said
the stepsister. She doesn't look much like you at all.

"The daughter studied it. Tried to think what she had seen.
The closer she looked, the less sure she was that she had seen her
mother. Perhaps, then, all along she had been the one haunting
the swimming pool. Why should hauntings happen in linear time,
after all? Isn't time just another swimming pool?

"Now, Andy, it's time for you to go to sleep. But if you like,
though I don't care for stories, I'll tell you one more."

Rose Red says, "Once upon a time there was a house that Death
lived in. Even Death needs a house to keep himself in. It was indeed a very nice house and for much of the year Death was as
happy there as it is possible for Death to be. But Death cannot stay
comfortably at home all year long, and so once a year he found
someone to come and keep it for him while he went out into the
world and made sure everything was as it should be. While he was
gone from his house, it was the one place that Death might not
come in. He knows this, even though, at times he wants nothing
more than to come home and rest. And while Death was gone
from his house, all of those creatures who, by one means or another, had found a way so that Death might not take them yet,
might come and pass a night or two or longer in Death's house
and not worry he would find them there. In this way many may rest
and find a bit of peace, though the one who follows them unceas-
ingly will follow them once more when they put their foot onto the
path again. But this isn't your story. As a matter of fact, those who
come and stay owe a debt of gratitude to the one who keeps house
for Death while he is away. Even Death will one day pay his debt to
you as long as you keep your bond with him."

Andy sleeps. He sleeps long and wakes, again, before his laptop.
Has he written what he reads there, or has someone else? Well.
Bears can't type. It's morning and there is no one in the house but
Andy. There's a pile of bear shit beside the farmhouse table, cold
but still fragrant. The puzzle is back in its box.

And now the story is almost over. Andy continued to work in
a desultory and haphazard way on his dissertation. No one else
came to the kitchen door while he stayed in Skinder's house, but
one night the bell woke him again. He went first to the kitchen,

thinking he might see one Rose or the other, but truly this time there was no one there. It came to him that the bell he still heard ringing was not the same bell as before. He went, therefore, to the door at the front of the house, and there, on the porch, stood Skinder with his dog.

How did Andy know it was Skinder? Well, it was as Hannah had said. You would know Skinder, whether or not the dog—small, black, regarding Andy with a curious intensity—had been beside him. What did Skinder look like? He looked exactly like Andy. It was as if Andy stood inside the house, looking out at another, identical Andy, who was also Skinder and who must not be allowed inside.

There was a car in the driveway. A black Prius. There was a chain on the front door, and Andy kept it on when he opened the door a crack. Enough to speak to Skinder, but not enough for Skinder to come in, or his dog. "What do you want?" Andy said.

"To come into my house," Skinder said. He had Andy's voice as well. "My bags are in the car. Will you help me carry them in?"

"No," Andy said. "I'm sorry, but I can't let you in."

The black dog showed its teeth at this. Skinder, too, seemed disappointed. Andy recognized the look on his face, though it was a look that he knew the feel of, more than the look. "Are you sure you won't let me in?" he said.

"I'm sorry," Andy said again. "But I'm not allowed to do that."

Skinder said, "I understand. Come along." This to the dog. Andy in the house watched Skinder go down the steps and down the gravel driveway to the car. He opened the door and the dog jumped up onto the seat. Skinder got in the car at last, too, and Andy watched as the car went down the driveway, the little white stones crunching under the tires, the car silent and the headlights never turned on. The car disappeared under the low, dragging hem of leaves and Andy went back upstairs. He didn't attempt to sleep again. Instead, he sat in the red and white bedroom, in a chair in front of the window, watching in case Skinder returned.

Hannah came back two days later. She sent a text before her overnight flight: *Margot's still in a cast, but we've agreed it's better if I go. No one happy and house is too small. Neighbor going to help out. See you tomorrow afternoon!*

He hadn't finished his dissertation, but Andy felt he was well on the way now. And he was going to see Hannah again. They'd catch up, he'd tell her a modified history of his time in the house, and maybe she'd ask him to stay. There were plenty of bedrooms, after all. She could even take a look at what he had so far, give him some feedback.

But when she arrived, it was clear that he wasn't welcome to stay, even to Andy, who wasn't always the quickest to pick up on cues. "I'm so grateful," she kept saying. Her hair was blue now, a deep, rich sky-blue. "You were such a lifesaver to do this."

"I was happy to do it," Andy said. "It was fun, mostly. Weird, but fun. But I wanted to ask you about some aspects. Skinder, for example."

"You saw him?" Hannah said. All of her attention was on Andy, suddenly.

"No, it's fine," Andy said. "I didn't let him in. I did what you told me to do. But, when you saw him, I wanted to ask. Did he look familiar?"

"What do you mean, exactly?" Hannah said.

"I mean, did you think he looked like me at all?" Andy said.

Hannah shrugged. She looked away, then back at Andy. "No," she said. "Not really. Okay, so I've already paid the fare back on the Uber. It'll take you to Burlington and you can catch a Greyhound there back to Philly. But you have to go now, or you'll miss the last bus. I already checked the schedule—there's nothing if you miss that one until tomorrow morning. Don't worry about cleaning anything up or changing the sheets. I'll take care of it."

"I guess if you're sure," Andy said. "If you don't need me to stay."

She gave him an incredulous look at that. "Oh, Andy," she said. "That's so sweet. But no, I'll be fine. Come here."

She gave him a big hug. "Now, go get your stuff. Do you need a hand?"

He left the ream of paper behind. He hadn't really needed to print out anything. That got rid of one of the canvas bags, and he lugged everything else out to the Uber. Hannah came down the steps to give him a sandwich. She took a look at his Klean Kanteen and said, "Is that tap water?"

"Yes," Andy said. "Why?"

"Ugh," Hannah said. She took the canteen from him and opened it, pouring the water out. "Here. Take this." This was bottled water. "It's from the fridge, so it'll be nice and cold. Bye, Andy. Text me when you get home so I know you're there."

She hugged him again. It wasn't much, but it was better than nothing. The way she smelled, the feeling of her hair on his cheek. "It's really nice to see you again," he said.

"Yes," she said. "I know. It's been such a long time. Isn't it weird, how time just keeps passing?"

And that was that. He turned to get one last look at the yellow house and at Hannah as the car went up the driveway, but she had already gone inside.

When he was at last back at the apartment in Philly, it was morning again. Andy was tired—he had not slept at all on the bus, or in any of the stations in between transfers—and he could not shake the idea that when he opened the door, Skinder would be waiting for him. But instead here was Lester on the futon couch in his boxer shorts, looking at his phone and slurping coffee. It was much hotter in Philly. The apartment had a smell, like something had gone off.

"You're home," Lester said without much enthusiasm. "How was Vermont?"

"Nice," Andy said. "Really, really nice." He didn't think he'd be able to explain what it had been like to Lester. "Where's Bronwen?"

Lester looked down at his phone again. "Not here," he said. "I don't really want to talk about it."

From this, Andy gathered they had broken up. It was a shame: he felt Bronwen might have been a good person to talk to about Vermont. "Sorry," he said to Lester.

"Not your fault, dude," Lester said. "She was not the most normal girl I've ever been with."

Occasionally over the next week Andy noticed how Lester sometimes looked as if he were listening for something, as if he were waiting for something. And after a while, Andy began to feel as if *he* were listening too. And then, sometimes, he thought that he could almost see something in the apartment when Lester was there. It crept after Lester, waited patiently, crouched on the floor beside him when he sat at the table. It was mostly formless, but it had a mouth and eyes. It reminded Andy of Skinder's dog. Sometimes he thought it saw him looking. He felt it looking back. But Lester, he thought, could not see it at all.

It wasn't entirely bad to have it in the house. It meant Andy worked, at last, very hard to finish his dissertation. Or perhaps it had been Vermont that had gotten him over the hump. All that had really been needed was for him to get out of his own way. When he was nearly done, Andy began looking for higher-ed listings, and then, very soon, he was defending, and he was done, and he had graduated at last and had his first interview. He was very ready to leave the apartment, and Philly, and Lester, and Lester's ghost, behind.

The job interview did not go as well as he'd hoped. There were other candidates, and he was quite surprised when, in the end, the job was offered to him. But he took it gladly. Here was the path which led toward tenure and a career and all the rest of his future. Years later, one of the older faculty members who had been on the hiring committee got very drunk at a bar they all frequented, and told Andy that he had almost not gotten the offer, in fact. "The night before we met to discuss, Andy, I had the most peculiar dream. In the dream I was in the woods at night and lost, and there was a bear. I couldn't move I was so scared. The bear came right up and I knew that it was going to eat me, but instead it said, 'You should hire Andy. You'll be glad if you do and you'll regret it if you don't. Do you understand?' I said I did and then I woke up. And then at the meeting no one wanted to say much; there was a very weird feeling, and then someone, Dr. Carmichael, said, 'I had a dream last night that we should hire Andy Sims.' And then someone else said, 'I had the same dream. There was a bear and it said exactly that. That we should hire Andy Sims.' And it turned out we had all had the dream. So, we hired you! And, in the end, it turned out for the best, just like the bear said."

Andy said that this was extremely peculiar, but yes, it had all turned out all right. When, later, he went up for tenure and got it, he wondered if the committee had been given another dream. In any case, he was content to have what he had been given. He caught himself, once, at the end of a lecture, saying, "Much to think about." But there wasn't, really. His students gave him adequate ratings. It seemed to some of them that Professor Sims really looked at them, that he seemed to see something in them (or perhaps near them), none of their other teachers did. What exactly Professor Sims saw, though, he kept to himself. It was, no doubt, an unfortunate after-effect of the water he'd drunk so much of one summer.

There was this, too: although his children asked him over and over why they could not have a dog, Andy could not bear this idea. Instead, he got them guinea pigs, and then a rabbit.

As for Hannah, he ran into her once or twice at conferences. He went to both of her presentations and took notes so he could send her an email afterward with his thoughts. They had drinks with some of their colleagues, but he didn't ask her if she still housesat in the summer in Vermont. All of that seemed of another life, one that didn't belong to him.

Lester had dropped out of the program. He went and worked for a think tank in Indonesia. Andy didn't know if anyone had followed him there.

And then, years later, Andy found himself at a conference in Montpelier, Vermont. It was fall and very beautiful. He found trees quite restful, actually, now that he'd lived on the East Coast for so long. The last day of the conference, he began to think about the parts of his life that he hardly thought about at all, now. He'd given his panel, had heard the gossip, talked up his small college to fledgling PhD candidates. Back in his hotel room, he looked at maps and car rentals and realized it would not be unrealistic to drive home instead of flying. It would be a very pretty drive. And so he canceled his plane ticket and picked up a rental car instead. He thought perhaps he might try to find the yellow house in the woods again, and see who lived there now.

But he didn't remember, as it turned out, exactly which highway the house had been on. He drove down little highway after little highway, all of them lovely but none the road he had meant to find. And, toward dusk, when a deer came onto the road, he swerved to miss it and went quite far down the embankment into a copse of trees.

He wasn't badly hurt, and the car didn't look too bad, either. But he thought it would require a tow truck to get it back up again, and his cell phone had no reception here. He went up to the road and waited some time, but no car ever came past and so he went back down to his rental, to see what he had to eat or drink. He saw, close to where the car had ended up, there was quite a well-trodden trail. Andy decided he would follow it in the direction he felt was the one most likely to lead toward St. Albans.

The trail meandered and grew more narrow. The light began to fade and he thought of turning back, but now the trail led him out to a place he recognized. Here was the patio and here was the Adirondack chair, grown even more decrepit and weatherworn. Here was the comfortable yellow house with all the lights on inside.

He went around to the front door. Well, why not? He wasn't a bear. He knocked and waited, and eventually someone came to the door and opened it.

The other Andy stood in the doorway and looked at him. Where was the little dog? Surely it was dead. But no, there it was in the hallway.

"Can I come in?" Andy said.

"No," Skinder said, and shut the door. Andy waited a little longer, but all that happened was that the lights in the house went off. It was dark outside now and the wind was rattling all the leaves in the trees. There wasn't much he could think of to do, so after a while Andy went back to find the path again.

JUSTIN C. KEY

The Algorithm Will See You Now

FROM *Vital: The Future of Healthcare*

ALAINA HARRIS DIDN'T look depressed. The twenty-eight-year-old Black woman smiled at our receptionist and showed bright interest in the paintings on the waiting room wall. Why was she here? The algorithm assessment of her neural scans from her primary care doctor were unhelpful. Her referral note simply read: "odd presentation, in need of therapy, no medical issues." I sighed. "Odd" wasn't a treatable disorder.

I pulled up my own emotional calibration app on my phone, brought my heart rate down a few beats, and flattened my anxiety curves. They spiked whenever a Black woman like myself came through our door for a new appointment. The noise cleared. I called her in.

"Dr. Hairston." Alaina offered a warm, light handshake. "You're Black."

"Last time I checked."

"I'm sorry. It's just, this is great. I didn't know what to expect and . . . oh god, I'm rambling."

"It's nice to meet you too," I said.

There was so much to gather from that first human interaction. From how she addressed me to where she sat in the room to her palpable energy. She wore a sweater despite us being at the height of summer. She took in what seemed to me every corner of my office, noting the decor, checking for the windows and the doors. Cautiously curious. She paused at her neural display gracing the wall behind her seat. A patient's response to this was also informative.

"So," I said. "What brings you to see a psychiatrist?"

Off that one question, she told me about growing up in the city, her parents' loveless marriage, her difficulties in college, the way her mind often worked against her. An open book, she was yet uninterpretable. The way she described her childhood in vague, distant terms suggested a repressed trauma. I didn't expect to get there in the first session.

She finally sat back and sighed. "I just feel like everything is hard, you know? Work is hard, friends are hard, living is hard." She glanced at me, as if just remembering where she was. "Not that hard, though. Don't get me wrong. I love life."

I smiled. She relaxed.

"You mentioned things at home being stressful," I said. "Tell me about that."

"I live with my best friend. Lauren. We've been besties since college, and I love her. I really do."

"I sense a 'but' coming on."

Blues shifted to orange in some of her neural clusters. I focused on her body language, which spoke a similar message. The change in position. The nervous smile. This was the topic.

"We're very different people," she said. "I love her. I need her. I just . . . I don't know if she's a good friend for me, you know? If I'm good for her. Seems I can never do enough."

"You feel as if you're not being a good friend?"

"She says I'm not." She laughed, not pleasantly. "Lauren always ends arguments by going on one of her drives. And when she's upset she's probably drunk or high or both and . . . it's just not smart. It's selfish."

A faint blue light flashed in the bottom corner of Alaina's display. I shifted to hide my distraction and tapped the side of my chair twice.

Are you sure you want to disregard this clinical warning?

I tapped again. *Yes.*

"That sounds really hard to deal with," I said.

"It is. Because I try. Really hard. It's a lonely place to be. I'm never alone, though, not really. I'm always the one listening. Except here, I guess."

"I'm glad you're having the chance to be heard," I said. A beat of silence hung between us. "There may be times where you feel differently in our sessions. Alone, unheard. If that happens, I invite you to let me know. It could be important for us to work through."

We finished. I didn't mention interventions. Frankly, I wasn't sure she needed it and, if she did, I didn't yet know what we would be treating.

Once she was gone, I skimmed the automated intake draft, which included all the essentials for billing and legal purposes. Most of the data—like eye-movement analysis—only needed review when flagged for significant abnormalities. The meat was in the formulation, diagnosis, and proposed treatment. I frowned. The algorithm homed in on abnormalities in the brain's language and emotional centers and interpreted this as a psychotic process, which was clearly wrong. The algorithm could be way off base, especially with Black patients. I deleted the assessment and wrote my own, spending some extra time noting that the benefits of continuing with her as a patient outweighed the risk of the compatibility flag.

I checked my emotional-state readout. I was slightly angry and anxious, foreign attributes in my own office. I recalibrated myself, went out to our reception area, and poured myself some herbal tea to enhance the calming effect.

"A tough new?" Michael said from his doorway. We had started the practice together out of residency, decades ago, right as the cluster-based treatment revolution swept through psychiatry. We were some of the only private psychiatrists left who still did face-to-face interactions.

"Straightforward, actually," I said. "Algorithm pegged her as psychotic, but she's definitely not. Just some depression and anxiety."

"The algorithm conflated psychosis and trauma with one of my patients the other day."

He gestured towards the blue warning lights through the office door I'd failed to completely close. "You want me to take her? I have space on my panel."

"Oh, that? No, nothing significant. She's African American."

Michael nodded and left it alone. The blue indicator warned of a potentially undesirable result from a patient's neural network paired against the provider's. Subconscious biases, uncanny similarities, all could theoretically interfere with a healthy therapeutic alliance. For years the algorithm had conflated race with shared experience. The latest iterations supposedly addressed this, but old glitches died hard, and Black patients were still underrepresented in data pools because of continuing disparities in mental healthcare access and engagement.

Regardless, some things we didn't challenge each other on. We knew where my Blackness ended and his Whiteness began. It's why we'd always worked well together.

Back in my office, I replayed the part of the intake that sparked the warning: Alaina recalling Lauren's criticism. The printout identified neuronal clusters indicating shared experience, similar neuroanatomy, and a high percentage of paired firing between our respective mirror neurons. The computer essentially posited that our brains were too much alike to achieve a successful balance of objectivity and subjectivity. Specifically, the algorithm predicted that I would deter her from getting ablation therapy despite analysis showing it to be the most beneficial treatment long-term.

I read it over again to be sure.

I considered Michael's offer. The International Psychiatric Association hadn't released any official recommendations since the seminal study on the pairing technology showed a clear parabolic correlation between therapist-patient neural pairings and outcomes. Like many things, the algorithm gave no insight into the "how." Many speculated that the lack of boundary setting, regression, and poorer physician decision making contributed to this phenomena.

But handing over her case was the last thing I wanted to do. Because, for the first time in years, I was intrigued.

The ride home was a good in-between time to reflect, rediscover, and digest the day's patients. Today, though, I needed some me-time to recalibrate.

I waited until I was on the freeway to run the anxiety module. I gritted my teeth against the pressure emanating from my temporal implant and swiped through the files that came up on the car's display, sorted by emotional state, impact, and then date. Ah, there it was. I frowned at the algorithm's attempt at a title: Fear of Misdiagnosis.

"Play back, quantity thirty." My fingertips dug into the well-earned grooves in the main passenger seat's armrest as the machine soaked my brain in the sensory input that provoked anxiety.

It's all your fault.

A woman with brown, fluffy hair and dazzling hoop earrings sat in the seat beside me. When I looked at her, she was gone.

I gasped and reflexively yanked off the probe.

What the hell had happened?

A notification blinked on the frozen display.

Origin of emotional dysregulation identified. Would you like to link to it?

Yes. A crude representation of my own neural network materialized in a faint hologram that zoomed into a black, foggy void with only scant, roaming particulates. I'd seen this many times before, but never in myself. The visual representation of an ablated past.

The ablation procedure had been pivotal in my development and making it through the second half of college. But what else was there? I blinked. I couldn't recall. First generation, on scholarship, my family's expectation of *"there goes Dr. Hairston!"* followed me from childhood to college. Neural Cluster Ablation had only just entered clinical trials. The procedure hoped to magnetically target select neuronal clusters correlated with distress and remove them permanently. The study gave me my first neural probe, a device now ubiquitous for neural self-regulation, especially amongst mental health workers.

You were never good enough. Not then, not now.

Softer now. The faintest shadow of a woman's image lingered and then disappeared with a blink. I began to reach out and then stopped.

Sensory hallucinations were known artifacts from memory recalibration. My connection with Alaina had somehow stirred up a random remnant from that black void. The ghost of a past I decided not to think about. I *paid* not to think about.

I shut off the program.

Alaina was early to her next appointment. I turned off my neural upload as she walked into my office. She wore a sweater similar to the week before.

"I've been thinking about your situation with your roommate," I said after we had settled. "How was it talking about her?"

"Exhausting," she said. "We're just different people. 'If you can't do anything about it, then why worry?' That's what my dad used to say, at least."

"It's obviously been affecting you."

"Sometimes I get really upset about the things Lauren says. I try not to let her see that it gets to me."

"You must let it out somehow."

"I'll go for a walk. Play the piano. Sometimes I snack a little. Well, a lot, if I get stressed enough. But that's a whole thing." She waved a hand. "Mostly, I just deal."

"This relationship means a lot to you."

She smiled, then sobered herself. "It does. Me and Lauren always been like *this*. We helped each other through some shit coming up." Scant blue and orange lines cascaded through Alaina's limbic system. "I screwed up. And I can't leave it like that, you know?"

"How did you screw up?" I said.

She shifted. Distress grew.

"Can we talk about something else?"

My usual response would be to explore this resistance. The real work of therapy happened in these moments. But I, too, was uncomfortable. And I was afraid of losing the patient's trust. What if she didn't come back to her next appointment?

I didn't press. We spent the rest of the session talking about whether she would call her mother for her birthday even though they hadn't spoken since her mother cursed her out for forgetting her birthday the year before.

I canceled my next patient and ran provider analysis on Alaina's session. My heart rate and temperature had peaked several times. The suggestion to change topics threw me, yes, but what else caused a response? I zoomed in on one of the spaces. When Alaina said *I messed up*, my parameters leapt.

Would you like to flag these for future sessions?

I closed the app.

Tunde worked with an investment company based overseas. His days started as mine ended. I entered quietly, changed into evening clothes, and found myself in the kitchen. Nini, our house's virtual assistant, suggested a vegan salad with light dressing from the Rude Girl, a new place just down the street. I no longer wondered how the machines came to their decisions, much less if they were right. The algorithm knew my blood markers, genetic risk, the daily change in body composition, and a slew of other factors that, when put together, predicted this specific meal would give me the best chance to live until I was old enough to regret living. How could I argue with that?

After his work, right when I was beginning to doze beneath

the now-warm sheets, Tunde slid into bed beside me. The hum of some television series leaked from his earbuds. I stirred. A soft *click* as Tunde switched to his reading app.

I noticed a long time ago that Tunde feigned reading financial periodicals around me. I'd looked for couples' therapy but gave up when I couldn't work in both our schedules. Hell, what had that been? A year ago now?

My hand went to my phone and the regulation app. Instead, I put it aside.

"Can't sleep?" Tunde said.

"Why do you always read in bed?"

"Because reading in the shower would be silly."

"Is talking to me not enough stimulation for you? Am I not enough?"

Before Tunde could respond I got out of bed, took some sheets from the closet, and went to sleep on the couch.

I continued to see Alaina weekly. Our topics ranged from her loving but misguided single father, her fluctuating motivation to execute on a long-standing business idea, and wondering if life out in the country would "be much simpler."

Branching lines sprouted and thickened after every session, a testament to the connections made. I felt genuine joy when Alaina, who had come to me without experience expressing herself or her emotions, began to consciously make these connections.

"Maybe that's why I let this Lauren thing bother me so much," she said after recounting a best friend who moved away in the third grade. Alaina glanced back at her neural map and lightly traced the new, thin tendril as it branched out from her current cognitive state to the memory cluster highlighted on that very first session. "Because I'm afraid of being alone, see? I just wish I could make things right."

I didn't speak. Many things—good and bad—were born in silence.

"She was dating this guy. They were engaged. He was an asshole. The type who hit on her friends when she wasn't in the room. She must have known about it. In fact, I'm sure she did. He tried to kiss me while she was throwing up in her bathroom. I *had* to say something. She confronted him, and he broke it off."

"She blamed you?"

Alaina wiped her eyes and then laughed at her wet fingers. "Not at first. She started dating again and seemed genuinely happy. She was definitely a lot better. Stopped drinking too. Then those relationships didn't work. She'd say little things here and there. 'Another Saturday night, me and you, just like you wanted.' Drinking got bad again, and then we'd argue about that."

"Does she drink a lot?"

"Not anymore. Just when she gets really upset. Then she goes for her drives."

I made a mental note to return to one of Lauren's "drives." "You mentioned rectifying the relationship. What do you think that would look like?"

"Being here, for one. It was her idea. She thinks that if I get help, her life will be easier. That, and I quote, she'll be able to 'live.'"

"So it's your responsibility to make her happy?"

Alaina smiled. "Aren't we all a little bit responsible for someone's happiness?"

Tunde and I committed to a home-cooked meal one night a week. Our calendar chose the day well in advance, and it usually coincided with Tunde's sometimes erratically scheduled days off. I got home later than usual. Tunde sat on the couch, reading his periodicals. A dirtied dinner plate rested beside him.

"You ate already?" I said.

"Was I not supposed to?" I put the plate in the sink and, as I left, Tunde rose. "I didn't know when you would be home. You didn't send me any—"

I closed the door behind me. No one yelled. No one threw anything. I often heard of those types of antics when patients talked of their childhood. For us, only silence.

Sometimes, I wondered if that was worse.

"Insurance notice," Michael said one morning. Both of our nine o'clocks had downgraded their in-person sessions to neural upload review and treat. He flicked the notification over to my device. "That new one you've been seeing. You going to take her on pro-bono?"

"You know we can't afford that." I quickly read the notice. I'd expected this, sooner or later. Had it already been twelve sessions?

"I want to explore your relationship with Lauren," I said once Alaina was situated in my office.

"I don't want to talk about her today. She gets on my last nerves."

"I think it would be beneficial to bring her into the room with us." At Alaina's look—and her reddening neural map—I spoke quickly. "Not the real her. Just your experience of her to help us get to the root of the issue."

"The issue is she's stubborn as a rock. Will it hurt?"

"It won't hurt," I said. "It'll be emotionally uncomfortable. But that's the point. Discomfort, we can work with."

I picked up the remote to the neural simulator and held it for her to see. "May I?"

She nodded. There were no probes to place. The same functional-MRI sensors used to create her neural map could tell the molecular structure of the nutrient from her breakfast that made it across her blood-brain barrier.

"Think about your last altercation with Lauren. Try to remember it exactly as it happened."

As the patient explored her own memory, I ran the Neural Amplification and Recreation Protocol. The system used Alaina's sensory input and neural response data to create a personalized "key" that could reverse-engineer experience from Alaina's memories.

A soft triple beep warned of impending output. Then, a new voice came to life.

"It's all your fault," a woman said. The tone was incongruently friendly. "If you had just minded your own business everything would be fine. You always thought you knew best."

The NAR protocol was one of the most jarring experiences for patients in any setting. It essentially took one's memories and thoughts and brought them out into the open. So I expected a reaction. Only not this one. Because Alaina wasn't frightened or surprised or scared. Alaina was angry.

"He wasn't good for you," she said.

"Is anyone?" the NAR produced. I moved to turn the program off, then stopped myself. "You just want me to be alone. Like you."

"Leave, then. Go back to him. You two deserve each other."

"I will."

I stopped the protocol.

"How—" I cleared my throat, took a deep breath. "Excuse me. How is it hearing that?"

"Hard," she said.

"How often does that come up with her?"

"Daily."

I can't leave because I'm all you have. Without me you'd probably kill yourself.

I spilled my tea fumbling for the controller. "Sorry, I thought I had turned that . . ." But the NAR was off. Alaina hadn't spoken. What's more, the voice wasn't quite the same as Lauren's.

"She says that all the time. That I'd be alone without her."

"You heard that, just now?" I said.

"Of course I did," she said. "Am I not supposed to?"

"No, you are, it's just . . ." I shifted. "It sounds like there's a lot of conflict with her. You really value this relationship. That's why it's taking such a toll on you."

As I said the last my mind tallied up the truth of it, what I had been gradually noticing over the last several sessions. The way Alaina's clothes hung loose, something I noticed because she wore the same weeks before. The steady decline in weight every week. The picking of her fingers. The soft rock back and forth in her chair. Alaina wasn't doing well. Perhaps the insurance was right to push me.

"Treatment can help," I said.

"I thought this was treatment."

"It is. But it may not be enough."

"I don't want pills."

I smiled. "No pills. We've come a long way."

I pulled up her display and showed her the highlighted area in her amygdala linked to the cluster of memory and association cells that represented Lauren.

"This is your friend. This is the effect your friend has on you." Thankfully, there were still strong positive associations that connected to pleasure and joy. I focused on these first. "You would still have your positive responses to her. All the things you enjoy about your relationship. It's these areas, where you're experiencing anxiety and distress, that we can dampen."

"To make me numb?"

"No, not numb. More resilient."

"Is this what you did?"

I frowned before I could stop myself.

"There are other, stronger treatments, but I don't think you need them right now. The dampening process is a lot less invasive. It basically takes all of the data we've gathered here in therapy, the work we've done, and multiplies the benefit a hundred-fold."

"I don't want to care less," she said. "I just need to be better."

I tried another angle. "You think Lauren's criticisms are valid?"

"I do."

We agreed on no treatment for that day. I noted that I was still assessing the need for intervention and uploaded a small clip of our in-session conversation, which I knew insurance would request. I marked the NAR protocol as a procedure. I hoped to delay the conversation of out-of-pocket payment as long as possible. Insurance often cared little about my hopes.

That done, I considered replaying the moment of the unexpected voice. *I can't leave because I'm all you have.* Did I really need to? *Without me you'd probably kill yourself.* No. The explanation was simple: NAR often created echoes in a patient's mind as part of the neuronal intervention.

Why, then, had I heard it as well?

The algorithms responded to some change in me. Nini suggested food with more carbs and eliminated some morning and evening workouts to increase my sleep. Self-regulation increased. I checked my regulation app constantly, adjusting as soon as it swayed from normal. I did this so often that security asked me to verify my identity to make sure the app hadn't been hacked.

Tunde and I were intimate for the first time in years. Afterwards I felt a sense of emptiness, like giving someone deprived of sugar just a taste of some blandly sweet thing, a shadow of what used to be.

"Something's on your mind," he said as I got up to shower and get ready for work.

More like something was *in* my mind. The voice inspired by Alaina's neural recording was full and near constant now. What's more, it had evolved from the original stranger to something more familiar, something from my past.

"If you could remove your worst memories, would you?" I said.

"Is this a philosophical problem or a practical one?"

"I'm asking you, would you?"

"If I needed it, I would," he said.

"You don't know this, but I overheard you talking about it back

in college. You said it was like killing a part of yourself. You compared it to the Ship of Theseus."

A pause that he tried to cover with a cough. He should know
better.

"Hey, you needed it. You did what was best for you. What was
best for us. As for the ship, I'd rather ride around in one with a
few stand-out patches than rotting wood." He put his tablet screen-
down on the bed. "What brought this on, babe?"

I ignored the algorithm's pre-set outfit choice for the day, neatly
centered in my closet, and picked out an older blouse in need of
ironing. "Nothing."

"You seem distracted," Alaina said in the middle of our session,
less than two hours later.

She was right. My mind was elsewhere. I brought my full attention back to Alaina and smiled. This was what I trained for.

"You're right, I am a little distracted. I've had a couple rough
nights lately, and it's harder to keep my mind from wandering.
How does it make you feel, thinking that I'm not listening?"

"It feels like criticism. Like you have better things to do, and
I'm a waste of time."

"I wonder where you've learned such a reaction?"

After some thought, Alaina talked about Lauren's drinking and
driving. The session was back on track. I offered to see her a second time that week on Thursday. She obliged.

Although handled well, in truth Alaina's observation annoyed me to no end. I unsuccessfully attempted to adjust my
modulation many times that night. After another bout of un-
fulfilling intercourse, I used Tunde's snoring as cover and went
into the den to access my patient records. I pulled up the moment of distraction with Alaina, viewed it from her perspective,
and cursed. My eyes were glassy, my gaze off. And when she
called me on it I looked less in control and more like a pupil
being reprimanded.

The computer flagged this section for "embarrassment," "resentment," and "doubt." I selected "doubt," saw a cluster of neurons glow in the frontal lobe, and then connect to another cluster
in the thalamus.

I looked up. "Babe?"

Soft snoring answered. I pulled up the security system. All en-
tryways were locked and there was no recent spike in noise levels.

Two voices. Whispering. Far away, but clear. I crept out of the den and into the kitchen.

You're drunk.

No shit. A good friend would take the keys. But not you. You only act like you care.

The closer I got to the door leading out to the garage, the louder they grew.

Give me the keys, then, Laura.

Don't be concerned now.

I crept up to the door. Soon I'd be leaning against it. The voices were clear now. I knew they came from inside me somehow, but that didn't make them feel any less real. I touched the reinforced metal and flinched at the initial, wood-like feel of it.

Slam!

I jumped. Something behind me shattered. The voices stopped. I didn't go to the app to analyze my emotions or cluster connections. I just left the kitchen as fast as I could without panicking. As the door closed behind me, underneath the slide of metal was the faintest rev of a gas-powered engine.

I didn't sleep more than twenty minutes that night. Thankfully, the next day was one of my virtual algorithm consultant days, a gig I picked up that paid well and offered some intellectual curiosity in a sea of monotony. I reviewed algorithm assessments and briefly checked in with patients. At times there were glaring errors, like recommendations based on misgendering, but mostly I was just there to give a human face to medicine.

A light ping startled me as I turned off the monitor. Just my secretary. On an adjacent display, her likeness materialized in a hologram.

"Zachary Parker called. He's demanding an earlier appointment because his 'life is falling apart.'" My schedule appeared under her.

I responded to such requests with a five-minute video call to explore boundaries and ultimately deny. But after a night of phantom memories and tortured dreams, I took the easy way out.

"Give him Alaina's Thursday slot," I said.

I immediately knew what was happening. Alaina had gotten to me, I'd failed at hiding it, and now I was punishing her for it. She was evoking in me the role that Lauren played in her life.

I dialed my secretary.

"Let's keep Alaina's appointment."

"Oh. Dr. Hairston, I already rescheduled her for next week."

"I see. How'd she take it?"

"Fine," she said. "She wasn't upset or anything."

The week went on at a crawl. Zachary Parker didn't make it to his appointment. I cleared the hour after Alaina's next visit so that we could spill over past our time if the topic allowed.

But Alaina never came. She was a no-show.

She didn't show up the next couple of weeks. My secretary called at first, and then me. Voicemail. I considered calling from either a blocked number or pretending to be someone else, but quickly shot down both ideas. That was crossing the line. Patients fell off all the time.

Self-recalibration increased; I surrendered some of the settings to automatic adjustments. Sleep came easier. Home disagreements quieted. My thoughts were once again clear. I distracted myself with work. Helping others with their problems allowed me to postpone the need to address my own.

If scheduled outpatient appointments were a kind of cruise control, then working in the emergency room reminded of the power and the stakes of being active behind the wheel. It also reminded of the cost of hospitalizing someone. I made sure to do at least one shift a month.

I put out a call to the community hospitals with my hourly rate and requested length of work. Of the several options that appeared almost immediately, I chose Michelle Obama Memorial. With fewer resources, the work would naturally be more involved. As a Black provider, the unique patient experience often made it worth it.

I started with clearing out the holdovers from overnight. Individuals in need of sobering up, others contemplating the knife or the phone until the early morning, and the manic episodes that seemed immune to treatment. Each had a computer readout that aggregated data from all their medical care across the country and analyzed them against a global database of various clinical presentations, treatments, and outcomes. This produced a nice little table of risks, scores, and suggested interventions.

I only looked to the notes for guidance on the last three. One I discharged because their craving for death had been induced by alcohol, another I marked for admission to a sister hospital with open beds, and the third I set up for in-house guided psychedelic therapy. This last patient, a social media influencer, recently lost half his followers after his now ex-partner posted a video of his candid, transphobic rant. His elaborate plan for suicide included a livestream.

Inpatient admission, the algorithm suggested. Though he was a clear candidate for guided psychedelic therapy, the algorithm considered available resources in its calculations, and Obama Memorial didn't have any licensed therapists. It would be way too much at my hourly rate for me to sit and do it, so I called a video service I contracted with. After a six-hour trip I could reassess him on my way out and, if I was right, potentially discharge him.

"Busy morning," I said as I entered the shared workroom just outside the overcrowded emergency department.

The senior emergency medicine resident sighed. "Always. Air quality's been low the last week. Lot of algorithm-induced anxiety around lung cancer predictions. So a lot of these 'shortness of breath' should be in and out."

"What you got for me?" A purple tag—psychiatric services— marked several of the triage bay video feeds.

"I discharged a few. Secondary gain, most of them. Their suicidal thoughts magically resolved when they heard we didn't have a guide."

I leaned forward and tapped the icon in blue, still pending evaluation. Lauren Roberson, Room Three. "And this one?"

"Young Black woman picked up by the Community Response Team. Crashed her car into the guardrail, got out, and tried to enter passing cars. They found an empty bottle of liquor in the car. She reeked of the stuff."

I was already looking over the drug screen, which included analysis of blood and urine. "Alcohol level is zero."

"Crazy, right? No pun intended. No drugs in her system, bizarre when I talked to her, rambling, kept going on about some issue with her friends. Seems like the real deal."

"They're all the real deal," I said, not unkindly. I expanded her room's live feed. She was in the standard hospital gown; a blue sweater lay across the foot of the bed. Red lines ran the length of both forearms. I squinted, though there was no need. With the video quality, she might as well have been right in front of me.

"Did she come in with some other name?"

"Huh?" the resident said.

"Like Alaina or something like that?"

"No. Is that a psychotic thing?"

I reviewed the video uploaded by the Community Response Team. Shortly after contact she rushed at the main responder, yelling *Where is she? Where is Lauren?*

"It is, isn't it? I thought it was weird she was screaming her own name when the CRT picked her up. You're thinking multiple personalities?"

Blue and red lights flashed in the background of the feed. A characteristic siren just touched the audio.

"Why did they send the police to get her?" I said.

The resident frowned and leaned forward. "That's the CRT."

"That was definitely police. See." I rewound the video. "Huh. Weird. I thought there were lights—never mind."

I continued to watch. The community responder pulled out a gun as Alaina closed the gap. I blinked. No, not a gun. I closed my eyes.

Get on the ground! Get on the fucking ground!

Pain in my knee and wrist. The smell of hot tires and spent gas.

I paused the playback, checked to make sure the resident couldn't see, double-tapped, and then circled my neural chip to mitigate the anxious thoughts.

My pulse and my breath slowed. I resumed the playback. There was no gun. There were no police. The response team restrained my patient and safely got her into the padded car.

"She's drunk," one of the responders said after.

"No shit. Let's take her to MOM. They'll know what to do with her."

I watched it again and then sat back. It looked like Alaina. Sounded like Alaina. If I checked her neural print against Alaina's, it would be one and the same. But Alaina wasn't homeless and Alaina wasn't psychotic. What was she, then?

"Uh-oh. She's not happy."

Alaina approached the front of her room, which was offscreen. She screamed soundlessly and waved her arms.

"First cranial pulse of the day, you think?" the resident said.

"Not yet. Charge it up, but wait." At the resident's baffled look, I clarified. "I know her. She's one of my private patients."

When I arrived, Alaina stood on the opposite side of Room Three in full defensive stance. She wielded one of her shoes while two orderlies tried to talk her down.

"Alaina," I said. Her eyes widened and then welled with tears. She dropped her shoe, sat back on the bare bed, and began to weep.

"She got me good," one of the orderlies said. He had a long, thick scratch down the middle of his arm. "I wouldn't get too close."

I nodded and pulled a chair up to the side of her bed.

"You heard it, too, huh?" she said.

"Heard what?" I said, though I wasn't surprised at the accusation.

"I have to know if Lauren's here. If she's okay. Did she tell you where she was going?"

"Why would she tell me?"

"Because you heard her, that day in the office. You didn't ignore her like everyone else."

"I work here," I said. "No one told me to come."

"Yeah, okay," she said. "I know when I'm being lied to. I don't fucking like being lied to."

Anger: a newcomer in our therapeutic relationship. I wished we were in my office. I felt blind without the insights of the neural mapping. She must have taken something that wouldn't show up on the drug screen. With a change so quick, there really was no other explanation. But if I went that route, I might lose her.

"You checked in under Lauren's name," I said. "Why?"

"Because *she* should be here. Not me!"

I looked away, let the air cool.

"What happened between you two?"

"She ran off again because I wasn't going to take her shit. I was looking for her, and they brought me here. I don't know what she wants." She put her head in her hands, massaged her temples, then squeezed. "What do you want?"

On a whim, I asked, "Is Lauren here right now?"

Alaina laughed. "You're really trying to play me. She's not here, even if she should be."

"Can I talk to Lauren? Do you have her number?"

Alaina shook her head.

"No, I can't talk to her or no, you don't have her number?"

"She doesn't have a number. She doesn't need one. I don't want to talk about this." She shook her head, looked around, and shrank. "Are you keeping me here?"

"Do you want to stay?"

"You ask like I have a choice."

"Because you do." I could easily petition for a Treatment Despite Refusal claim. Given her presentation so far, the lack of drugs, and already what would be considered a violent act, the algorithm would grant me permission to force a wide range of treatments. "You're on a hold now, yes, but I can release that hold."

"What do you think I should do?"

"Spend a night or two in the hospital. Get some rest. Figure some things out."

"Will you be here?"

"No. But they . . ." They what? Would take good care of her? They'd offer her a bunch of treatment options that would all seem scary and big, and she'd leave the hospital in a couple days never wanting to see a psychiatrist again. Though studies on neural overlaps between provider and patient showed clear negatives, there were less discussed positives. The automatic rapport between two Black individuals, for example, present from our very first handshake and laughter of relief. I was her only mental health provider, and this was her first emergency department visit. I didn't yet know what to make of her symptoms, but if it was something long-term, it probably wouldn't be her last. I couldn't abandon her to the mercy of the system.

"I think you can go home," I said. "But I'm worried about you. I want to see you in my office this Thursday. And we should start treatment. More treatment."

Her eyes widened. "You think I need it?"

"You're stressed. And whatever reason it may be, whether some imbalance in your brain or you ate something that didn't quite agree with you, I think it's time for some relief."

She considered in silence. I let her.

"I'll think about it," she said finally, her voice a little more sure. "If I can go home, I'll think about it."

"Where will you stay tonight?" I said.

"Family. I'll stay with family."

I debated with myself. I needed to know more, and this wasn't the setting to do it.

"I need to talk to Lauren."

"I told you, she's hard to contact."

"Let me be the judge of that. I'll sign the discharge papers and drop the hold, I just need a little assurance here. Give me her full name."

"Lauren," she said. "Lauren Daniels."

"Birthday?"

"January twenty-fourth, two thousand forty."

I went back to the workroom. The resident was finishing a call. When he saw me, he checked the video feed.

"I knew they taught psychs magic," he said. "I swore she was going to swing on you."

"Sometimes patients just need a little talking to."

"You said she was yours. I didn't know you treated psychotic patients."

"I don't," I said.

"Should I put in admission orders?"

"No. Discharge."

The resident lifted an eyebrow.

"No hospital's going to take a psychotic patient refusing treatment, so she'd likely be here all night. You're working a twenty-four, correct?"

He lifted his hands. "Discharge it is. You know I'm with it."

I sat at the computer to see if I could track down this Lauren Daniels. I put in her name and the DOB. Nothing. I tried just the name. There were a few matches. I picked one in proximity to Alaina's age. I opened her chart.

A warning popped up. Ice went down my spine.

It's your fault.

I turned. "What did you say?"

"Nothing," the resident said. Then he laughed. "Careful, or I'll have to admit you."

"Then maybe I could get some rest," I said, going with it.

I went back to the warning. *This patient is deceased. D.O.D 01/24/2040. Are you sure you want to open their chart?*

Was I sure?

I opened it and, while I waited for it to load, checked the transcript of my interview with Alaina. I'd heard two thousand fourteen but, no, she said forty.

My insides turned to stone as I read the details about the motor vehicle accident that had taken Lauren's life seven years ago.

"Get Acute Ablation Therapy ready for Room Three," I said. I repeated it, this time louder.

"Is it a little soon? He just got here."

I sat up, scrambled at the controls, and brought up Room Three. A man with lazy eyes in need of sobering occupied my patient's bed.

"Where's Alaina?" I said.

"Who?"

"Alaina. Lauren. The damn woman who was in Room Three!"

"She left."

"What?"

"You told me to discharge her."

I ran out of the room, down the hall, and threw open the back fire-escape door and went out into the night. I yelled for her, but it was of no use.

Alaina was gone.

The rest of my shift was uneventful.

Tunde and I rented a private boat off the coast of Playa del Rey and were well out into the ocean just in time for sunset. I left my dampener in the car. Whatever I felt was far from pleasant, but it was necessary. The rest of the shift had been uneventful.

"Something's on your mind," Tunde said as we walked out onto the deck. Dinner had been quiet. He ordered his usual at seafood restaurants: crab legs and coleslaw. I tried something new, the seared scallops, and hated them.

"I had a rough shift," I said.

"Not just today," Tunde said. He looked out to the sea. Judging from the nervous tilt in his voice, he hadn't self-regulated in a while. "When you're with me it feels like your mind is someplace else. Or wants to be. Part of me wonders if you've had any inappropriate relationships lately."

I laughed. Sneaking in an affair while trying to figure out Alaina and the effect she had on me? Absurd. "I should be offended."

"Offended is good," Tunde said. He laughed out toward the darkening horizon. "I'll take offended."

"Something *has* been going on," I said. I continued to smile to keep my husband at ease. "Does the name *Lauren* mean anything to you?" I saw the lie forming behind his eyes. "Whatever it is, it's out there already. I didn't know my ablation therapy included a memory wipe. I guess that was the point, though, huh? Who was Lauren?"

"Laura," Tunde said. "You were roommates. In college."

"Laura. Laura Chisholm." I tasted the name, felt its tremble on my lips. I hadn't spoken it in decades. "She always had the big hoop earrings and the hair everyone wanted."

"That's her. Everyone knew Laura."

"Did she die?" I said.

"Yes."

"Car crash?"

"You remember a lot more than you should."

I shook my head. "I don't remember."

"You lost me."

"One of my patients. Her best friend died in a car crash seven years ago. The friend's name was Lauren. She was intoxicated."

"Jesus," Tunde said. "Laura was killed by a drunk driver. That's definitely too close to home. You're going to stop seeing her, right?"

"Yeah," I said. "Definitely."

Silence. Whatever Tunde and I had become, he knew when I was lying.

"You used to tell me about your cousin having schizophrenia," I said. "That it came on after she lost someone. You told her story sometimes when my path got hard, and I thought about giving up."

"I remember," Tunde said.

"I don't recall you ever having a cousin." I turned to him. There were no sensors. No displays. Just the two of us under the dying light. "Was it me? When you talk about this phantom cousin, are you just talking about me?"

"You inspired me," Tunde said after some time. "You inspired us both. You got help. And look how far you've come."

A dorsal fin briefly broke the surface some hundred yards away. I waited for the rest of the dolphin's pod to show. None did.

"What was I like?" I said. "Before?"

"Smart. Beautiful. Creative. All the things you are now."

"Liar," I said.

"It's no lie." Tunde shifted. "You were suffering. Before Laura died, it was manageable. You had a light episode every now and then, but we got through it. No one knew, unless they needed to know. Laura's death was . . . tragic, for the whole school, but for you it kept happening over and over because you still heard her." He shivered. "The stuff her voice would say . . . You have to stop seeing this patient. It's taking a toll on you."

The last of the day's rays warm on my skin, I leaned over and kissed my husband. Our lips lingered long enough to let sparks fly between us, like all those decades ago when he proposed as we watched an ocean sunset. But, alas, nothing but stubble and cognition.

"That's why I need to keep seeing her."

Though the *why* of anything in life was complex, the *how* of the situation was clear. I had developed symptoms consistent with mild schizophrenia shortly upon college matriculation. My once benign psychosis dramatically worsened after the tragic death of my college roommate. The ablation therapy did its job, and core memories surrounding the psychosis—including Laura—had been purged. Decades later, the pairing of my cognition with Alaina's facilitated a free stream of emotions between the two of us. Her experience gave life to dormant parts of my past, similar to the classic case studies describing late-stage dementia patients showing transient moments of awareness and memory. I hallucinated because the awakened part of my brain also facilitated bouts of false sensory information decades ago.

Alaina and I started in very much the same place. If I wasn't specially equipped to help her, who was?

I came into the office two hours early to prepare for Alaina's next appointment. I went over her files, algorithms, and used the cognition extraction technology to see an emulation of my own logic analyze the details of her case.

Alaina was fifteen minutes late. She wore the same baggy sweater from the hospital three days before. She stank of insomnia.

"You look how I feel," she said.

"We both had a rough week. I wanted to bring up a sensitive topic. How did Lauren die?"

"She told you she was dead?" Alaina said.

"I saw it in her records." I leaned slightly forward. "What goes through your mind when I say that? When I mention her dying?"

"She's manipulating you. To get what she wants. Everyone thinks she's dead. Everyone gives her sympathy." Alaina huffed disgust. "She wasn't ready to go. And she didn't. I keep her alive."

"Maybe that's true. But do you think she wants to live at your expense?"

Alaina began to cry. I handed her a tissue. When she was done, I showed her where Lauren's voices lived in her brain. Delusions—or fixed beliefs—were the hardest things to combat in psychiatry. For some people, showing their physical derivatives went a long way.

"This is the sensory part of your brain lighting up when I talk. It comes all the way from the nerve anchored in your eardrum and links back to here, where memories are." I switched from live feed to a previous recording. "See, here, that's your sensory portion lighting up independently. No input from the outside nerves. It does, however, have an intimate connection with this cluster, where your memory of Lauren lives."

I turned off the recording. "Do you hear her now?"

"I only hear you." She kept my gaze for only a few moments before looking past me. Her neural read shifted.

I leaned forward. "I am not here to judge but to explore."

"She needs me."

"She's gone," I said. I turned off the session recording device. "I had a friend too. She died in a car accident after one of our arguments, like Lauren. I can help you be at peace. I think she would have wanted that."

I clipped the earpiece behind her ear.

"You think I'm crazy," Alaina said.

"Oh, no. No, no, no." I shook my head. "I think you need help. And I have help."

"Will I be like you?"

I shifted. "I don't understand."

She took the earpiece off and gestured around her. "All this, just to function. I see you dampening yourself and dampening yourself. Do you even feel anything anymore?"

"Alaina, I know this is upsetting, but—"

"You're broken," she said. "And I'm whole. It might be a rotting whole, but it's my whole, and it's all there right now. You had a piece of you taken. And now you have to depend on technology just to get through the day. I've seen you!"

For the first time in our many sessions, I was unintentionally silent. Alaina looked to me for the same therapeutic expertise I had shown before to make this moment into something productive, but I had nothing.

"I'm sorry, I—" Alaina began to say.

I held up a hand. "It's fine."

Alaina missed her next three appointments. I took on more shifts at Obama Memorial and kept an eye out for her. She popped up from time to time in the medical charts. Still presenting under different names, still refusing treatment, still looking for her friend, Lauren.

Three months later I had another ablation treatment. Not only to eradicate any resurfacing remnants of Laura but to also clear my memory of Alaina.

I made sure my notes on her were airtight in case of any unlikely future litigation. As I waited for the machine to do its work I took the final chance to reflect on Alaina's words. The Ship of Theseus was replaced piece by piece until it was something completely new. Was I the same person as before the ablation? Of course I wasn't. Would I have become a doctor?

Alaina's choice bothered me the most. We were so alike and yet chose completely differently at the most pivotal junctions in our lives.

Why?

No answer came, only ignorance, and therefore, bliss.

KAREN RUSSELL

The Cloud Lake Unicorn

FROM *Conjunctions*

BEFORE I STARTED living on extraordinary time, I used to set my watch by Garbage Thursday. My landlady often jokes that Garbage Thursday is my Sabbath. Garbage Thursday is a secular ceremony of reckoning and forgetting. You hear the same hymn booming across our leafy block each Thursday evening: the trash bins bumping and scraping over asphalt, the rolling harmonies of a neighborhood remembering in unison that this is our weekly chance to liberate our lives of trash. Smells and peels, used neon condoms and yolky eggshells, kombucha six-packs and leopardy bananas—down the driveways they come, our open secrets straining at white Hefty bags. Clink-clink-clink, we rattle together, the Ghosts of Garbage Thursdays Past, Present, and Future.

Via neighborly telepathy, I always reach the curb at the same moment as my friend Anja. She lives in Unit B of the Cloud Lake apartment complex across the street. The name "Cloud Lake" is like a cemetery marker for the acres of water that once flowed here, drinking in the sunshine of the last century; we live in Mult nomah County, Oregon, where the names of the dead can be found on condominiums and athletic clubs and doomed whimsical businesses. Anja says she can feel the lake water rippling below the pavement. What I see as early-morning mist, she says, is actually the vaporous ghost of Cloud Lake. Anja vibrates at a special frequency. She emigrated to Portland from Sarajevo, and tells me she was epigenetically altered by her childhood experience of the Bosnian War. She smokes pre-rolled joints and has a secondary addiction to deep-dish pizza. We have developed a kind of whistling camaraderie on Garbage Thursday, what I imagine to be a gravediggers' rapport, like something out of Shakespeare. "What's good, Mauve!" she waves to me across the street, centaured before her own overflowing bin. "Disposing of the evidence, I see!"

The curb is like the diary where we record our hungers. A diary slated for weekly erasure. The amnesiac's log of "refuse." This used to strike me as a squeamish euphemism, but now I think it's the perfect word, noun and verb, for the toxic mosaic we make in our ad hoc collaboration on Ninth Avenue. Through the upstairs window on Thursday nights, I watch a small, ephemeral mountain range building itself on either side of the street. Everything my neighbors have refused to hold on to that week—our dubious purchases and irreparable mistakes, the husks of daily life. On my pilgrimage to the curb, I've seen an imploding piano gusting sheet music like autumn leaves; an artificial lemon tree; a still-running Roomba vacuum cleaner, flipped onto its back like Gregor Samsa; family-size KFC buckets and like-new KETO LIFE diet books; a Lynchian arrangement of IKEA "Malm" dressers, the Stepford Wives of furniture; ferrous badminton rackets and mossy novelty bongs; a silver cage into which a wild crow had flown, sleekly pillaging some poor ghostbird's uneaten seeds; an unlucky vanity mirror with a lightning crack; a bucktoothed donkey piñata, mysteriously intact; red rubber galoshes, size 14, that made me picture a barefoot giant wandering into the rain; a crushed VHS machine next to a box of *Time*, a stack of unspooling tapes; a live bait cooler from which a dead prawn hung like a pirate earring; a child's Civil War diorama; many desecrated Swiffers; deflated kiddie pools in summer; toothy shards of sleds in winter; confusingly geometric sex toys in every rainbow hue; a flattened pyre of Fisher-Price tricycles. It amazed me, each Thursday, the sheer heft of what we could not digest, the aftermath of our appetites. Anja bent to stack her pizza boxes into a cheese-and-rain-cemented tower, while I arranged my bottles into a calliope in the blue bin. Ruby and indigo and emerald glass, so pretty in the moonlight. Sometimes I wonder if it was these jeweled colors that first drew the unicorn to our street.

Strange prohibitions govern what can be said between two neighbors, even friendly neighbors, on a slab of asphalt in haunted October. Anja claims that she knew I was pregnant before I did. "But I didn't want to say anything, Mauve. You weren't showing yet, and the beginning is so touch-and-go . . ."

The tell was not subtle. Anja watched me collapse in my driveway. Last October, I was dragging the bins to the curb under a jack-o'-lantern moon, enjoying the lullaby of the little wheels, when something twisted sharply inside me. Pain dragged me to my knees. Anja ran across the street to help me up. When I could breathe again, I walked down the hill to the Cloud Lake Pharmacy. I am almost certain this "drugstore" is a mob front. They sell hemorrhoid creams and medicated lollipops and almost nothing else. Once I'd tried to buy Advil and the sheepish clerk suggested that I try the Walgreens on Holgate. But, incredibly, these likely mobsters had a single pregnancy test for sale.

"What's gotten into you, Mauve?" asked Edie that evening. "You seem nutso lately. More than usual, I mean."

Something had, indeed, gotten into me. This new life marked reality so faintly—a watery pink line on a test. I held it up to the light, watching the pale line firm and darken. What a strange way to take the temperature of one's future. It seemed impossible that a life had planted itself inside me without my awareness. I had been moody and queasy, cratered with surprising acne, but these signs seemed far too subtle to herald a baby's arrival. The mildest augurs of a stowaway. I felt the mind-body split acutely that night, studying my thirty-nine-year-old face in my landlady's mirror. The glass stared beyond me to the night sky in the window, where a full October moon bobbed over my shoulder. Trick or treat, I thought.

Next came the cold thrill of betrayal. A positive result meant I had already been pregnant for several weeks. You'd think women would be alerted at the moment of conception, receive an unmistakable sign, like the crystal ball dropping on New Year's Eve in Times Square. We should levitate above the bedsheets; our eyes should change color. Instead, my body had behaved like a surly teenager—cranking her music behind a locked door, bass shaking through the walls, none of the lyrics intelligible. Why hadn't my body trusted me enough to say, "Mauve, we are pregnant"?

A line of poetry drifted back to me then, something I'd memorized in college for a grade and managed to hold on to all this time—"And of ourselves and of our origins / In ghostlier demarcations, keener sounds." To figure out the age of my possible baby, I turned to Google. Older generations felt connected to their foremothers by handwritten diaries, the ghostly wheel ruts of the Oregon Trail; I had Autofill. Millions of other women at this same phantasmal threshold, it seemed, had also typed my question into the search engine. Google directed me to a dubious oracle: the Pampers Due Date calculator. I plugged in my dates. The Pampers genie congratulated me: YOUR BABY IS SIX WEEKS OLD! The illustration of the embryo looked like a scowling pencil eraser. I waited to feel whatever you were supposed to at this juncture—something, surely. I realized that I was freezing, chilled to the bone. Perhaps I had been for some time. I went fishing in the hamper and borrowed two of Edie's sweaters, pulling one on top of the other. Out here I struggled to do a load of laundry, and yet somehow in the deep privacy of my body, an embryo had built itself a spine. It was braiding neurons into a brain. Soon it would discard the tiny comma of a tail, which was vestigial and marvelous, tadpoled between two futurelegs. With every heartbeat, I realized, a stranger grew stronger inside me. More human and more animal.

I was afraid to leave the computer screen, afraid to blink, as if I thought that by freezing myself in one location I could bring Time to heel. I would need years, I felt, to prepare for this pregnancy—an event that had already happened. For an hour or more I sat there, sick with vertigo. A belly growl broke the spell. I tossed the pregnancy test in the wastebasket; I'd been holding it midair like a demented conductor. Then I walked downstairs and began to eat. I opened jar after jar with the blank ravening of a bear. I stole and ate Edie's raw wildflower honey, which moved like liquid amber and tasted sweetly green and prehistoric—eating it, you could imagine crunching down on a trilobite. I sprinkled sea salt onto the black honey, picturing my baby's tail. Under my conscious mind, a longing began to spread—a hope I was afraid to speak out loud, even to myself. Was it possible I could be the mother of a child? A violent desire took root—and this time I felt it. I wanted to know my son or my daughter. I wanted to be this baby's mother. Later I'd remember this moment as a second conception, the one I was sober and awake to register, although no less mysterious to me. Alone in the dimming kitchen, I licked the salty honey from the spoon and continued digging, wrenching amber from the jar, waiting for my stabbing hope to dull.

When I finally called the doctor, the receptionist said breezily that they would see me in six weeks for my first ultrasound. The rider to this appointment lifted out of the silence on the line: *if you are still pregnant in six weeks' time.*

*

My first trimester unfolded inside green parentheses. A long-held breath, where I tried only to think about my baby in italics. *Your baby is seven weeks old today. Eight weeks. Nine weeks.* Your baby is the size of a pomegranate seed, a blueberry, a red grape. Every pregnancy chart I consulted compared the size of a human fetus to fruit. Figs, papayas, rhubarbs. As the weeks advanced, your grocery basket grew heavier: a lime at week eleven, mango at twenty-three, a cantaloupe at thirty-four, until at last there was a triumphant exit from the produce aisle. At week forty, the fruit bowl of metaphor abruptly disappeared, and the analogy sutured itself into a circle, beautifully tautological: your baby is the size of a baby.

Why fruit? In the OB-GYN waiting room with Caro, we debated this. Maybe, I said, the makers of these fetal charts loved fairy tales. Perhaps, like Milton and the Brothers Grimm, they understood the power of a seedling taking root inside a woman.

But my sister had laughed angrily and told me, "Mauve, don't give them too much credit. These charts aren't relics. Someone thinks that mothers are too dumb for the metric system."

For the past four years, I'd lived alone in the basement apartment of a house I shared with Edith Stone, a white woman in her early sixties who had grown up in Walla Walla, a lifelong smoker of Kools cigarettes and warm misanthrope. In our time as roommates I had never once heard her apologize to anyone, for anything, which I viewed as a feat worthy of a trophy. Edie was a kind of Social Olympian that way—she refused to dye her blue-gray hair and had a parroty rasp, and she said yes only when she meant yes, and no the rest of the time. She made enemies everywhere she went, including places where this seemed impossible, like the St. Stephen's Religious Bookstore where she worked. She was as dedicated to her God as to her vices. No nicotine gum for Edie. She lived with a bald-faced integrity I could barely imagine—I had grown up believing it was a woman's job to be the sugar stirring through life's lemonade, and I who often said "Yes" when what I really meant was "Go away," or in the more extreme cases, "Please don't kill me."

I asked Edie to be the godmother of my baby.

"No way," she told me. "How much longer do you think I want to stick around here?"

"Do you mean 'here' as in our house? Or 'here' as in life?"

"Both," she said, after a moment's reflection. "But rent is still due on the first."

I didn't see the unicorn until the tenth week of my pregnancy.

One Garbage Thursday in November, facing a curtain of lightly falling snow, I put my boots on and pulled the compost bin through the slush—a quiver of arrows that week, amputated cherry boughs. I'd rescued one of Edie's quartz rosaries from the trash, where it had snaked around the deadest branch. Too cheap to call an arborist, Edie had taken to hanging these discounted rosaries from the ailing foliage. Now our yard looked like an Uber driver's windshield. She bought them in bulk with her employee's discount from the St. Stephen's Religious Bookstore; she left a lot to God's care, and sometimes I had to step in for God with the pruning shears. At the curb, I stopped to catch my breath and stared up our driveway in time to see a feral creature lifting its pale skull from Anja's garbage. A single antler speared out of the middle of its brow. A deer, I thought at first, squinting through the fog. I had never seen a deer on Ninth Avenue before—certainly not in the dusk light of November, a blue hour when the porch lights switch on but the moon is unrisen and the northern stars are few and aloof.

Was it a snow-covered doe? Could snow cover any creature so completely, from ankles to skull, eyelids to hooves? The antler wasn't an antler after all. It was a horn, long and cetacean, white as the birches that stood sentinel on our leafy block at night.

"Anja?" I called shyly from my side of the street. Her windows were dark. Then I remembered Edie was volunteering at the women's shelter until ten, and so I had no saner pair of eyes to summon to my side as night fell around the Cloud Lake apartment complex. As far as I knew, I was the only person to witness this eerie scavenger as she cantered down our block toward the highway, an ancient piece of pineapple pizza dangling from her lips like one of Edie's cigarettes.

I decided not to mention her to anyone. I was afraid that I would chase her back out of time and into eternity if I spoke the word "unicorn" out loud.

Craving salt is a survival mechanism, said the doctor. But in you, it's gone haywire.

Cookies, kiwis, ice cubes, salad, bread, the webbing of my hands—I was salting everything. I bought a spice rack and filled it with garlic salt, turmeric salt, black lava salt, red chili salt, a keg of your good old-fashioned Morton's salt. Food became a vessel for iodine, and if there wasn't a shaker on the table I wasn't interested in eating.

Dr. Barretto told me that I was severely anemic, and that I should remedy this with iron supplementation, not an ocean. "Try cooking on a cast-iron pan," he suggested. Dr. Barretto was a portly Argentine man in his fifties who seemed to feel I was ridiculously old to be having a first baby. He always hit on Caro when she accompanied me, even when we spoke loudly about Caro's girlfriend, Nieves. He scheduled my delivery for July 2, and it astonished me to learn that we could choose my daughter's birthday. Because I would be forty in July—a *geriatric mother*, he kept repeating with increasingly angry emphasis, as if this were a punch line I'd failed to get—he would be performing a Caesarean section.

"Perform" is a disconcerting verb to hear in relation to one's surgery. It made me think of sad circus seals and belligerent stand-up comedians. Caro teased me about this, the medicine she mixes for me when I'm afraid; her jokes are more potent than anything the gangsters stock at the Cloud Lake Pharmacy. "Catch the June 2 performance—live, for one night only! Standing room only, your C-section!"

When I made it to week twelve, that spectral mile marker when a miscarriage becomes less likely, we had a small party. My sister bought me a Himalayan salt block. I'd never seen one of these things before, although she told me they were bougie fixtures in all her Vancouver friends' backyards. It was a twelve-foot-by-eight-foot slab of salt, crystal pink and twinkling in the night air. Caro held up a candle so that we could see the waves of rosy inlaid mineral. It looked like a mountain sunrise planed into a rectangle, or a doorstop for an archangel.

"Wow, Caro," I said. "Thank you. Where did you buy this thing, the Narnia Gift Shop?"

"You're going to love it, Mauve. Everything you cook on it will have your favorite taste: brine." She handed me a cookbook filled with pictures of raw meats sweltering on the sunburn-pink block. "It's also a present for my niece," said Caro, touching my belly. I'd been crediting so many of my strange appetites to this fetus, including the insatiable need for salt. Did these cravings originate with her, or with me? I no longer knew.

At another office, they did a high-tech new test. A vial of my blood disappeared into a sterile back room and got shaken down for information. "You are having a daughter," said the friendly, bored technician, a middle-aged Black woman with a photograph of twin girls in blue school plaids on her desk, and a yawning conviction about my baby's future reality that I wished I could feel.

One night at the start of my second trimester, alone in our yard, I bent to lick the salt block. I don't know what possessed me. The pink crystals scraped at my tongue. Under my rib cage, the baby began to kick. We developed a rhythm: *lick, kick, lick, kick.*

When I rose from the salt block, the unicorn had reappeared.

It had been hours since dinner, and the block had cooled, its color changed from sandy pink to Martian lake. The plants in the yard were a uniform blue. But the unicorn was lit unsteadily from within, flickering from white to gray, the wattage jumping each time she snorted. I recoiled in an awe that was also revulsion— what was a unicorn doing in our backyard?

"Deer are vermin out here," my boss, Steve, told me when I first moved to Oregon from Florida, eager to live closer to my sister and to work for a real newspaper. My boss was one of Seattle's jaded children—a transplant like me—an ursine white man with a combustible ratio of insecurity to entitlement. He seemed to find it hilarious that I was so enraptured by the sight of a doe and her two fawns. I could see them from our office window, grazing in the alley of daffodils beside the Willamette River. "You grew up with sharks and alligators, and you're creaming yourself over a *deer?*" (Steve's teasing could make even my hairline flush. He made a blow-up doll's face to mimic my stunned expression, fluttering his eyelids. I couldn't recall how I'd responded that day. Said nothing, probably. Possibly I'd laughed. I beamed a prayer of thanksgiving to the pantheon of deer that Steve was not my baby's father.)

"Girl," he'd chided me. "Put your camera away. Don't you know that miracles are regional? To us, a deer is like a big antlered rat."

Now I wondered if the same was true of unicorns in the west. Could a unicorn be rabid? Were their eyes always this feverish? I stared into her bottomless pupils and I felt dizzy with echoes, filling with some kind of primordial déjà vu; my arms shot out as if I were wheeling over a stairwell. As I crept closer I could see gray scuff marks on her hooves and horn; they made me think, insanely, of bowling shoes. Parts of her were emaciated—her wishbone haunches, her thinning white mane. The unicorn whinnied once, exhaling spume. Her rib cage lifted like a shipwreck at low tide, the long bones curving up with each breath, while her large belly swung heavily below her. It sounds silly to feel sorry for a unicorn, but I did then. Time pre-dates unicorns, just like the rest of us. Eternal beings, it seems, are not exempt from aging. The unicorn kept changing as she walked toward me. Like a hologram, she seemed to flicker between realities. Now she was a scabby trespasser, now an otherworldly traveler. Ordinary, extraordinary, beautiful, ugly, starving to death, and luminously alive. Each time I blinked, her status shifted on me. Even her shadow seemed to change on the grass, elongating and twisting, melting and transforming, molten with light.

"Oh!" I shouted like a *Jeopardy!* contestant, startling us both with my *eureka!* syntax, having recognized her uncanny condition. How had I missed it? "Are you pregnant?" I hadn't guessed that an immortal could get knocked up. I wondered what the gestation time for a unicorn might be: hours, centuries? Now I guessed the reason she'd come bounding out of the mists to nose at Anja's pizza boxes.

Cravings are ephemeral, but also undeniable.

She trained her dish-huge eyes on me and began to steadily blink, like a carpenter aiming a nail gun. If she'd hoped to bolt me to my shadow, it didn't work. I could still move, but I did so slowly, not wanting to scare her off. I took a few steps backward, snapping my fingers to beckon her to me and instantly regretting it—a unicorn is not a lost puppy. And I wanted to earn her trust. I wanted to soothe the concave ache that had driven her out of the ultraviolet and into the range of my senses. This hunger I believed we had in common, me and the unicorn.

Carefully, I negotiated backward through the shining rosemary, around the dented meteor of the BBQ lid, making my way to the salt block. I watched her lower her long face to the illuminated surface, which glowed more intensely by the second, brighter than the porch light, brighter than the cloudy moon. It was her phosphor, I realized. She had suffused the block with her strong light. In my own body, I could feel her blood pressure rising, iodine funneling to her starved cells. Branches were caught in her dirty

hair. I wished I had something else to give her: a garland of flowers, a heating pad. I smiled as I watched her purple tongue rowing
across the block: "So you're a salt freak too?"

On an ordinary night, our yard is a thoroughfare for tame raccoons and stoned Anja. I had never been visited by a beast before.
Her horn had the bioluminescence of marine life, and her tongue
seemed almost prehensile. She ran it around the edges of the salt
block, snorting with pleasure. Salt and thirst go hand in hand, I
thought as I turned on the sprinklers and watched her lap at the
whiskers of water. Then she shook a cape of droplets from her
mangy, magnificent coat and took off. She went soaring over the
hedge, knocking a few more branches off the dying cherry tree as
she disappeared into our neighbor Jessa's yard.

I was never a horse girl. I was never even a mule girl. The sound
I made to call her back to me was my poor ventriloquy of the child
actress in *Black Beauty*. It didn't work. She did not return. Did the
unicorn know I was not a virgin? Probably, I thought. Any stranger
could tell.

I'd grown up believing that I was infertile, and the hundreds of
uncontrolled experiments I'd conducted over many sozzled nights
seemed to bear this out. I had hosted boyfriends and girlfriends
and bartenders and AA sponsors and wizard-like poets and party
acquaintances and true strangers inside my body, and for decades
none of these visits had ever resulted in a pregnancy, or even a
"scare," as teenaged Caro used to call them. I had gotten a single
period at the age of fourteen; our family doctor had discovered
that I had a rare hereditary mutation. Everyone had seemed so sad
for me, even the guy who cut my mom's hair, even my aunt Rhea,
who loved her life as a happily single and childless engineer, and
so I'd had to reassure these adults that I was much more excited
about being a mutant than being a mother. The diagnosis was a
relief to me—a nonfatal answer to the case of my missing menstru-
ation. They'd sent me home with a peacock fantail of glossy bro-
chures, thin legends about married couples overcoming infertility.
"Help will be available, Mauve, when you're ready to have a baby,"
the doctor told me. But that day never came. I had never longed
for a child like some of my friends, whose crisp, adult voices went
doughy at the sight of baby hands. It was strange to feel this new
appetite growing at pace with the fetus inside me. *Fifteen weeks.*

Sixteen weeks. At night, I paced my basement bedroom, sweaty and nauseous, flush with the terrible hope. I felt as powerless over the longing to hold my baby as I did over the hunger for salt.

Garbage Thursdays excepted, I would ordinarily never spy on my neighbors. But that night I could not resist peering over the hedge to look for the unicorn. I saw Jessa's Jacuzzi and cheerfully unseasonable Christmas lights, and beside it the two giant raccoons that split their time between our yards. Usually these twin behemoths move in slow, panda-like circles between our properties, carrying greasy Styrofoam shards from the Lucky Devil dumpster in their mouths. Sometimes, I swear, they wave at me. I love their tiny, sleek hands, which make them look like lady assassins. Tonight, however, the raccoons were standing straight up on their hind legs, bristling all over. Had they just seen her, the horned interloper?

They stood shoulder to shoulder, staring forlornly down the empty road like tiny stockbrokers watching the market plummet. "You two look the way I feel," I told the raccoons. It reassured me to know that other animals also felt surprised by a unicorn manifesting on our residential block, and bereft at her disappearance. Under my navel, the baby woke into a somersault—she was most active at night. I loved the sharp surprise of her foot discovering my ribs. This alien metronome inside me.

"Come back anytime," I called softly over the hedge. The sprinklers were arcing water over the grass in liquid scimitars, unlit rainbows in utero. "I'll leave the salt lick out for you."

"Are you worried about people calling your daughter a bastard?" Edie asked me one warm night in the backyard, where the hedge shivered suggestively but kept its secrets. "Jesus, Edie," said my sister, but I laughed to let her know this brusqueness was just Edie's way of stamping a valentine. Her frankness makes me think of a lizard's throat—that bright scarlet bulging out, as irrepressible as life itself.

"No," I said. "Besides, she has the best aunt in the world. And the best . . ."

"No honorifics, Mauve. I can't be a godmother, OK? The houseplants are already too much for me."

At the twenty-week ultrasound, Edie and my sister flanked the bed. They stood there quiet as the Secret Service while the techni-

cian murmured, "Good, good, all good. Would you like to see inside
her heart? Let's count the chambers together—one, two, three . . ."
She clicked a long ellipsis against the roof of her mouth. "Four!"

"Fuck!" said Edie, who never whispers to be polite. Cigarettes
have thinned her voice. "Is four too many or too few?"

"Just the right amount of chambers."

We watched the pinprick of light that was the baby's beating
heart. It pulsed on the dark screen, the cosmically black screen,
and I shut my eyes between blinks and saw our unicorn's horn
moving off into the distance.

In mid-March, I harvested six sullen-colored cherries from the sick
tree. A week later, I nearly lost the baby. At the ER, the first doctor who examined me was cagey as a carnival psychic. "The pain
and bleeding may go away and you can continue to have a healthy
pregnancy and baby. Or things may get worse."

I was discharged and told to take a "wait-and-see" approach—
was there another option? I wanted to ask the nurses. Edie prayed
for us, Anja sat in silence with me on the basement couch, Caro
stayed over and made us dinner on the salt block: the baby stayed
inside my body, and after seventy-two hours I began to breathe
again. But the fear never left me. After that scalding day and night
at the ER, trying to mentally separate the six gloomy cherries and
the blood clots in the toilet bowl felt like pulling magnets apart.

Not an omen, said Caro. You read too much into the world,
Mauve. You think everything has to mean something. But you're
not the addressee on the envelope here, OK? Mostly, the world is
talking to itself.

I knew my sister was right, and yet I could not make myself believe her. A part of me felt certain that I had been punished for
trying to become a mother—for failing to listen to the world as it
whispered and shouted "no."

"Hope can be agonizing," Anja told me one Thursday night, three
weeks after I'd been discharged from the ER. "But you have to
keep hoping."

I was still pregnant, but Anja was losing her mother to a long
battle with ovarian cancer. We stood bracketed by our garbage
bins, staring down the hill toward Mount Hood and a wall of ad-
vancing rain. I wished the unicorn would come galloping into view

to frighten flowers out of the mud, to bring Anja comfort from a world beyond this one. I combed my memory for something true and consoling. In one deep pocket I found the lint of a half-forgotten poem.

"Hope is the Thing With Feathers . . ."

"Is that the Obama book?"

"Emily Dickinson. Wilin' out with the Capitalization."

I managed to reassemble most of the first stanza for Anja, the only one I still knew by heart.

"The Thing." Anja smiled. "God, I used to love that movie as a kid."

We riffed for a while: Hope is a dolphin's fin. Hope is a cherry lip balm. Hope is an unwritten Rihanna song. This week, your hope is the size of a mustard seed, a blackberry, a four-headed dragon.

Hope is a salt lick, I said. Muscle and mineral. Hope is a habit that the living can't quit. Anja was right about the verb and the noun of it. Hoping was nothing to romanticize. It was a necessary, excruciating activity.

I was thinking about the pink slab waiting outside our house in the rain. All the women in history before me who had tried to tempt a unicorn out of a glen. I was remembering the sound of my baby's heartbeat faltering, the lengthening hyphens; we had watched her ultrasound on a large black screen, the ER residents crowding in as if we were the football game. The ice-water voice of the weekend nurse who told me, "Your baby is performing poorly." The sound that wrinkling paper makes under skin, the disposable hospital sheet tearing as I swung my legs wider for another stranger's gloved hands. The melody of our tiny wheels on Garbage Thursday going up and down a thousand driveways. In the taxonomy of losing, these must be the two fundamental categories: those things we lose and believe we might find again, the sting of grief lightened by the hope of retrieval; and those losses that are final, insoluble, eternal.

April rains covered Portland in a steady mist. I reached Week 28, my third trimester, another spectral mile marker—even if the baby was born prematurely, the odds were now very good that she would live. At 4:00 a.m. when the baby and I were both awake, I prayed a two-word prayer to her pummeling fists, to her head butting at my ribs in the womb's windowless darkness: "Please, come. Please, stay."

I had not seen the unicorn for eleven weeks. Not an omen, I told myself in Caro's voice. She is an immortal ungulate. She has a life.

There are events for which I fear I'll never find language. Whole years of my childhood that have lost their magnetism, sending the alphabet clattering to the floor, a pile of symbols that won't stick to the door. Even talking to my sister, I often feel like a clumsy surgeon botching the operation—using the wrong-sized tongs for certain slippery red truths. I must be constantly underestimating and misreading everyone in my life if I can't describe one painful hour to Caro, or even to myself. Every human body must be a library of silent experience. Glaciers go sinking through us before we can utter a word.

But now I know that the unspeakable can also be beautiful. Delicately, deliriously joyful. Secrets can sieve through a heart, fine as stardust.

Here is a secret I am happy to share, even if I can only do so in this galumphing sentence, which is too coarse, too clumsy, too earthbound, too human for what I wish I could evoke: the unicorn came back.

I had no history of miscarriages, I told the first and the kindest of a rotating cast of ER doctors on the night of the blood clots. (I continue to see these in nightmares, dark red and gnarled as tree roots.) Yes, I'd confirmed when the doctor's eyebrows lifted. I was turning forty, and this was my first and only pregnancy. Gravida 1, para 0. He pushed his eyebrows down politely and hid his face behind the clipboard. He was a handsome Black man who looked to be half my age, his shy eyes lassoed in spearmint-green glasses. His hands were as reticent as his voice during my examination, prodding only where necessary, taking great care to avoid causing me additional pain. I told him that I was surprised to be a gravida too; I had grown up believing that for me, pregnancy would be impossible. The nurse who had been tightening the black cuff on my arm, a white woman with veiny hands and beautiful smile lines, paused to stare at the side of my face. "Would you have made different choices, honey, if you'd known you could get pregnant?" she asked me, with the mild, automated curiosity of a waitress inquiring, "Cream or sugar?" I answered honestly. I said: "I don't know." As I've mentioned, I haven't always been aces at safety. I had a history of "kamikaze promiscuity," as my sister calls it. That's a longer story, but suffice it to say that I have no interest in solving the mystery of my baby's paternity—the main suspect has already informed me he wants nothing to do with me, which is really the best possible outcome. I don't want to disparage the possible fathers of my baby, so I'll follow Thumper's mother's sage advice and say nothing at all. My daughter had so many arms waiting to hold her. My sister Caro, whose love is infallible. Anja, hostess of the best CBD pizza parties. Edie, who couldn't fool me into thinking she didn't love me and my baby.

We had the blessing of a unicorn.

And if our unicorn looked a little like a curbside sofa left to molder in the rain, a FREE sign disintegrating on its soaking cushions? Well, I thought, I'm no spring chicken myself.

At the OB-GYN, they treated me like an audacious cadaver. The twentysomething nurses spoke to me with a tenderness reserved for the terminally infirm. I began to feel so self-conscious about this that I bought a push-up bra and cream blush. "Uh-oh!" said Caro. "What happened here? You look like Mel Gibson in *Braveheart*." "Thirty-year-old Mel?" I asked hopefully, and she declined to answer. I wondered how the pregnant unicorn felt about her own growth and decay. I'm sure there must be ups and downs on the trampoline of eternity.

I didn't wash the Himalayan salt block before I cooked on it again. For the first time in my life, friends treated me like a master chef. My sister said, "You seasoned this perfectly!" Even Edie asked for seconds, then thirds. I demurred, shy with pleasure—I credited the salt block. I thought we were tasting her magic, but I knew better than to tell anyone about the visiting unicorn. Everything I grilled on the salt block had a lavender taste now, ineffably fresh and bright as graveyard bouquets. I wondered if we would all live forever.

Sodium chloride, I've since learned, can bring on muscle contractions.

On the night the unicorn returned, we both went into labor. Week 36—four weeks before my scheduled delivery, when my daughter was the size of "a large jicama"—I left the house to take out the trash and found myself drenched and speechless on the damp grass. Nothing I had read or heard about labor could have spoiled the surprise of my water breaking; for a moment I thought I might be dying. The unicorn was watching me silently from the shadow of the cherry tree. She chewed the bark off the sickly trees with the

nonchalance of an old pro; I thought she must have given birth
many thousands of times before. At one point, she craned her neck
over the hedge and dipped her horn into my neighbor's Jacuzzi,
purifying it forever. I considered lumbering through the hedge into
Jessa's yard, naked and hairy as the Sasquatch, and lowering myself
into the bubbling tub. The Portland water birth that nobody wants
to see cannonballing into their Thursday evening.

Then the unicorn shouldered through the thin branches to the
salt block, and I crawled over to join her, hunched on all fours, gathering my strength between what I realized must be contractions.
They seemed to be happening everywhere that night, not only in
my body. The black sky curved into an hourglass above us, opening
outward in twin parabolas, forcing the constellations earthward; I
waited for stars to fall on our heads like grains of sand. A warm,
mammalian calm filled me. My breaths synced themselves to the
accordion inhalations of the laboring unicorn. Anja's ghost lake
under the Portland streets, hidden moons and satellites, pregnant
strangers moaning as they parted the glass hospital doors, every laboring animal, bats dreaming under bridge trestles and matronly
whales skimming Antarctica—I felt myself expanding and contract-
ing in secret solidarity with so many near and distant bodies. That
night I drew as close as I ever have to the wordless domain of the animals. Carnality without estrangement, knowledge without thought.

Dead light came slingshotting across the galaxy; Edie's automated sprinklers turned on, dousing us with chittering water.
Whatever was earthquaking down the length of the unicorn's body
did not seem to frighten her, which helped me to welcome my
own spasms. (She seemed, if not bored by them exactly, casually
resigned; I saw with horrified awe that a coltish leg and hoof was
now dangling from her lower body.) Between contractions, we
bent and licked at the salt in tandem. I wondered if Edie could
see us from the upstairs window, if she was sitting at the typewriter,
smoking her Kools and questioning her sanity. Knowing Edie, if
she was still awake she would most likely be out here on the deck
shouting instructions, reminding me that she was not liable for
any injuries sustained if I was gored on her property.

As the unicorn shuddered beside me, I wondered for the first
time if she'd come to me specifically, despite my slovenly habits
and erratic employment and inability to apply cream blush at age
forty. Maybe so, I let myself believe. We had a powerful lifewish in

common. We had formed and carried the same heavy dread inside our minds. Eternal life is no guarantee, it appeared, of delivering a live baby. Her gray belly swayed, and I saw the unspeakable possibility shining in one inky eye.

I was too shy to stare directly at the unicorn, but I watched her in profile. The huge eye was all pupil, with the thinnest rim of violet around it. Soon I could only see her in flashes. Pain was blanking us out of the canvas. Her dilated eye swallowed me into it. A full moon floated in the center of the vanished iris.

My hospital bag was packed and waiting by the door. Caro had volunteered to drive me to the labor and delivery ward months ago, but I didn't want to bother her until things were further along. And I didn't want to leave now—who could abandon a unicorn? My own contractions were becoming faster and stronger, waves of hot crenellated pressure that pinned me to the ground. I could still sing, which I did. The O of my mouth echoed down, down, down, a wild guttural sound, threading through the tree roots and the ghostly lake. I should call Caro now, I decided, just before my body caved in on itself. Then I understood with a piercing shriek that I would not be having my baby in the hospital.

When I recovered from the final push, the cherry tree had split down the middle, and a new voice came wailing into the world. My daughter was born on a nest of sticky red grass beside a raccoon-masticated Frisbee and the balding rosemary bush, where the pink quartz beads of a rosary glowed like tiny berries. I'd awoken the entire neighborhood, it seemed, with my final scream. Six minutes later, an ambulance came roaring down Ninth Avenue, whisking panic out of the dark firs and the silent bedrooms with its spinning red siren. But the emergency has passed, I wanted to tell them. My daughter is here with us, alive.

What fresher salt lick exists in our universe than a newborn's eyelids? The unicorn leaned over and licked the angry tears from my daughter's blossoming, astonishing, ocean-blue eyes. Then she dissolved from sight a final time. In her place was a warm, blood-wet, tiny mortal. A verifiable miracle. Her fists windmilled everywhere as the paramedics put her onto my chest, her wrinkled face furious and waxy, ashen white as a Pompeii survivor. I was afraid she would vanish as mysteriously as she'd arrived. Diffusing into the void again, like the unicorn. "Please stay," I begged my daughter that night in the garden. So far, she has.

Proof by Induction

FROM *Uncanny*

PAULIE RUSHES OUT the elevator doors the moment they part, only to skid to a halt at the sight of his father's wife. She shakes her head, but he doesn't need the confirmation. If Tricia is out here and not in the hospital room with his father, it can only mean he has passed. He numbly accepts a hug from her.

When she releases him, a woman in a tweed jacket clears her throat. "Mr. Gifford, we are all very sorry for your loss."

"Thank you," he replies automatically, focusing on her crucifix. He swallows. "This is probably a dumb question, but what happens now?"

The chaplain draws herself up. "Now we all go back to the room where your father passed, unless of course you prefer not to." She begins walking as she talks. "You can enter into his Coda and say any goodbyes you'd like to say, or ask him any questions you have about his end."

Paulie follows her, wondering dimly if there will be fallout from the meeting he had to cancel with Professor Tappert. Paulie's father was a professor emeritus at his same university, so certainly they should be sympathetic. He doesn't kid himself about how this meeting was going to go, however. Tappert is on his P&T committee, and with his scant publication record and mediocre yearly reviews, his tenure prospects were already dim. They're even dimmer now.

Inside the hospital room, Paulie stares. He isn't sure what he expected, but he almost believes his father could open his eyes at any moment—except for the endotracheal tube stuck in his mouth. He's never been this close to a dead body before. Is he supposed to touch it or not? Paulie puts a hand on his shoulder; it feels like his father.

He grips the bed rail.

The chaplain gestures toward Tricia. "Mrs. Gifford elected not to enter his Coda. If you would like to, you can see him there."

Paulie eyes the console and cables behind the bed. "Is it really him?"

"Yes and no. The human mind remains aware of stimulus for up to five minutes after what we consider to be the moment of death. The Coda does for his consciousness what the rest of his telemetry does for his vital signs—takes a snapshot that we can look at later. The Coda allows you to interact with a simulacrum of your father, with his memories and personality at the end of his life." She gesticulates awkwardly, as though the topic is distasteful. "He can tell you if he had a life insurance policy, where the will is, things like that. The Coda cannot change in the way that a person can, however; it cannot learn or grow." Her eyes meet Paulie's. "Your father's soul is not in there. Your father has moved on."

It was early morning when Paulie put the headset on, but pre-dawn when he blinked into the virtual environment. He had only left the hospital to go home and get some sleep about five hours before the end. Now he could almost believe he had turned back around and found his father waiting here, as though the five a.m. phone call from Tricia were just a dream.

Gone was the endotracheal tube. The room was eerily silent, with none of the sounds he'd associated with the hospital from his visits over the past week.

He met his father's eyes. "Hey."

His father smiled ruefully. "Hey."

"Are you—"

"Dead?" His father gestured toward the inactive monitors. "Apparently so."

"Does it hurt?" *Are you afraid*, he wanted to ask, but he knew better than to talk to his father about emotions.

"Nothing hurts," he said, picking at a scab on his leg. "I guess they have a way of turning that off."

"Did the doctors mess up? Should I ask for an autopsy?"

His father shook his head. "Nah. I'm seventy-one, diabetic, and with a bad heart. You're not going to win any lawsuits here."

It occurred to Paulie that Codas could be programmed to give whatever answer benefitted the hospital.

Paulie stared out the window, over the parking lot, to the eerily empty expressway. "I really believed we were close on that Perelman proof."

"Maybe nobody's meant to find it."

Easy for him to say. He'd already been beyond questions of tenure and publication; now all of that was even more meaningless for him. For Paulie, though, Perelman would have been the home run his tenure dossier needed.

He turned back toward the bed. "Okay. Well." He put a hand on the chair he'd sat in last night while his father complained about his breathing. He should say something. Something like *I love you*, he supposed. But his father had never gone in for the mushy stuff in life, so why start now?

"Goodbye, then," he finished instead.

"Bye, Paulie," said his father. "Thank you for visiting."

Thank you for visiting. The same as he'd taken to saying every time Paulie came to him since his health began to decline last year. Paulie waited, hoping this time his father would say something more, until the moment dragged on awkwardly, and then he pulled the interface off his head.

"What happens to his Coda when we leave?" he asks, leaning against a counter.

The chaplain sighs. "The equipment will be cleaned and re-used, except for the actual leads that connected to his scalp, which are disposed of."

"I don't mean the equipment."

"No," she agrees. After a moment she continues. "The simulacrum itself will be digitally compressed and sent to a data storage facility."

"Will he be . . . awake?"

"He's not actually conscious now, so no, he will not be conscious in storage."

"Okay, well I suppose that's . . ."

"Mr. Gifford?"

Paulie lets his vision rest on the blinds, absentmindedly counting. Three straight blinds. Two twisted. Five straight. The rest in a mass, discrete, but not countable from here. Three two and five. Prime numbers. Two that add to the third.

"Can he think creatively? In the, uh, simulation, I mean. Can he do math? Can he have insights?"

"Again, that's not your father in there. That's a slice—"

"Yes, I know, a snapshot of who he was in his last moments. Last night when I was here he was arguing with the nurse about whether or not he should have to wear that oxygen mask. He was capable of thinking critically right up until the end."

The chaplain winces. "I hate to remind you, but he was mistaken."

Paulie nods. "He was no doctor, but he *was* a mathematician. Can his Coda still think mathematically?"

"I suppose, Mr. Gifford. I'm no scientist."

Paulie pushes off from the counter. "I'd like to take him with me. That should be possible, right?"

She bites her lip. "This hospital is affiliated with the Presbyterian Church. While we are not opposed to the Coda on a theological basis, obviously, our ethics committee has concerns when it comes to the appearance of attributing personhood to what should be a temporary means of gathering information and comfort."

Paulie crosses his arms. "If it's not a person, then it's data. I'm next of kin, so the data should be my property."

"Technically his wife is next of kin." She holds up a hand at Paulie's intake of breath. "It is possible to take ownership of the simulacrum, with proper paperwork, if his wife agrees. You would be billed for the computer and interface, and insurance will not cover the expense. But Mr. Gifford, I don't recommend it. The healthiest thing you can do is move on. Let go."

He meets her gaze. "Thanks for the advice, but my mind's made up."

Gina wraps him in a hug when she comes home from work. "I'm so sorry," she murmurs. "I assume you told Maddie."

"Yes."

"How did she take the news?"

He thinks back to his daughter's return from school. How much harder she took the loss than he, even though he's the one who lost a father. "Not well. She's up in her room."

Gina eyes the computer console on the coffee table. "What's that?"

"The hospital let me take his Coda."

"You mean—is he in there?"

"Kind of. Not really."

She shudders. "Wow. Okay. If this helps your grieving process, then I'm all for it."

"It's not about grieving."

"What, then?"

"The Perelman Hypothesis."

She frowns. "I thought you'd given up on that when your father retired."

"He only retired from lecturing. From office hours and meetings and committees and grantsmanship. You never retire from thinking. We were working on it together. It was going to be his last big result."

"Paulie, people have been trying to prove that conjecture for ninety years. Whoever finally does will be some grad student in their twenties, using techniques that don't exist yet."

"We were close, Gina. I know it."

She meets his eye and holds the glance a long time before replying. "And you think you're going to accomplish this by spending time inside a computer with your father."

He winces at the inaccuracies, but he doesn't correct her. "I think so," he says instead.

"Okay, Paulie," she says, though she shakes her head. "But do me a favor. Keep it in the den, okay? I don't want Maddie anywhere near it. I don't want her confused about whether Grandpa's really gone or not. Just let her grieve."

The hospital room was dark once again in the simulacrum.

"Hey. Thank you for visiting."

He nodded at his father. "Do you remember me, uh, visiting you here before?"

His father seemed puzzled. "You mean last night? Yes."

"No, I mean here in . . . in this thing. In your Coda."

"The last thing I remember is not being able to breathe, and my chest hurting like a motherfucker, and then I was sitting up with all the cables and hoses off, and you walked in."

"Do you understand that you're dead?"

His father nodded. "Either that or I'm suddenly cured."

"What's the square root of i?"

Paulie's father stared. "What?"

"The square root of i. In any form you like."

"Paulie, why?"

"I'm trying to see if it's really—" Paulie turned away, his fists clenched. "They say this simulacrum knows everything you knew at the last moment. This is something you could have done in your head."

"Okay, Paulie. One over root two plus i over root two. And its negation. Or would you prefer the answer in polar form?"

Paulie breathed a sigh of relief. "Okay, so I've been working on Perelman. Help me find something to write with." He started digging in drawers, but all of them were empty.

"Are you serious?"

He looked at his father. "Don't you want this?"

"Want?"

"We could still have that breakthrough. One last result to rock the mathematical world. Make everybody learn your name."

His father smiled faintly. "Your name too."

Paulie put a hand on the bed. "Your legacy. My career. There's something for both of us here. Do you have anything better to do?"

"I guess I really don't."

He returned to searching the room, but every compartment was empty. Nothing existed in this simulation except what could be seen on the surface. Finally he hit upon the dry-erase board the shift nurses wrote their names on. He pulled a cap off a marker and tested it, half expecting it not to work as in the real world. To his relief, it left a clear line on the board.

"That's not a lot of space," said his father.

"No," he agreed. "I can't bring anything in with me or take anything out, though. Whatever we come up with has to be in small enough chunks for me to remember and replicate in the— replicate outside. So it's just as well."

"Okay, show me what you have."

Paulie started filling the little board with equations. "We know how to generate particular examples—"

"Trivial solutions," his father interrupted. "Perelman referenced a dozen himself, in his publication. We can't enumerate an exhaustive set, though."

Paulie nodded. "Right. Now, before you went into the hospital the first time, we had taken the approach of looking for a relationship between the cardinality of the Ricci set and the number of solutions it generates. We started by considering finite sets."

His father rubbed his forehead. "I vaguely remember, but this was right before things went downhill."

"That's fine—I've been working on that without you, so we don't have to repeat it, we only need to figure out the next steps. I've been approaching it as a series, trying to tie the value not merely to cardinality, but to its h-value. This feels right to me."

His father perked up at that. "Not an equation," he said. "A series."

"Right. Call it H and see what it converges to as n approaches infinity."

Gradually the board filled with arrows and sigmas and integrals.

"I wish we had a bigger board," Paulie said.

"Write on the wall. What are they gonna do, yell at us?"

Paulie stared. "Goddamn, that's brilliant."

After another hour or so they hit a dead end.

"If we had a generalized solution for hyperbolic equations," Paulie's father began.

"We don't, though."

"No, but look up Brumbaugh Manifolds. Doug Brumbaugh was working on this the last time I saw him. He may have made some progress."

"Okay, that's something to try. I won't be able to hold much more in my head anyway."

"I bet if you talk to the company that makes this, they can find a way for you to email yourself from inside or something."

"No way," Paulie said. "I don't want anyone to know what we're working on here. I don't want someone to go find every mathematician who's died in the last five years and hook all their Codas up in some kind of screwed-up massively parallel computer and beat us to the punch."

His father's eyes widened. "Shit."

"Yeah. Only a matter of time before somebody else thinks of it, though."

"So you might as well be first?"

Paulie chewed his lip. "Do you not want to do this? Do you think this is wrong?"

He grinned ruefully. "What do I know from wrong?"

Paulie dropped into the bedside chair. "What's it like?"

"What?"

"Being dead but being conscious. Does it make you upset?"

His father shrugged. "It is what it is."

"You had plans," Paulie said. "You were going to remodel the house."

"Guess now I'm not."

Paulie gripped the bed's footboard. "Don't you feel anything at all?" He couldn't remember if his father had ever had a feeling in his damned life.

"Would it change anything?"

Paulie flips through images on a tablet in the mortuary office. "Somebody told me you had an option to put a Coda interface in the niche with his ashes, but I don't see that here."

Next to him, Tricia winces, but she schools it quickly.

"We don't include Coda ports in the regular lineup," the funeral director says, "but yes, it is a choice we offer. This is not a service that has caught on yet. Many people find the idea disturbing, as though we are preventing our loved ones from moving on. Or preventing *ourselves* from moving on. If you elect to equip the niche with an interface, you will have to choose the special columbarium we have set aside for that. It's, ah, not near the other niches."

Paulie glances at Tricia, but apart from insisting on a fancier urn for her husband, she's let him make all the decisions.

"Do it," he says.

At the cemetery Paulie kisses the urn, and Tricia does the same. Then he watches as an employee places it into the columbarium and closes the marble cover.

A minister selected by her side of the family drones on. As far as Paulie remembers, his father wasn't religious, but this isn't for *his* benefit, after all.

On the way to the car he grabs Maddie and pulls her into a tight hug. "You know I love you, right?"

She sobs and nods against him.

"You know I'm proud of you, right?"

"Paulie," Gina says, "you're upsetting her."

"I just want to make sure she knows."

*

"Hey."

His eyes adjusted quickly to the dark. "Hey."

His father gestured at the silent equipment by the bed. "Guess this is the end. I had an insurance policy. There isn't much, but it should pay for a cremation. Tricia should be able to find the paperwork. You're the beneficiary."

"Yeah, we took care of all that."

"Oh. How long have I been gone?"

He stepped over to the dry-erase board. "About three weeks."

"Then . . . what are you still doing here?"

"We've been working on the Perelman Hypothesis."

"Are you serious?"

Paulie uncapped a marker. "Don't make me go through it all again. It's fifty degrees out, we only have so much time, and I need to walk you through what we came up with last time. Trust me, you're on board."

His father blinked. "Okay then. Go ahead."

The clock on the wall ticked off seconds, while the hour and minute hand relentlessly pointed to eight minutes after five the entire time it took Paulie to run through the connection to hyperbolic equations.

"I reached out to Professor Brumbaugh like you said, but he pointed me to the Jagadish-Rajput conjecture."

"I haven't heard of that. Are they working on Perelman also?"

"No, they're working on node forms, but their conjecture is that hyperbolic equations correspond to node forms. They've tested several hundred terms using a supercomputer and they've all checked out."

His father shook his head. "How's that help us?"

"Node forms converge. Supposing we can prove their conjecture, we can use that to prove Perelman."

"This isn't math. This is grasping at straws. A supercomputer says it works—*so what?* That's not theory. Where's the proof?"

Paulie capped the marker, even though he suspected it could not dry out. "Don't you see? If the correspondence holds, then—"

"Are you trying to give me a heart attack in the afterlife? Do Jagadish and Rajput have the basis for a theorem, or just a coincidence they can't explain? Even Euler had conjectures disproven after three hundred years!"

"Well, fine then—" Paulie lowered his voice. "Fine. Help me find a counterexample, then. Or better yet, help me prove Jagadish-Rajput true, because *that* proof will make us both famous."

His father crossed his arms. "Fine. This conjecture is bound to have consequences for other node forms. Maybe a proof by contradiction is our angle."

Paulie and his father toyed with a variety of extrapolations, looking for a counterexample. At least the false starts could be erased—and Paulie wouldn't need to remember any of them when he got out of the Coda. All he'd need to remember would be a working approach, if they found one.

"The department voted on my tenure application this week," he said during a break. "They voted to advance it to the dean." Paulie suspected strongly the vote was not unanimous, which boded poorly for the next level of the process, but he kept that part to himself.

"Huh."

Huh? That was it?

"You could congratulate me. You could wish me luck."

"Okay. Good luck."

"Thanks," Paulie muttered. He added a few more lines to the board. "Maddie has a dance recital next week. She misses you a lot."

"Wish her luck too, then."

"It just . . . it reminds me of my piano recitals."

His father leaned on his bed railing. "Is that what this is really about, Paulie? Are you here to tell me I was a shitty father? I know. I already acknowledged that, after the divorce."

Paulie dropped into the chair by the bed. "No," he said at last. "Sorry. I keep thinking of what other people use the Coda technology for, and I keep waiting to hear you talk about something besides math or life insurance. I keep hoping you'll have something profound to say."

"I'm not the mushy type."

"You could fake it."

"You're the smartest person I ever met. You would see through any faking."

Paulie blinked. A compliment.

"I wouldn't have blamed you if you didn't want anything to do with me," his father went on, "after not being there for you as a kid. But then you made me a part of your life and we got along okay. You treated me like a colleague, so I tried to treat you the same. Now you're mad at me for not acting more like a father? I didn't think you wanted that from me."

Paulie waited to see if he would say anything else. That was about as close to "mushy" as he'd come since the night twenty years ago when he'd apologized for abandoning him.

After a quiet eternity, he got up from the chair. "Okay, well, I think I have enough to work on for now. I'll come back when I have some progress."

"Bye, Paulie. Thank you for visiting."

"Jesus, Paulie, I don't mind driving home, but if you puke in the car, you're cleaning it up."

Paulie clinks his empty wineglass against Gina's still-full one. "The free wine is the only thing that makes these parties worth attending."

She rolls her eyes. "*Our* holiday party's at the Olive Garden. You should appreciate what you've got."

He smiles. "I think that's what I just said."

"Just pace yourself, okay?"

"It's a deal."

She gestures toward the food table. "I'm gonna get some crudités. You should get some food in you too."

"I will."

As she walks away, his phone buzzes. Paulie takes another glass of wine from a server and heads to one of the standing tables.

His pulse quickens as he reads Jagadish's name in the Sender field. He skims the text, but the message is too long and too dense to try to absorb on a tiny screen. The sooner he can leave this stupid party and go home, the better.

"Dr. Gifford!"

He tears his eyes from the screen to meet the gaze of his colleague, Professor Hewett.

Her expression softens. "How've you been holding up, Paul, since, well, since your father?"

"I'm doing all right, María."

She nods and is silent for a moment, as though considering. Finally she plunges on. "How's your research going? Anything promising? I know a bunch of us have been hoping to see something new from you."

"Did I hear you say Paul's working on something new?"

Shit. Dr. Tappert. The senior professor changes course to join them as though pulled in by lasso.

Paulie chugs the rest of his wine, as much for a moment to think as for an excuse to look away from Tappert's idiot face.

"Yeah," he says at last. "I'm looking into Jagadish-Rajput."

"Oh!" says Hewett. "I met a Peruvian mathematician at a conference who was working on that. His name is Segami—you should reach out to him."

Paulie nods. "Thanks. I'll look—"

"Wait a minute," says Tappert. "I remember reading something about—please tell me you're not still tilting at the Perelman Conjecture."

Paulie's throat tightens. "It's a perfectly valid area of research," he spits out. He steps away from the table and flags down a server for another glass, hoping to lose Tappert in the process.

No such luck. "Dr. Gifford," the older professor says, resting a hand on his arm, "Perelman's a valid area of inquiry for a young man, maybe. Or for an old man, playing at being a professor emeritus. Not for a mathematician seeking tenure."

Hearing Tappert's disavowal of his scholarly value is all the confirmation Paulie needs. No way had he signed off on Paulie's tenure application.

"I disagree, Dan," says Hewett. "I have a lot of respect for people going after tough things. After all, that's kind of what math is about." Turning to Paulie, she adds, "Going after Jagadish-Rajput is perfect, too, because if you don't make it all the way to Perelman, at least that's an approach that can get you some intermediary results. You just can't go silent for this long a time."

Tappert shakes his head. "It's a fool's errand. Paul, I hated to watch your father waste his later years on this, but not nearly as much as I hate to watch you throw away your career. At least your father had tenure."

Paulie slams his glass down on the table. "I really don't need you to—"

A gasp goes up around him, and Hewett points at his hand. "Dr. Gifford!"

Paulie looks down to realize that he has smashed the wineglass and lacerated his hand. The moment he sees the blood, the pain sets in.

Some police procedural natters away on the big screen in the living room, but neither of them pays much attention. Gina makes incremental progress on her cross-stitch while Paulie rubs the label off a bottle of beer and lets his mind wander.

The officers on the screen, with their private dramas and backstories, make him think of his father—alive again in the hours Paulie spends in his Coda, and nonexistent when Paulie looks away. Or maybe the experience is more like a very lucid dream. Paulie hopes not, given how many seemingly profound middle-of-the-night insights have turned out, upon waking, to be nonsense.

Then again, he's basing all his hopes on the assumption that deduction works the same in-Coda as outside of it.

No, this is beer-fueled nonsense. The whole point of deduction is it works for any set of starting assumptions. It doesn't matter whether space is Euclidean or not—what matters is what axioms you proceed from and whether your logic is rigorous. A theorem that's true in the Coda is true outside of the Coda. And if it turns out this life is a simulation, as Paulie has seen posited online, Perelman is just as true in the reality outside this one. Even if it's simulations all the way up.

Induction. Paulie is certain that if the deductive process is solid for a reality n, then it is equally true for a reality n plus one. If he can prove Perelman in-Coda, he'll have his n equals one. He'll have everything.

On the coffee table, his phone buzzes with an incoming notification.

"Don't," Gina says.

Paulie checks his screen. "It's my work account."

"I know. I always told you it was a mistake putting that app on your phone."

"This'll only take . . . shit."

"What's wrong?"

"The dean's office updated my dossier." He swallows. "The School of Arts and Science denied my tenure application."

The television goes to commercials, the volume seeming to double. He can't think.

Gina strokes his forearm. "What are you going to do?"

He sighs. "I can ask my chair to appeal, take it to the provost, but as things stand right now, I don't see a reason why he would."

"What then?"

"I've still got a year on my existing contract. After that . . ." He shrugs. "With my evaluations and fizzling research, I'm probably not looking at a tenure-track position. I could teach community college or high school, or somehow find a job in industry, but . . . hell, I wouldn't even know where to begin. Being an academic is all I know."

She mutes the television. "Oh God, Paulie, please don't tell me you can't find something around here." Gina manages a nonprofit educational foundation. Paulie can't even guess at what starting over would look like for her. "I want to support you, Paulie, but you have to understand that's asking a lot."

"We've still got time before we have to worry about that." He takes a breath. "I still have one chance."

"What do you mean?"

"If I can prove this thing. Technically I'm past the deadline to add publications to my dossier, but Perelman is such a big deal, I'm pretty sure they'd find a way to let me."

She runs a hand through her hair. "Is this . . . is this about the math or is this about something else?"

"What else would it be?"

She takes a breath to answer, then stops and faces away. Paulie considers repeating his question, but then she looks back at him. "Is this about living up to your father? Or about proving yourself to him?"

He swallows. "It's about the math, Gina. It's always been about the math. We're close, I know it."

She nods slowly. "Okay. Prove your theorem then."

He stepped into the darkened hospital room. "Hey."

"Hey."

Paulie ran a hand along the back of the chair by the bed. "You got a nice, uh, write-up in the AMS *Proceedings*. A lot of mathematicians said some pretty amazing things about you."

"I'm not going to see it; makes no difference to me."

"No, I guess it wouldn't. You never were the mushy type."

His father chuckled. "You can say that again."

Paulie erased the shift-nurse board. "I know you don't remember, but we've been trying to prove the Jagadish-Rajput conjecture."

"The what?"

Paulie began filling the board. "I'll catch you up on the broad strokes."

They were approaching a point of diminishing returns. Every visit was going to have to begin with Paulie summarizing all their past conversations, as well as the work he'd done between visits. There would come a point where recap would take all the time he could reasonably spend in the Coda. Then he would really be on his own.

"We should consider a proof by contradiction, then."

Paulie shook his head. "I tried. It hasn't gotten me anywhere. I reached out to a mathematician named Segami, who's been working on a proof by induction, though. It's trivial for n equals one."

"Of course it is. Can you prove it for n equals n plus one though . . . Show me what you have so far."

Paulie cleared the board again, and filled it with differential topology, Vila Groups, and half the Greek alphabet.

"What about Suárez Theory?"

"How's that apply?"

"It's about group automorphisms. We might be able to apply it to these Vila Groups of yours."

"Walk me through it."

Paulie took notes while his father dictated, stopping to ask for clarifications or to offer his own suggestions. The little board got cleared four times—each time a chance to mistranscribe something or miss an assumption. But finally Paulie capped his marker and stared at their work.

"I think—" He swallowed and tried again. "I think we just nailed down Segami."

"Looks like."

Paulie wandered toward the window, with its predawn view of the empty expressway. Softly, hardly daring to say it, he added, "and that gives us Jagadish-Rajput, which takes us to—" Somewhere he had raised his voice to the point where he was practically shouting. He turned back to his father. "To Perelman," he concluded, in a more conversational tone.

"That's good," his father said.

"*Good?* Holy shit, we've slayed the dragon, and all you can say is 'That's good'?"

His father shrugged. "Paulie, I'm dead. The moment you leave, I'll forget we even had this conversation. I can't get all emotional about this."

Paulie sagged into the visitor chair. "What was your excuse before you died?" he muttered.

"What?"

"Nothing. Fine." Paulie met his eyes. "Anyway."

"Yeah?"

"I was just . . . I mean, I should go. Try to write this up before I forget it all."

"Makes sense."

"Maddie misses you," he blurted out. "And Gina. Gina sends her love."

His father nodded.

"Maddie had her dance recital. She did great. She was graceful and confident. She didn't get that from me. I was so proud."

"That's good."

Paulie stood. "Yeah. I should go . . . I was wondering if there was anything you wanted to say."

"Uh, bye, I guess? Thank you for visiting, Paulie."

Maddie squeezes cement on a plastic wing, making the clear liquid bead up.

"Not so much!" Paulie blurts out. He reaches for a sponge. "Here, let me fix it!"

"Dad! You said you weren't going to take over! This is *my* model!"

Paulie puts his hands up in surrender. "Fine, do it your way!"

Maddie frowns, chews on her lower lip, and attaches the wing.

He experiences an odd sort of reverse déjà vu, back to his first chemistry set, working through the experiments in the instruction manual—or rather, watching while his father worked through the experiments. Paulie winces and rests his hand carefully on his knee. Then he does the one thing his father never would have done. "You're right," he says. "I'm sorry. Keep going."

Maddie snaps the next piece of plastic off and trims a bit of flash from it with an X-Acto knife. "Mom showed me a vid about your, um, the math problem you solved. Are you famous now?"

He smiles. "Famous among a very small group of people."

"That's still something. I bet you feel super proud."

Paulie doesn't answer. He's not sure what he feels. After spending decades imagining the aftermath of proving Perelman, it's possible he burned out his ability to feel anything at all about it. The reality can't match all he imagined.

"Maybe I could be a mathematician," she says. "I'm good at math. Grandpa said so too."

"You definitely are," he says. Funny how his father could say to Maddie the things he couldn't say to him. Maybe it was easier when it wasn't his direct offspring he was talking to.

He squeezes her shoulder, the n plus one to his n. Just like he was the n plus one to his father's n.

Paulie frowns. What conjecture would he be hoping to prove? That mathematical talent runs in his family? That's trivial. He thinks instead about the things he wishes he could prove. Did his father feel anything for him like what he feels for Maddie?

Deduction is useless here.

Maddie holds two pieces together and blows on them to dry the cement. "Is it true the university gave you back your tenure?" She says the word awkwardly, like she's testing out the concept. "Does that mean you can't be fired?"

"It's, ah, a little more complicated than that. Close enough, though."

She swallows. "So we don't have to move?" She focuses on the model with faux intensity.

Paulie shakes his head. "We never decided that we were definitely moving."

"But now we're definitely not?"

Paulie picks up a brush and taps the back end lightly on the table. "We're . . . still talking about it." Still avoiding the subject, if he's being honest.

Maddie nods and attaches another piece.

He accidentally fumbles the brush. "How about you? What do *you* want?"

"I want to stay," she says. "All my friends are here."

Everything's so simple from her perspective. Paulie doesn't know what *he* wants. Since his proof—since their proof—passed through peer review, the math world has been buzzing with the laying to rest of a decades-open question. He's gotten informal offers from schools across the country, including a couple of top-twenty departments. And, sure, his own university. Does he really want to stay someplace that hadn't wanted him?

On the other hand, Gina has her career, and Maddie has her whole life.

He squeezes her shoulder. "I'm not sure what's gonna happen, but I'll make you a promise. We won't decide without talking to you, okay?"

"Okay."

"I love you."

"Love you too, Dad."

He entered the hospital room and marveled at how unchanged it still was after all these months.

"Hey," his father said.

"Hey."

He shivered, the hospital's cool seventy degrees feeling like an ice bath compared to the warm day outside.

"You're not going to remember this, but we proved Perelman. Here in your Coda."

His father's eyes widened. "Really! Now, that's something!"

Paulie nodded. "Got it published. Both our names are on it. It's all anybody can talk about—not just the proof, but, uh . . ."

"Proof by simulacrum? I bet that'll shake things up."

"So that's *two* things you'll be remembered for. I'm not actually sure which will have the bigger impact."

"That's something."

"Yeah."

The two men fell silent.

"You don't . . . I mean, you can't remember any of the things we talked about, can you?"

"I'm sorry, Paulie, the last thing I remember is not being able to breathe."

Paulie shook his head. "No . . . yeah, that . . . that makes sense."

"Did you find the insurance policy?"

"Yeah. It took care of everything. Thanks for having that."

"Good."

Paulie fidgeted with the rod for the blinds.

"Is there something else?" his father asked.

"No, I guess . . . it's exciting, huh?"

"I suppose. I mean, I don't get to see all that."

"I just thought you might be . . ."

His father inclined his head. "Might be what?"

Paulie walked around the bed. "No matter how many times I come back in here, you're never going to say the things I want you to say, are you?"

"What do you want me to say?"

"Never mind. Look, it's blazing outside. I have to get back in the car, or I'm gonna get sunstroke."

His father nodded.

"Goodbye. Dad." The word tasted funny on his lips; he didn't think he'd said it once since his father came back into his life two decades ago.

"Bye, Paulie. Thank you for visiting."

Paulie runs the air conditioner in his car for several minutes, letting it cool down inside. While he waits for the temperature to get comfortable, he checks his phone. The congratulatory emails tapered off weeks ago. In their place is a grocery list from Gina, and a drawing of a horse, against a backdrop of hearts and stars, from Maddie.

Finally he puts the car in gear and rumbles off, watching the columbarium disappear in the mirror.

CAROLINE M. YOACHIM

Colors of the Immortal Palette

FROM *Uncanny*

Lead White

I will always remember the view of Paris from his window. Snow, pure and untouched, softens the outline of the buildings and covers the grime of the streets. White, the color of beginnings. His canvas is primed and ready to be painted, and stark winter sunlight glows bright on his undead skin.

The studio is cramped, drafty despite the heat radiating from the stove. One corner is clean and lavishly decorated, the rest a cluttered chaos of painting supplies and personal effects. He studies me intently as I take in the room, evaluating me much as he did at the Café Guerbois when I'd first caught his eye.

I wait for him to ask how I came to be in Paris. Artists are so very predictable that way—no trouble at all accepting this pale immortal creature as one of their own, but a woman of my mixed ancestry? Utterly implausible.

"You should hear the stories they tell of you at the café," he says. "If Émile is to be believed, you arrived here as an ukiyo-e courtesan, nothing more than paper wrapped around a porcelain bowl. A painter—he will not say which of us it was, of course—bought the bowl and the print along with it."

"And the painter pulled me from the print with the sheer force of his imagination, I'm sure," I reply, laughing. "Émile is a novelist and can hardly be trusted to give an accurate account. The reality of my conception is vastly more mundane, I assure you . . . though it does involve a courtesan."

"A grain of truth makes for the best fiction." He waves his hand at a worn-looking dressing screen. "Nude, but leave the jewelry and the shoes. I'll paint you on the chaise. We'll have three hours in the proper light, and I will pay you four francs."

"Victorine gets five!" I protest from behind the screen as I get undressed.

"Victorine is a redhead."

I step out from behind the screen and go to the chaise, running my fingers along the elegant curves of the walnut frame. The cushions are firm and covered in soft green velvet. I arrange myself carefully. Hopefully he will like what he sees. Often what the artists demand is a relaxed-*looking* pose that is hideously uncomfortable. Like novelists, they require only a grain of truth. The rest is purely of their own creation.

"My name is Mariko, by the way, but everyone calls me Mari." As if I could pass for a French girl simply by changing my name. Though, particularly with the artists, there is a fascination with all things Japanese. Several of Hokusai's views of Mount Fuji decorate the wall behind me, the ukiyo-e prints crammed together with neoclassical portraits and a few realist landscapes of the Barbizon School.

He remains facing the window, his attention fixed on the snowy landscape.

"I'm on the chaise," I tell him, and finally he turns.

"Bring your left hip forward. No, not that far. Bend the leg a bit more, yes." He paces back and forth, frowning. "Turn your head to face the canvas."

I smile knowingly. "Like a Manet."

His frown deepens into a scowl.

"Don't like a model that talks while you work, huh?" I've posed for that type before, honestly not my favorite sort of job, there to be seen and not heard. If the artist is talented enough I can still pick up a technique or two watching them work, but—

"I don't like being compared to other artists."

I laugh. More of an ego than usual, this one. Though perhaps he's earned it. If Victorine was to be believed, he's been painting since the Renaissance. "Then you must paint me so well that I forget about the others."

"Tilt your head into the light." His voice is softer now, and he steps forward to cup my chin, shifting the angle of my head ever so slightly to refine the pose. "And look at me intently. Intensely. As though I were the one naked on the chaise."

His touch sends shivers down my spine. It feels as if he is reaching into me, beyond the surface of my skin. Intimate. I'm not above a dalliance with an artist if he pleases my eye, or if I need the money or a place to stay . . . but this one is different.

His eyes are as dark as the Seine at night, darker even than my own. I'm laid bare before him in more ways than my mere lack of clothing. The canvas is reflected in the window behind him, and he is painting me in deft strokes of vivid color—as other artists have done before him—but this time the image holds the promise of an understanding. His skill with the paint is breathtaking; his movements simultaneously wild and precise.

It is exhilarating to watch him work.

My back aches and one leg is going numb, but I'm disappointed when he sets down his brush.

"You did better than I would have expected."

"Oh?" I stretch and, still nude, go to take a closer look at the canvas. Even with the work unfinished, I can see that he is more talented than any of the other artists I've known, and his intensity sparks my interest, draws me almost inevitably closer. "There are other poses I could show you, if you like?"

"Hmmm . . . ?" His gaze is fixed on the canvas, studying a streak of bright winter sunlight that cuts across the upper corner.

I'm about to give him up as hopeless when he turns to look at me. I'm lost in the darkness of his eyes, drowning in the intensity of his attention. I can barely breathe, but I repeat my invitation, "I could show you other poses."

"Yes." He sweeps me into an embrace that is strong and cold. White. He is snow and I am determined to melt it.

The sex builds slowly, deliberately, like paint layered on a canvas in broad strokes—tentative at first as we find our way to a shared vision, then faster with a furious intensity and passion.

After, when other artists might hold me and drift off to sleep, he dissipates into a white mist that swirls in restless circles around the room, chilling me down to the bones when it touches my skin. His mist seeps into me and pulses through my veins for several heartbeats. I feel energized, an exhilaration more intense than watching him work, a connection closer even than our sex.

He withdraws, and I am diminished. I hadn't known until this

moment what I was lacking, but now I am filled with a keen sense
of my incompleteness. I long for him, for the sensation of vastness
I felt when we were one.

He does not return to the bed.

I sleep alone and wake to windows white with frost.

Viridian Green

The park is vibrant green with budding leaves and delicate spring
grass. Birds are singing, the sun is shining, and my lover sets up his
canvas on an easel in the shade.

"Must we really have those other girls?" I ask.

"You on your own isn't enough for a picnic," he answers.

"I used to be enough, all on my own." I sound like a sullen child.
I'm tempted to tell him that for composition's sake he should have
more models, some of whom should stand to balance out the towering height of the trees, or that the setting he's chosen bears too
strong a resemblance to Monet's *Le Déjeuner sur l'herbe*, which was
in turn inspired by Manet's notorious painting of the same title . . .
but instead I bite my lower lip.

"I'll let you sit in front," he says. "And I'll take you to the Louvre
afterwards."

I sit at the edge of the white picnic blanket, taking great care
to crease my skirt at an awkward angle. I open the book that I
have brought—*Orgueil et Prévention*—and I cannot help but marvel
at the degree to which Mr. Darcy resembles my immortal artist.
I shall have to ask sometime if he's ever made Austen's acquain-
tance, though if I recall correctly from his occasional ramblings on
history he'd spent most of the relevant time period in Verona, trying to hide both himself and his paintings from Napoleon's army.
Or was it Venice? I have such difficulty keeping it all straight, I
truly do not know how he is able to recall several lifetimes' worth
of memories.

The three models he's hired are chattering incessantly about
the latest fashions—tassels and bustles, hemlines and hats. The
three of them have no opinions of their own and are simply par-
roting some column from *Harper's Bazar,* as if Americans knew
anything about fashion beyond having the good sense to look to
Paris for guidance. They mock my choice of reading material and

attribute the poor taste in literature to my being Portuguese, and I do not bother to correct them. They will shun me as an outsider regardless, and I have no desire to make friends with such insipid tarts.

"Suzette, lean in towards Claire, yes, better." He paints a few strokes and then strides over to where I am sitting to fix the hem of my dress so it drapes more gracefully. He gives me a pointed look. I return his silent rebuke with a look that is halfway between "apologetic" and "fuck you for inviting these other girls." That might seem like a big range, but as a model I've learned to do a lot with my expression.

He laughs and goes back to his canvas without taking away my book—though my reading it will render my pose too similar to a painting of Morisot's depicting her sister—and these wretched girls make it hard to focus on the text. One of them complains that there are ants in the grass, and another that being in direct sunlight will burn her glorious fair skin. I try not to grit my teeth. I'm supposed to have a serene smile, as if this was a delightful picnic with friends. Self-absorbed, shallow friends that I have never met before and who will not leave off of talking so that I might read my book in peace.

Now the third has joined the first two in their complaining. He is quite clearly not painting their faces right now or he would tell them not to move their mouths, which would be dearly welcome.

"And honestly why wouldn't you try," the least irritating of the three is saying. "After all, youth is fleeting if you're mortal, but if you can get someone like him to turn you—" She waves her hand in the general direction of the canvas.

"Keep your hand on the blanket," he says, not responding to her words.

"He doesn't turn models," one of the other women says. "That one's been at it for over a year now and if he won't even turn her—"

"I'm right here, and I have a name," I say. I turn the slightest fraction in the direction of the irritating woman before I catch myself.

"Don't move your head," he tells me.

"Wouldn't it be glorious to be young forever?" asks the woman who had declared her own fair skin glorious and I wonder if she even knows any other words.

She's wrong, anyway. Contrary to what everyone assumes, I have never asked him to turn me. Not yet, not yet. I do not want to die into being forever young. If he turns me now, it will be so that I remain a beautiful object to adorn his canvas, and I have grander goals.

"Keep your expression soft," he says.

Only then do I realize that I am scowling down at my book.

"Wonderful, Suzette," he adds.

Suzette is younger than I am and has a classic Western beauty. Wonderful, Suzette. Wonderful Suzette. What will happen when I am too old to be his model? He remains forever fascinated with youth, and rarely paints women beyond a certain age.

I do not want to be the art, I want to be the artist. There are women who manage to do both, yet I hear them so often described as models who paint—and this despite the fact that their talent far outstrips the men . . . who sometimes do appear in each other's paintings, but never once do you hear *them* categorized as models. No. They are painters who did each other tribute and documented each other's lives in masterful works of art.

Think of the time I would have to develop my art if he makes me immortal. So many of my hours are lost holding perfectly still to be immortalized as an object in someone else's paintings. I want it desperately, the gift of so much time. But when to do it, that is the trick. Eventually he will lose interest and cast me aside, but if I die into immortality now I will be horridly young. Not to mention the question of children, which I do not believe I want, but I am reluctant to give up the option.

Suzette laughs, but I have lost the thread of their conversation so I do not know why.

What if I have missed my moment? If his fancy turns to this woman with her *glorious* fair skin glowing like a diamond against her emerald-green dress, where will that leave me?

By mid-afternoon I am hot and hungry and his attention is fixed only on his work, on capturing the grass and the grapes and the girls. I can smell the fruit practically baking in the afternoon sun, but I am determined not to move or even complain. I do not even turn the pages of my book, reading the same ballroom dance on an endless loop, angrier each time that the Bennet sisters are having a lovely time dancing while I am sitting. in. the. sun. not. moving.

"Take me to dinner when we're done?" Suzette asks him boldly out of nowhere.

I hold my breath.

"Oh, I'm done with your part now, you can go," he answers, not looking up from the canvas. "All of you can go, I have what I need from you."

Suzette flounces off, the other two models following her at a distance, giggling.

I let out a soft sigh of relief when they are gone.

"I'm doing the trees now, and then after that the bowl of fruit, so you can go with them if you like," he says.

"But what about the Louvre?" I demand.

"Another time," he says. "I have to finish this before I lose the light."

His promises are a perpetual first day of spring—like daffodils that remain forever buds.

Chrome Yellow

I have no trouble convincing Louis to take me to the Salon. He is both a painter and a critic, and *unlike a certain other artist with whom I have parted ways*, he showers me with attention and treats me as a person rather than merely an exotic object to be painted. We are quickly separated in the jostling crowd, for as usual half of Paris has turned out to gawk at the paintings which hang from floor to ceiling.

The immortal artist—and yes, I am sufficiently petty not to name him even now, for his artistic legacy does not need more help from me than I have already given—is here at the Salon, of course, though I am pleased to note that despite him having taken part in perhaps a hundred Salons, the hanging committee has placed his work poorly. Not at the ceiling, quite, but high enough to strain the neck should anyone wish an extended viewing.

"I was quite fond of Naples yellow," he says, speaking loudly to some potential patron over the general buzz of the crowd. "The paints now are so exuberant, which has its place of course, but there's a subtlety to the older pigment, and I do sometimes miss the ritual of mixing it myself."

His words trail off as I approach. Perhaps it is only my imagination, but for a moment his edges blur, as though he is fading into mist. Even the merest suggestion of it makes me ache with longing. He was stealing away my life, but in those moments, in that process of the taking, I felt so complete. And who hasn't chosen, at one time or another, to do what feels good in the moment, even knowing that they might live longer if they were more virtuous?

"Mari," he says. Only the name, nothing more.

The painting that hangs behind him is titled *Woman, Reclining (Mari)*. Being familiar with his other works, I know that the reason my name appears in the title (shortened and in parentheses) is not because he believes my name is in any way important to the piece, but merely that he has many other works that bear the title *Woman, Reclining*.

I study the woman on the chaise, illuminated by the bright winter light streaming in through the window. The painting captures things about me that other artists have missed. There is a wry expression on my face and a bold invitation in my eyes.

He has changed the decor of the room. Gone are the eclectic mix of ukiyo-e prints and neoclassical portraits that would have been the perfect background for a woman of my parentage. Instead he's created miniature renditions of his own paintings from the past several decades. The entire composition is a collection of his work, and my form is but a piece in this collection.

"What do you think of it?" he asks.

I shrug, knowing full well that his question is a bid for my approval and my indifference will infuriate him.

"I've captured you so beautifully, and your response is to shrug?" He knows that I am baiting him, and his voice is light, but he cannot keep his face from falling.

"Yes, I should be so very honored, to appear here in the Salon," I say, unable to match his lightness. "Naked, no less."

"Ah, so that is it then," he says. "You had another painting refused. This is the third time?"

"The fourth." I'd thought to hide that unpleasant fact from him, but he was, as ever, a keen observer. "My style is not so rigidly traditional as to please the jury. And I—"

"—have a great deal of company." At some point during our conversation Louis has jostled his way through the crowd to join us. He catches my dismayed expression and hastily adds, "But your work is far better than that of the others who have been refused, of course—"

"This is Louis." I interrupt him to make the introduction before he can start ranting about the failings of other painters. "He writes for *Le Charivari* and, as you have heard, he appreciates me for my art and not only for my looks."

"Good."

With that one word it is now *his* indifference that infuriates *me*.

"My latest attempt at pleasing the jury was a harvest scene of two women working in a field, deep in conversation—"

"Which against my advice you signed only as Mari," Louis interjects. "You should sign with your surname if you want the jury to take you seriously."

"My father's name has no place on the art he so thoroughly disapproves of. Besides, it would be too similar to Camille's signature, and you've seen how everyone confuses Manet and Monet."

Louis opens his mouth to argue, then thinks better of it. Instead he starts ranting about Monet, and neither he nor my immortal artist notices when I leave. Half the reason I had asked Louis here to begin with was to make my immortal artist jealous, and he does not seem to care.

I am invisible, even as my naked form hangs upon the wall. As a model I am a footnote in the story of the artist, and as a painter I cannot win over the Salon jury. What I want most of all is to be remembered, but I cannot even manage to be seen.

Vermillion

"Surely he will change his mind and paint you again?" I'm sitting with Victorine at the Café Guerbois, nursing my coffee as she sips absinthe. It is Thursday, and Manet is here, presiding over his Batignolles group—this is no coincidence, of course, for I am familiar with their usual schedule . . . and having parted ways with Louis, I could use the work. The smoke-filled air inside the café still holds the day's heat, and by all appearances the discussion at Manet's table is similarly heated.

Victorine gives a bit of a shrug. "Perhaps. And what of your vampire friend?"

My eyes widen. "Victorine! You must not call him that. People will think he drinks blood."

"As you like," Victorine replies, "but that doesn't answer my question."

"I want to be the artist, not the art. Surely you of all people understand." I take a sip of coffee and try to hold back my jealousy that she is taking art classes at the Académie Julian.

"You and I," she says, "do not have the advantages afforded to women of means and social standing. Morisot and Cassatt need not give music lessons or pose nude to pay for paint. Surely *you* of all people understand *that*."

I bristle at her tone but the observation is true enough. Worse, a young woman with fine features and a striking green hat has entered the café and captured the attention of the Batignolles group. Renoir in particular seems quite taken with the girl, who looks not a day over fifteen.

"What you need," Victorine continues, paying little mind to the new arrival, "is to make a connection with an art dealer. You've had no success at the Salon, but Paul Durand-Ruel has had some success selling paintings in America, where the tastes are less refined."

"What a horrid thing to say!"

Unrefined. My paintings? I should stay in hopes of getting work but I cannot bring myself to spend a moment more in her company. I storm out of the café, my mind churning with accumulated insults. Victorine's barbs, the indifference of the painters I had hoped to charm, the deplorable youth of the woman in the green hat.

The heat rising from the cobblestones makes the world shimmer, as though the air itself is melting. It reminds me of all the times my immortal artist turned to mist and everything around us melted away. I crave the cold white snow of that first winter, the thrill of his embrace.

I am on his street before I have even truly decided to see him, and I knock upon his door quickly, before I lose my courage.

He is there, and Suzette is not, thank God.

"I wanted . . ." I trail off into silence because I am not entirely sure what I want, and I am even less sure that he is the one who can bestow it. Recognition? Respect? A way to be seen as more than an exotic courtesan who graces the canvas of painters.

"Time," he says.

He is staring at me, dissecting me not into shapes and angles or light and shadow but deconstructing my ambitions and my dreams, seeing a pattern that I cannot because once, centuries ago, he was not entirely unlike me. A mortal artist, striving for something greater, grasping without knowing what it was he sought.

"Time?" I echo weakly.

"Where were you, before you came here?"

"At the Café Guerbois," I admit.

"Trying to secure work from Manet and his lackeys, no doubt." He scowls at the mere thought of Manet, which I find rather heartening, that even he, my immortal artist, is jealous of his rivals.

"I need money for paint," I tell him.

"Ah, and now we are back to time again," he says. "Immortality is, obviously, all about time. When you come right down to it, time is the thing that everyone most values, even you mortals who have so little of it. You simply shift it around instead of trading it directly. Three hours of work for five francs, which then can be used to buy paint.

"An art collector is hoarding time. Time spent by the artist applying paint to the canvas, yes. But there is more to it than that. Each successive painting contains something of the time that went into all the previous canvases, not to mention the time spent studying, practicing. And the art holds other time as well—the model that sits for the painting, holding a pose for hours on end. Time that she has devoted, perhaps, to keeping a certain figure, or creating an appealing hairstyle."

I scowl. "Time spent building the resentment that burns in the model's eyes as she glares at the painter."

He tilts his head, thoughtful. "Perhaps."

"The other girls say you have never turned anyone." The words slip out before I can stop them, my heart racing, knowing the conversation is in dangerous territory now, territory that I have always scrupulously avoided. "They say that you drain away your models' lives and leave them with nothing. That all you care about is light and paint."

"Light and paint. Legacy and time." He leans in so close that I can feel his breath against my ear as he speaks. "You have a good eye for light, and with time you could master the rest."

"No one tells Jean that he has not mastered the rest, or Jules. People praise them for work that is nowhere near what I do." I gesture at his wall, largely covered with the works of his fellow Frenchmen, paintings ranging from brilliant to mediocre. There is a sunspot on the back of my hand, a single dark freckle that I had never noticed before.

"Time," I whisper.

"I cannot give you everything you want," he admits. "But I can give you time."

This. This is why I have always been so careful to avoid this conversation. I have always known that he would offer. And that I would accept.

"Yes."

He dissolves into mist and seeps through my skin. It is different than it always was before. His impressions of the world are mine to take, not mere glimmers at the edge of my perception but a clear vision of his entire being, like slipping into a photograph that holds his centuries of experience, living through a lifetime in an instant. Everything I have thirsted for since our first meeting— knowingly and not—all of it is here in this moment of connection. I am complete as I can only be when he is with me, and I absorb all that I can, drinking from him as deeply as I dare, taking him into myself and pulsing with the sheer power of it.

There are but wisps of white mist remaining when I realize that I must let him go. When he withdraws he does not steal a part of me, as he always has before. Instead he leaves behind what I have taken.

He has given me the gift of time.

Energy courses through me like a vermillion flame. I am no longer a mere model from whom he draws inspiration, but an artist, immortal. Time stretches out before me and I long to take him to bed that both of us might burn hot with passion.

But he has vanished, just as he did that first night, winter white and cold. As he always does when I most crave his presence.

I wait the entire night, but he does not return.

Cobalt Blue

I paint the English Channel at Étretat, shortly after sunrise. The sun is a fiery vermillion and the water shimmers cobalt blue. It is roughly my hundredth impression of a sunrise, spread across the year on whatever days I can gather up the energy to greet the dawn with my easel at the shore.

I have painted skies both cloudy and clear, water in a variety of hues. When the tide permits I paint from the beach and include the white cliffs, and when the tide is high—as it is today—I paint the vast expanse of the channel from atop them. Sometimes the dark silhouettes of ships break the line of the horizon, and sometimes there is fog, a thin white mist that gives me shivers not entirely accounted for by the crisp morning air. Monet set off a movement with his *Impression, Sunrise*, painted not far south of here. Monet, and before that Manet, changing the world of art forever. Or so the historians like to spin the tale, imposing order onto the chaotic jumble of the past, pulling a single narrative thread from the fabric of time. Providing a focal point, like the bright orange sun that hovers above the water. And their focal point, of course, must always be a man.

"You could have painted a hundred portraits of me, and instead you paint the sunrise." Victorine has come up the trail behind me, carrying her own easel, which she sets up next to mine. Her hair is like the sunrise reflected on the water, vermillion streaked with silver. She arrived here last week, at my invitation.

"Manet painted the definitive portrait of you years ago," I say, teasing.

"And Monet painted the definitive impressionist sunrise," Victorine replies. "Yet you seem to have no issue painting those. Besides, *I* painted the definitive picture of me. They showed it at the Salon. Honestly it is unfair that you should be immortal and I am not. Clearly I am the one with all the talent."

Her voice takes on an edge of bitterness as she says it, cobalt blue tinged green, like the underside of a wave in the bright light of a midday sun.

"I would turn you if I could." I hadn't known how precious the gift was that my immortal artist gave me, or how rare—he had gathered time for all the centuries of his existence, and even so had only barely enough to share his gift with me. The process had nearly destroyed him, leaving him unable to take any form but mist for over a year.

"Then paint me," she says. "Give me that at least."

I cannot paint her without stealing precious moments of her

time, and I cannot bear to lose my oldest friend. She is already slipping away so fast.

"Please," she says. "Just this once."

I let her convince me because in my heart of hearts I long to paint her. I direct her to an outcropping of rock and have her look out over the water, her face glowing in the morning light. Her dress is a pale blue, the perfect contrast for the orange-streaked sky, and, of course, her hair.

The wind has freed a lock of it and when I go to pin it back in place the edges of my hands thin into mist and I can feel her energy, the wildness only barely contained beneath her skin. Where my immortal artist was cold and white, she is a fiery vermillion, and this neatly composed painting is entirely wrong.

"Let your hair loose in the wind, and take off your hat," I tell her, my fingers still brushing against her face, the tiniest sliver of my hands still within her, our energies pulsing together, her passions tempting me to drink deeper, to take more of what she unknowingly offers. So sweet and heady, this sensation of pulling her out of herself.

I force myself to withdraw and she gasps.

She stares off into the distance and for a moment I am not sure if she heard my request.

"Is that always what it's like?" she asks. "The thrill and then the loss."

"Yes."

Victorine removes her hat and takes down her hair, then tousles it—carefully but with a result that looks careless. The hat she lets dangle from her hand. Everything about it is exquisite, and I paint in frantic dabs of color to capture it before we lose the light. Victorine holds her pose flawlessly, and I know from experience how difficult it is to stand so long, especially in the sun. I highlight the graceful curve of her shoulder, the determined set of her jaw.

I have always signed my paintings Mari, but this painting of Victorine captures her with such honesty that on impulse I sign this one with a name I have not used since my mother died—Mariko. In red as a nod to tradition, but spelled out in the French alphabet for I do not trust my ability to write the kanji even for my own name. That, too, is honest—an admission that I am of neither world and of both.

"This is your best work so far," Victorine says, admiring the painting. "We can go in turns—you shall paint me and I shall paint you. It will be a series of a hundred portraits and historians will speculate about—"

"No, I cannot. Never again." I know the longing she feels. It was cruel of me to paint her. Cruel of me to invite her here, to ease the loneliness of being fixed in time as the world keeps passing on. And in truth, I hunger for her as much as she does for me, for the taste of her humanity. I can feel my fingertips thinning into mist, reaching out for her . . . but no. Already her life flits away far too fast, and I will not speed her to her grave for the sake of my art. I will find another way.

"I cannot stay, knowing what I will not have."

"Take the portrait, if you like." I turn away from her and look out over the English Channel, pretending that I don't care what she chooses.

She leaves without another word. She doesn't take the painting. The water stretches out before me, an endless chasm of blue.

Cadmium Yellow

My work is on display at the Art Institute of Chicago, thrilling for the venue but disappointing for the exhibit—Cassatt merits an exhibition composed entirely of her own work, but I am tucked away in *European and Oriental Art*. Still, they have invited me to the opening, and I have done my best to look fashionable though I cannot pull off the yellows that are quite popular this season and the angular lines of flapper dresses are better suited to women who are straight where I am rounded. Never have I paid so much for so very little fabric, though I must admit the beadwork is lovely and the freedom of movement compared to the dresses of my youth is divine.

The exhibit is laid out so that I must walk through the European artists in order to reach my own work, and I am startled to encounter a painting with which I am intimately familiar—*Woman, Reclining (Mari)*. It is, to my surprise, exactly as I remember it from the Salon. By now the varnish should have darkened and the yellows should have shifted brown, for he had favored the cheaper chrome yellow during that period.

"I had them restore it." He has appeared from nowhere. Like

the painting, he is exactly as I remember from our last meeting—only his clothing has changed. "It seemed fitting, given the subject. An unchanging painting of an unchanging model."

He means it as a compliment, but I am half a human lifetime away from being the woman that graces his canvas, and no longer mortal. To imply that I am static and unchanging simply because I do not physically age . . . I had thought him more insightful than that.

"I'm surprised to see you here," he says.

"And I you." I'm flooded with emotions. Surprise, yes, and also a longing that I thought I'd put behind me, that old, familiar yearning to connect with him, to let our energies flow together and feel the pulse of time itself. But I pity him, too, because for all his success as a painter, he is not keeping up with the world, and his popularity is fading. If he cannot come up with something new, he will be swept into the past as a historical footnote, or perhaps be forgotten entirely. "What are the odds that we would finally be in the same exhibit, after all these decades?"

He shakes his head. "What I meant was why Chicago? Why not San Francisco or Seattle? You could blend in there."

"The handful of Japanese living in Chicago are a curiosity, like kimonos displayed in a department store. People aren't as hostile to me here as they might be on the West Coast because they do not see me as a threat. I've taken up correspondence with a young artist there—Chiura Obata, who is doing some promising work—and he says resentment for the Japanese community there is building. Besides, it isn't my intention to blend in. I want to be remembered."

There are three of his paintings in the exhibit, and the other two both feature Suzette. Time has not been kind to these. The thick strokes of paint are cracking, darkened in places with grime, faded in others from light.

"Yes, but you want to be remembered for your art. Being so out of place will only distract people from your paintings—"

"And yet you are also here, some three hundred years older than everyone else." I tire of looking at Suzette, indeed I tire of looking at his paintings at all. I drift deeper into the exhibit as we continue our conversation, searching for my own work. It is quieter here, away from the growing crowd of patrons who have not yet made their way this far in. "Why must I blend in when you do not? Why is your story so much easier for them to accept than mine?"

"They can see themselves in me. Envision themselves as immortal. I am what they wish to become. You are the foreigner they fear. The outsider."

"And a woman besides," I mutter. "If I don't carve out space for myself, they will steal whatever inspiration they like from my culture and my art and erase me from the conversation entirely."

There is only one of my paintings on display, which I had been excited about before I'd known that they had three of his. My sole piece in the exhibition is the painting of Victorine, standing on the rocky shore, surrounded by the cobalt blue of sky and ocean, and seeing it I am filled with sadness.

"Have you seen her lately?" he asks. "Victorine, I mean."

"Not for many years, though she writes me letters occasionally."

"She must be very old now, yes?" he says. "She and Monet are the last of your mortal cohort. It is easier to bear after that, the fleeting nature of the lives around us."

His expression is sad and I wonder about *his* mortal cohort, the people he had known when he was still alive. He never speaks of them, which I thought was for lack of memory but perhaps he is trying to avoid the pain of his loss. I put a hand on his shoulder, cold against cold. When he does not speak further on the subject, I turn my attention back to the exhibit.

The curators have opted to hang my painting at the transition point, the very edge of the European artists, for though I am French—or was, at the time of the painting—they clearly do not see me as having been truly European. Worse, they have placed my painting alongside two others, not a trio of my own work but with a pair of paintings that share the same model—Victorine's self-portrait . . . and Manet's *Olympia*, which bears more resemblance to *Woman, Reclining (Mari)* than it does to Victorine.

"Of the three of you," my immortal artist says, "Manet has captured her the most realistically."

Of course he would think so, for he sees the world through the same male gaze that Édouard once did, antiquated and narrow, dismissive of women. To him, Victorine was a model and a prostitute, elevated only by her inclusion in Manet's painting. And I was similarly unchanging in his view, an object to be painted.

"All three paintings have elements of truth and falsehood," I argue, "for each artist comes to the canvas with our own artistic vision and personal biases. How we wish for the audience to view the subject, the context in which we are working, the details we choose to include. And what is truth, anyway? We cannot capture the entirety of a person's life on a flat piece of canvas. No matter how skilled the painter, there are only hints—suggestions which the viewer of the painting will fill in with whatever it is that *they* believe . . ."

I cannot quite articulate what I want to say; perhaps that there is no underlying truth at all, only a myriad of perceptions, each slightly different from the rest.

"Yes," he agrees, "that is exactly what you are missing, the ability to draw upon the perspective of the viewer, to give them an experience that is both familiar and new, to evoke in them a shared experience. That is the thing you must learn—to depict the universal truths."

"Your truths are universal but mine are not," I say, and he nods as though I am agreeing with him. "I've lived in two countries that do not consider me one of their own, and the lesson I've learned is that *I* must adapt, that *I* must learn to act as other people do. I did it as a young girl in the French countryside, and again when I came here. They will not make allowances for me as they have done for you—I am not permitted your eccentricities. I must behave as they expect, always, flawlessly."

"You say the right words, but you don't believe them," he says. "You are fighting the inevitable, the world is what it is, and you are who you are. It cannot be helped."

"But the world can change. It has changed. And so have I. You're the one fighting the inevitable, not me."

"There's no audience for what you do, this blend of styles and inspirations and . . . perspectives," he says, convinced that he can sway me to his way of thinking if only he can find the right words, the proper argument. "It's too complicated, muddled—like mixing too many colors, overworking the paint."

"When other impressionists were influenced by Japanese art there was an audience for that. Monet, even now, is painting a grand mural of his beloved water lilies, in a garden inspired by Japan."

"Monet's paintings are relatable."

Relatable. Monet filters the world through a background

that these art patrons understand. European. Male. He is relatable in ways that I will never be. My mere existence requires an explanation—how is it a woman like me came to be in France, why am I in Chicago and not San Francisco? If the story of my life focuses on the art it will be rejected as implausible, but if I pause to explain the truths of my existence the story is no longer universal.

Patrons and donors file past, many of them stopping to stare at Manet's painting, which is here on loan from the Louvre. It remains provocative even now, though there is less scorn and more admiration in the bits of conversation I catch. They barely glance at Victorine's self-portrait, or at my own painting.

None of these mortals has ever met Victorine, so the truth of the depiction matters to them very little. They only experience the art, whatever it might convey, and their attention is drawn to a naked form, a confrontational stare, a famous artist's name.

I don't need to capture the truth of my subject, I need to capture the attention of a broader audience, convey a deeper underlying truth . . . and I do not know how.

Ultramarine

It's a cold March afternoon in 1927 when a Western Union courier hands me the small yellow envelope of a telegram. It comes from a woman I've never met, though Victorine often mentioned her in letters. It bears sad news that I have known for quite some time was coming.

I had planned to paint the sunset from the shore of Lake Michigan today, so I force myself to go out with my easel, but the colors are wrong. Rosy pastels streak the sky above the water. Some other night I might have found it beautiful, but tonight I cannot think of anything but vermillion, and I let the light fade to the deepest blue without so much as opening a tube of paint.

The world has been a week without her in it, but her death did not become a truth for me until the telegram arrived. She is the last. Even Monet has ceased his endless paintings of water lilies, having passed in December. I've not seen either of them for decades, but tonight I feel the loss as keenly as if I'd sat with them yesterday, all of us gathered at the Café Guerbois, Victorine and I engaging the men in passionate discussions on the purpose of art, the role of the model, and whether critical outrage was an attack on the honor of the painter, this last being a topic that always irritated Manet.

They were my cohort—Édouard, Émile, Claude, Paul and Camille, and of course Victorine. I met them not knowing that I would outlive them, and without having the distance that knowledge brings. My immortal artist was right—I don't get quite so close to mortals now; I no longer see myself as one of them. But I'm accustomed to navigating a world I do not feel a part of, a place where I am unlike all the others. This has always been my truth.

I sit all night beside my canvas, a lonely vigil for the last of my cohort. The sunrise is reflected on the square windows of the city skyline. It's a fitting tribute. My memories of her life are fragmented as if by steel and concrete, everything but the fiery window-glass moments are lost to the passage of time.

I cannot paint the sunrise. Vermillion is her color and she is gone.

If my immortal artist is to be believed, I will grow accustomed to this. The pain that burns sharp within my chest will fade to a dull ache, not just for Victorine but for all mortals. Their passing will be easier when their lifetimes are but the merest fraction of my own. I will never share the length of history with them that I do with my immortal artist, and by comparison the loss of such shallow relationships will seem trivial. Or so he says. He is an ass, of course, and making excuses for his own inability to connect with those around him.

But the fact that he is an ass doesn't mean that he is always wrong. Those things he'd said at the Art Institute, what if all of it is true? Maybe my perspective is muddled with too many influences, perhaps I have failed to synthesize such disparate parts into a cohesive whole. Maybe the failing is in my execution.

I have outlived my friends, my colleagues, and for what? All my paintings combined have not garnered the renown of *Olympia* or *Impression, Sunrise*. I am best known as the model from *Woman, Reclining (Mari)*, and maybe my lack of success is not—as I have always told myself—because I am a woman and an outsider, but because I am lacking in talent.

Even being immortal, which should be simple enough, is a task that I am failing for I cannot bear the thought of stealing time from mortals whose lives are already so fleeting. I take just enough here and there from models—always with their consent—to maintain a human form, but if I cannot create beauty, cannot leave my mark on the world of art, their time is wasted, and nothing is so precious as time.

I've never done a self-portrait, but I am determined to purge these wretched truths. I paint the portrait and quite literally put myself into the work, thinning my fingertips into mist and leaving a sliver of my very being in the darkest shadows of ultramarine. I create the portrait in shades of blue, abstract and dark, shadows overpowering the light. I call the painting *Futility*, and I do not sign my name because despair is never done, it is unending and can never be complete. Critics will no doubt call it a feeble imitation of Picasso, but I cannot bring myself to care.

Alizarin Crimson

I'm still fighting the ultramarine depths of despair some fifteen years later, when I meet Joshua at the Club DeLisa. We get to talking, a fragmented conversation to fill the space between sets. He's a singer and he used to play trumpet in a swing band, up until he got caught in Chicago by wartime travel restrictions. Little Brother Montgomery and the Red Saunders Band are playing tonight, along with a comedian and some dancers.

"I love the music, but what really brings me here is the energy. It reminds me of the Café Guerbois—in Paris. I used to go there with some artist friends of mine, painters who wanted to push boundaries and create something new." There's something about him or the music or the energy of the club tonight that compels me to keep talking. "The way the musicians build on each other, changing the nature of music, it fills me with nostalgia. They have a passion that I've been missing for a long time."

He gives me a strange look. "You're one of those immortals, like Pops."

"Yes." I'd heard him play once, back in the '20s before he moved to New York. I hadn't realized he was immortal, but that did make sense of all the tall tales and inconsistencies when he talked about his childhood. I can't help but wonder who turned him.

"You must really be something special then," Joshua says. "Show me your paintings?"

"Only if you'll sing for me." I'm flirting without meaning to, leaning in close as we try to talk over the noise of the club. He has the same vibrancy the performers here have, and I long to taste him, to connect at a deeper level.

We stay late, almost until dawn, drinking beer and discussing everything from the gorgeous poems in Georgia Douglas Johnson's *An Autumn Love Cycle* to Archibald Motley's vibrant paintings of nightlife—both in Paris and here in Bronzeville. Our conversation turns to the war, and he talks about the delicate dance of supporting the war efforts while simultaneously pushing for civil rights for Black folks here at home; the *Pittsburgh Courier* was calling it "the Double V Campaign." At some point he mentions the Japanese internment camps, and we both go quiet for a moment.

"Must be hard," he says, "having family on both sides of the war."

"Honestly I've always felt more French than anything else. But I'm defined by what other people see, not by who I am. I have so little connection to Japan—to me it is courtesans in a ukiyo-e, brightly colored kimonos in Paris shops, faint memories of warabe uta my mother sang for me a long long time ago. And yet I'm still the enemy."

"Tell me about it," he says, and both of us drink.

Joshua walks me home, and I invite him to come in. I haven't had anyone over in ages and there is clutter everywhere. I scoop up fabric scraps from the assorted seamstress jobs I've been doing on top of waitressing to make enough money to pay the outlandish rent—so high it's illegal under rent control but who am I to challenge the landlord? And he knows it, knows just how far he can push and get away with it. Boarding at the Eleanor Club had been cheaper *and* the shared bathrooms there were cleaner . . . but I couldn't bring men home with me. I sigh. There are always tradeoffs. "Sorry about the mess."

He laughs. "You don't have to—"

"I do." Not so much for the mess but because I need to shift my focus away from his delicious energy. He is too much temptation, but I can't bring myself to ask him to leave.

While I try to tidy up, he studies the art on my wall. The oldest piece is a woodblock print, *Night Scene in the Yoshiwara*, by Katsushika Ōi, one of the few tangible items I have that belonged to my mother. I wait for him to guess, incorrectly, that it is my work, but he turns his attention to a far more recent piece.

"Is this?" he asks, leaving the question unfinished.

"The Tanforan Assembly Center." I set down a handful of empty paint tubes. "Chiura Obata sent it with his last letter. Sumi on paper. I'm not sure how he managed to get it past the censors, maybe smuggled it out with one of the couriers that brings him art supplies. He's starting an art school. I don't know how he can make art in a place like that."

"Maybe the art is what saves him, the thing that keeps him from breaking. Besides, if you wait for the world to be perfect, you'll be waiting forever."

He's right, of course. There is always something—a war or a plague, a widespread catastrophe like the Great Depression or the more personal tragedy of a friend's passing. Being immortal, it is so easy to put off the work, to drift aimlessly because there is no urgency without the ultimate deadline of death. "The frustrating thing is that Chiura can make art when I cannot. That he's stronger than me even though I'm the immortal one. I'm angry about the camps but I'm not forced to live in one. I have only the most tenuous ties to Japan. My mother died more than a lifetime ago when I was young."

"After Ma died, back in '37, I couldn't . . ." Joshua waves his hands as he searches for the right words, "I just couldn't anything. I'd open my mouth to sing and nothing came. There was too much joy in a cheerful song and too much sorrow in a sad one. Ma sang the blues like nobody's business, taught me everything I know. She was forty-three when she died and I was so angry with the world for taking her."

"I'm so sorry."

"Yeah. Well it's not about strength. Music is the thing that saves me, usually, the thing I escape to. But when Ma died, everything I tried to do reminded me of her, and the pain was still too raw."

"So what did you do?"

He laughs. "Enlisted in the National Guard. Powered through basic combat training. That's probably not going to work for you, Mariko. But mostly what I needed was time. I found my way back to music again, and you'll get back to the painting. That's where your heart is."

"How do you know, you haven't even seen my paintings—"

Then I notice what he's looking at.

Futility.

I never even tried to sell it, and I haven't finished a single painting in the decade and a half since I'd poured my depression onto
the canvas in blue paint. It's a painting of my heart, and my heart
is broken. The canvas isn't hung or even framed, it simply leans
against the wall in the darkest corner of my apartment.

"This is amazing," he says. "Powerful."

As he studies the painting—intensely, intently—I can feel the
barest shimmer of a connection, a faint suggestion of how it might
feel to take a fragment of his life, and like a shark frenzied by a
drop of blood in the water I am suddenly overwhelmed with need.

I draw him close and we kiss, deeply, bodies pressed together. I
tremble with desire and with anguish, for I am determined that I
will not consume him. "No, this is wrong, I have to stay away from
mortals. You burn so bright, so briefly."

"Are you protecting us, or are you protecting yourself from the
pain of losing something so fleeting? How can you paint if you
refuse to live?"

"I can't," I admit.

"It's okay," he whispers, his breath hot as fire against my skin. "I
want to know how it feels, how you feel. Live with me. Everything
in this one moment."

I slide out of my dress. "We can have the one without the other.
I've heard what people say about immortals, about stealing away
people's lives with sex. That's not how it works."

"Never?" He unbuttons his shirt.

"Almost never."

We have sex in broad strokes of fiery vermillion shading into
crimson, building to a deep connection, something beyond the
raw intensity of our physical passion. I transform into mist at the
moment of his climax and bask in his passion, his energy, his
health, his life. When I withdraw, I try not to take anything with
me, though I'm not sure I entirely succeed.

Unlike my immortal artist, I do not disappear into the night. I
return to human form and sleep in Joshua's arms.

In the morning, I start a new painting. A Black man, talking to
a woman who has her back to the viewer, both of them standing
under a streetlight in front of the Club DeLisa. The streets are
empty save the couple, and I paint the center of the canvas in a
realist style reminiscent of Edward Hopper, but as I move out from
the light into the shadows, surrealism creeps into the painting—

the buildings in the background morph into barbed wire and the full moon hangs crimson in the sky.

I title the painting *Night Club* and sign it Mariko. It is both bleak and beautiful. Chiura would be proud. At Joshua's encouragement, I sell it to the Art Institute of Chicago, along with *Futility*.

Full of life and finally painting again, for three months I am the happiest I can remember being since I became immortal. Then Joshua is called to service with the 370th Infantry Regiment. He goes to a training camp in Arizona. In his last letter before he ships off to Italy, he proposes.

I accept.

Zinc White

When Joshua returns from Italy, he brings me a gift. An enemy parachute, salvaged by a fellow soldier. He'd traded some cigarettes and a pair of wool socks from one of my care packages to get it. There are twenty panels of usable silk in the canopy once I've discarded the burnt bits. The material is thin and slippery and difficult to sew, but I manage to make myself a wedding gown. The color is a delicate cream, a beautifully warm tone—zinc white mixed with cadmium yellow and the barest hint of alizarin crimson.

It is a warm August afternoon, and raining, which they say is good luck for weddings. Ours is a quiet Sunday afternoon affair. A few of our musician and artist friends attend, and three soldiers from his company. No family because all of mine passed away before Joshua was born and none of his relatives that live near Chicago approve of our relationship. He wears his uniform and I wear my gorgeous parachute gown. Looking at us, no one would guess that I'm three times the age of my groom.

The cake is a cardboard cutout, but Joshua surprises us all by opening it up to reveal a stash of Hershey's Tropical Chocolate Bars he'd saved from his rations, enough for each of our guests to have one.

They are not at all what I expected, difficult to chew and far less sweet than what I remembered of the chocolate I'd tasted before the war. I must have made a face because Joshua laughed. "Why do you think I had so many left?" He lowers his voice to a conspiratorial whisper. "And these are the *new and improved* variety."

We can't afford a honeymoon but we both manage to get Monday off work and we spend the entire day holed up in our apartment, newlyweds basking in the joy of being together after spending so much time apart.

It isn't until I leave for work Tuesday morning that I see what has happened, sprawled across the top of the *Chicago Tribune* at a corner newsstand: *ATOMIC BOMB STORY!* The news is a stark and chilling white—the flash of the weapon itself, the coldness of a headline that speaks not of the people killed but of the power the American country now wields.

I let the white consume me. I transform into mist and careen through the streets of Chicago, then out over the vast ultramarine depths of Lake Michigan. Yet even here I cannot escape the war, for I find myself sharing the sky with warplanes from the naval air station, pilots training to fly in formation and land on aircraft carriers. Pilots not unlike the one who flew the plane that dropped the bomb.

What right do I have to feel this pain, I, so distantly removed? I feel guilt for being free instead of interred, for being American instead of Japanese, for failing to connect with my mother's country. Her country, never mine.

And then, Nagasaki. The city where my mother was born.

There are no words to describe the horror. I am only at peace when I transform into mist, mingling with the clouds above the city. It would be so easy to remain this way, to disperse in the atmosphere, to thin into nothingness. I am immortal, yes, but only so long as I choose to endure.

If not for Joshua, I might never have returned to human life. He is my anchor in the endless sea of time, my shelter from the nightmare storm of mushroom clouds. And I, in turn, am his calm harbor when the flashbacks hit, his comfort from the pain. We fight together against our demons from the war, stronger for being able to lean upon each other.

I paint Nagasaki in abstract, a monstrosity of crimson and white. It is passion and anger without form, in a style I have not mastered, and the result is garbage. I destroy canvas after canvas, unable to paint but determined nonetheless to try.

"Would it help to talk about it?" Joshua asks.

I'm painting over a ruined canvas, making it ready for my next attempt. I stop partway through, leaving streaks of color in be-

tween the broad stripes of white. "They're the only ones who start
with a blank white page. Their story is the default, invisible, a crisp
new canvas. Our stories, our history, our pain—that's color already
on the page and we have to work around that, we have to explain
why there's a burst of crimson seeping through where our people
bled, why there's a vermillion rage underneath the calm surface
of white."

"And then they'll tell you that they don't want your explanations because it complicates the story, sullies the art. They're always erasing the past—that's how they get that fresh white page
they like to start with."

"Like snow covering the filthy streets of Paris," I say, remembering the time so long ago when I looked out the window of my immortal artist's studio. I wonder where he is right now, where he's
hiding from the war, for that has always been his way, to withdraw
when the world of mortals was too intense or dangerous. "The
memories are harder to visualize now, there are so many of them
and they blur together. I suppose I wasn't meant to remember
more than one lifetime."

"You should write it down," Joshua says. "Tell your story."

"I thought they didn't want my explanations." I study the canvas, partially repainted.

"Since when do you care what they want?" he replies.

"Never. And always." I leave the canvas to dry, my previous failed
attempt still showing in the gaps. It is better this way, somehow,
with white to cover the things too horrible to bear. Pain avoided
and erased. There is truth to that, in the things we hide, the things
we omit, the things we do not even think to include. Words unwritten.

I title the painting *History* and sign it white on white, nearly
invisible, erasing myself before anyone else can.

Emerald Green

For thirty years I live an almost human life. I can't bear children,
but after the war there are so many orphans, and particularly un-
wanted are the mixed-race children, the children most like me.
We adopt Midori when she is four years old and Joshua is forty and
I am one hundred and six.

They grow and change and age and I—well, I don't age but having them as a family alters me forever. I learn more about Japan, my interest spurred not by my past but by Midori's future. She looks like I did when I was young, and I want her to have the connection to her birth mother's country that I have always lacked. I try to give her a sense of belonging to both places instead of neither—and it strengthens my own connections as well. Maybe what I needed, all this time, was an excuse to explore a culture that never felt like my own. But it seems fitting, somehow. As a tree grows, so too do its roots.

It trickles into my paintings, as everything always does. Art has a way of absorbing all that I am—in its content and technique, but also more literally, for ever since that ultramarine night of losing Victorine I always leave a fragment of myself in the paint. In one color of each painting, as the emphasis, a focal point. When I paint my family, I am in the crimson, the color of love and passion.

The mortals around me begin to see the truth in my paintings. It is the most miraculous of things, for as I pour myself into the paintings they begin to sustain me, stealing brief moments from the audiences that study them, only the tiniest sliver of time from each but adding up to eternity as my popularity grows.

Three precious decades, vibrant like springtime, warm as summer, beautiful and fiery even in the autumn, when I know that Joshua's eternal winter is near.

He is laid to rest in Graceland Cemetery. Whatever my immortal artist might say, Joshua is no less for being one lover of many, our marriage no less meaningful to me for being a smaller fraction of my existence than it was of his.

On a sunny spring afternoon, I go to visit Joshua's grave. I'm sitting in the shade of a cherry tree, reading the latest John le Carré novel—Joshua had developed a fondness for spy stories in his later years and sharing a book seems more fitting than leaving behind a bouquet of wilting flowers—when my immortal artist finds me.

"I tire of the endless cycles," he says without preamble, "the constant turmoil of the world."

We've exchanged the odd letter here and there over the years, but I haven't heard his voice since we'd shared an exhibit at the Art Institute, for he travels widely and hides from mortal society for years at a time. He can't stand such newfangled technology as the telephone or the ever-present cars, never mind flying from one place to another in planes. No, he travels by shifting into mist, he communicates only by post, and hearing him again for the first time in so long I am struck by how thin he sounds, almost hollow. Like an echo of the immortal artist I once knew.

"Hello, old friend." He hates when I call him old, and I love to tease him. As usual, he doesn't take the bait.

"There's an impatience in the mortals now, as they rush through their fleeting little lives, and all I desire is a peaceful time to paint. To retire to a garden, perhaps, as Monet did in his final years."

"Then find a garden, or make one." I remember something Joshua once told me. "If you wait for the perfect moment, you will wait forever. Even we immortals paint in stolen bits of time, for the demands of the world expand to fill whatever time there is, no matter how vast. We must fight for it. For art. For time. Even when our lives are endless."

"I am weary of the fight."

I realize that I can't remember the last time he's exhibited a new painting, and his more recent letters have not mentioned models or even lovers, only his travels. "You've stopped painting."

"You've finally won them over to your way of seeing things, your muddled mix of influences, that complex stream of new ideas and techniques." He stares at a mausoleum in the distance, and I wonder if the pillars remind him of ancient Greek ruins.

"I'm persistent," I tell him.

"Stubborn."

"Yes. And I've learned to care less what others think." I run my fingers over Joshua's headstone, letters and numbers cut deep into the granite, shadowed in ultramarine.

"Is that the man you married?"

"Joshua," I say. "He died a few years ago. I miss him dearly. But I'm glad he's here and not in one of those crowded city cemeteries like the ones in Paris with graves practically stacked one atop the next. He loved plants. Trees. Gardening was one of his many attempts to escape from the horrors of war. We had a beautiful garden out behind the house. It looks a mess now because I've never been able to create plants from anything but paint."

"He was also a painter?"

I shake my head. "No. A musician, a composer, a civil rights activist, and, for a time, a soldier. He was the one who suggested I take control of my narrative, preserve my memories in writing. I haven't quite the knack for prose that Émile did, of course, but I want to have a record of my past."

"You've kept your connection to the mortals," he says, his voice wistful. "Yours was the last generation that really moved me. The last to draw me in."

He speaks of my entire generation, but I'm better at seeing the negative spaces now, hearing the words that aren't said. No one since me has moved him, there is no one but me in his heart after all these years . . . and I have well and truly moved on.

I can't help but think how far we've diverged. He is tradition, isolation, stagnation—all things I see within myself but which I fight so hard against. It leads me to think about duality, the way we often divide ideas so neatly into opposing pairs. Artist and subject. West and East. Life and death.

When I return to my studio, I paint a canvas on both sides: one a lively picnic in Burnham Park and the other a funeral at Graceland Cemetery. The grass of both is a vibrant green, and instead of placing opposing elements on opposite sides of the canvas I jumble everything together. There are hints of death at the park, and life in the cemetery. Even the style of the painting is a chaotic mix of impressionism and realism, ukiyo-e and abstract expressionism.

I call it *Two Worlds*, and it is what some consider my greatest masterpiece.

Titanium White

The latest fashion in Paris is voluminous and flowing, with hidden pockets and hooded capes. A decade ago it was sleek minimalist cuts in patterns reminiscent of Rothko. It's fascinating to watch the way trends disappear and return, the throwbacks and the updates, the new combinations and perspectives.

The city itself follows a similar cycle, though far more slowly since a building is less easily changed than a frock. The arrondissement of my mortal youth is recognizable again, re-created as a historical preserve. They've managed to keep something of its underlying character, though the streets are far too clean, and the towering mid-millennium arcologies block the morning sun and make the light all wrong.

The Café Guerbois is a museum—a static re-creation of the buzzing artistic scene it once was—but there's a dive bar around the corner called le Salon des Refusés, where artists gather in their various groups and have heated discussions on the nature of art.

I sometimes go on Thursdays.

The new generation isn't weighed down by centuries of history, the experience of how far we've come. Their basis of reference is the time of *their* childhood, not of mine. They are at once refreshing and infuriating, and they inspire me to push forward—in my paintings and in my life. My once-immortal artist would have liked this bar, for the nostalgia of it if not for the modern conversations. It is strange to think of a world that doesn't have him in it.

The Musée de l'Orangerie houses the last remaining trace of his existence—*Woman, Reclining (Mari)*. The museum has continued to restore it for centuries, using the best technology and the most skilled conservators.

On the surface, the painting is much as I remember it, faint though the memory is. But he is gone from it, the paint that he himself applied replaced bit by bit like a colorful Ship of Theseus until little of the original remains. His other paintings are lost and have probably long since crumbled into dust. Poor Suzette. She'd thought herself immortal at least in paint, but that tribute is fleeting. History has forgotten her, even as a footnote. It's hard to imagine that once upon a time I'd been jealous of the attention he'd paid her, so many lifetimes ago. And jealous of him for being an artist when I was a model. Now his painting is preserved, not because it was painted by him but because it is the earliest known depiction of me.

Time eats all things in the end. Entropy brings everything back to white—a chaotic jumble of all the colors mixed together, if you paint with light. Now even my once-immortal artist has succumbed to the unending white. An artist must struggle to find meaning, to put order to chaos—and he no longer wished to fight.

He is a mist too thin to ever recohere; the strongest notion of him that remains is the splinter of his being that lives on in me. His model and his student, shining so brightly that I can never again be placed in his shadow.

In honor of his passing I paint *Entropy* in a palette of colors I mix myself, using formulas from both ancient times and modern, carefully applying the colors so the painting will change as it ages—chrome yellow that darkens to brown, red lake pigments that quickly fade, an ordivant green that will darken through emerald and into a deep blue over the course of several hundred years. I put myself into the titanium white, mist into paint, adding nuance to the crisp bright hue.

It is a self-portrait, though my physical likeness is not in it. It is a historical painting, though it does not depict any recognizable moment in time. Even the signature will shift, as mine has over the centuries—briefly it will read *Mari* before the rest of my name emerges. *Mariko* means truth, so this appeals to me conceptually: over time, the truth will be revealed. Then eventually the letters will fade until only the M remains. The details of history, given enough time, are mostly forgotten.

I have the Musée de l'Orangerie display the painting in carefully specified values of light, with strict orders never to move it, repair it, or alter anything about the painting or the room. Its true glory cannot be appreciated within a single human lifetime, but mortals flock to see it nonetheless.

And even now the doubt remains, the lingering fear that I will be forgotten. Perhaps the time has finally come to share my story. I've been writing it in dribs and drabs ever since Joshua suggested it, the words accumulating like dabs of color on a canvas. There are moments I choose to describe and moments that I omit, deliberately or otherwise. When you outlive everyone you've ever known, there's no one to remind you of the things you've forgotten, and no one to contradict your version of events. I find myself always returning to white. Beginning, again and again.

White

This is not the end. I'll leave my mark on the blank page of history, and I'll paint the world in colors so bold and bright they cannot be ignored.

There is beauty in my truth, and I have so much to share.

The Future Library

FROM *Tor.com*

18 August 2125
Kløfta, Norway

You wonder what this letter could have to tell you, because you think you already know everything about the Future Library. Who doesn't? It's the only story on NewsLens, every day, all the time. They're making yet another movie, and another virtual reality experience, and even a porn game. You can make anything into porn, I guess. Even forests. You've probably even entered the library's Forever Contest yourself, in the hopes that you're one of the one hundred who is selected each year, out of billions. One of the one hundred who will become immortal.

I didn't participate in the official documentary, because the whole thing was a lie. And also because I was in prison on "ecoterrorism" charges at the time. I put this in quotations on purpose. Because of the nature of my crimes, I had no computer access or right to be interviewed during my trial, or after. The Future Library's lawyers made sure of that.

It was a life sentence, until Gunnar came to see me at Ullersmo Prison.

Nothing is for forever. Not a life sentence, not a forest.

Not even the Forever Contest.

They have hidden so much from you, but no longer.

My name is Ingrid Hagen, and I'm the one who discovered that the trees can talk.

*

I'm not good at telling stories. I started out as an arborist, not a librarian. Leaves, sure, and roots, but words were never really my thing. Well, until they were.

I have to start at the beginning, so you'll understand.

I grew up in Oslo, in the Grønland area just north of the central train station. My mother went into labor early in the summer of 2050, when half of the Americas and a good portion of southern Europe were on fire. All the drought, and so much heat, they said. The icebergs had melted too much, the transportation industry was still using too many fossil fuels, and so on. It was being called the "Red Summer" then, because no one could know at that point that it wouldn't burn out before the end of that summer. That it never really would burn out, per se. It would just eventually run out of trees to devour. But it was still gray and wet in Norway in those days, and even cold some of the time. Some of my earliest memories are of begging to borrow my mother's iScreen so I could watch Operation Green's joint international effort to protect the rain forests.

I didn't understand the politics of climate collapse, being a child, but I liked the clips. The rousing speeches, the big tractors building protective fences around the land, the water drums being hauled from the cloud-seeding factories in China, where they could grow rain. And the arborists, most of all. They looked so adventurous, in their scuffed boots and sweat-stained neck gaiters, climbing spikes and ropes dangling from their utility belts. I would watch them shimmy up and down the trees for hours, until my mother demanded I go eat dinner or do homework.

By the time I got to university, arboriculture was a dying art. Earth's remaining trees were precious, but there were just too few of them to need many arborists. I had to go all the way to the University of Tennessee, in the United States. After graduation, I ended up in Brazil with the rest of our dwindling industry, trying to stop the mass extinction process there in the Amazon. But it was like trying to save a car crash victim with a Band-Aid. I have never felt wind so hot and sweltering as there, with sun that could sear your flesh through clothes—even in muggy Tennessee. I felt more like I was swimming than walking through the Amazon. Like everything was underwater, if the water was boiling.

We tried and tried, until Operation Green started laying us off too. All funding was being diverted toward stopping the CHA7-MRSA superbug that was decimating urban populations, and then toward the global air pollution crisis. We lost the rain forest.

Ten months later, I was in a grocery store back in Oslo—no, let's be honest about it all, if we're going to be honest about any of it—I was in the discount aisle of a Vinmonopolet, spending the dregs of my pitiful bank account on enough liquor to erase at least a full week from my existence, when I first saw Claire Nakamura.

"Champagne," I noted, mostly because it had been so long since I'd had anything to celebrate in my own life. Operation Green had promised that as soon as they resecured funding they would hire us all back, but I knew the day they sent us home that they never would. The rain forest, the trees I had loved, were gone.

"Is this bottle good?" she asked me in English. She sounded a little like Awhina, one of the arborists I had worked with in Brazil, who was from New Zealand. Claire was already incredibly famous by that time, a renowned novelist from Auckland, but like I said, words were never my thing. I didn't recognize her. I only knew that she was the most beautiful woman I'd ever seen.

"It doesn't matter," I replied. "If the occasion is good enough, it always tastes good."

That made her smile. "I've just inherited a forest," she told me. *Forest.*

"That's incredible," I said. It had been so long since I'd heard that word spoken aloud. Just the sound of it made my heart stir.

"That's not the reaction most people have," Claire laughed. "No one, in fact."

"I'm an arborist."

The skin on my hand burned with white-hot fire where she took hold of it—surprised, giddy. I can still feel exactly where her fingers first touched me if I concentrate. She smelled like salt, and the rain from outside the door, and ink.

"Do you believe in fate?" she asked me. She was joking but not really, I could tell. Later I learned it was that way with writers, that everything seemed like fate or magic to them, and it was always totally normal.

"I believe in champagne," I said.

It was a terrible joke, but it worked. Or at least, it didn't ruin my chance.

She bit her lip, suddenly a little shy, as if working up the courage to say something. Finally, she held up the bottle. "I was going to drink this alone because my friends are all still in Auckland," she said. Her eyes were deep, deep green, like a juniper in spring. "Do you want to come see my forest?"

I did. But to be honest, in that moment, even with the prospect of a forest, I really just wanted to see her. The entire train ride from Sentralstasjon, I held the fancy bottle for her, heart racing, my fingers gripping the neck of it so tightly I thought it might shatter.

"So, it's a forest, but it's *so much more* than that," Claire was explaining, breathless with excitement.

That's how I ended up working at the Future Library.

It might be hard to believe, because the Future Library is all anyone talks about these days, but back then, I'd never heard of it. This was some thirty-plus years before it would officially become a library, after all. The trees were still growing then. Just little saplings.

Claire had inherited custodianship of the Future Library from its founder, Katie Paterson, who had just passed away of old age. Katie started the project decades ago, back in 2014, nearly half a century before Claire or I was even born. Back when the world's forests were beginning to die, but there were still plenty. Claire had learned of the library herself because she'd been asked to write a novel for it. She'd come to Norway because she'd wanted to choose her tree.

You've read it already, of course. *The Song of Leaves.* The first book the Future Library released.

I'm getting ahead of myself.

Katie Paterson originally created the Future Library as a literary and environmental public art project, before the board twisted it into what it is now. After receiving approval from the Norwegian government, she came from Fife to purchase several acres of land in Nordmarka Forest, a few hours north of Oslo. There, she planted one thousand Norwegian spruce trees—*Picea abies*, known and harvested for their quality wood, for obvious reasons—in addition to continuing to care for the thousands of juvenile birch, *Betula pubescens*, and pine, *Pinus sylvestris*, already flourishing in the area. Then she began inviting the authors.

The idea, Claire had said that night as we walked between the dark trees, our only light the moon and the tiny beams from our phones, was to convince one hundred authors to each write one new work, to remain unpublished and unread, and held in trust by the Future Library for a hundred years. At the end of those one hundred years, in the Spring of 2114, long after the authors and Katie Paterson herself would have passed away, the new custodians of the Future Library would cut down one hundred of the thousand trees she had planted, and print these one hundred books on the paper made from their wood for future generations to read.

The authors were free to write whatever they wanted, with "a thematic emphasis on imagination and time," Claire explained as she popped the cork off the champagne, her smile so beautiful. She was the fifty-seventh author invited to write for the Future Library—one of the last ones Katie Paterson had selected before she died in the early 2070s—but she was the first one to ask to come to the forest to choose the tree that would become her book. By the end of Claire's short trip, the aging and ailing Katie had already decided to hand over custodianship of the Future Library to her.

Claire went home to pack up her life into a suitcase and apply for a Norwegian residency visa. It wasn't but a few more months before the Future Library's secretary Ikká called her with the news that Katie had passed away in her sleep.

Even with the partial travel bans due to the canine-avian-equine influenza outbreak from Greece, Claire could not be stopped. She made it back to Oslo after a forty-hour, six-transfer journey and a twelve-hour wait at the border, plus two temperature tests, three blood draws, four nasal swabs, and a ten-day wrist tracker in lieu of a quarantine. Her first stop, after not having slept for nearly two full days, was that Vinmonopolet.

There was no sign on Claire's tree, the one that would be for her book—nothing to mark it out from the others in the grove—but I burned its shape into my mind after that first night. It was one of the newer Norwegian spruce saplings, one of the many planted by Katie, in a particularly sunny clearing. Good sun exposure through the canopy, excellent root spread, and ample shelter from the wind, even being as deep into the north of the forest as it was.

"What do you think?" Claire asked, leaning back against the bark of its trunk and grinning up at me. Dawn was breaking, just enough that we could see each other in the muted glow of the sunrise without our phones anymore.

I wanted to ask her to marry me. Instead, I asked her for a job.

"Trunk measurements, leaf samples, soil pH, all of it requires very precise knowledge and experience," I bragged desperately. "I would check every sapling every single day, from root to tip."

I tried to make it all sound as serious as possible, but it was sort of a lie. The trees in Nordmarka were exceptionally healthy, even with the Amazon already dead ash, and forests in Earth's subtropical and temperate zones withering. But I worried if I told her that I already wanted to be with her for the rest of our lives, it would have spooked her. We'd known each other all of eight hours.

Then again, maybe not. She was the one who believed in magic, and fate.

She was the one who kissed me first.

We were never apart from each other after that. We took the train back to Oslo the next day so I could pack my clothes and give up my apartment, and then I moved into the library's modest residential cabins just outside the forest, into the one beside Claire's. Three months later, I moved into hers, and six months after that we married, right there among the trees, with her favorite librarian, Gunnar, officiating.

For three decades I had her as my wife, and I had the forest as its head arborist. During the days, Claire would be wrapped up in a cardigan in her office, she and her librarians nearly hidden by their piles of books and papers and stacked mugs of tea, and I would be outside with the other arborists, covered in mud, climbing up and down our trees. At night, we would sit together in front of the fire, and she would tell me everything about her side of the library's work, about words and stories and books, and I would tell her everything about mine, about roots and rain and leaves.

It was perfect.

Sometimes I can't believe how quickly it went, and sometimes I can't believe I was ever allowed to have been so happy for so long.

I'm sorry. It's just that when I think of Claire, even now, it's hard to think of anything else.

If you go back into the news archives to look for mentions, mostly no one cared about the Future Library project in the beginning. It was something that no one alive in 2014 would still be around to see. But by the late 2090s, when the Future Library was only about twenty-five years away from maturing, suddenly a quarter of a century didn't seem so long. Visits to the forest ticked up, and literary outlets began to run culture articles. Someone even created a countdown people could keep running in the corners of their NewsLens devices. I did not, because it bothered my view when climbing, but Claire did. She would tell me the count first thing every morning even though we both had it memorized, giggling gleefully as she snatched her NewsLens off the nightstand to peer through it at me.

"Are you sure you can do it?" she asked me, exactly one year before the Future Library was to officially open. Her voice had grown so weak by then, it was barely more than a breath.

Earlier that afternoon, I had taken the train from Frognerseteren Station back to Oslo, to buy the same champagne from the same Vinmonopolet where we'd met half a lifetime ago and bring it back. At this time next spring, my arborists would begin to fell the trees of the first authors, and prepare the logs to be processed into paper, so their words could be printed.

And Claire would not be there to see it.

"I promise," I assured her.

Before, I had meant it. The library was her dream. I could have allowed them to cut down the one hundred trees destined for their books and been at peace tending to the rest of the forest that remained. I could have done it together with her.

But now . . .

Claire tried to take the tiniest sip from her glass, and gave up.

I could tell she didn't believe me, either. She had watched me care for the trees every day for three decades, as closely as a mother might care for her children. And she knew how even more precious those trees had become. By that point, early 2113, Nordmarka was the last forest remaining in the world, and had been for some time. The Valdivian rain forest in Argentina and Chile, the Miombo Woodlands in central Africa, Arashiyama Grove in Japan, all gone. We'd heard that in the hermetically sealed bio-vaults in the New Tsimshian Collective in former western Canada, there were a handful of lab-grown saplings struggling to put down roots in the synthetically enhanced soil substitute the Tsimshian botanists were trying to perfect, but they always curled inward and died a few years after germination. Outside their vaults, the last scattered wild specimens that had survived whatever killed their forests had also slowly weakened and shriveled to husks, despite the UNEP's best efforts to save them. Every so often there would be a report of a living tree, but it always turned out to be a mistake, or a hoax. The ground was just too poisoned, the rain nonexistent, the sun too corrupting.

Nordmarka was truly all that was left. Every tree that remained in the world lived in the Future Library.

"It's all a cycle," I finally said. Gunnar, whom Claire had chosen to take over management of the library for her, set the syringes and IV bundle down on the table beside us, and kissed her on the forehead before withdrawing to wait with the physician outside the room.

Her lung cancer had become so bad that she could no longer bear it. Not for even one more night, let alone one more year. The Crackles, they were now calling it, because of the sound. Without the rest of the world's forests to help Nordmarka clean the air, the PM2.5 particles were so dense that even with respirator masks, which were at a shortage anyway, the Crackles had become an international epidemic.

"All things must grow, and then die, so that new things can grow. No tree can live forever, just as no person can," I told her, taking her hand.

"But a book could, my love," she whispered desperately.

I knew what Claire was hoping. She was hoping that a year from then, when her tree fell and they turned it into her book, that when I finally held a copy of it in my hands I would feel that I had the last piece of her, after she'd gone.

But I already had the last piece of her, in her tree.

It was not that I loved the forest more than I loved her. It was that to me, they were one and the same.

"For Claire," Gunnar said to me a year later, the day of the Future Library's opening, as we stood in the early morning light on a make-shift stage. The audience clapped while my arborists waited beside us, handsaws politely clutched behind their backs. Gunnar and the librarians had decided we would start with her tree, to pay respects to her. Her book would be the first one the library would publish.

"For Claire," I echoed.

I had walked us to the far shady corner of the Future Library's grove at dawn that morning, where the roots ran close together and the branches of the sibling spruce brushed against each other in the breeze. I had pointed out the tree they would cut, and Gunnar tied a little gold ribbon around one of the low branches, so they could find it again with all the press watching.

They did not know this forest like I do.

"You're sure you're all right?" he asked again.

"I am," I said, as the saws began.

I was crying, and he squeezed my hand, and I saw that his eyes were shimmering too.

"You'll get the first copy," he told me as the trunk began to bend.

It wasn't until that first tree toppled, and we saw the exposed rings of its inner wood, that everything fell apart.

Here is the first thing they have hidden from you: the idea to plant the authors' remains in the dirt under each tree was mine.

The official Future Library website gives credit to Claire. Which is fine. She was the one who did the work to make the whole thing happen. We'd been together a few years by that time, and even though she'd just been diagnosed with her Crackles, she was busier than ever finishing her list of the remaining authors to ask to write a book for the Future Library, looking for new and interesting voices, and I was busy caring for the saplings. At first, I'd thought that one hundred books sounded like an impossible amount—I don't think I've read even ten books in my life, let alone a hundred—but the longer I was with Claire, the more she opened my eyes. I began to understand that one hundred isn't that big of a number at all, even for books, just the same way that she came to realize that a thousand trees is also hardly a large number. We were both tending to such small, precious things.

"I wish there was some way they could come meet their trees, too, like I did," she sighed one evening as we sat on the porch after dinner, overlooking the forest as it grew dark and shadowed in the sunset. The last oil wars were at their peak then, and the aviation industry was completely grounded. Our staff who rode the train back and forth from Oslo had said a flight could take weeks to get, and cost more than a down payment on a small apartment somewhere in the outer exurban zones.

I tried to muster a reply, and failed. Even though Claire's Crackles was only Stage I and she was responding well to treatment, I was still reeling from her diagnosis.

But Claire could always draw me out of a mood, no matter how dark. To comfort me, she started talking about books and immortality, about how she felt that an author and their art were one and the same. That an author's works were not like children, but more like incarnations. They *were* their authors. And that as long as people continued to read them, they would live on. "*When writers die, they become books,*" one of her favorite authors was famously attributed as having said, she told me. Jorge Luis Borges had died far too long ago to be asked to be part of the Future Library, but it didn't stop her from wishing she somehow could invite his ghost to write another novel for her.

That was when I'd gotten the idea.

"Maybe they could still visit their trees, in a way," I said.

Claire loved the symbolism of it. She set to work at once, calling the still-living authors who had submitted their work to the Future Library and the families of the ones who had already passed away. We already knew everyone was either planning to be cremated after death, or had already been cremated, because burial had been too expensive for decades. Ashes essentially last forever in their urns, and the authors and their families were surprisingly touched by the request. It wasn't hard to convince them to send a small portion of each person's remains to us, or promise to, once they passed away.

In their undiluted state, human ash is incredibly harsh on plant life, even in small doses. Too much sodium, too high a pH level. I figured out how to mix it with a special soil blend of my own creation to neutralize the sodium and bring the acidic levels to base.

After each little urn arrived and I combined it with our blend, Claire and I had gone to each chosen tree, where I dug a hole at the base of the trunks, careful not to damage the root systems or disrupt the ground cover too much. We "planted" the authors beneath them, and then smoothed the earth back out.

"Now they will get to meet their trees," I told her after we finished the first one, holding her close. It takes only a few months for a tree to leech such a small amount of nutrients from the dirt. In forest time, that was practically no time at all.

She kissed me. "You have to do it for me, too, when I'm gone," she said. "I want my ashes to be buried beneath my tree."

I wanted to argue that it would be years, hopefully decades, before we had to consider that, but it wasn't the time. "I will," I replied, and kissed her back.

As we stood there embracing, I thought about the cremation and soil mixture fading into the warm, moist darkness below, but I know Claire was imagining something spectacular, like the remains turning into letters as they decayed and then creeping in tendril sentences around the roots, absorbing into the trees.

"Clear!" my deputy head arborist shouted, jolting me back to the moment. The creaking gave way to a rumble, then a whoosh, and the sky brightened and the world shook with a boom as the Future Library's very first spruce fell to the earth.

You can tell the age of a tree by the number of rings it has in its wood. Every year it grows another, an infinitesimal widening of its trunk. A tree could sort of be read not unlike a book, it occurred to me then as I watched it crash downward. Which years had drought. Which had fire. When water was plenty. When the sun was strong. The rings on this first tree were perfect. Impossible symmetry and grace. Love is not something that happens to a person, but something a person does for another person, every day, every moment. A labor, not a feeling. These rings were a record of my deeds.

I went forward as soon as the ground stopped shaking, to put a hand on the tree. The smooth, round shape of the inside of its trunk looked back at me. Its rings circling and circling, one hundred times, a dizzying, mesmerizing spiral.

No.

Those arcing lines in the wood were not rings, I realized then.

"What in God's name . . ." Gunnar whispered.

They were words.

Next, I was sitting in a chair in Claire's old office, somehow. There was a mug of tea on the armrest, its tail of steam long dissipated. Gunnar was not with me, nor my deputy head arborist. Only Hsiu was there, our most junior arborist, nervously twisting their neck gaiter in their hands as they watched me. They were new, our last hire, just five years on the job.

"Where is everyone?" I finally asked.

"Outside, with the reporters," Hsiu answered. "The prime minister is on her way up from Oslo to see."

To see what? I almost asked, but I already knew.

Do you believe in fate? I could hear Claire's voice in my mind, as crystal clear as it was the first day I'd met her, in that old, crumbling Vinmonopolet on the corner of Nordre gate and Markveien.

"I need," I said to Hsiu. I was trying to stand up. "I need."

"I know," they said. They eased me back into the chair and went to the desk. On it was a perfect disc the size of a giant serving platter. A slice of peach-golden wood encircled by dark-brown bark. "Gunnar had them cut a piece for you before they were swarmed by the crowd."

It was a cross-section of the trunk of the tree we had just felled. "Claire's tree," Hsiu said. They held it out. "Her book."

The Song of Leaves, the title along the outermost ring read.

I looked at Hsiu. "It's not," I tried to say. "It can't be." I couldn't finish.

Hsiu was still staring at the disc, eyes full of wonder. "I guess we don't need to print and bind it as a book anymore. It's already . . . it's already done."

Over the rest of the day, Gunnar supervised the felling of four more of the authors' spruce as I tried to collect myself, and all four were the same. Instead of mere growth rings inside the trees, there were words, impossibly small yet somehow still legible, in one long, spiraling trail from the center out to the very edge where the bark began. Poetry and shorter novels were large enough to read with the naked eye by squinting, such as *The Song of Leaves*. Longer works required a magnifying glass. They were in all languages—Norwegian, Korean, Portuguese, Arabic—some changed midway through, the way that a ring might warp due to drought or flood. Some told stories so long, minor branches also had to be cut off the main trunk and sliced into discs themselves to reach the end.

How was this possible? What did it mean? The media went wild with investigative articles, opinion pieces, personal essays. We let the same photographers we'd cleared for the opening ceremony continue to photograph the new trees, and they licensed some of their lesser shots to the open market. NewsLens was flooded with them. They were so ubiquitous, so inescapable, that I stopped using my device altogether. Put it in the drawer of Claire's lonely nightstand and never got it out again.

That first week, there were so many meetings. Meetings with the prime minister and the king, meetings with Operation Green—revived again at last, and with WWF, EDF, UNEP, every acronym possible. Gunnar went over and over the daily operation of the Future Library from the administrative side, and I detailed endlessly the care I and my arborists had provided to the trees. I gave them our logbooks, our weather records, our rainfall charts, everything. They grilled me about the planted cremated remains, made me explain our exact method again and again. The world had been charmed by the sentimentality of what we'd done with the ashes when Claire had put out the original press release, but now they were obsessed with the plantings. Consumed.

But there was no magic to it, I insisted. Just Claire and me, the night, some nutrient-dense soil mixture, and a little too much wine. It was romance, nothing more. Whatever had happened, it had not been because of us.

They said they agreed with me. I believed them.

The project continued forward, and the library still released the novels, but the entire process had to change. Instead of felling the trees and pulping their wood into paper to print the books, we simply took each trunk and cut it into thin discs, and sold each disc as the book. We made each disc about 1.25 cm thick, and thus could create approximately 1,500 to 2,000 copies of a book from each tree.

Within a month, every one of the one hundred novels in the Future Library had been "published," and sold for thousands of kroner. Millions even, sometimes.

They were beautiful, I have to admit. I've never been one to particularly think books were beautiful, but these books were. Buyers hung them on their walls like art, and would sit or stand in front of them for hours with magnifying glasses, reading the stories. People felt connected to nature again. To trees. There were ShareLife videos of readers talking about how every time they passed by their book, they would touch the wood with their fingers, feel the words therein. There was something magical about them, they said. It reminded them of their closeness to the Earth.

I don't have my copy of *The Song of Leaves* anymore. It was confiscated from me when I was arrested. I don't know what happened to it, but I'm sure the temptation to resell it was simply too great. I was languishing in purgatory, the courts too busy with Crackles lawsuits and climate refugee resettlement appeals to hear my case. And even if they had, I already knew I would be convicted. I would never see the light of day again. I imagine there was a quiet auction somewhere, a sum I wouldn't even be able to comprehend for all the zeroes, and that was that. It was gone.

It doesn't matter. We're almost to the part where I tell you why.

*

The day of my arrest—the day I tried to expose everything—was at the end of that first month. We'd just cut down the final, hundredth tree, and my arborists were hard at work measuring and dividing its trunk to produce its books. After this, there would be no more. That was what I foolishly believed. After all, Katie and Claire had only ever intended there to be one hundred books in the Future Library and had only invited exactly that many authors.

But could that really be it? NewsLens asked, constantly and through every device and screen and portal, impervious to all ad-blocks. The world was poised, breathless for what might happen next.

"Technically, one thousand trees were planted in Nordmarka at the start of the Future Library project. But only one hundred actually were cut down," Klima-og Miljøvernministeren Kristoffer Berg, the minister of climate and the environment, said to the rest of the room, leaning forward on the conference table so he could reach his microphone. Daily briefings had gone from being just the librarians and the arborists in Claire's modest office to extremely formal things in a hulking, hideous temporary structure the government had assembled. They had created an official board to oversee us, full of their own people.

"Exactly," I said. "The other nine hundred weren't meant to be additional inventory for the library. They were meant to make up for the one hundred we knew we would lose to this project. Nordmarka has the only trees remaining in the entire world."

"I'm not calling for a culling of the entire forest," Minister Berg argued.

"Any allowance is too much. The Future Library was not just supposed to publish a hundred books a century later, but also to protect the forest in which those books were grown," I replied.

"Just one more," Director Pak suggested. "As an experiment."

I shook my head. "If we cut down the one hundred and first tree, what's to stop us from cutting down the one hundred and second? The third? We've already destroyed every other forest on the planet. When will we stop?"

They all said noncommittal things. That's when I knew it *would* never stop. That this was not the completion of the Future Library, but rather, the beginning. The beginning of the end of our last forest in the world. Even if they were to plant a hundred more tomorrow in exchange for each one they cut down today, trees grow so slowly that we would never catch up to ourselves. The forest would be gone within our lifetimes.

I had to do something. I had to show them.

I had to tell the truth.

Because I'd kept something from all of them, a secret, because I hadn't known it would matter so much.

That night, I took Claire's keys from her nightstand drawer and let myself into her darkened, silent office, and then into the small, even darker, even more silent room at the end of it.

Each book submitted by the one hundred authors of the Future Library was stored on an encrypted server somewhere for safe-keeping until the project came to fruition, but originally, the plan also had been to print and display the manuscripts in an exhibit in the Deichman Library in downtown Oslo, until the trees were cut down and pulped into paper. The manuscripts were set into boxes and locked, so visitors could pick them up and hear their pages clack against the sides of their containers, but not read them. To enhance the mystery, Claire had told me with a wink. The outer layer of the boxes was made of wood, in keeping with the theme of the project, but Katie Paterson had possessed the foresight to line the inside of each of them with stainless steel. When closed, the boxes were watertight and airtight, so the manuscripts would never decay—at least not for a very, very long time. Long enough that vis-itors to the Deichman Library could handle them and spread the word about the project, anyway. It was a very clever publicity tactic.

But after the power shortages in the early 2100s, the Deichman Library was turned into a homeless shelter, and the manuscripts cast aside, the exhibit scrapped. Their boxes were moved back here to our offices. The only place left for them.

With all the surprise and the awe at the trees, it seemed that everyone had forgotten those original manuscripts were still here. Tucked away in a dank little closet that no one had opened for decades, and now no longer had any need to.

I counted fifty-seven boxes and slid the slim wooden shape out from its place in the middle of the collection. Claire's book was slight, perhaps just two hundred pages or so. Trembling, I inserted the smallest gold key from her keyring into the lock and turned. The lid eased open with a tired creak to reveal her manuscript inside. The book she had written decades ago—the story that was meant for her tree. My eyes were so blurry from the tears, I could hardly read the title across the yellowing, slightly faded cover page, but it didn't matter.

I already knew what it would say.

Or rather, what it would not.

Here is the second thing they have hidden from you: *The Song of Leaves* is not Claire's book.

I know this because the day the Future Library opened, when Gunnar and the rest of the staff told me they'd decided to honor Claire by publishing her book first, I made a choice. Perhaps it was the wrong one, but it was the only one I could have made. I couldn't stop myself. I had to protect the last thing I had of her.

The tree I took them to that morning—the tree we cut down and found those impossible words inside—was not the one I had marked in my mind as special, not the one I had tended to every single day with more care than I have ever tended anything else. That tree's branches reached for the sky, its gnarled roots crept through the darkness below, with nothing but sun and rain and earth to sustain it. No cremated ashes, no Claire, had been planted there.

Because it was not her tree.

The next day at the morning meeting, I raised my hand to speak before Prime Minister Sjur or Vice-Director Oliveira could begin with the minutes. I needed to tell them the whole story. To tell them the truth, before they destroyed the forest attempting to discover it.

But before I could start, Minister Berg leaned forward to his table microphone, cutting me off. "I'd like to talk about symbols," he said slowly.

"Symbols?" I asked, surprised.

Minister Berg cleared his throat and smiled.

Suddenly, I could tell that whatever he was about to say next had been rehearsed. That the other officials already knew. There was some sort of plan, and they had already all agreed on it.

"Of hope. Of the future. That a human's life might continue even after their body is gone."

"But—" I paused, tried to remain collected. I looked at Gunnar beside me, but he was looking at Minister Berg, not me. "That's not what's happening here, with the ashes and the words. It's not the truth—"

"Truth for truth's sake is academic, at best. But we live in the world. The most noble purpose of truth is to benefit the greater good," Minister Berg continued, voice echoing through the ugly gray room. "I think, with the right balance between environmental protection and humanitarian considerations, the Future Library might be able to do even more for the forest—and mankind—than we'd previously hoped."

"I have evidence," I tried to say, but I was already panicking. "I can show you."

Evidence of what? I expected him to ask, but he said, "A proposal, for the board's consideration," instead. He was facing the rest of the table now, not me. As if I hadn't spoken at all.

I looked desperately at Gunnar again as Minister Berg began to describe his idea for the Forever Contest. Of holding an annual call for cremated remains from the global public, and a drawing to decide which to "plant." Of allowing just a few of these last trees to be cut down each year, so we could read the words written inside their wood—the last words of the planted person. Words from beyond death, words that meant that a person was never really gone.

They already knew it would become the single greatest event in human history. You could see it in their eyes. Earth was spiraling toward death, and people were terrified. There wasn't a person still alive who would be able to resist entering.

I tried to argue, but it was useless. What politicians can do with words seems like a kind of magic Claire might have invented in one of her novels.

"The funding would continue indefinitely this way," Minister Berg was saying, and the rest of them were nodding. "Each tree in Nordmarka is certainly precious, but we still have thousands of them. If we're careful, if we create a strict annual maximum number . . ."

Gunnar still would not look at me. "Gunnar, please," I said to him as the minister continued his speech. I touched his arm to force him to pay attention. "This is important." The words were hot and sharp in my throat. "It's about Claire's book."

"I'm sorry, Ingrid," he sighed. His voice was so soft.

It took me a long time to believe it. That they had swayed him too. Gunnar had been a part of the Future Library project for nearly all his professional life, the same as Claire and I had. I thought of anyone, he'd understand time like we did.

But I guess even one hundred years is not very long, compared to the ages of the elder trees in the Future Library forest for which I'd also cared.

We held a vote. A sham of a formality. I was the only dissenter. The library would announce the Forever Contest the next day, and begin taking submissions immediately. Every year, the remains of one hundred winners would be planted, and then the year after, their trees would be cut down, so we could read their immortal words. And sell them.

I ran back to the storage closet, to take as many of the manuscripts as I could carry. I had to go public. I had to tell the truth. I threw open the door to the room so quickly the wall rattled.

But the manuscripts, and their little wooden boxes, were gone. The space was as bare as the day it had been built, just an empty square.

I turned around. Gunnar was standing there in Claire's office, hands in his pockets. He still could not look at me.

I was arrested.

I realize now that the board already knew what I'd been trying to tell them. That at some point, amid all their excitement, someone on staff must have remembered that according to procedure, our off-site server with the electronic copies of the manuscripts would automatically unlock that first week, to allow for printing. Perhaps Gunnar had gotten a system-generated email about it. They must have checked the trees against the files. They must have known since nearly the beginning.

Initially, my charges were listed as something to do with business fraud. But then someone convinced the other arborists to gossip, and stories were exaggerated, idle chatter inflated, until the accusation was not that I simply had complained about how the newly formed board was handling the administration of the Future Library, but rather that I had outright threatened its members. Suspicious tools and materials—saws, knives, fertilizer mix, batteries for my head lamp—never mind that all arborists use such things in the daily undertaking of their profession, were found in my room.

Eco-terrorism had a much more serious ring to it.

The library's lawyers likely figured I would use my chance on the stand to expose the Forever Contest rather than defend myself, so they never let me near the courtroom. A safety concern petition had been filed. I watched the proceedings from prison at Ullersmo, in cell 144. My roommate was serving a seventy-year term for double homicide, ten years into her sentence. Even she had heard of the Future Library, from inside there.

"So, anyone can enter the contest?" she asked, leaning over from her top bunk to look down at me.

"Yes," I said. There wasn't any point in trying to convince her of what I knew. That it didn't matter. That no one was winning anything, even the winners. "But how would you even enter your name, from here?"

"There's a whole computer room in the education wing," she said. "Everyone gets one hour of internet access a day. Haven't they taken you to see it yet?"

Of course they hadn't. And they never would.

"Why did you try to kill them? The Future Library board?" she asked. "For the trees?"

I shrugged. *For truth,* I should have said. "For love," I did instead.

She smiled crookedly. "Me, too."

I was sentenced to life without parole.

I had nothing but time to watch what happened to the Future Library, and the forest, after that.

The board kept cutting down trees, our precious Nordmarka dwindling as the earth became even more polluted, the droughts even worse. More pandemics, more wars. Sometimes, inside Ullersmo, it would get so hot that even with the fans spinning as fast as they could go, prisoners would just drop to the floor, their eyes rolling back in their heads, their withered bodies so overheated they could no longer function. It was like being back in the dying Amazon again. Struggling to breathe, sweating so much but that sweat making no difference, because the air was so hot and humid that your sweat simply clung to you like a curtain of steam, making you even sicker.

And still, every spring, the Future Library felled one hundred more trees for the Future Contest.

Whenever my roommate went to the education wing for her hour on the computers, she let me give her a few questions to look up, as long as it didn't take more than fifteen minutes of her allotted time. There had been some conservation attempts in response to feeble complaints from independent environmental bodies, she told me. The board apparently once tried to send seeds from Nordmarka to the biovaults in the New Tsimshian Collective, but the spruce wouldn't grow there. They also tried cutting and examining smaller plants under a microscope, *Vaccinium myrtillus* and *Hylocomium splendens* and *Oxalis acetosella*, to see if other flora might also be capable of producing words, but it seems that only the trees can do it.

And they've noticed style differences between the species, as well. *Picea abies* tend to hold sad stories, and *Pinus sylvestris* grow sweeter, happier ones. *Betula pubescens* often reveal poetry, or sometimes even music, the notes floating between the rings as they go round and round, flats and sharps, halfs and wholes, as though the lines are composition staffs. The Bergen Philharmonic Orchestra performs them all in a concert every autumn. I've heard their recordings playing in the mess hall during dinner hours, crooning softly over the intercom system—a benevolent gift to us from the wardens on days when our already meager rations are exceptionally low.

The songs are so beautiful, it's hard for anyone to do anything else while they play. Cutlery and conversation still, and we all just sit in silence for hours, lost. I have never felt such a profound ache as when I listen to those songs. The loneliness suffuses every cell of me even more than it did my first night without Claire. It's like the birch understand even better than us what it's like to grieve something precious. Maybe they do. After all, I'm only seventy-five years old. We've been destroying their forests for millennia.

All of this art is passed off as being thanks to us humans, of course. Our remains, our lives after death, sent to this sham Forever Contest. The board has already lied about so much, it's not that hard for them to lie about this too. How would anyone prove it? The "winners" are all dead before they even win.

The day of the Future Library's opening, I truly had no idea that there would already be words inside the spruce tree I had pretended was Claire's. No one did. Who could have? I thought it would be pure, plain, untouched wood, just the same as the wood in her actual tree—if wood was wood, what difference would it make? I'd thought. All I'd been doing was trying to save the tree I loved like I had loved her. To let another one be made into paper for her book. Readers would still be able to have her words, her pages. And I would still have her tree.

But when they cut into it, when we saw the words, that was when I understood what we were doing.

Here is the last thing they have hidden from you, which by now, if you believe that what I've told you about Claire's tree is true, I think you can no longer deny.

The Future Library doesn't plant our remains. Or even if they do, it doesn't matter. The stories they cut down and release each year aren't our stories.

The truth is that all of this has nothing to do with people, or with hope, or immortality.

The truth is that the Forever Contest is meaningless. Because every single tree in Nordmarka already has words inside of its wood.

We are not writing them.

The trees are.

Even as used to time on an unfathomable scale as I am—the time of trees and forests, where one of our lifetimes is but a blink compared to theirs—I thought the relentless monotony of my incarceration would never end. I longed for death at times, mostly just to stop the boredom. The unchangingness of every day. Of having to live without being able to save my trees.

Then, finally, one day last year, I woke up to my roommate hovering over my bunk, gently shaking my shoulder.

"Ingrid," she whispered. It was very early. Her brow was furrowed with concern. "That noise you're making."

I drew another strained breath, and listened. That familiar sound, like tiny bubbles or wrinkling paper.

The Crackles.

I will never know exactly how Gunnar managed to secure my compassionate release. Even with things as bad as they were outside, part of me still can't believe he managed to circumvent the need for the board's approval without them noticing, and then hide it from them until it was too late. But perhaps they truly were so distracted, he barely had to try at all.

My heart swelled with surprise and tenderness when I saw it was him waiting for me in the visitation room, clutching his hat. Even after everything that had happened, I couldn't help it. He'd been like a brother to Claire and me for so many years before it had all gone bad. And our discovery had been so incredible, so beyond the realm of possibility, that no one could have comprehended it.

"You look terrible," I said, after we pulled back from the embrace and wiped our eyes.

Gunnar laughed, more of a snort, and shrugged. He was so gaunt, his hair so white and thin, mere wisps. "Food shortages."

We always had food shortages inside Ullersmo. I'd had no way of knowing if it was the same outside, or simply that we were the last priority. "So bad?"

He nodded. He looked at me and gave a long, tired sigh. That's when I heard it, in his lungs. The Crackles had gotten him too.

"It was all the time you spent going into the city," I said sadly. In that last decade before the Future Library's opening, Gunnar had been so dedicated to ensuring our licenses and permits stayed current, he'd traveled down to Oslo to file our paperwork even during the rioting that had released ancient, burning asbestos from damaged historical buildings, and during the water contamination crises, when none of it was safe to drink.

But Gunnar just shrugged again. He said it could have been anything. Everyone was getting the Crackles these days. The scientists had modeled it out, how much more quickly things were going to get worse now that we'd been without any trees except those in Nordmarka for almost fifty years. What it would be like at eighty years, at one hundred. The models didn't really go beyond that, he said.

"Why did you come?" I asked, not unkindly. "Why now?"

"Truth," he said.

The board had been cutting trees for years now. But lately, he said, the stories had become more and more strange. They were having a harder time finding ones that sounded like they were written by humans, and having to cut more and more trees every year in order to hide their lies.

"What do you mean, more strange?" I asked. How could anything be even more strange than it already was?

Gunnar looked uneasy. "I finally realized something about their stories," he said.

It took him time to figure it out, because the Future Library did not necessarily cut down the trees in the same order in which they'd been planted by Katie Paterson or had seeded themselves naturally by wind and rain centuries before. The board was mostly doing it by health—cull the weaker ones in the grove first, let the strong ones keep growing longer.

But enough years had passed that Gunnar was able to start putting it together. He knew nothing about trees, remember, but he knew all about words. He was a professor of literature at the University of Oslo, before it was defunded under national emergency measures and he'd come to the Future Library at Claire's urging. And Hsiu knows just as little about words as I do, but they know the trees very well indeed, after all this time. Hsiu had been his head arborist for five years now, Gunnar told me. Most of the others I knew had already died from the Crackles.

Together, poring over the wooden discs of each tree's book in the library, and the pages and pages of logs from the arborists, stretching all the way back to when Katie's original team planted them in the forest in 2014, Gunnar and Hsiu noticed a pattern.

"It's all one story," he told me. "Each one of them, each tree, contains just a tiny piece. What we have is obviously incomplete— but they've cut down enough now that we can see the pattern." He reached for my hand. "It's all part of *The Song of Leaves*. All of it. Every tree that's ever lived. They've always been telling this story, in every language. It's only recently they've started learning ours."

I stared at him in amazement. It was not the Crackles this time, why I could not catch my breath.

I could feel the ghost of my trees again. The way their needles used to delicately brush my shoulders as I walked between them, and the knotty turns in the ground beneath my boots where the roots peeked through. I could hear the wind rush through their branches.

"Have you read them?" Gunnar asked. "The pieces that have come out since you've been here?"

I shook my head. "They don't let me use the computer."

"The board believes . . ." He trailed off. "The board believes that the trees are trying to tell us something, about Earth. Things we can't tell with our instruments. Things about the air, the water. They're so much older than we are. They believe . . ."

I was gripping his hands so tightly it was hurting us both. "Tell me."

He looked down. "They believe that if they can read the complete story, in order, that the trees can tell us how to fix things, before we all die."

No.

No.

I could not bear it.

"Gunnar," I tried to say.

"I know," he said. "I know. I tried to tell them. But they're obsessed with the idea. And Minister Berg says that even if it doesn't work, it doesn't matter anyway. Even if Nordmarka was still its original size, in its peak centuries ago, it wouldn't be enough anyway. As far as the scientists can tell, humanity is almost doomed to go extinct in the next fifty to one hundred years no matter what."

It was hard to see him through the tears in my eyes.

"They're going to cut them all down. This summer. In the hopes of learning the end of the story." Again, Gunnar could not look at me. His voice shook. "There is nothing I can do to make up for the damage I've already done. The terrible choice I made. But they can't be allowed to destroy the forest."

A round of terrible coughs broke him off for a moment. He reached for his handkerchief, and it came away from his lips speckled with red.

"Yesterday evening, they just cut down another," he finally continued. "One of the youngest so far. Possibly a natural seeding, according to Hsiu. A recent offspring of the trees Katie originally planted. I read its rings late last night, before the board would see it today. There's a line in its part of the story . . ." he paused. "It asks for you."

I stared, spellbound. "For me?"

Gunnar nodded. "The trees know your name."

We sat in silence for a long time, too amazed to speak. I tried to picture the forest instead.

Slowly, I became aware that Gunnar was trembling. I put my hand on his back, then touched his face. He was crying, I realized.

"I'm sorry the only thing I can do to help stop the board is petition for your parole, given your diagnosis. I'm a director now, my signature will work for that. For at least a week, anyway. It'll take them that long to even get to the paperwork to see what I've done." His shoulders hiccupped. "It's not enough."

"It is," I said.

"It's not. Not by far."

I kissed his wasted cheek. "Gunnar." The skin there was as cold and gray as mine. "It is."

Finally, finally, he looked at me. "I understand now, Ingrid. What you were trying to get us all to see, all those years ago. This story is not ours. They are not telling it for us. They are telling it for each other."

At last, we come to now.

Today is 18 August 2125. The second day of my freedom.

I have returned from Nordmarka to my little hovel of a flat outside Kløfta just this morning, before dawn. Gunnar rented it in secret for me, as his last act. Then he went back to Oslo, where they've moved the board meetings, and has likely already emptied the syringes from his euthanasia package into his veins. He is gone. They can do nothing to him now, and neither can the Crackles.

The dirt of the forest is still under my fingernails, and in the treads of my boots. It was a long hike, difficult in the darkness, but I've done it many times before. The first time while carrying a champagne bottle, the second while carrying a bunch of little urns of ash with Claire, and struggling with the shovel as she laughed. The third, with the shovel again, and only her remains. And the fourth, the night before I was arrested. I was all alone, and carrying only one thing that time.

No, not all alone.

I had the trees.

I will bet that even after learning all of this, you still don't want to believe me. Not about the cremated remains being worthless, not about the stories inside the wood not belonging to the people you think made them. Not about it being the trees having done it, all along.

But I can prove it.

Because I still have Claire's manuscript. Her book.

Not the one that everyone thinks is hers, the words inside the first felled tree—but rather the one she truly wrote. The one she gave to Katie Paterson so many decades ago, that was sealed in the wooden box for display at the Deichman Library, and then forgotten in the storage closet of her office until the board destroyed the rest of the boxes to protect their secrets.

The night I went into that closet to read the manuscripts, I should have known better and taken them all then, but at least

I did one thing right. I did take Claire's with me. I went straight out from that room into the darkness. No coat, no flashlight, no shovel. I walked the way I had walked the first night she brought me to Nordmarka, by feel of the gnarls of wood poking through the undergrowth beneath my feet and the touch of the rough bark of branches around me, by the rush of the wind as it whispered around the trunks.

"Isn't it beautiful?" Claire had said, even though we could hardly see anything under the dim moon. She had meant the library, the idea of it.

"Yes," I'd agreed. I had meant her, and the trees. The sound of her voice and the sound of their leaves, blending together.

Alone, in darkness, as the board was closing in around me, I dug a hole with my hands and planted Claire's box beneath her tree. Her *real* tree. The tree she showed me that first night, she nearly breathless with excitement as she tried to tell me everything about the library, me clutching the champagne bottle so hard my knuckles were white, so nervous to be so close to her that I could hardly hear her words over the waterfall rush in my ears. The tree I loved as deeply as I loved her, for just as long.

I knew they'd never find it amid all the others, tucked into a distant corner of the grove, because they would have to know which tree was really hers first out of the thousands and thousands. And none of them know the forest like I do.

"Do you ever wonder what they would say?" Claire asked me, just before the medication put her into an endless sleep. *"If the trees could tell stories like us?"*

"Yes," I'd said. I had spent my whole life wondering that.

She laid her head back on the pillow and grimaced at the needle in her vein. I touched her cheek. *"It seems impossible that we're the only species who can."*

"Do you think anyone would really listen, if it were true?" I'd asked. I did not have faith in humans the way Claire did.

I will never forget that last smile she gave me, before her eyes closed. *"You would, Ingrid."*

Tomorrow, I will release this letter, and then Claire's book. You will finally be able to read it, the way the Future Library always intended.

It's a love story. A slim, bittersweet thing. It's about a marriage, a husband who loves his wife very much and a wife who loves him back but is disappointed he's not more romantic. She finds their quiet newlywed life boring, and wishes for grand surprises and cinematic moments, but he doesn't know how to give them. His love is in the little things, every day, too small for her to notice. She is a fire, burning fast and bright, and he is an ocean, slow and long. Or perhaps, a forest.

Some years after they wed, the husband becomes sick and dies. The wife is bereft, mourning his quiet, everyday love that she will never feel again.

But a week later, a letter arrives in the mailbox. It was written by the husband long ago, on the day they found out he was sick. He reminds her that at their wedding, he promised to love her every day, for her whole life. Not his, but hers. The letter tells her that he will write more—many, many more, and will save them to be sent after his death—that this way, he can still love her for her whole life.

In the moment, each letter by itself will seem small, just a little thing. But all of them together will fill a room, he swears. That the longer she waits, the more she will finally be able to see the truth, that his love has always been very big indeed.

Did Claire know even then, somehow, in some way, I wonder? She was always so full of magic.

I am finally, finally starting to believe.

Within instants, Claire's work will infiltrate every corner of the networks, embedded in everyone's NewsLens and EyeScan. I will let the media organize a lab sample when they inevitably come rushing to me, so they can test the paper and the ink and date it to the year that Claire submitted the pages to Katie Paterson, as the fifty-seventh author of the Future Library. But even before those results are released, you will already believe. Scholars will comb through her bibliography and compare her style with her previous works. Claire's words will shine through.

You all will know *this* book is truly hers—not the one in the first tree we cut down. Because those words were there all along. This will prove it.

And then, you all will believe me when I reveal to you Gunnar and Hsin's list. He told me the order of the trees, the order of *The Song of Leaves*, over and over, until I memorized it. When you read their story so far in sequence, you won't be able to deny it.

You will finally understand who is writing *The Song of Leaves*, and what it is about.

You will understand that cutting the forest down to have every piece doesn't make the story go on—it makes it end. That we will only know the rest of it by watching the trees grow.

That the story will only save us if we let them keep telling it.

Claire's box is on the table beside me, mud-stained, its outer wood gone soft and gray. But the steel inner case peeking out between the warps in its seams is still strong. This is the closing of my story, and of Claire's, but only the beginning of the trees'. This is what I will leave behind. Her words, and mine, as well. I wish the forest could read them.

Who would have guessed that at the end of my life, words would become the most important thing?

L'Esprit de L'Escalier

FROM *Tor.com*

First Step

Orpheus puts a plate of eggs down in front of her.

The eggs are perfect; after everything, he finally got it just right. Oozing, lightly salted yolks the color of marigolds, whites spreading into golden-brown lace. The plate is perfect: his mother's pattern, a geometric Mediterranean-blue key design on bone-white porcelain. The coffee is perfect, the juice is perfect, the toast is perfect, the album he put on the record player to provide a pleasant breakfast soundtrack is perfect. Café au lait with a shower of nutmeg. Tangerine with a dash of bitters. Nearly burnt but not quite.

Strangeways, Here We Come.

Eurydice always loved the Smiths. Melancholy things made her smile. Balloons and cartoons and songs in any of the major keys put her out of sorts. When they first met, she slept exclusively in a disintegrating black shirt from the 1984 European tour. He thought that was so fucking cool. Back when he had the capacity to think anything was cool.

She's wearing it now. Nothing else. Dark fluid pools in patches on the undersides of her thighs, draining slowly down to her heels.

Her long black hair hangs down limp over Morrissey's perpetually pained face. The top of her smooth gray breast shows through a tear so artfully placed you'd think they ripped it to specs in the factory. Sunlight from the kitchen windows creeps in and sits guiltily at her feet like a neglected cat.

Orpheus never once managed a breakfast this good when she

was alive. If he's honest with himself, it wouldn't even have occurred to him to try.

"Darling," he says softly, as he says every morning. "You have to eat."

But she doesn't, not really. They both know that. She lifts one heavy, purplish hand and drops it, settling on the only thing she does need: a peeling, dishwasher-tormented limited-edition 1981 Princess Leia glass filled with microwaved lamb's blood. Forty-five seconds on high.

Orpheus winces. She retracts her hand. She is very sorry. She will drink it later, congealed and lukewarm, alone.

Eurydice picks up a slender and very clean fork. The problem has never been that she doesn't want to get better. Her short fingernails have black dirt under them. No matter how she scrubs and scrubs in the sink, no matter what kind of soap she buys. Orpheus hears the water running at three a.m. every night. The trickling, sucking song through the pipes. The negative space next to him in the bed, still cold from her body. But it doesn't matter. On Sundays he paints her nails for her, so she doesn't have to see it. But today is Saturday. The polish has chipped and flaked. The constant crescent moons of old earth show through.

She slices through an egg and lets the yolk run like yellow blood. Severs a corner of toast and dredges it in the warm, sunny liquid, so full of life, full enough to nourish a couple of cells all the way through to a downy little baby birdie with sweet black eyes. If only things had gone another way.

Eurydice hesitates before putting it between her lips. Knowing what will happen. Knowing it will hurt them both, but mainly her. Like everything else.

She shoves it in quickly. Attempts a smile. And, just this once, the smile does come when it is called. There she is, as she always was, framed by tall paneled windows and vintage posters from his oldest shows:

OPEN MIC FRIDAY AT THE CLOTHO CAFE, $5 COVER!
SINGING ROCK MUSIC FESTIVAL, JULY 21ST, ACHERON, NY.
LIVE AT THE APOLLO.

And for a moment, there she is, all cheekbones and eyelashes and history, grinning so wide for him that her pale, sharp teeth glisten in the rippling cherry-blossom shadows.

Then, her jaw pops out of its socket with a loud *thook* and sags, hanging at an appalling, useless angle. She presses up against her chin, fighting to keep it in, but the fight isn't fair and could never be. Eurydice locks eyes with Orpheus. No tears, though she really is so sorry for what was always about to happen. But her ducts were cauterized by the sad, soft event horizon between, well. *There* and *Here.*

Orpheus longs for her tears, real and hot and sweet and salted as caramel, and he hates himself for his longing. He hates her for it too.

A river of black, wet earth and pebbles and moss and tiny blind helpless worms erupts out of Eurydice's smile, splattering so hard onto his mother's perfect plate that it cracks down the middle, and dirt pools out across the table and the worms nose mutely at the crusts of the almost-burnt toast.

He clenches his teeth as he clears the dishes. Eurydice stares up at him, her eyes swimming with apologies.

"It's fine," he says, curt and flat. "It's fine."

Somewhere between the table and the counter, the tangerine juice stops being tangerine juice. It thickens, swirls into silvery-gold ambrosia, releases a scent of honeycomb, new bread, and old books.

Orpheus dumps it in the sink.

Second Step

Marriage isn't what he thought it would be.

She didn't even thank him for making her breakfast. He doesn't want that to annoy him the way it does, but he can't shake it. She owes him. She owes him so much.

Orpheus remembers the days when he was so full of her nothing else would fit. And then when she was gone, and he dreamed of her so vividly he woke with her scent pouring from his skin. When nothing was innocent. Every chair just an inch to the left or right of where he'd left it the night before. Every book opened to a different page than the one he'd marked. Every lost key or wallet or watch not misplaced but *taken.* Every flicker of every lightbulb was her, couldn't be anything *but* her, his wife, calling out to him, begging him to hear her, pleading through the impassible doorway of her own final breath.

He was so young then, young, stupid in love, unaware that there were certain things he simply could not have. Limitation was for other people. All he'd ever needed to do was sing and the world opened itself up to him like a jewelry box—and she was there when it did, the little pale dancer on the velvet of his ease, spinning inexorably round and round on one agonizingly perfect, frozen foot. If the world declined to open for others, that did not concern him.

When she is back, he dreamt then, *when I have her back, I will be happy again. She will be whole and laughing and warm as August rain and she will look at me every day just the way she did when we first met, as though nothing bad ever happened. Her eyes will be the same shade of green. The span of her wrist will fit between my thumb and forefinger. We'll go to the movies every night. I won't even want other girls. We'll drink ourselves into a spiral of infinite brunches. She will put her hand on the small of my back when we are photographed just the way she used to. Her smile will be full of new songs. When I touch her again, time will run backward and gravity will flee and pain will be a story we tell at parties, a fond joke whose punch line we can never get quite right. Everything will go back the way it was.*

She won't remember anything. Like in the soaps. She will be so grateful and so relieved and she won't remember any of it. Not dying. And not . . . the rest. I will bear the weight of our past for both of us. I am strong enough for that.

When Orpheus wakes in the night, she is never beside him. She stands at the window, looking out into the chestnuts and the crab-apples. The moon blows right through her. He can see mold flowering along her spine. Where she touches the curtains, it spreads, unfurling as luxurious as ivy.

Third Step

They have a little house on a busy street in a desirable school district. Chestnut and crabapple trees frame a chic midcentury modern bungalow in a neighborhood where poor but brilliant artists lived twenty years ago. Orpheus has other properties, more convenient to the city, more architecturally stimulating, more impressive for entertaining. But she's only comfortable here.

Whatever *comfortable* has come to mean for either of them.

He bought it from a day trader who lost both legs in some kind of vague childhood equestrian incident, a year or so after the second album hit like a gold brick dropped from the heavens and money became an abstract painting, untethered to concrete expressions, a defiance of realism, meaning whatever Orpheus wanted it to mean. It still had all the custom railings, ramps, lifts, and clever little automated mobility features installed and up to code. The previous owner joked that it was haunted.

It is. And it is not.

Eurydice doesn't handle stairs well.

After breakfast, she makes her way to the second-floor studio, gripping the silver safety rail with desperate tension. Her ashen feet squeak and drag on each step as she pulls herself up hand over hand. Orpheus watches her from the foot of the staircase. Her lovely legs beneath her nightshirt, the hardened, bloodless muscles of her calves, the curls of her hair brushing the backs of her thighs like dozens of question marks hanging in space, so much longer than before.

Hair keeps growing after you die. He remembers reading that somewhere. In a green room. On a plane. It doesn't matter. He used to watch her bound up to the bedroom, a kind of joy-stuffed reverse Christmas morning, reveling in the shine of it, of them, waiting to catch a playful peek before chasing up to catch her, two steps at a time.

Orpheus hears her fingernails crunch on the stainless steel. She hauls herself up another stair. She pulls too hard; flesh sticks against metal. The skin rips right off her palms, leaving a trail of black, coagulated sludge. Eurydice doesn't notice. She doesn't feel it. She doesn't feel anything. Her gray, marbled flesh rejects material reality wholesale. Those circuits just don't connect anymore.

"Baby . . . ?" Orpheus calls out softly.

Eurydice's head whips around. Her eyes are not the same shade of oaken green. They are black, silvered with cataracts. But they still burn. She stares down at him. He stares up at her. They have been here before. Another staircase. Another hall. Without a handrail, without plausibly candid family photographs at pleasant intervals, without Tiffany glass sconces dripping peacock mood lighting onto their path.

Eurydice turns around to see Orpheus behind her on the stairway. Blue-violet fungus uncurls along her jawline. Silver moss bristles along the stairs like new carpet wherever she's walked. Her pupils swallow him whole. She hears his voice and pivots toward it, instinctively, a reflex outside thought or ego.

"See?" she says in a shredded, raw, sopping voice. "It's not hard."

Fourth Step

They get a lot of visitors.

If Orpheus and Eurydice were a rising It Couple before, always ready with an open door and a seasonally appropriate plate of canapés and an incisive opinion on the events of the day, now they are the number one five-star-rated tourist destination for their particular and peculiar social circle. The commute doesn't seem to bother anybody. Friends, colleagues, family, fans, people they haven't heard from in years suddenly tapping on the windows, peering into the back garden, offering to help around the house, pick up groceries, medications, her favorite shampoo, his brand of whiskey. Anything at all, poor dears, just know we're here for you both in your time of need.

Rubberneckers, Eurydice calls them all.

At least they bring presents.

And they ask questions. Orpheus used to get asked questions all the time. *What are your influences? What was it like growing up with a famous mother? When's the next album coming out?* Sure, they were always the same questions, over and over, at a million pressers, in a thousand TV studios, but he had charming, humble, yet flirtatious answers for each one, and the interviewers always laughed.

Now it was only one question, still repeated, but with no good answer: *How is your wife?*

Ascalaphus brings organic fruit baskets.

Hecate brings three-scoop ice-cream cones.

Rhadamanthus keeps showing up with DVD box sets even though Orpheus has told him about streaming a hundred times.

Minos brings puzzles from the Great Paintings of History series. Adult coloring books. Something to occupy her mind, keep her sharp.

Charon is forever trying to talk Orpheus into going Jet Skiing with him on a lake upstate. *Come on, man, it's not like you were a homebody before. Do something for yourself. She's not going anywhere.*

Even the rivers come, though never all at the same time. Sopping wet, clothes clinging to their skin. Acheron with an asphodel blossom in his lapel; Phlegethon smoking constantly; Cocytus in jeans, her huge bone-pale headphones keeping the lamentations piping in; Styx, runway thin, bespoke black silk from top to bottom, always asking for change; and Lethe, her wet hair dyed blue, her long lashes inviting the universe to drown itself in her.

They never say anything about the mushrooms growing in the fireplace, on the windowsills, crowding spotted and striped between the books on the shelves.

And they bring booze. Not the cheap stuff, either.

Fifth Step

What does she do all day?

Mostly, Eurydice practices fine motor control.

It was all explained to him at the time, though Orpheus didn't want to hear it then. She has to stay active. Mentally and physically. She has to keep moving. Rigor mortis sets in again so fast. And she forgets. Not just how to move her fingers, but what fingers are and why moving is a good and desirable goal.

Orpheus remembers Persephone in a power suit, standing with one strappy red heel in the shallows of the Styx and one on land, in both worlds and neither, a bridge in girl form. So terrifyingly organized. The brutal corporate efficiency of death. Handing him stacks of neatly indexed and collated instructional materials with bold graphics and a four-color print job. *Don't look at me like that. This is all new territory for us too. None of our orientation paperwork was designed to handle it. I was up all summer. Now, turn to page six. We can put her back in there no problem, but a corpse is a corpse, of course, of course. Sorry, that was insensitive of me. Office humor. I'm not usually so . . . forward-facing with the clients. It's just that bodies aren't really our market focus. I'd recommend putting her on blood thinners, just to keep everything . . . liquid. And the blood, every day at mealtimes. Or she'll forget who she is. That's just standard. It's the same down here. Goes with the territory.* She pointed a ballpoint pen at a huge black stone drinking fountain on the beach. A long line of dead faces waited their turn to drink. He shuddered, watching blood bubble out of the spigot and into the basin. *Sheep's blood is fine. Pig is closer to human, though. Unless you can get human! No? You're right, bad suggestion. Are you listening?*

But Orpheus hadn't been listening. He'd been looking at her. Seeing her face again, her lips, the birthmark on her throat. Everything just as it was. Seeing them on picnics, reading to each other, taking cooking classes, standing in line at airports. Seeing her sitting cross-legged in the studio listening to his new songs, her adoring eyes reflecting his brilliance back at him. Seeing their kids. He didn't hear a word.

So now Eurydice does the newspaper crossword, to keep the neurons firing.

She cleans the house, always in the same pattern, starting with the downstairs bathroom and working her way outward in a mandala of bleach and orange oil.

She text banks for local political candidates.

She plays online baccarat and mines cryptocurrency.

She runs a couple of miles a night, hood drawn up, headphones in. It tenderizes the meat. Orpheus has tried to tell her it isn't safe for her to be out alone. She laughed in his face.

She works in the garden, weeding out the mint and asphodel that constantly threaten to take over everything. Asphodel isn't native, it isn't in season, this is the wrong kind of soil altogether, but nevertheless, the white, red-veined blossoms stretch like hands toward the house.

She spins and dyes yarn to sell at the farmers' market on Saturdays. She writes out the names of the colorways on little gray cards and ties them to the skeins with scraps of ribbon. *Die Like Nobody's Watching. Live, Laugh, Languish. Whatever Doesn't Kill You Is a Tremendous Disappointment. Thanks, I'm Cured. L'Espirit d'Escalier.*

It took Eurydice a year to be able to write again. And when she did, though her lettering came elegant and careful, it wasn't *hers.* It wasn't anyone else's either. It was just new.

But no matter what she writes on the cards, whatever color she pours into her big glass dyeing bowls, the skeins all come out the same shade of black, and no one buys them.

On Thursdays they have couples' counseling. They hunch together on the couch so they can both be seen in the little black eye of the webcam. Orpheus talks and talks. *I just want you to be happy. Why can't you be happy? After everything I've done for you. You're so fucking cold.*

Eurydice never says much. *I'm sorry. I'm sorry.*

The therapist gives them worksheets about Love Languages. Eurydice fills them out. Orpheus does not. So she answers for him.

His says: *Physical Touch.*

Hers says: *The Soul-Consuming Fires of the River Phlegethon.*

Once, Orpheus came home to find the crossword left out by the fireplace, every square filled in with the same tidy, alien letters. *Fuck you. I hate it here. Fuck you. I hate it here.*

He tossed it into the grate and flipped the switch. The pilot lights along the fake log popped to life and devoured the puzzle, the mushrooms, the deepening, ripening mold.

Sixth Step

Orpheus's mother comes whenever her book tours bend their way. She can never stay long. Calliope is a household name; the arts are the family business. She never stops working. She writes sprawling doorstoppers about war and romance that lounge effortlessly atop the bestseller lists. She doesn't knock.

Calliope breezes in, all sensible heels and comfortable beach dresses, reading glasses hanging on a strand of pearls around her neck, a faint forgetful hyphen of lipstick on her teeth, a full color spectrum of pens stuck behind her ears and in her hair. She sets up a battle station in the dining room: stock to sign, contracts to go over, laptop, tablet, phone, a headset like a crown of laurels into which she dictates her next project while she bakes and cleans and runs the soundboard for her son in the basement recording studio. She brings a bag of thick, hideous hand-knit sweaters for Eurydice, who is always, always cold, even with the furnace playing at top volume. She raised Orpheus alone, a single mother in an era when that was an impossible ask, bouncing him from auntie to auntie whenever she had to hit the circuit. He adores her. She smells sharp and warm and welcoming, like a used bookstore.

And she takes over bath time.

It has to be done every night. Otherwise the mold gets ahead of them. It flowers deep in her joints, thick enough to pop her shoulder out of the socket or a tooth out of her gums. Once, in the early days, he stayed up working and forgot her bath. Eurydice didn't complain. She never complains. He woke up and found her on the front porch holding their newspaper. The rot had colonized her eye sockets in the night. Eurydice stared at the headlines through a sheen of black mold tipped in blue spores, spanning the bridge of her nose like a starlet's sunglasses.

"There was an earthquake," she'd said quietly, without looking up. "In Thessaly."

Somehow Calliope always knows to visit when Orpheus doesn't think he can bear to lift Eurydice into the tub one more time. It's not safe to let her do it herself. Her heart no longer has the capacity to keep everything churning along thump by thump, so a stubbed toe or a bruised elbow is a potentially catastrophic hydraulic leak. But Calliope doesn't mind. She has enough energy for everyone. She lifts her daughter-in-law naked into the clawfoot tub and pours in bleach like bubble bath. She scrubs the little fractal spirals of mildew from Eurydice's livid back, her hair, under her arms. The water is warm, but it doesn't matter. She doesn't feel it.

Calliope sings to the beautiful corpse of Eurydice as she washes away the evidence of her nature. She sings like a cake rising, a dove's egg hatching, a memory of goodness. The anthurium on the bathroom sink stretches its crimson heart leaves toward the song. So does the clay in the tiled floor. One by one, the black hexagons crack and buckle, straining to get closer to her. Even the tiny threads of fungus on the nape of Eurydice's neck prickle like hair, erect and aware, moronically yearning without understanding toward the profound thing Calliope is.

She squeezes the sponge out against her daughter-in-law's mottled shoulder. Water trickles backward down along her spine and forward over her sternum, and somewhere between the two, before it splashes down into the bath, it forgets to keep being water. It thickens, turns pale gold. The ribbon of bleach twists into honey. A sudden smell of apples and asphodel exhales from the tub: sharp, autumnal, crisp red skins and crisp white wind. Eurydice sobs in recognition, an ugly, stitch-popping sound. She cups her hands and lifts them to her chapped lips. But the cider-mead of Elysium does not want her. It shrinks back, the bath begins to swirl down the pipe the wrong way round, and where her mouth catches some meager slick of the stuff, it catches a cold blue flame. The faint fire spreads, burning off the alcohol, licking at her knees. Eurydice wails in horror and hunger, trying in vain to stop up the drain with her feet and suck the wine from her fingers at the same time.

Calliope strokes her wet, sweet-scented hair and nods tenderly.

"I know, my love. Marriage is so hard."

Seventh Step

Orpheus and Eurydice met at a party thrown by his agent. A hundred thousand years ago. Yesterday. A blur of balconies and city lights and swaying earrings. A fizzing, popping, positively carbonated evening. Discontent was simply not on the guest list.

"Darling boy," his agent had crooned, guiding Orpheus by the shoulders around a river current of oyster puffs and mini souffles and out-of-season vegetables cut to look like birds of paradise. "Everyone is just *dying* to meet you." Hermes hit his stride in sneakers so white and new they glowed like angelic wings, discussing cheeks and kissing percentages, managing the room as no one else could.

And finally there she was, drifting between little clutches of conversation. Spangles and crystals the color of olive leaves shimmered down her body like rain, a thin fringe that danced every time she laughed. She wore her hair up in a complicated twist with a jeweled comb, and when Orpheus remembers this, when he dreams of it, he sees them all at the same time, overlaid like double-exposed film: the dress and the comb and the twist and the long, limp, greasy hair as it is now, strands stuck in the milky fluid of her dead eye.

"Have you met Eurydice?" Hermes's voice trips down the halls of that other life, that correct life, the life he'd been promised. "You absolutely must, she's a treasure."

And she'd turned away from some studio exec pestering her and offered him her gorgeous hand tipped in gold polish. A faint blackbird of a bruise rising already on her forearm. Hearing her voice for the first time like hearing a song you just *know* is going to hit hard.

"Well, aren't you something?"

And what were you doing at that party? their therapist asks later, so much later. Eurydice shrugs and stares at her knees. Cypress trees cast shadows like black arrows on her face. They never planted cypress. But thick green spear heads crowd the windows on all sides now.

She doesn't remember, Orpheus sighs.

I'm asking her. Active listening, Orpheus. You'll get your turn. So what was happening in your life that night? Were you in college? Working? Promoting your own music?

She was never in the industry, Orpheus says. *It was one of the things I found so refreshing about her, considering her father and all.*

Eurydice picks at the scabs between her fingers. Finally, she rasps: *I . . . I used to sing.*

No, you didn't.

Okay, she surrenders quickly, as she always does. *I didn't.* They used to fight till the rafters came down and make up on the ruins. Orpheus usually won, but he enjoyed the battle. Now he gets his way so easily.

You never told me.

Okay.

You could have come into the studio with me. Put down a backup track.

I didn't ever sing. I can't sing.

Eurydice, do you want to talk about the man who grabbed your arm?

No.

A small bubble of trapped gases slowly inflates her cheek.

But he *was* something. And so was she. He was famous. She was beautiful. What else did anyone need? They were young and it was easy. Orpheus saw himself as he knew he could be reflected back at him in that heated, shimmering stare. He wanted it. He wanted that ease forever. He wanted himself as she saw him.

Just because he went home with a maenad that night and had to be reminded of her name when they met again a month later doesn't make it any less love at first sight.

Orpheus has repeatedly explained that to their therapist.

Eighth Step

Orpheus knows they're here before he even gets to the foot of the stairs. A guitar case leans casually against the wall next to the guest bathroom, perfectly centered in a spotlight of morning sunshine.

It's not one of his. This warhorse is more stickers than leather by now, held together by memory alone.

Orpheus sighs heavily.

Eurydice's father and his dirtbag friends don't call ahead. They don't bake, they don't help with chores, they don't come bearing takeout, and they definitely don't do baths. They just turn up. Once or twice a year. Orpheus rounds the banister today to find the boys all smoking around his living room, feet up on the coffee table, a random girl asleep on the piano bench, empties stacked into green-and-brown hecatombs on every surface. He recognizes the labels.

Orpheus and Calliope are merely famous. The old man is a legend. Seminal. Iconic. No one comes close to his influence, his sheer ubiquitousness. He *is* music.

He lounges in the big swayback armchair, a man mostly his haircut, perpetually stuck halfway between Robert Plant and David Cassidy, a catwalk in the form of a man, leather jacket, leather pants, massive paparazzi-proof hangover shades, a big golden sun stamped on his black T-shirt, herpes sore like a kiss below his lip. A face that invented magazines, a voice that filled them to the brim. He laughs wolfishly at something or other one of his strung-out friends said and puts out his cigarette on a sunbeam as though it were solid stone.

"There he is!" Apollo brays. "Big O! We were just talking about you, weren't we, boys? And where's my beautiful baby girl this morning?"

"She'll be up soon," Orpheus mumbles.

Apollo pats his ribs for more smokes. "Call her down. Lazy, cow-eyed lump." He finds one and jams it unlit between his teeth. "I'm up every morning at the crack of dawn, you know. No excuses. Sleep is for the dead, kiddo!" He catches himself and grins sheepishly, a grin so pretty even Orpheus finds himself trying, once again, to like the man. "Whoops. Awkward. Don't want to offend. You know how sensitive the youth are these days. Can't say anything anymore. Oof. I'll want a drink. You want a drink, mate? Probably need a drink before she . . . ah . . . before *that*." He digs in his pockets for a light. "How's things, anyway? Everything back to normal?" Apollo's eyes glitter suggestively. "Back in the saddle, so to speak?"

Orpheus stares. He coughs out a hollow laugh.

One of the old gang leans forward from the depths of the plush gray couch. He winces; his stomach's wrapped in sterile pads and medical gauze signed by the whole band like a cast. Prometheus flicks a lighter for Apollo's wobbly cig.

"Yer a life saver, thanks," the legend mumbles.

Dionysus heads for the kitchen. Orpheus tries to tell him they barely keep anything in the house, but he opens the fridge with a *Hey, hey, hey* straight out of afternoon reruns. Row after row of wines so old they could draw a pension. The crisper drawers packed with Harp lager—the old man doesn't do wine. His sister favors Blue Moon, but they haven't seen her since the wedding.

It's always like this. Prometheus and Dionysus and Pan, hiding his horns under a fedora, along with whatever nymphs they were shacking up with that week. Ransacking the house, talking about themselves and the old days until you wanted to rivet their mouths shut.

Apollo throws back a beer in one long swallow and gestures for another as they wait for the dead to rise. "When are you going to start touring again, son?" He taps out his ash onto the sleeping girl. She's gorgeous, but they always are. The gray flakes drift down to land on her necklace, a chain of silver laurel leaves looping around her perfect, warm, and living neck. Orpheus stares. He can see her pulse faintly beneath her skin. He'd almost forgotten people's bodies did that. She smells like a river, a forest. Alive.

"Don't want to wait too long between albums. I should know. Can't go radio silent just because the going gets a bit uphill, eh? Gotta get back out there."

"I couldn't stay cooped up like this." Dionysus shudders as he upends a bottle into his gullet. "This house gives me the creeps. And I think you've got a serious mold problem." He wrinkles his nose at the ceiling. A delicate charcoal filigree mars the drywall. Orpheus doesn't have to look. He knows. He'll call someone. To-morrow. Soon.

Orpheus grimaces. Pan glances up from his endless scrolling through whatever hookup app he's on this time. *Swipe, swipe, swipe.* "You can always open for us. The fans would lose their minds." *Swipe.* He lowers his voice. "You can't stay cooped up like this, poor thing. It's not healthy. Life goes on, yeah? There's only supposed to be five stages of grief. What are you on, stage twenty? Does she even . . . does she even know you're here?"

"Of course she does," Orpheus snaps defensively. But she steps out behind him as soon as his voice hits the air.

Eurydice's face glows with health. Her lips shine ripe and red. Her cheeks blush. Her hair shines. Bare, tanned legs delicate as knives beneath a loose skirt and the oversized mustard-colored sweater Calliope knit for her, a friendly cartoon snake on the front and GNOTHI SEAUTON, Y'ALL! sewn on with black thread in a circle around its winning smile and forked tongue. Orpheus's chest throbs. It is her, it is her, as she always was, as the sun made her, as he dreamed of her over and over until it wore a groove in his brain. She clasps her hands to her chest like a little girl. Moves her shoulders up and down slightly so it looks like she might really be breathing. But she isn't. Of course she isn't. It's all a show, all for *him*.

Apollo looks nauseated. His throat works to keep the bile down. He looks his daughter up and down, his dancing warm eyes gone distant, flat, glassy. The words he doesn't say hang in the air between them. *I thought you would be different this time, but I guess not.*

She forgot to do her hands. Her father can't help but goggle at them, fish-colored, embroidered with black veins. She ran out of foundation, couldn't find her gloves. Prometheus goes to open a window—there isn't enough Red Door in the world to fix the smell, rich and putrid and earthen.

"Why don't you play us something?" Dionysus suggests.

None of them can take it, they're so fucking fragile. Orpheus hates them. He hates her. He hates how hopeful she gets. Every goddamn time, and for what? They're so empty, they need something pouring into them all the time just to escape knowing it, into their mouths, their eyes, their ears. Music is just the sound of time blowing across the lip of their nothingness.

Eurydice never puts on the makeup for him. She'll take off the glossy, thick wig as soon as they go. The contacts, the fake lashes, all of it. A pile of girl on the floor.

"Yeah, come on, give us a little song," Apollo agrees eagerly. Anything, anything to avoid having to be here and now. "You must be getting brilliant material out of this whole mess. Deep, experiential stuff. Raw, authentic, blah blah blah, the whole aesthetic. I'm here for it. Front-row center. Can't wait to hear your new sound. Hey, you can even play my ax if you want." He signals for

Prometheus to go get it from the hall. The titan hops to it like an eager spaniel. "Would you like that?"

Orpheus doesn't want to do it. He knows what will happen. So does she. But Eurydice's blown-out pupils bore into him from behind green contacts. She can take it. She doesn't mind. Anything, if it'll make Dad happy.

Apollo puts his guitar into Orpheus's hands. What is he supposed to do, then? It is an instrument made of forever. It is the beginning and end of song. Eurydice fixes her silvered eyes on her father. She puts her cold, heavy hand on his knee and the great man flinches. He fucking *flinches*.

But Orpheus's fingers do not move on the strings. He doesn't want her to know. He doesn't want her to hear. *I haven't done anything wrong*, he tells himself. But nothing in him answers back. So he begins to play a slow, lilting version of an old Smiths song. For her, for them. "Pretty Girls Make Graves." A good joke or a bad one. Who cares? Just let it be over. The voice that moved rocks and trees to life and even the fish to dance fills up a living room with wallpaper twenty years past chic. The girl on the piano bench opens her startlingly green eyes.

He's not even through the first verse when he sees it. Eurydice trembling, vibrating, barely able to hold still. She's shut her eyes. Her jaw clenches so hard they can all hear teeth cracking. But she does not, cannot cry.

Her fingertip blossoms with blood. Real, living blood. Just under the skin. It goes pink and brown, the nail a little round moon, warm, soft. The rest of her hands remain skeletal, ashen, moldering. But her fingertip wakes to the sound of his music, like the rocks, like the trees, like the fish of the stream and the sea.

Finally, she cannot bear it. She cannot be a good girl any longer. She howls in pain. She claws at the living tissue. Her eyes roll back to find some path away from anguish. She drags her hands down her face, smearing away the careful makeup, the meticulous lip. Chunks of flesh come away. Orpheus stops; the color ebbs away. The nail blackens again, little lightning bolts of mold snaking back up out of the cuticle.

Her family scatters like raindrops.

Orpheus and Eurydice sit alone in an empty room.

The carpet has turned into long silver grass. A wind from somewhere far off shakes tiny seeds into the air.

Ninth Step

Orpheus has tried to touch her a thousand times. She has never said no. She has never covered up or cried or told him she needed time. She'll let him do anything he wants.

But he doesn't. Not often. Not anymore.

Once she slid into bed with him and the touch of her flesh shocked him almost into the ceiling. She was as warm as the earth in July, hot, even, the air around her oily and rippling. Orpheus wept with relief. He kissed her over and over, drinking her up and in, so grateful, so stupidly grateful and urgent and needy. She was back and she was his and it would all be fine now, it would all go back to the way it was and when he sang to her she would dance again, she would dance and drink her juice and eat her eggs and maybe they would get a cat. A big fat orange tabby and they'd name it something pretentious and literary nobody else would understand. *I knew you were there*, he whispered into her hair. *I didn't doubt it for a moment. You're always there.*

Only afterward, when he was brushing his teeth, did he notice her slick silver hair dryer left plugged in by the sink. He felt the barrel. She'd run it so long the metal was still almost too hot to bear.

So when Orpheus starts sleeping with the maenad from his agent's party again, he tells himself it's not his fault. It's not her fault either. It's not even *about* her. He tried. He really tried this time.

Let me hear the new song, the maenad says, and rolls over toward him, tangled in sheets like possibilities, everything about her so alive she glows. Her apartment is so clean. No grass or mushrooms or fine purple mold in the ceiling roses. She runs her rosy, licorice-scented fingers through his hair.

And when Orpheus sings, it doesn't hurt her, not even a little. *I love you*, the maenad breathes as she climbs on top of him. *You're amazing. You deserve so much more than this.*

Tenth Step

Every night at nine thirty sharp, Eurydice opens her lavender plastic birth control compact and presses down on the little blister pack with the day of the week printed over it.

In those moments, Orpheus always wants to ask her what she's thinking, why she bothers, what's the point. But he never does.

A pomegranate seed pops out. She closes her eyes when she swallows it.

Orpheus goes to the coffee shop down the road most mornings. He gets a latte for himself and one for Eurydice, then drinks them both on a park bench between here and the house. Cinnamon on top. No sugar. He likes all the sugar himself, but that's what she used to drink. So that's what he drinks now forever.

He tells the cute young barista behind the counter his name. She has a nose piercing and huge brown eyes like a Disney deer. She spells his name wrong on the cup.

"No," he says with his most charming half-cocked grin. "Like the singer."

"Who?" the girl says innocently. "What singer has a weird name like that?"

Orpheus puts the coffees down on his bench. He squints in the sunshine. Watches some kids fight over the tire swing. Pulls out his phone and jabs at the keyboard with his thumb.

Are you around? I need you. I want you.

She texts back right away. Quick as life.

When he gets home that night, he has to step over the green-black river that churns through the foyer, separating the land of the living room from the land of his wife.

Eleventh Step

It's afternoon and there are crabapple blossoms all over the front walk like snow and a smart knock at the back door.

Orpheus feels a rush of excitement prickle in his chest. He knows the face on the other side of the glass. His friend. Maybe his only real friend. The only one who gets him completely, who understands what he's had to go through, who can make it an hour without saying something that makes Orpheus want to punch them in the mouth or beg them to take him away from this place forever.

"Hey, fuckbrains," Sisyphus says fondly as Orpheus turns the bolt and lets him into the kitchen, sporting three days of stubble, ripped jeans, steel-toed boots, and a faded black T-shirt that reads ROCK 'N' ROLL FOREVER in white letters with lightning-bolt tips.

And a dog. Three dogs, actually. German shepherd puppies, maybe four or five months old, all gangly teenage limbs and ears that don't know how to stand up straight yet.

"Hey, crackhead," Orpheus answers. "They give you a day pass?"

The pups sniff at Orpheus. They gag and growl, showing tiny bright teeth. They look past him as one, curious, black-nosed, alert. Past him toward the brand-new river of ash slowly flowing up the hallways.

The ash weeps audibly.

Eurydice hovers behind her husband in another of Calliope's grotesque sweaters. This one with a doofy purple horse and MENIN AEIDE THEA. Three canine heads tilt toward her at precisely the same time. One dog. Three bodies. They move like a stutter.

Sisyphus sinks into the breakfast nook, a heap of handsome limbs. He rolls a milky gray marble over the tops of his tattooed fingers, back and forth, back and forth. His left hand says PRDE. His right says FALL. He nods at the dogs and mumbles:

"Well, I had an idea."

Eurydice holds out her blood-purple fingers to the puppies. They advance slowly, uncertainly, huffing her ashen, green-veined hand. Then they fall all over her, snapping the leash, their movements identical, licking her face, wagging great shaggy tails they haven't grown into yet, howling in recognition and joy. Eurydice beams, grave dirt showing between her teeth, caking her gums.

"I thought, you know . . ." Sisyphus says sheepishly, holding one of the leftover cans of Harp between his threadbare denim knees and cracking it with one hand while the other rolls his marble knuckle to knuckle to knuckle. "Emotional support dog. Worth a try."

"You thought *that* would make a good emotional support animal for my wife," Orpheus deadpans as the three hounds loll in Eurydice's lap, their furry bellies as white as death.

Sisyphus gestures with the beer. "Hey, Cerberus is a good boy! He's had loads of training. Sit, stand up, shake a paw, do not chew souls, do not let the living cross into the realm of the dead, the whole package. And nothing spooks him." His voice softens. "He wanted to come. He misses her. They got to be quite good friends, you know. Nobody pays much attention to the old fella once they're settled in. But not our girl. She brought him snacks."

"The fuck does he eat?" Orpheus asks.

"Kindness," Eurydice growls. Cerberus licks her nose and whimpers in furry ecstasy. "Don't we all," she says into his downy ear.

Sisyphus rolls his stone back and forth. "She took him for two walks a day, every day, and not short ones, either. All down the new riverfront walks, along the Lethe and the Phlegethon and the Acheron." He glances toward the sobbing hallway, but Sisyphus is far too polite to say anything. "She let him stop and sniff whenever he wanted. The shops and galleries started leaving out bowls of water for him."

"I never heard about any of this. What shops?"

Sisyphus lifts an eyebrow. "Didn't you have a look around while you were down there, man? See the sights while you were in town?"

"I was a little busy."

"Who is that busy? It's hell. You weren't even curious?"

Eurydice laughs hoarsely. It is not a kind laugh, and Orpheus doesn't like it at all. She would never have embarrassed him like that in the old days.

"Well, yeah, shops. Saltwater taffy and glass bowls and shit. Revitalization. It's Persephone's whole thing. You do *not* want to let that woman get bored. The saltwater still comes from the rivers, though, so it'll make you forget or be invincible or relive every lamentation of your life just the same. It's just . . . nicer now. Oh, and her yarn. All the shops carried it. They couldn't get enough. She called each lot the funniest things, had us all in stitches. Even Clotho had a standing order. So soft! And the *best* colors. I made this shirt out of it. Do you like it?"

"*Whose* yarn?" Orpheus asks in confusion.

"Who do you think?" Sisyphus laughs.

Eurydice heads out the side door without a word. The dogs walk primly on their leash, heeling perfectly and staring up at her in abject adoration.

"Be honest, man," Sisyphus says, leaning forward. "How's it going?"

Orpheus's eyes burn and his chest crushes in on itself. "It's like I don't even know her anymore."

"Well, I mean, yeah." Sisyphus chuckles.

"What does that mean?"

"Look, I love you, you know that. But did you ever really know her in the first place?"

"What kind of bullshit is that? She's my wife. How can you even ask me that, after everything I did to get her back? Just to be with her again? Of *course* I knew her. Know her," he corrects himself.

"You didn't know she had a dog."

"What happened down there . . . it isn't important, don't you get that? It was a horrible dream. A bad trip. I don't want to know about it. Neither does she. That's all behind us now."

Sisyphus shrugs. "Okay, what's her mom's name?"

Orpheus blinks. "It . . . I don't know, it never came up. But that's not fair, it's not like I don't know her family. Her dad's around all the time. He's never mentioned her either."

Sisyphus sighs, gets up, and helps himself to the vintage Star Wars glasses in the cabinet. He picks Lando. "Where'd she go to college? What was her major? She have any siblings?" The dead man looks around awkwardly for a moment before Orpheus snatches the glass out of his hand.

"I'll do it," he snaps. He gets a blood bag out of the fridge and sticks it in the microwave for forty-five. They stand on the ceramic floor while the machine hums toward its inevitable beep. Deep-green mold crawls through the cracks between tiles under their feet toward the river in the hallway.

"A little bleach will probably take care of that," Sisyphus says quietly.

"Yeah," Orpheus mumbles, pouring the blood out for his friend. "You'd think."

"I don't mean to pry—"

Orpheus laughs in his face.

"But did you ever ask her?"

"Ask her what?"

"If she wanted to come back."

"Why the hell would I ask her? Nobody wants to be dead. I did the right thing. For us. For her. You were there. It was heroic. I was selfless. I was strong."

"Were you? Or could you just . . . not accept that something pretty was taken from you? Did you know her? Or was she hot and rich and uncomplicated?"

"Fuck you," Orpheus whispers.

"Okay, okay. Calm down. I'm not accusing you of anything. I'm just asking questions."

They sit in ugly silence, letting the sunlight through the dusty, spore-spackled windows say the things they cannot.

"How's the new album coming?" Sisyphus asks finally.

Orpheus grabs the rough cut out of his bag, sliding the disc across the table. A fine mist of silvery pollen puffs up in its wake.

Upstairs, asphodel flowers explode out of their bed, a detonation of white-and-red petals like blood and skin. They spread and spread, tumbling onto the floor, nosing the curtains, suckling the wallpaper.

Sisyphus rolls his stone across his knuckles, patiently, endlessly. With his other hand, he touches the disc and knows every song in a moment.

"Wow," Sisyphus whispers. "Oh, wow."

Twelfth Step

Orpheus decides to leave on a Wednesday. Not markedly different from any other Wednesday. She can have the house, he doesn't care. He stops giving her the lamb's blood in the morning. *It'll make it easier,* he tells himself. *She'll forget. She won't suffer. I'm not hurting her. Not really. I'm doing what's best for both of us.* Fuck the house, fuck the cars, fuck his outstanding record contract. None of it matters. If he doesn't come back, that's just fine. But he doesn't know how to start. Where to go. What to take. This isn't his gig. It isn't anyone's gig.

Orpheus asks his mother. She tells him the obvious: *the entrance to hell is always in your own house, silly billy.*

The house didn't have a basement when he bought it. It sure does now. A door between the studio and the library that was never there before. A door and a long, long staircase leading down into lightlessness.

Mold has colonized the house. Tiny blue mushrooms on the fireplace. Carpets of pink fuzz climbing the stairs. Black water flowing past the front door. Weeping ash rippling down the hall. A gurgling stream of fire between the kitchen and the dining room. Asphodel everywhere. Ambrosia in every takeout container.

The rivers visit all the time now. They don't even speak to Orpheus anymore. They just go straight to her.

Eurydice doesn't clean anymore. She and Cerberus lie in a pile together and watch the country inside the house grow by candlelight. When Orpheus asked if she felt like pulling her weight on even the most basic level, she turned her head like a stone door and stared in the direction of his studio, panting like a wolf.

Cerberus doesn't let him into her room anymore. If he tries, the three pups growl and drool and their eyes flash green in the dark.

Orpheus sings for his wife. He sings for an audience of two: of death and death's great love. The most important studio boss there is. He sings everything she ever was or could be. He sings every moment of their life together, every kiss and whisper and quiet joke, every intimate space that opened between them like dark flowers, every good day, because they were all good days. He sings her heart out. He sings what will become his comeback anthem, a song no one can get out of their heads, topping the charts for years, used in every film about love and loss and even an antidepressant commercial. Orpheus strips Eurydice of Eurydice and transforms her into a song so perfect death gives up and life buries him in laurels.

The song of them, that she never hears. He simply never thinks to play it for her. It's his. His best work. Besides, she never asked what he sang to get her back. He'd have shown her, if she'd asked. Probably.

And what he sang for her and only her, what he sang before the great starry, unweeping face of death, is sitting on a rough-cut demo in his leather bag as he walks out of his house on a Wednesday years later, in a padded envelope with his agent's address on it.

"Do you still love me?" Orpheus asks her Tuesday night, the night before he leaves her. She sits on the porch with her dogs, putting together a puzzle of *Starry Night*.

Eurydice runs her fingers over the black half-assembled chapels and cypress trees. She hasn't had lamb's blood in two weeks. Sometimes she forgets she is dead and starts screaming when she sees herself in the mirror. But today was a good day. They watched TV together. She watched Cerberus play in the backyard. One of him ate a bee. She laughed.

"I see my love for you as though it hangs in a museum," Eurydice says slowly. "Under glass. Environmentally controlled. It is a part of history. But I am not allowed to touch it. I am not allowed to add anything new to it. I am not even allowed to get close." She puts a golden star into place without looking up. "Why didn't you turn around?" Eurydice whispers.

Orpheus tells the truth. "I knew you were there, baby. I never doubted it for a minute."

Children yell and play in the neighbors' gardens, high-pitched giggles fizzing up into the streetlights. "You didn't know. You assumed I was there. Behind you. Like I'd always been there. Behind you. You couldn't even imagine that I might not do as I was told, that I might not be where you wanted me to be, the moment you wanted it. That was my place, and you assumed I would be in it. What in your life has ever gone any way other than as you wished it?" She glances toward the house, toward the demo still sitting where Sisyphus left it. "And now you have what you want from me. What you always wanted. I am no longer necessary. And yet. I am still here."

Her hand settles down on the leftmost puppy. Cerberus wears three weighted coats, to help with his anxiety. Maybe Orpheus should have gotten her one. He thinks of that now, and dwells on it long enough that there's no easy way back into the conversation, and Orpheus just tells her to shut the lights off before she goes to bed.

Orpheus and Eurydice step blinking into a summer's day. The blue of the sky throbs in their eyes. He takes her into his arms and swings her around. *You're back, you're back, and it'll all be as it was, you'll see. I saved you. I did it. Aren't you happy? Baby? Put your arms around me. Don't you want to?*

Orpheus walks down the porch steps of his house. It is dusk, and he can smell everyone's dinner. He can see all their lights, the illuminated windows of their worlds. Owls are heading out to hunt. Business on the West Coast closes in an hour.

Orpheus stops on the stair. For a moment, just a moment, he thinks that perhaps she is there. Asking him not to go. Eurydice as she always was, adoration in human form, the way he remembers her. The way she should have been. Maybe it will all be all right, and this was just the last test, the last barrier between life and death.

His phone buzzes in his pocket. He knows without looking that it's his maenad, warm and rosy and waiting.

Orpheus turns around on the staircase. For old times' sake.

Eurydice stands in the window, watching. Acheron and Phlegethon kiss her cheeks, lay their heads on her shoulders. She smiles with such tenderness, but not for him. She shuts her eyes in their embrace.

Orpheus straightens his shoulders. He turns away. He has places to be. A maenad. A record. He has a life. He has a legend to become. He knows it's all there, just waiting for him.

Behind him, asphodel devours the house whole.

Tripping Through Time

FROM *Dark Matter*

IT'S THE GREAT Fire of London and I'm serving biofarmed eel canapés. Smells and sounds don't get through the bubble, or I guess they call it the chronofield, but I can see plenty: thatched roofs going up like match heads, blue-and-orange flames licking and crunching on wood, smoke tunneling up into the hazy sky, people running for their lives. It's a trip.

I shouldn't be watching, though. I gotta sling these canapés and then get more champagne flutes out the chiller. Clay, who is now head server, stuck her whole bony neck out to get me this job. I spot her across the way, offering appies to three musty old men posted up at the shimmering edge of the chronofield. She's auto-smiling and hide-the-pain laughing at whatever junk they are saying to her.

Usually her hair is a rust-colored buzzcut, but today she's wigged up, all straight and glossy and long, because it's one of *those* gigs. They also got us in period costume, which is not falling-apart sweat-pants but instead these stiff, soot-smeared dresses that actually, me to you, look somewhat good in an aggressively retrobomb way.

I waltz over to the riverbank where our employer, Mrs. Silver-wright, is holding court like some kind of primeval sea goddess. She's wearing this unbelievable half-holo gown that looks like a perpetually crashing wave, all foamy and whatnot, and her bass-clipped hair is billowing in perfect tendrils around her face, and her cheekbones are so, so deadly. Sometimes I just stare at them.

"That's the issue, isn't it," she says, plucking a canapé off my tray. "If we hosted at, say, the building of the pyramids? It could be an entire day spent watching one slab of rock get hauled up a sand dune. The signing of the Declaration? Over in minutes."

Her admirers nod and tutter.

"I'm afraid destruction simply schedules better than creation." Mrs. Silverwright gestures over her shoulder, where the river's reflecting the orange flames in a ripply dance. "And it's not as if we're the only ones drawn to the spectacle. People came from miles around to watch London burn."

I can see another boatload of people rowing through the dirty water, smeared with actual soot, eyes bright and panicky. It's shitty for them, but like Mrs. Silverwright told us while we were setting up, these people have been dead forever. And we can't leave the chronofield anyways.

An old woman does the classic forearm grab, clawing me up with her nails. "Excuse me," she says. "Is this eel or elver?"

In my head I'm like, *It's whatever you want it to be, baby.*

In real life I'm like, "This is eel, ma'am. Imported from a bio-farm in Andalusia, served on crostini with a balsamic reduction and sesame-seed topping."

She hucks it right in the Thames.

But all in all, it's not a bad gig. Me and Clay keep circulating, and every so often we pass like two satellites in orbit and beam each other information about who's getting too drunk, or too handsy, or just keeps saying the stupidest shit. People are really into watching London burn down, so they're easy to please. Honestly, the hardest part was probably the pre-job testing.

Rich folks already got all these custom telomeres and whatnot, which makes it easier to get modified for the chronofield. Us caterers do not, and apparently some people have a real rough time inside that pretty, shimmery bubble. Like, the girl before me just started bleeding out her nose and ears one night, gushing all over the white linen tablecloths and babbling about how sorry she was.

I've got the right genetics for the mod—as proven by a shitload of tests in this little bunker slash office where I had to wear a big circuitry-swatched apron—but I still feel woozy when we zap back to reality, which is a big antiseptic-white tent. Me and Clay keep the smiles stapled on while all the guests flit away to their limos or quaddies. Then we help our chef-slash-serving captain and her bot load up all their shit, and then we finally hit the detox.

The magnetics make my skin grow goose bumps and tug my hair all over the place. Clay's gets lifted straight up for a second, and I can see the edge of her lace front. The scan blinks green.

"That's some good money," she says, stepping out of the booth. "And it's rad, right? Seeing the past. I mean, you can't touch it, but it's rad."

As soon as I get out of the detox booth, I grab my phone from the storage locker and see she was right: the money is good as hell. I pump my fist a little. "Hey," I say. "Thanks for getting me this, Clay. This is *big* necessary right now."

"Hey," she says. "I know." She pauses. "Mrs. Silverwright likes you too. We could get you on regular. Sisterhood of the time-traveling pants type shit."

I blink. "She *likes* things?"

"Micro-expressions," Clay says. "Gotta be watchful."

We bump elbows, mask up, and part ways: Clay to her ride, me to my metro. There's another virus going around, so every second seat in the tube has one of those 3-D printed spike pads glued to it to keep people from sitting too close together. But of course that just means more people are standing crammed up in each other's mouths. I try to face the corner the whole ride.

The apartment block's in quarantine mode when I get there. The door sprouts me off a little swab to run around my nostrils, then I sit tight on the stoop while it does its thing. It's a warm, muggy night, warmer than London on fire, which seems backwards to me. The bubble must be climate-controlled.

Finally, the door chimes me through and I scurry up the steps. Me and my mom are on the third floor—one of those half suites with an epoxy wall installed to double the number of units. Sometimes at night we hear our neighbors on the other side moving around. Mom used to joke with me about them being ghosts, or maybe creepy mirror versions of us with black button eyes. She got that from a book she read me as a kid.

The door to our apartment has another quarantine warning blinking on it, like maybe three flights of stairs was long enough to forget. I shoulder it open and head straight for the sink.

"Hey, is that my little time traveler?" my mom calls from the next room. Her voice is a little scratchier than usual. "Is that my little quantum jumping bean?"

"Woman, what does that even mean?" I call back.

I don't come out of the bathroom until I'm fully scrubbed and my outer clothes are in the laundry. Mom doesn't get flare-ups too often anymore, but she's on immunomodulators all the time—colitis—so I've been washing my shit good for years already. The coconut-scented disinfectant gel is pretty much my signature fragrance.

Mom is at the kitchen table, peering at her work tablet. When she looks up, I can tell she's relieved to see me in one piece and not, like, turned into a fetus or something. "Hey, hon."

"Queen of England says hi," I tell her.

"Unbelievable, the shit they use it for," she says, sounding grudgingly impressed more than angry. "Parties! Just sitting there watching a city burn down."

"Can't really do nothing else," I say. "We're all stuck in the chronofield, right?" And I think, *They dead anyways*, but I don't say it, because it's the kind of thing that'll get her actually angry. I'm tired and achy and I want to just chill and enjoy the fact I got paid. "You test today?" I ask.

"Just now," she says, nodding at the kit magnetized to the fridge. "Clean as a whistle."

I wrap both my arms around her and give her a big squeezing hug. We smell like the same soap, but she has her mom smell going on too. There's this safe, warm feeling when you're with someone you love and you're both clean, especially after a couple weeks doing distance and isolation, and you know you can hug them. Me to you, I think it might be the best feeling in the whole fucking world.

Next party I work is a week later, and also like six hundred years ago. It's some famous battle: big muddy hillside, people clanking around in armor, arrows flying everywhere. The rain sleeting down doesn't get through the bubble, but some of the guests are going around with fashionable black umbrellas anyways. I'm a little distracted tonight and Clay notices; she intercepts me right as I run out of deconstructed patatas bravas.

"You good?" she asks.

I nod.

"Your mom good?"

I don't want to burden Clay with this shit, not when she's already burdened with her own shit, but she has those big soulful

eyes you just want to confess stuff to. "Tested red yesterday morning," I say. "Not IDed yet. I keep thinking I must have brought
something in, you know?" I whirl my finger. "Like, maybe even
something from here?"

"No way," she says. "Detox, remember? And you wash hard, girl.
You wash better than my brother, and he's a nurse."

"Thanks, Clay." I pause. "Your parents okay?"

"Holed up and healthy, yeah," she says. "Just jealous I'm out
here breaking physics while they stuck inside playing canasta."

She spots someone's glass running low and darts over before it
hits critical empty. I circle back to the kitchenette to restock my
tray. I'm just starting to feel better when a soldier eats shit right in
front of me, staggering out of the mist and collapsing just outside
the chronofield. He's so full of arrows it should be funny, he's got
six, no, seven, one's broken off in his belly.

But his blood is bright red, leaking down into the mud, and
the shimmer distorts his face but for a second I swear he's staring right at me. I know he's been dead for hundreds of years
already. He doesn't look dead, though. He looks desperate. It's
not funny.

A drunk man shows up, one of the guests who was placing bets
earlier on who was going to get trampled by their own horse. He
has a wine stain on his crisp white sleeve. "Oh my God, that's horrible," he says. "Hold this. I want a souvenir."

He hands me his glass, sloshing half of it into the dirt. I'm too
shook to do anything but take it. The functional part of my brain
figures he wants to take a snap of himself with the dying guy in the
background, but instead he slides this metallic prong out of his
sleeve and pushes it against the chronofield.

A poison-yellow warning holo pops up. He shunts it aside, keeps
pushing, and suddenly a small hexagonal chunk solidifies in the
shimmery surface of the bubble. The node falls away. The guest
gives a grunt of satisfaction, eyes fixed on the arrow sticking out of
the dying guy's back.

"Heath? What are you doing, man?" His slightly more sober
buds have spotted us. "What's he doing?"

Heath snaps a glove on, wriggles his fingers, and shoves his
arm through the chronofield. Everybody shouts and jumps and
rushes forward at the same time, everybody except me, because
I'm still standing there holding Heath's wineglass and watching

the soldier bleed out. The shouting cuts off. Heath is staring at his arm, which is intact on the other side of the bubble, with that drunk, bleary kind of self-amusement. Someone does a nervous laugh.

Then Heath starts to scream. His lanky arm is whipping around like a popped balloon, and somehow it's shrinking like one too, collapsing in on itself, bones crunching bones and skin slurping skin. He staggers back, and only a stump comes with him. He's screaming, I'm screaming, everyone's screaming. The little medi-drone me and Clay helped load up comes whirling over to see what's going on. It clamps itself to the blood-spraying end of Heath's not-arm.

One of his idiot friends is shaking me like, *Why didn't you stop him?* like, *You overserved him, you overserved him!* Which is so fucking absurd I will laugh if my throat ever gets unstuck.

Mrs. Silverwright sweeps in and detaches him, shoves him away. "Are you okay?" she asks. It takes me a second to get she's asking me.

"Yeah," I say. "Yes. Ma'am."

We both look down at Heath, who is still writhing around on the dirt. The thing that he used to open the hole, the metallic prong, is lying beside him.

"What a fucking clown," Mrs. Silverwright says. "One in every family, I suppose." She gives me a pat on the arm, then turns to her clustered guests. "The party's ending early today, darlings."

When I get back to reality and back to my phone, there's a message from my mom telling me she got her bug IDed and it's a SARS variant. I don't show it to Clay. She's still buzzing about what happened with the chronofield, how that dumbshit deserved to lose more than one limb. I nod and nod and nod, and even laugh, and then we go our separate ways.

The whole metro ride I got this dread in my belly, and guilt for the dread, which feels bad too. I walk slow from my stop, saun-tering down the empty street. Halfway home a drone flits up, yammering about curfew, but I got an employment blit from Mrs. Silverwright so I'm in the clear. A couple minutes after that, I'm waiting on the stoop for the apartment door to read my swab, and the dread's getting worse and worse.

The scan blinks green and the door opens, which also opens my lungs, at least a little. I head down the hall. Our door's got a new pictogram now—a notification that says, *Infected individual in isolation.* I shoulder it open and beeline for the bathroom.

"Well, well, I have been blessed with a visitor from the distant past." My mom's scratchy, cheery voice is coming from the portable speaker on the kitchen table—she's already gone full iso in her room. "How was Agincourt?"

I think about the man full of arrows, and Heath the rich drunk clown reaching for him, and Heath's arm turning into flesh-spaghetti and disappearing.

"Rainy," I say. "You okay? Still flaring?"

She doesn't answer, and that makes me scrub harder, like I can squeeze a reply out of my slippery hands. "I'm okay, hon," she finally says. "But I'm on Waitlist for a hospital bed."

I get the trapdoor stomach thing, where it feels like all your guts just dropped out the bottom of you. I pull my phone out of the disinfectant tray and pull up Waitlist. Friends and family notifications: a great-uncle here, an old classmate there, and sitting buried in the 932 spot, my mom.

"Bad timing," she says. "They just got a big surge."

My mom had me late and she turned sixty last year. That, plus colitis and other IBDs getting reclassified as comorbidities a while back, means she's low priority.

"Company can't bump you up?" I ask.

"They barely cover my immunos and liver checkups. They're not gonna up and find me a bed." She bites back a cough, and that spikes all the little hairs on the back of my neck.

"How you breathing?" I ask. "What's your peak flow?"

"If I link you all my numbers, you're just going to worry. You can't change the numbers, hon." She pauses. "I'm reading the complete works of Tennessee Williams. How about you make something to eat, get cozy in bed . . ."

I go to the kitchen and fix up some food and clean everything on automatic. Spray, wipe, spray, wipe. Mom got a drone delivery while I was working. A big box of my favorite knock-off Nesquik cereal is on top of the fridge. Same taste, fewer atrocities—I said that when I was a kid and Mom never let me forget it.

I don't go to my room, though. Instead, I go sit with my back to my mom's door, so I can hear her shifting around in her room, so I can almost feel it. We do up the camlink so we can see each other. Her liver-spotted hands are holding an old, battered book of plays. She's halfway smiling. She can tell I'm not in my bed, but I think she gets it.

Me to you: Tennessee Williams is not my thing. I kind of doze off, shoulder blades slowly sliding down the door. But I do hear that one part I always remember, from the very start of *The Glass Menagerie*, where their eyes fail them, or they fail their eyes, and they get their fingers pressed forcibly down on the fiery braille of a failing economy. That shit has been happening for centuries.

Mom works in contact tracking, for a company called Hund. They mostly take care of her meds—colitis is not cheap—but they don't have provisions for virus season. While she reads, I split off a new tab and start searching around Hund's policy site, which is basically all fucking nonsense.

But when I move up to their conglomerate's policy site, I spot something co-signed by Aline Silverwright.

I get my shot during the Toba catastrophe. Mrs. Silverwright breaks away from her flock and goes over to the edge of the chronofield, checking something on her embedded wrist screen. She looks as regal and beautiful as ever, with her heartbeat and other organ functions transposed to the fabric of her dress in an elegant anatomical collage.

Outside the bubble, a bunch of people in extremely retrobomb attire—animal skins and bark type shit—are staring off into the distance at a growing pillar of smoke. Earlier I heard somebody say that they're not *Homo sapiens*, they're some other kind of hominid, but they look human to me.

Anyways, I'm glad me and Clay are wearing chamsuits instead of period costume. It's a weird feeling, only being able to see your gloved hands, everything else just a blur. But you get to pretend you're a ninja and it's not like the guests treat you much different.

"Mrs. Silverwright?" I say, from a distance so I don't startle her by accident. We're out of earshot of the other guests.

"Hello, darling," she says. "What is it?"

"My mom works for one of your companies," I say.

She gives a tight smile. "Small world."

There's no smooth chill way to say it, and I have to say it now, before she gets distracted. Before I lose my nerve. Before I start thinking about how she might freak and dump my contract, dump Clay's contract, too, just for good measure.

"She's sick with the new bug and she's high risk," I say. "She needs a bed, or a medidrone, and her company won't pay out, so she's stuck on Waitlist, and I was hoping you could help."

Mrs. Silverwright fixes her apologetic eyes just to the left of where my head actually is. "I'm sorry to hear that, darling, but now's really not the time," she says. "The magma's about to start. Make sure everyone's got a glass. Boris will probably try to do a toast of some sort."

She walks off, and I realize I been wearing a chamsuit my whole fucking life. I go get the champagne. The guests are congregating at the edge of the bubble, most of them sitting on little modular stools we helped the bot unload. On the other side, the people who are hominids are agitated, some muttering to each other, some just watching, stock still, eyes wide, as the sky gets dark.

Everyone's got a glass. I back away to the kitchenette, because I don't want to watch a volcanic eruption kill people who are already dead. I'm hoping Clay will circle back, too, and we'll get a slice of time to talk, and I'll tell her what happened.

"This shit is so barbaric."

Not Clay's voice. I look up and see this girl in a swirling lime-green holojacket holding a vape to her pouty lips. She's got the same cheekbones as Mrs. Silverwright.

"They could have viewed it from anywhere, but they pick a village, so they can see people being fucking terrified," the girl says. "What's next? The Tulsa massacre?"

I just stare at her.

"I'm only here for my dissertation, but I don't know if it's even worth it, like, morally?" She turns her head and blows smoke. The volcano's still billowing ash into the sky behind her. "If the chrono-field failed, they'd deserve it. Honestly."

"Huh," I say, deploying the all-time safest, most vanilla word on instinct.

"I feel so bad for you, having to watch this kind of shit," the girl says. "I'm sorry. Just wanted to say that. I should get back to the jackals now."

She thrusts out her pale, moisturized elbow, pretending like she's a chill, normal person and half her bloodstream is not composed of artificial leukos. I bump her back. It hurts so bad. She smiles, like she did me some kind of favor, then stumbles back to the party.

The volcano blows and I can see Mrs. Silverwright's heartbeat racing on her dress. I remember how she looked like a goddess to me the first time I saw her.

Fuck.

My mom is playing music when I get home, streaming some electrotango, the kind of stuff she used to dance to back when social dancing was a thing. Sometimes I hear the floor creak a certain way and I know she's gliding around in there. Sometimes, when we're both clean, she'll get me to be her follow, and I'm pretty damn bad at it but it's okay.

I go to the bathroom and scrub. She'll be pissed if I tell her what I tried with Mrs. Silverwright, because it was risking my job and whatnot, but at the same time I want to tell her.

I want to tell her how Mrs. Silverwright apologized to the space beside my head, and how her heart started racing when she saw the volcano blow, and how the hominids, the people, were so scared but nobody really gave a fuck—not the girl with the holojacket and not me either.

It was a bad, bad trip. I dry my coconut-smelling hands on a fresh towel, then pick up my phone, wiping the last of the disinfectant off its screen. I send Mom a little door-knock pictogram.

No read, no reply.

For a second I imagine it's because she's dancing, sweeping up and down the narrow space between her bed and her closet, but she showed me her lung function yesterday and I know she's not. I go to her door and knock for real.

"Mom? I'm back to the future, or whatever." My voice is all high and tight and I can't fix it. "You okay?"

No reply.

I get these dreams, sometimes, where I'm climbing a tree or a ladder and I fall, and there's this gut-lurch, and this horrible knowledge that you can't take it back. You can't redo the rung, or the branch. Your hand slipped and you're done.

I open my mom's door, wrapping my hand in my sleeve on automatic, and I start falling. She is smaller than I've ever seen her, curled up on her bed in the middle of this big damp wet spot. Her skin has gone gray. Her phone is lying on the floor where she must've dropped it, back cracked so the battery is peeking out. She is holding her breath, the same way I am, like it's some kind of contest, and I think maybe if I just give up and exhale, so will she. I breathe. Her rib cage does not move a millimeter. I am falling, falling, falling.

New strain. More aggressive. Can't touch her. Can't touch her. I call the emergency line and then I do it anyway, stumbling over to grip both her hands. They're cold. I start rubbing them, like that might help, the same way she did for me when I was little and I would come in from the snow and she would say, *icicle fingers!* and rub them warm again.

The AI on the emergency line is asking me to scan and link her vitals. She's dead, though. And I get this horrible thought: she was dead anyways. She was outside the bubble.

The next party is in Venice, back before it was underwater, but it doesn't even matter because I'm not even there. It feels like I'm a drone hovering along behind myself, watching me talk to the chef, watching me refill trays, watching me smile. Clay would know something's wrong. She would know it in an instant. But she's home iso-ing with the same bug everyone's getting now, same SARS variant.

So I float around the party, slinging feta zucchini gratin, and nobody can tell the ice truck finally came for my mom yesterday. Some of the guests are wearing little masquerade masks. A few have these black goggle-eyed ones with hooked beaks. Heath the clown is back, showing off a flexy new artificial arm, all sleek and white and Apple. The girl with the vape is here again, too, and she doesn't look at me.

Outside the bubble, the cobblestones are crowded with partiers, packed shoulder to shoulder how they never are now. Men and women in costumes are marching through the street. People are waving lanterns, spilling wine, playing bulgy-looking guitars. They look so happy.

"Poor dumb fuckers," Heath says, slurring even though I haven't served him any alcohol. "Getting their ticks all over each other."

This is the last big carnival before the Bubonic Plague hits. I heard Mrs. Silverwright talking about it with the sponsor earlier, like she was talking about cloudy, chance of showers. These happy people are going to be digging mass graves soon. This is the last night before the course of European history is altered forever, and it's a chance for solemn reflection on the ephemerality of some-thing, something, something.

I watch myself get another bottle of Chardonnay out of the chiller. I'm wearing a checkered serving apron that looks dumb but has a pocket. In the pocket, I have this pointed metal thing that keeps poking at me.

Mrs. Silverwright is wearing a dress with photosensitive stalks that swivel around to follow the light, and it makes her look like she's made of snakes. She smiles at me when I serve the wine. Heath is pretending to put on a puppet show with his artificial arm, wrapping his real one around the girl with the vape, who giggles. I can hear my mom's voice reading that Williams line, *fingers pressed forcibly down on the fiery braille,* and I understand it now.

Some people will never feel anything until their hands get pushed down onto it. I wander to the edge of the chronofield and take the sharp thing out of my apron. It's a short metallic prong inlaid with circuitry and loaded, from what I can tell, with the other kind of virus. Me to you, I don't remember why I snatched it off the ground at Agincourt. Maybe I wanted a souvenir.

Maybe I wanted this. I push it against the shimmery wall of the chronofield. Wave after wave of warning holos pop up and I slap them all away. Heath the clown had it set to target one specific node. I simplified things: I got it set to target all of them. A beautiful Italian woman in a beautiful, filigreed mask dances past me, so close we're almost the same person.

Little hexagons start to appear, not just where I'm pushing but everywhere, all across the bubble, sprouting like metal flowers. A tremor goes through the whole chronofield. I hear panicky shouts. I keep pushing, but I look back over my shoulder. Mrs. Silverwright is running at me. The girl with the vape is shrieking at me.

"I didn't mean it!" she howls. "I didn't mean it!"

And that's true too. They don't mean it. But they still have to—

The Frankly Impossible Weight of Han

FROM *khōréō*

Case #*1*: Grant

Four hours after Grant Rutherford completes his life's work—a machine that extracts energy and matter from ambient sources to create exact copies of anything it scans—he passes out behind the wheel of his 2025 Ford Fusion, crests a highway embankment, and flips into a ditch.

Grant hasn't slept since his wife died the previous week, the victim of a tumor caught too late. This diagnostic failure was partially attributable to the closure of the more accessible—but less profitable—local primary care offices in favor of a surgery center forty miles away, and partially attributable to Mrs. Rutherford's doctors, who transmuted her fear and pain into the subversive signs of a traitor in their war on opioids.

Shamed, Mrs. Rutherford returned home and pulled herself up by her bootstraps until it was too late for anything other than palliative care, and Mr. Rutherford passed Christmas Eve by his wife's bedside, watching as the color slowly dissolved from her face.

In the weeks before his fatal crash, it is Mr. Rutherford's intention that the first thing copied by his Frankly Impossible Machine™, or FIM, will be an orange. He owes this sentimentality to his undergraduate days, when he fell in love with the work of Pablo Neruda. (And indeed, in another reality, Mr. Rutherford is a poet—but here, he blooms to adulthood in a grim place, one where publishers drive libraries to extinction and poetry is not considered a valid avenue for the investment of one's professional time. Mr. Rutherford instead becomes a scientist—a pursuit better leveraged towards profitable ventures.)

As he enters his first career, his resolution to hold on to some shred of ethics narrows his choice of employer. He and his wife make the best of this. They have no children due to an amassed collection of student loans (and if there are grumblings of *personal responsibility* in the audience, I'll remind you that you're welcome to stop reading at any time).

For the Rutherfords, work is both life and legacy, and it is perhaps for this reason that years later, on the eve of his death, Mr. Rutherford still desires to replicate this orange, to put a carpel of himself inside this machine he will give to the world.

In the moments before he presses the button—four hours before his death—he decides he needs some part of his wife to be present, and so he also inserts her gavel.

Consider, if you will, this noble machine, still running in the basement when he leaves his house for the last time. We know now that the replication time of an object is proportional to its mass and the complexity of its composition. Far smaller and simpler than Mr. Rutherford's noble piece of dimpled fruit or the well-worn wood of his wife's gavel is his grief, which now forms a patina coating the inside of their home.

Perhaps Mr. Rutherford should've known better, but I would argue his failure belongs to us all.

I hope you will allow me some leeway here: in order to comprehend the events that are soon to unfold, we must accept that the next thing copied by Mr. Rutherford's FIM *is the machine itself.*

How does it manage such a thing? Especially with Mr. Rutherford's body lying in a ditch? (At the exact moment of replication, Mr. Rutherford's core temperature has already dropped to 90°F due to the snowy conditions on that particular January night.) We may never know, although there are a number of theories involving a second, never-discovered machine, or tricks with a mirror, a rogue photocopier.

The point is that once we accept the existence of the second machine, we can begin to grasp the monumental shift in power dynamics that has just occurred. A single machine is a choke point, something for a government to leverage for its own purposes. But a second machine means an end to scarcity itself—or would have, if only things had turned out a bit differently.

My theory is that the machine knows this, has debated the ethics of such a revolution, and found it lacking. That it's aware its creator is dead—and, in a moment of mourning and self-consolation, decides to copy itself, a thing it knows inside and out.

It makes copy after copy after copy, its entrails humming and whirring as it slowly sucks the warmth out of the room. There is nobody present to observe the way the air grows thinner and thinner, the way the room grows colder and colder (surpassing, even, the drop in temperature of Mr. Rutherford's body, despite the brave struggle of the household thermostat). There is nobody to ask the machine whether its intentions are to destroy us or to save us.

I suppose, in a way, it achieves both.

Case #2: Mi-Young

And now, a day later, we come to a truly pivotal moment, like a spinning coin that balances precariously on its rim. If, for example, the police officer that comes to Mr. Rutherford's house to make the death notification to his wife gets on his hands and knees and peers through the privacy-glass blocks of the basement window, he might notice something amiss and kick in the door. The FIMs find their way into the hands of local law enforcement, and who knows what the outcome will be?

The machines could just as easily be discovered by the stream of overworked and underpaid temporary relief rural mail carriers who shove letter after letter into the Rutherfords' unattended box, desperately hoping it won't fill before the regular carrier comes back from sick leave. (He never does, as he was the first to visit the house. Although he will eventually stop crying, he'll never feel safe delivering mail again.) So many unexplored avenues exist in which the FIMs become the boon or the nightmare of either the state or the giant corporations that form its equivalent—but instead, the FIMs are found by one Mi-Young Cho, Mr. Rutherford's old college roommate and sometimes friend.

Unlike Mr. Rutherford, Ms. Cho has chosen poetry and the poverty that comes with it—although it's of the romantic sort, as her family would willingly rescue her, should she ever find herself in real trouble. This bifurcation of careers drives a wedge between Ms. Cho and Mr. Rutherford, one only recently removed. As a final olive branch, Mr. Rutherford has given Ms. Cho a key to his home, a bittersweet gesture of semi-patronage—and his way of putting his past to rest. At some point, we must all live with our choices.

And so, we arrive at Ms. Cho, her heart racing as she turns the key. She has a poem to read to Mr. Rutherford, and he hasn't answered her calls, her texts, her email—and although she doesn't expect him to be home and tells herself she is only leaving a note, perhaps some small, fearful part of her longs to see his face. He chose a life in which he is a scientist married to Mrs. Rutherford over a life of poetry with Ms. Cho, but that doesn't mean she accepts his choices.

She pushes open the door and steps inside. Immediately she smells a curious ripple that reminds her of ozone. She tracks it to the basement door, which is cold to the touch. (Permit me, in this moment, another suspension of disbelief, for while no standard household door seals tightly enough to create a vacuum, when Ms. Cho's ghost is interviewed, she will swear that when she turned the knob and pulled, the basement opened itself to her with a pneumatic white hiss. As she was the only witness present, we will have to take her at her word.)

She trails down the steps, spelunking into the basement's frigid interior, and finds the machine, which has by now made exactly 422 copies of itself, each the size of a shoebox.

(In her interview, the ghost of Ms. Cho will staunchly maintain that the room sounded like new snow—deathly quiet, save her own panting breath. As if the machine was waiting to see what she'd do next.)

She looks at the room, packed floor to ceiling with boxy machines, arranged as neatly as a delivery on a pallet. She picks one up and looks inside. It's empty.

Then it whirs. An instant later, an orange appears in the air directly in front of the machine. It drops to the ground, a bounce that becomes a roll—*thud, thud, thiddle-thiddle-thiddle.*

If, perhaps, the machine had created some other object, we would not be as lost as we are, although I doubt it. Some things are inexorable. When Ms. Cho picks up the orange and peels it, the sweet citrus spiking the air, she's transported back to a night six months ago—the memory of getting sloppy drunk in a bar as Mr. Rutherford loudly proclaimed that being downsized from the NIH didn't matter, anyways, because his machine was nearly complete.

That night, Ms. Cho had looked into her glass and contemplated how Mr. Rutherford would react to her leaning in for a kiss. She'd had a chance in college and blown it. Mr. Rutherford had immediately moved on, but Ms. Cho never gives up on the things she wants.

What machine? she'd asked. The sibilance of the word had been intoxicating, the way it mingled with the sounds of pouring liquid, of ice in glasses.

He had explained it. Told her the first thing he'd copy would be an orange. She had nodded shyly and moved in for the kiss, and he'd rebuked her and fled the room.

The evening had been so hot, she'd heard her sweat sizzle as she walked home. She had written that night, a poem about an impossible machine and an orange, and when she'd read it the next morning, it had contained a seed of brilliance (his, not hers, but she had ignored this fact). She'd sent it to a literary magazine before calling him, intent on either mending fences or giving him back his key.

Straight to voicemail. At first, she had taken it as a sign he wanted to be left alone—but then why not answer and demand the return of his key?

In their acceptance letter, the magazine's editors had commented on their appreciation for the Neruda homage. Ms. Cho had pinned it to the wall, and in the intervening weeks, she had tapped it as she exited and entered the house—a sign that her luck was changing, a constant reminder of the meaning of an orange.

In a fit of pride, she'd called her whole family, even the distant cousins still in Korea. "Come visit me," she'd said, the half-known language awkward in her mouth.

Ms. Cho apprehends the machine's implications at once—and, like all artists, she believes she is uniquely qualified to save the world. She backs her car up to the garage and loads as many of the FIMs as she can fit into the hatchback. (She originally intended the vehicle to be a safety net in case she should ever find herself homeless, but clever Ms. Cho has always managed to find a way.)

By now, the machines are behaving differently. They still make copies, but more slowly, and the inside of the car is warmer than the house. Even so, Ms. Cho drives with the window down, because something about the FIMs makes her breath come in gasps. When she glances in her rearview mirror, there's an odd pattern to the way the light falls over their square bodies, as if the laws of optics don't apply to them. And once, when she's cruising along at a steady seventy miles an hour, she looks back and sees a red glow spark in the corner of her vision—and then it races across the back of the car, machine after machine blooming and dimming in sequence, as if passing along some missive.

Despite the open windows, the car fills with the scent of oranges. Occasionally, a fruit shoots out at an angle and bounces before coming to rest on the floor.

Ms. Cho drives the six hours to Chicago, stopping once at a gas station and once at a grocery store for snacks. In both places, the staff can barely meet her gaze—and while she wonders why, she finds that examining their faces for too long makes her think about the creep to whom she gave her virginity, and this unnerves her enough that she looks away.

On her way out of the grocery store, she brushes past a family, and each child bursts into tears.

Ms. Cho locates the homeless shelter with the best reviews on Yelp (terribly dated, but technology isn't her strongest suit). For the next week, she does her best impression of an undercover agent, sleeping on an uncomfortable cot and handing out machines from her car to those she feels are the most deserving. By then, she's come down with a malaise she assumes is a cold, and before the shelter can kick her out, she drives the six hours back to the comfort of her own apartment.

She taps the acceptance letter pinned to her doorway one last time before lying down for a nap. Only then does the wave wash over her—of sadness, hollow and bitterly cold. She pulls the blankets up to her chin and comforts herself with the knowledge that she'll soon see herself in print.

Before long, Ms. Cho hears the distant voices of women singing. The tune is so familiar that she can taste its sweetness, and yet for a moment she struggles to place it.

Arirang, she thinks, closing her eyes.

Her body never leaves her bed again.

A list of the ten things first copied by the FIMs:
1.   Grief
2.   An orange
3.   Mrs. Rutherford's gavel
4.   A $20 bill (copied 10 times in a row)
5.   A pack of cigarettes
6.   A vial of insulin
7.   A baggie of heroin
8.   One box of Kraft macaroni and cheese (copied six times)
9.   A cell phone
10. A mouse (emerges cold to the touch)

After every seventeen items, each machine produces a copy of itself—although the speed of production varies, of course. (And again, I must impress upon you that while this may have been Mr. Rutherford's intent, I believe it represents some agency on the part of the machine.) At the moment Ms. Cho takes her last breath, she has spent two weeks in bed, a figure that seems quite ludicrous—two weeks without food or water?—but her ghost, when interviewed, will be quite adamant on the subject.

If it really is two weeks, then by that moment—according to a number of mathematical predictions and extrapolations that we cannot hope to untangle—there are an estimated 7,289 machines in circulation. By now, news is spreading, from tweet to texts to machine tutorials on YouTube, comment after comment declaring the replicating boxes a hoax.

A number of agencies have slowly stirred awake, alert levels changing from jade to a medium olive green: information specialists tracking trending keywords, weather outlets noticing the rapid, unpredictable formation of cold fronts in the Midwest, health agencies marking the uptick of symptoms in the greater Chicago area—respiratory complaints, headaches, fatigue—their data fettered by how slowly the matter ascends the bureaucratic hierarchy.

There are other, stranger symptoms spreading in ways not usually tracked by those same agencies: Reddit threads that explode with mentions of odd dreams, radios that bloom with the voices of recently dead loved ones, animals that stare at the clouds and whine. A particularly entertaining creepypasta about angels takes off like wildfire, its origins impossible to discern.

Nobody assembles these pieces until far too late, for the same reason that Mr. Rutherford never became a poet: profitability requires efficiency, which is supposed to require specialization and the elimination of all idleness. It's only when deepfake analysts begin to wage vitriolic war over a video clip of the replication of the Sears Tower—to true Chicagoans, it is and forever will be the Sears Tower—that some part of the FIM diaspora makes the national news. By then, there are only a few holdout skeptics: too many people have seen signs of the ghosts.

Case #3: Byeol-Seong

When Gang Byeol-Seong hops onto Flight 1821, it's with the clear intention of pilgrimage. Despite his means, he doesn't take a direct flight to Chicago, as such a thing has become impossible thanks to traveler after traveler desperate to confirm the existence of the new Sears Tower, which sits in the middle of the Magnificent Mile. Instead, he flies to the city that has usurped its status as the Midwestern hub for international flights—Detroit—and for the pleasure, he pays roughly six times the normal price. (This arrangement will ultimately prove untenable, as the FAA will soon ground all air travel.)

Mr. Gang doesn't know much about his distant cousin, only that she's American and that they share an ancestor best known for battlefield strategy during the time of the Three Kingdoms, the subject of a recent Netflix documentary. He knows she is a writer, and finds this ridiculous, as he believes in only two things: the power of money, and the power of Jesus.

But Mr. Gang's mother is a mudang (무당)—an urban shaman— whose refusal to find Jesus embarrasses him to no end, and she called him on Monday morning to tell him that she'd cast yut (윷). "The world might be ending," she said. "Might be starting in Chicago."

Despite his frustrations—yut isn't even a valid fortune-telling method, just the sticks from a children's game—cold trickled down Mr. Gang's back. He had just gotten off the phone with his cousin, was still contemplating that his English is better than her Korean.

It takes him two days, but he buys his ticket, because there's something odd and winding in his chest, a feeling not unlike the determined press of an index finger.

A few days later, he gets on a plane to Detroit. The flight takes the entire night, so long that Mr. Gang is forced to get up and walk the aisle, like a cow circling in a pen. Whenever he sits back down, the cabin seems to darken—and it's a darkness that feels full, not with the bodies that pack the seats but with the spaces between them. A darkness that watches him back.

He shuts his eyes and hears an odd tinkle, like bells. When he concentrates on it, his chest turns hard, as if it's lined with stone. Grief fills him, so thick and cloying he can barely swallow, and the scent of oranges suddenly spikes the air. He makes a note to call his mother, to visit the grave of his father.

His eyes fill with tears, but then—

Ding!

"This is your captain speaking. Though we were originally scheduled to land in Detroit in the next hour or so, due to unforeseen circumstances, we are being diverted to another location. We're sorry for the inconvenience."

The people around Mr. Gang groan. He blinks—his vision is blurry, his cheeks wet. He brushes his hand against his face and looks out the window, but he sees no lights in the dark.

The plane shudders suddenly, turbulence throwing a flight attendant to her knees. People scream as lights flare, as masks drop from overhead compartments, but the shaking shows no signs of stopping.

He prays to Jesus. Another wave of grief hits him, and his throat closes up—

The plane stops shaking.

(I submit that the following events are depicted as told by the relevant interviewees. Employ critical thinking when examining their accounts for veracity.)

Mr. Gang notices, then, how cold the air has gotten. How quiet it is, as if every person has stopped to hear his prayers—a quiet like new snow. He scans the seats—all empty—but when he swings his head back to the center, a spectral woman stands in the middle of the aisle, an empty metal box in her hands. She smiles and holds it toward him.

By now, the pain in his chest is so extreme, he reaches for his sternum and is surprised to find it intact. "Will this make it stop?" he gasps.

She nods.

After a moment, he reaches for the box—

And then he's somewhere else. A place filled with flowers.

Case #4: Geum Ja

When Kim Geum-Ja—who has long submitted to being called "halmonee," as any grandmother should—sits up in bed, it's with the certainty that her son is both alive and dead. She accepts this, because part of the path to becoming a mudang is a cracking of the soul that lets in the miasma and sickness that seems to fill the whole world. Geum-Ja had undergone this change in her twenties, but unlike most of those of her calling, her training had never completely restored her spirit, resulting in two odd effects: she was never given a new name, and she also now shares her life with a number of ghosts. Most days, she wishes they would just *shut up* for a while, but they sometimes make themselves useful.

There are machines, says Hibiscus (무궁화)—who, like always, has chosen to pop up without warning. Her hair is perpetually wet, a symptom of having drowned, and she resides in a giant metal bowl that Geum-Ja sometimes uses to make gimchi when she isn't around.

Geum-Ja is sitting on the heated floor, shelling garlic into a wooden bowl. She shrugs at the ghost. *So?*

So, you should probably draw down one of the goddesses and find out what's going on.

Geum-Ja rolls her eyes. *You could just tell me.*

Hibiscus smiles and shakes her head—not hard, but still, droplets trickle to the floor. Geum-Ja tries not to roll her eyes—it's hard to keep the linoleum clean when a ghost is always dripping on it, but if Geum-Ja doesn't wipe it up, the hot floor makes the room smell like a wet dog.

I can't tell you about the machines, says Hibiscus. *It's something I don't understand. Something new. She cocks her head. Something old, too, though. As if they're filled with han (한). And it feels like there are new ghosts all around me, but I can't reach them, even to talk. Strange, don't you think?*

Geum-Ja shivers. Han is many things—grudge and pain, anger and sorrow. It can be passed from person to person like a virus, and its ability to trap spirits in this world is the main mechanism through which ghosts are formed. *Where are these machines?*

Hibiscus shrugs. *America, mostly.*

Geum-Ja clicks her tongue. Lately, the Americans are always doing something to end the world. Still, she is old enough to feel pro-American, at least some of the time. *Who would be good?* She asks out of politeness; it's not like mudang can call down whoever they want. It takes time to build relationships with goddesses. With some of them, you just have to be a natural.

A pox goddess.

Geum-Ja furrows her brows. *I doubt one would answer me.*

For this, says Hibiscus, *one might.*

Geum-Ja pretends she's not worried about her son, but she is. She can feel the pressure of grief growing in her sinuses, and the television is reporting more strange phenomena now—pink hail, the growing cold, tremblings from within the earth. Swathes of animals abandoning their posts. People are disappearing, and the ones they leave behind start crying and never stop. Others lie down and turn sluggish, as if afflicted with a fever.

And as bad as all that sounds, it's nothing compared to what will come, given what Hibiscus told her. Bad things in the spirit plane are always bad for people. Geum-Ja pulls out all the stops to call down a pox goddess, despite the risk of pissing off the deities she consorts with the most. She makes the grandest offering table she's ever seen, packs it so full of food and fruit and flowers that they spill onto the linoleum and right up to the door. She sings and shakes her rattle of begged and borrowed metal. She beats a drum and jumps on a blade, and then something deep within her guts pinches, like the way that clothes stick to thighs on a hot day, and she decides to try something she hasn't in a long time— tying the knots that symbolize the first mudang's journey to the underworld.

Halfway through, she hears a voice. *Mother? Mother? Is that you?*

She freezes. *Son? What's happening?*

I don't know. I think I might be dead.

Geum-Ja almost cries out—but she's not fully herself anymore. Already, the goddess is stretching its limbs into her own, trying out

her fingers and her eyelashes. She manages an answer in her mind
only: *Hang on.*

And then she closes her eyes, and someone else opens them.

(And here, we must end our examination. Given the outland-
ishness of what follows, it falls outside the realms of our investiga-
tion. When the material falls short, what is left but belief?)

Case #5 (Because You Can Never End on Four)

It's hard, perhaps, to be a goddess of the pox. Very maligned, and
nobody prays to you unless they want something.

As soon as she awakens, the goddess recognizes that the air
around her is clogged with ghosts, each one pinned to its spot like
a butterfly to a board. They snatch things from the air and jam
them into their mouths, greedy to fill the gnawing void that forms
the center of every ghost.

She extends her slender fingers and pulls the pin out of one.
The ghost roars to life, goes wailing toward the horizon in hopes of
finding a wayward soul to eat. It leaves behind the object that held
it in place—a humming metal box, the air growing cold around it.

The goddess brings the pin to her celestial eye and sees it for its
true form. It resembles a bacterium, which is even more novel to
the pox goddess than antibiotics or microbes that eat plastic. She
shuffles it to her finger-pad and brings it to her tongue.

Her mouth fills with the flood of it. Pure, keening han. All at
once, she understands what's going on.

"Show yourself," she orders, and when she turns around, he
stands before her: the ghost of Mr. Grant Rutherford.

"Undo this," she says, pointing to the boxes, the ghosts.

He shakes his head. He is early in the spirit change and still
looks mostly human. "They killed my wife."

"Yes," says the goddess, trying not to sound exasperated. "They
are always killing things."

Mr. Rutherford shrugs. "I'm entitled to my grief."

She waves at the ghosts, the particle-pins, the metal boxes. "Perhaps, but this isn't just grief. This is han. You can't just . . . *manu-
facture* it."

"And yet," he says, his voice cold, "I have. It stays. And even if I
wanted to stop it, I'm—"

"A ghost." She purses her lips. He might be too far gone to be reasoned with, but she doesn't think so. "What if you could see your wife again?"

His face twists. *How hard his choice must be,* she thinks. For all he knows, she could be a liar, offering him a deal she has no intention of honoring—and he has so much to lose. The world didn't care whether his wife lived or died, but now he is making it feel his grief. That is power, more power than even the goddess has.

But then, from deep within, Geum-Ja nudges her. *Look in your pocket.*

The goddess sticks a hand in her robes and pulls out a small wooden hammer, like a miniature version of the mallets used to pound rice cake. When Mr. Rutherford lays eyes on it, he falls to his knees.

She approaches him and holds it out. He takes it and bows, forehead to the ground, the small hammer held to his chest.

The goddess waits a long time. Longer, perhaps, than most human lives—but here, in this place, they are outside of time.

Mr. Rutherford looks up. He has come to a decision. "Show me."

She waves her hand, and like the spread of night, they unfurl before her—the flower-fields of the dead. Filled with more blossoms than there are stars in the night sky, each of them named and legendary.

She plucks a flower and crushes it in her palm. The air fills with the scent of oranges, and then the blossoms part, and through them strides Mrs. Rutherford, beaming like the sun.

The goddess holds up her hand, and Mrs. Rutherford stops. She turns to Mr. Rutherford. "And now? Will you agree to let go of these machines?"

He runs for his wife. In doing so, he gives his permission—which means the goddess is free to reach out her hand and gather all the threads stretched between his spirit and the machines, the copies of his grief.

She does so. She pulls, hard.

All at once, the ghosts shake free of their pins. The machines fall silent, into eternal sleep.

"You know," she says, just as she takes her leave from Geum-Ja, "I don't have many followers these days. Others will tell this story; see that you tell it the best."

*

Mr. Gang awakens not on a plane or in a field, but on his mother's linoleum. She squats nearby, shelling garlic, and the scent dredges him into full awareness.

The sight of her face—dissolved into wrinkles, as if she's aged twenty years—fills him with alarm. He gasps and reaches for her. "What happened?"

She smiles, the new wrinkles soft under his fingertips. "You wouldn't understand."

He bristles. "Try me." After all, he now lives in a world where he can disappear from a plane and wind up in his mother's house. He's gained some flexibility.

She thumps a fist against her chest, an old sign of mourning. "Sometimes, we owe it to the world to help bear the grief of another."

The words flow over him—in, and then out, like the tide. "You're right," he says. "I don't understand."

But when he touches his own face, his cheeks are wet with tears.

Root Rot

FROM *Apex*

BY THE TIME I hear that my brother is looking for me, and has somehow scraped together enough credit to get on a commercial flight to New Tel Aviv, and that he's also brought his three-year-old daughter on her first interplanet trip, my insides are already rotten. Can't get to the doctor without citizen papers, but I know. I can feel it. Lungs, liver, stomach, whatever—they're done for. Most days I wake up, bleed, drink, bleed, and pass out. I am fucked beyond any reasonable doubt.

When the two OSPs are finished beating the shit out of me outside Farah's (only place in the Arab Quarter with a liquor license, which means what's happening currently, a beating that is, happens less frequently than if I was drinking somewhere else) one of them checks for warrants. I'm swaying like something in the breeze though the provisional government never fixed the generators so there isn't any breeze this part of the planet. Sometimes I blow in my own face just to remember what wind felt like.

"Hey, you got a brother?"

Word drops into me. Shakes me up bad to hear it and for a second I almost don't process what it means. Then I do and want to die. I spit out some blood and nod.

"Posted a bulletin. Yesterday, looks like. Asks if anyone's seen you. Want me to forward your location?"

I try to think and then try not to think, and for a second I am really still, and then that second is one of the worst things I've felt in years, so I stay quiet and make a gesture like I'm going to hit the OSPs and they start in again and, later, when they've gone and I get feeling back in my body and start to register the pain, I go back inside and then I pray and then I don't look at anybody and then I drink until I pass out.

When I start wishing I was dead I know it's morning. I spend a few minutes trying to work out where I am. Still at Farah's maybe. In prison maybe. In the street probably. As long I'm not at the house. Take a few minutes and press at my body. Feet. Stomach. Throat. Eyeballs. Thighs. Feel like crying but don't.

My fingers are crusted with blood, and I think one might be broken. For a second, I think the blood might be dirt, that red Mars soil, and I get confused and think maybe I've still got a job, maybe it's years ago and I've just been dreaming all of this pain, and maybe I'm still handsome and unbroken, maybe Farah and I are still in love and I can still make something grow, I can still get my fingers in the dirt and hear it, and then I shift slightly and get a bomb's worth of pain from my ribs and my vision blurs blue and when it clears I know the soil is blood. I know where I am and who and why.

I turn over and make myself puke, and it's that familiar yellow color with the little bit of blood threading through it like embroidery. Try and see my face in it but can't. I'm sure if I could I'd look worse than dead. Skin pale and covered in bruises, my hair falling out, a few teeth gone in the back and I swear I'm getting shorter too. Maybe if I just lay here for a while nothing will happen and then I can start drinking again.

"Get up."

Maybe not. Guess I'm at Farah's. He kicks me in the ribs and cusses me out until I sit up.

"Hi," I say. Voice sounds like a bad engine and I know my breath is probably toxic. I'm struck by the hugeness of how unwantable I am. Farah used to think I was pretty when I was clean. I used to think so too. Well nothing's inevitable but change and skyscrapers as they say.

Farah's just standing there and his arms are folded across his chest. I want to lick it like some wounded animal, him or me I don't know but there's some combination of animal and wound. "Hi," I say again.

"You can't come back in here."

When Farah and I were together we used to draw on each other's chests little maps. Plots of land we wanted to live on, spots on Mars we'd go and build our freedom. He would laugh and then when things got bad he wouldn't laugh so much. But the ones I drew on his chest were so real to me. I never laughed.

"I'm okay, I just need to rest today. I'll be okay. I won't come back tonight, I'll go somewhere else and cool off and come back tomorrow."

"You can't come back in here, ever."

Really detailed mine were with all the land sectioned off into what types of plants I was going to have and then I'd get so excited to tell him how I'd figured what they needed from Mars soil and sun and air and he would listen and smile or listen and look so sad when things changed and I did too.

"Okay."

"You haven't paid your tab in months. And when you get in fights outside it's bad for business. Offworld Settlement Palmach fuckers are over here constantly for you and no one wants to deal with that."

Farah was the one who was waiting for me outside Ansar VI when I got out but I didn't know what to say and neither did he so we didn't. And he took me back to the bar and poured when I asked and that's it and that's where we've been since.

"It's bad for business. And it's bad for me. They'll take the liquor license and maybe my papers too. And I don't want to ever look at you again."

I sit there like a puddle and try not to think. If I keep my eyes focused on the puke I won't let what's happening in. It'll stay out so I can move and breathe some. I stare at the little thread of blood in the bile and in the corner of my eye I see Farah start to go and the desperation in me rears up.

"Fathi's here," I say.

He stops and I can see he's being really careful with what's on his face. Blank like a stone wall.

"He's looking for me. OSPs told me last night. Please don't do this."

"Maybe you should see him."

"Don't want to see him. Please. I love you."

"Fuck you."

"Okay."

"You owe me too much for that. Just too much."

"Okay."

We both shut up and I know that we might not ever stop shutting up now. That we might be shut and closed forever and no openness ever coming back. Every day there are moments like this when whatever might have been waiting for me in the future just goes away, I can feel it just burning up. I wish I could stop drinking. No I don't. I wish I'd never come to this planet. No I don't.

"I'm going to code the bar's door against your breath until you settle the tab. Maybe Fathi can help you. I don't know. I don't think I can anymore. If I ever could. I'm sorry."

Yes I do.

"Please. I can't pay. I don't have anything left."

Farah and I touching the dirt before this was New Tel Aviv, when it was still new. Holding seeds. Playing with gravity and dreaming of freedom. Kissing. The way I could make him laugh like the sun was out and we could photosynthesize.

"You could always sell it. You know somebody in the city will pay good money."

It. Flash of red. Memory. Dirt. Petals. Whatever.

"Don't have it. Confiscated. All gone," I lie.

Farah shakes his head, really tired-seeming. Looks like he's going to say something, maybe argue, push me to do what I should, but he doesn't. I think I'm glad about that but I'm not really sure. It's a long time before he talks again.

"Either pay your debts or don't come in here again."

"Okay," I say. He reaches out and puts his fingers on my knee and I remember how much he used to like touching it, how he liked to feel where it'd been broken and reset. We hold still like that for too long so I say, "Can I have one more drink, just to get me going, for today?"

For a second his face looks like it's got something like pity on it, and for that I'm grateful. It's all I ever want.

I get out and sun hits me like a missile, and if anyone outside is looking at me with any kind of anything on their face I don't know it, I can't see anything at all.

Getting to the other side of the Arab Quarter means going through the New Tel Aviv settlement civic center but I really don't have a choice if I want to get some cash and keep drinking. If I had better papers and hadn't been in prison I could drink somewhere anon-

ymous and illegal and maybe fade away but oh well. Walking to
the delineation gate I stop by the dried-out water tanker (left over
from when we were still trying to fully terraform the Quarter, when
any of us thought this could be home) to visit the cat. She came up
on the second or third rocket from somebody's alleyway in Khalil
and when things were good she was adored and we joked about
making her mayor. Then we all got fucked and she did too. Once
the settlements got on the Mars train and surrounded what we
had we were all panicking and trying to stay free and in the panic
nobody took her with them. Now she's forgotten like me. Like all
of us I guess, but me especially I like to think. I check on her when
I'm sober enough to remember.

I crouch, eye the underside of the tanker. She's there looking
like I feel. We look at each other for a while and eventually I reach
out my hand to try and pet her. Too far back and I'm stretching
to just get a scratch, something to let her know I'm here. No luck.
Oh well. Yank my hand back out and go to look at her again but
she's gone. I stay down there for a moment because it's cool and
my head hurts. The space where she was, where my hand couldn't
reach.

Closer to the delineation gate I find some kid selling flasks. I
manage to convince her to take some synth watermelon seeds I
found in my pockets for a flask of arak, which is all I can afford
since nobody drinks it anymore. It does the trick and soon I'm
numb again. The thing about drinking a lot is that there's nothing meaningful about it. Just fucks you up and you're not in the
world anymore and there's no past or future really just one foot in
front of the other if you can manage that. And sometimes you can
still kind of experience what's around you only it's not as intense
on a personal level. Like now, when the arak's fuzzed me up, the
settlement drones flashing hasbara holograms aren't so annoying.
They're kind of like insects that aren't biting. Just something to
look at with corpse eyes.

At the gate the guard asks where I'm going and checks my papers, which are shit, obviously. I say I'm just going across to the
other side of the Quarter and I'm sticking out my arm before he's
even finished looking. Window opens and the little mechanical
arm comes out to stick my vein. Once they've got the liter of my
blood they approve a fifteen-minute pass to get through to the
settlement. The blood loss and the arak have really messed me up

but I think I can manage getting to the next gate into the Quarter in time. They're usually pretty good about getting the blood back in once you're there depending on the line, though once or twice I've gotten someone else's liter. Probably healthier than whatever I've got going on, probably might have saved my life. I don't know.

The settlement civic center looks the same as always. Clean and stupid. The glass looks terrible and it never lasts. And they've ruined all the landscape work they made us do in Ansar too, synthetic olive trees on every fucking corner like a postcard. And the synth poppies look as sad as I knew they would. I stop and bend down to feel them, the sickly genetic smell. None of the settlers know how to grow anything real here and none of the Palestinians have the resources even if they did know, which they don't.

Before the settlements when this was just empty planet it was so possible, just crammed to the brim with possible. It was going to be free and we were going to learn the land and find God again and all that bullshit. I believed it so deeply I left everything behind on Earth. The people who couldn't leave I cursed and tore from my heart. I was stupid and I thought things would be different. And when the settlers followed and they liked the wide-open planet so much they left the old land behind, they declared any flora from Earth contraband and put me away. Now we've got a provisional government I don't know or care about and my brother's been living in Reunified Palestine for years while I drink myself to death, which reminds me my brother is here for me, and I want to just pull up everything with roots on this fucking planet, just salt the ground and then salt myself too. But I've only got a few minutes before the blood loss passes me out so there's no time for being angry or anything else.

At the other delineation gate there's a protest on the Arab side. They're holding signs in Arabic I can't read. Somebody took down one of the hasbara drones and they're passing it around like a football though it doesn't really roll. People are dancing and something's on fire. I don't know what they want, not sure I can even guess anymore. Some days I'm sad about losing the language, but most days I don't mind it. Ansar policy is to reprogram prisoner consciousness with Hebrew once they wipe the Arabic, which serves me fine. I like not understanding things.

The blood bot gives me my liter back and I stand a little straighter. I'm looking at the faces of all the Arabs through the

light-meshed gate and I hear myself thinking they're idiots, they're
evil, we ought to just shut up and die and float out into space, cold
and empty as every day here, all we deserve. Sometimes I don't
know what's my voice and what's the guards at Ansar VI and what's
the drones and what's the drink and what's Farah and what's God.
All I know is when the protesters make space for me to stumble
through their anger, when they touch me and tell me to join them,
I loathe, I loathe every cell on my body that feels and I loathe every
second I'm breathing and the pit opens up in me and I want something more and I don't know what it is. So I push them away and
while they're yelling and spitting at me *collaborator coward fucking
drunk* I drain the last of the arak and I say thank you to the drone
when it passes out an Arab in front of me and I can pocket a few
loose coins that spill out from her hands like petals.

When I get to Abu Khaled's he's curled up on the floor and I can
tell he's soiled himself. Touch his forehead and it's hot as an iron.
Probably he'll last a few more days and then go. I wonder if he has
papers for the house or if it'll go to the settlers. Last place I ever
felt decent was in this front room of his—curled up a lot like he is
now and crying nonstop while I tried to dry out for the first time
in years. His hands on my head. His hands. Remembering feels
terrible so I dig a nail into my palm until the pain brings me dull
again. I need to get him stable and then ask for some cash. That's
it. That's all.

I get his pants the rest of the way off and drag him into the tiny
bathroom and into the tub. While I rinse him off and he's groaning, eyes floating open-closed like a camera shutter, I look at him.
Skin used to be brown but now it's some sick gray blue. Bruises
everywhere. So thin you could think he was just pastry.

When I'd stumbled in, that night I was trying to be good, he
was patient. I cried and he just sat there and touched me, just a
little, just to show he was there, and eventually I slept, and the next
day he fed me and we didn't say anything to each other since he
only spoke Arabic and I didn't. I was close to dead from trying to
stop drinking cold, but he kept me alive and I got back to normal.
I'd hated him for how kind he was and how it made me feel okay
for a moment so one night I drank enough so that I knew I'd do
something cruel, and I did, and so I left and knew that it was my
fault that I was leaving, which was right. After that I didn't see

him again, but I went back once, late at night when I knew he was asleep, and I worked for hours until the sun was just coming up, sweating and freezing and pissed myself but couldn't stop until it was right, until I'd made him these long wooden planters with bell peppers growing in them, real ones, part of the stash of seeds I'd hidden, or at least I hoped they were growing, but they were definitely there. I felt good, so I went and loitered near the border fence until the OSP spotted me and did what they do, and I fell unconscious feeling nothing.

Now he's shivering in the tub all wet. It takes me a while to get him out and into the bedroom because I'm starting to shake from not drinking since the arak a few hours ago. The room is nearly empty. Only things around are socks and his paintings and cigarette butts. Get him on the bed and pull the sheet over him and it pretty quickly gets soaked in his sweat, and a little after it's got some of mine on it too. Abu Khaled is shaking and I'm shaking and I can't think straight, and I'm trying to ask him how he is, or if he can hear me, or if he has any money he can spare, but I can't get the Arabic out though I really try and remember. So for a few minutes the two of us are just making sounds at each other, groaning a little like birds. He starts to sound like he's in a lot more pain, and I don't know what to do or say so I start crying and just touching him, his head, his neck, the soles of his feet, shoulders, stomach, just putting my hands on him the way I would put them on soil, just getting to know what it is. He starts trying to say something, and I'm listening harder than I ever have.

"Law samaht," he's saying, over and over, "law samaht, law samaht." I don't know what he means except that his voice sounds like he needs something. And I'm remembering what he did and what I've done and didn't do, and I can't fucking understand what he's saying and I'm a sorry excuse for flesh so I take some deep breaths and I leave him there crying out like I was an angel who turned away. And in the front room I find a few crumpled up shekels and stuff them in my pockets. Hold down some puke and try to stop shaking. Hear him still in the room saying what he's saying, needing what he's needing, and I walk out and I shut the door, and in the yard the wooden planters are empty.

Next morning I've got a few ribs broken. Last night I took Abu Khaled's money and went to a bar in the civic center. Wasn't enough money to settle my tab at Farah's, so I figured it was worth it and besides some settlers might beat me bad enough that I'd be passed out until my brother's gone back to Earth. No such luck obviously as I'm awake now. Neighborhood drone picked me up walking toward the bar and put me on the municipal timeline, so some settlers came by and I hit one of them kind of halfhearted but enough to get beat. It felt all right. I actually think one of them might have served as a guard at Ansar VI, but I couldn't be sure, passed out too quick and besides I can't remember much from those days. This morning the money's gone and I still haven't had a drink, so things are pretty bad. Can't even puke. Can still feel my insides breaking down. I'm willing them on.

Out of options, so I get up from the civic center street and limp through the delineation gate. Nothing left to do but go to the house. My head is killing me and something in my side is aching, in addition to the broken ribs. Maybe they're poking some organ, something fragile in there, just puncturing it with every step I take back toward the house. Or maybe that's just all my fuckups talking.

The breath scanner at the front door is busted, stripped for parts by someone since I've been here last, so I muscle down the door and get inside. Most of the inside's been stripped too. I stopped caring about it a long time ago so I let it happen, even encouraged it sometimes. Not much left inside the wooden walls, most of it synth wood but a few planks here and there real that I brought with me on the first rocket. Standing inside it's still, empty like the remnants of a ghost. A reminder of what gets left when I try, which is nothing. A wave of something hits me and I feel sick, really sick, a new level of pain and nausea. Get on my knees to wait for the puke to come. I know what to do in my throat to coax it out and I do, little burps and swallowing, and soon enough there's a new puddle of bile on the floor, some arak smell, and more blood than usual. Something in me knows there can't be much of this left. I rest my forehead on the floor. Red dirt tracked in by looters mixes a little with my sweat and I rub it around a little: Mars makeup. Almost pretty again. Don't want to get my head up from the floor or open my eyes so I crawl with my forehead pressed to the synth-wood floor like some protracted migratory prayer. Feel my way around to the little closet I used to keep seeds in. Check first for the liquor compartment— found, broken, and emptied. I figured as much. But I reach behind and underneath and open up the second compartment, the one nobody knows about, not even Farah when we shared this place as lovers and comrades and fools. Eyes closed I'm fumbling around in the dark trying to find the last part of the person I was and then I do. I stay still for a little, and feel the blood pump in my body and around my rotten organs and through to my bruised and broken and reset arms and into my fingers and then somehow a little bit into the soil that my fingers are feeling, and through the soil into the roots of the last real poppy on Mars, the last remnant of the place I thought this planet could be.

When they took me to Ansar I'd already started drinking. Already just a shadow and welcomed the Palmach vehicles, the shackles. Farah already gone even when he was with me, the country on Earth already reunified, free. I knew I'd missed whatever a person's life could be that was good. The ship had flown. I gave up everything and let myself conceive of the life held in the imagination of Ansar VI and that was all. But still I kept this plant. Sometimes, in that sweet spot when the drink loosens my mind but doesn't wipe it, I remember the little poppy and get wistful, swear to myself I'll find a piece of land for my own and get things going, start over, eke out home through the sweat and the tears, and then I take another drink and it all just seems too hard so I let go again. But here it still is, rare as all hell, almost impossible to keep alive on this planet. My last resort.

My hand still stuck in the compartment and illuminated by the artificial sunlight bulb I installed, the misters come on. Wet fingers, a little caked-up blood or dirt washing off, and when the sound is done I can hear somebody behind me in the room. I try to yank my hand out and turn around and get up off the ground all at once and do none of them, somehow end up hitting the ground face first. When I can open my eyes and lift up my head a little some things swim into view, two pairs of feet, one big, one heartbreaking small, and I know.

"Hi, Fathi," I say, trying to push up onto my hands and knees but not quite getting there. Suddenly my arms feel like spun sugar. Nobody says anything while I keep trying to get up, scoot over to the wall and sort of push up against it to get some leverage. Eventually I give up and stay on the ground. I shut my eyes and move my face so they're pointed where I know Fathi's face will be and then I open them and I keep them trained only on his face. I can't look at her. I don't want to see how she's seeing.

Fathi looks older but then he always did. People always used to guess he was the older one of us and sometimes I thought they were right. I was born first but Fathi was born smart. Born good maybe. He's dressed in nice jeans and a yellow collared shirt, and I start counting the hairs in his beard to avoid looking at her.

"I'm here to take you home."

Looking right in his eyes I try to smile a little. "Like that British song. Remember that? *Pack your things I've come to take you home.* Something like that right? Only I don't have anything to pack."

"Farah told me you're sick. Dying."

Fucking Farah.

"'Solsbury Hill,' that was it. Gabriel. You remember? Every time we'd play it Dad would tell us Peter Gabriel was pro-Palestine. Remember?"

"I don't want you to die."

My eyes are locked on Fathi's face like a leech but I can hear her breathing, I can feel her here with us seeing me and I don't know why these memories are coming to me now but I need Fathi to remember them with me. I know I smell like alcohol and blood, probably other things more vile and sick, but he's looking at me without any pity, without any anger even, and for once I let myself sit in that non-judgment, in that love, and I don't run away this time.

"Do you remember that? Fathi? The song?"

"I remember that. Of course I do." His eyes are soft and blue. I can feel one of my ribs poking into my skin and I wonder if it's bleeding but I can't look down to check because I might see her. "It's been a long time, habibi."

"Yeah." My mouth feels like brick and dust. "How have you been?"

"Good. Things are good."

Fathi used to cover for me when I came home late back on Earth. When the soldiers were looking for me after throwing rocks. When our parents were looking for me after boys. Fathi was my anchor and I've only been able to drift so long because I didn't have him here with me.

"You know things are different now, back home. There's a place for you there."

"I don't know. I don't know about that."

"I do."

Fathi and I playing football. Trying cigarettes together. The way he held me when my heart got broken. The way his face looked when I left him in the morning, asleep like an angel, and I took my bag of seeds and crawled through miles of tunnels to get to the rocket and held Farah's hand while we sobbed and the land got smaller and smaller and then gone.

"I left. I gave it up. It doesn't want me back."

"It doesn't want you dead either."

"I left you there. I left you all alone and I went away."

"Yeah, you did. So you're a piece of shit. What else is new."

Even sick as I am Fathi gets a laugh out of me. But the laugh hurts my ribs, which reminds me I've got ribs, which reminds me I'm a person and so on. I try to avoid thinking those things because they hurt so I say something to get this to stop.

"I'm glad I left. And I'm glad I didn't take you with me." I don't feel anything when I say it, because I'm staring at the corner of Fathi's mouth and praying he'll get hurt and leave. I don't want to do this. Fathi's eyes I can't read and he comes forward, leans down to me, and touches my forehead. Like some insect landing on a bloom. I'm blinking hard and he's wiping off the sweat from my brow. Fathi speaks soft to me while he holds my hand.

"I will forgive you no matter how hard you try to stop me. B'hebbek. Remember? B'hebbek. You can still come home."

The Arabic doesn't process in my brain, but it does somewhere else. And I know he's telling the truth. His mouth is in that little curve it makes when he's being sincere. It used to make me annoyed that his body was bad at lying and mine was too good. I want to shake him and tell him to lie for both our sakes, for her sake.

"I don't have papers. They've got me on no-transport. There's no point in trying."

"One of the port employees agreed to get you off-planet. They'll get you papers and a ticket on our return flight and you can live with us. You can come home."

"How much?"

"Sixty-five thousand."

His words are sieving through me like water, and the drink-guards-God-me voice is saying *You could get that for the poppy, easy. This is it. This is the moment. This is your soil telling you to come back. This is goodness finally coming to meet you where you are.* Trying my hardest to listen. To believe that this is my voice and that it's telling the truth.

"I'll try to get the money."

When I let myself say that my eyes almost waver, almost drop down to meet her gaze and let her see me. But I don't. Fathi looks down at her, and then at me, and his eyes get harder, sadder. I watch the muscles in his arm tighten, relax, tighten.

"The flight leaves at eleven. Meet us there."

He turns to leave, tugging at his daughter's little arm so gently, just the way I used to tug at his when we were kids.

"Fathi?"

He stops and looks back.

"How's the soil?" I say. He smiles.

"Lush," he says. "Waiting for you." Between the three of us, Fathi and his daughter and me, something almost begins to grow, something almost claws its way to taking hold. I close my eyes, and as they leave the little one says "Buh-bye," but I hear it for a moment as "alive."

Alive.

Now everything's a blur. The blood bot a blur. The still-raging protest a blur. Hasbara drones projecting blurs as I get close to the Import/Export and Contraband Office in the civic center, hands obsessively going to the little package of soil and life hidden in my crotch, making sure it's still there and I didn't break it. Now the IEC guard checking my papers and getting ready to jail me. Now whispering into their ear what I have and who I need to see. Now the higher-up. Now the little room and the surveillance bots blanked for a few minutes. Now I'm taking out the poppy and now the higher-up's eyes going wide and now "Name your price" and now I hear somebody's voice saying "Sixty-five thousand" and now one of the times I can't hear if it's me or God or drink or death or love but now the cash in a discreet little tote bag and now the poppy leaving my hand and now the last chance I had at what I'd dreamed of gone into the hands of a bureaucrat who'd sell it for more than I'd ever dare to dream. But, now, I don't care. I have what I came for. I know where I'm going. And all the way back through the civic center it's like I'm floating like the gravity's gone out again though it hasn't. And I get my rotten blood back and I keep walking and as I walk I'm shedding so much weight: the poppy, Ansar, the drones and the blood bots, the IEC, the beatings and the OSP, the settlers, Abu Khaled, the protest, the Quarter,

hope, home, hope. And then I get where I'm going. And I'm silent as I push over the tote bag of money. And I speak in the voice
of somebody too stupid and too wrong to do any different and I
want to say so many things but instead I say, "This covers the tab
and then some. I'm going to sit here and drink and I don't want
you to ever try and stop me" and Farah looks at me like the way
you look at something that's not there anymore, like the way you
look at where a plant used to be or a vase or a building, and then
something in his eyes changes and he pours me something clear
and unknowable and that's the end of it, and I drink until I can
barely speak, and then when I'm ready I go to the port.

Can barely stand. Make it to the viewing section and find the hole
Farah and I hacked into the lightmesh fence years ago. Sneak
through and collapse onto the bit of shadow on the edge of the
takeoff platforms and find the one rocket gearing up for a launch.
Where Fathi is. Where she is.

Pain in my back and in my stomach. I don't care. I take a swig
from whatever I brought from Farah's and things quiet down.
Just my rot and the settlement's rot and the planet's rot all com-
muning, all sharing a body. I'm blissful knowing I did exactly what
everybody with any sense thought I would do. I'm already somewhere floating outside anyone's jurisdiction. And then I look over
at the rocket and my eyes roam to one of the windows and there
she is.

It's too late to look away, I've already seen her and I swear she's
seen me even though I know that's not possible, I'm too far away
and it's dark. But I believe we're looking at each other. She's plain-
looking and sweet, a brown curtain of hair and her eyes like two
onion bulbs, little I mean, and light. If anything was left of my
heart she would break it. I can't remember her name, if anybody
ever told me in the letters to Ansar or on the bulletin or maybe
Fathi said it or fuck maybe she told me herself once but I can't
remember. The ship's starting to lift off and I send my soul with it.
I touch my empty knee and I whisper like she can hear me.

I tell her they're right about me. They always were. I'm bad and
I'm a criminal and a threat and I tell her it's okay, that she doesn't
have to be that way, that people disappear from your life and you
can forget who they were or what they did to you or what they
looked like drunk, I tell her she's home and she should know that

she's home, that her dad is good how I'm not, I tell her that God
loves her and the land loves her and I tell her that poppies need
lots of sun and not too much water and she just has to care for
them until they're gone, and I tell her that they self-seed so beautifully that she'll forget about them for years and then, so suddenly,
like heartbreak or hope or pain, just so fucking quick, they'll come
back, and she won't even remember they were ever so far gone.

Contributors' Notes

ELIZABETH BEAR was born on the same day as Frodo and Bilbo Baggins, but in a different year. She is the Hugo, Sturgeon, Locus, and Astounding Award–winning author of over a hundred short stories and around thirty novels. The most recent of these is *The Origin of Storms*, the final volume in an epic trilogy full of more dragons, metal men, and complicated politics. She lives in a rambling old parsonage in Western Massachusetts with her husband, writer Scott Lynch, and some charming cats.

• "The Red Mother" almost didn't get written. It's the second story to feature Hacksilver and was originally slated to be part of the Gardner Dozois–edited anthology *The Book of Beasts*. The first story, "Hacksilver," was meant for *The Book of Legends* and was already finished when Gardner passed away and the anthology project was canceled. Around that time, Jonathan Strahan invited me to be a part of his anthology *Dragons*, and I thought maybe I could finish the uncompleted story for that. It turned out to be more difficult to navigate the change than anticipated, and I couldn't find an ending for the story in time for that publication. Riddle contests require the author to be clever. Eventually I overcame my despair and solved the problem, and Jonathan was kind enough to purchase it for *Tor.com* despite the delay. I am thrilled that it's found some happy readers after its struggle getting born.

C. L. CLARK is a BFA award-winning and Hugo-nominated editor and Ignyte Award–winning writer, and the author of Nebula finalist *The Unbroken*, the first book in the Magic of the Lost trilogy. She graduated from Indiana University's creative writing MFA and was a 2012 Lambda Literary Fellow. She's been a personal trainer, an English teacher, and an editor, and is some combination thereof as she travels the world. When she's not writing or working, she's learning languages, doing P90something, or reading about war and [post-]colonial history. Her work has appeared in various SFF venues, including *Tor.com*, *Uncanny*, and *Beneath Ceaseless Skies*.

• "The Captain and the Quartermaster" started, actually, with an Ursula K. Le Guin exercise from her book *Steering the Craft*. I was spurred to finish it by a call for stories about "silk and steel" sapphic romances (a romance between someone with a harder, physical skill, such as sword fighting, and someone with a softer, mental skill, such as diplomacy).

I didn't want to write it as a traditional romance, though. Simply put, this story is about divorce. I love exploring the intricacies of queer relationships within fantasy worlds, and I especially love the bitter moments— some made all the more bitter because of how sweet the highs of romantic love are. In particular, I was thinking of the small moments that make up intimacy in a long-term relationship, those little joys and exquisite pains, and the way the couple navigates (or fails to navigate) obstacles together. I was also interested in the way people outside of the relationship may see something different than the couple experiences.

Structurally, I was inspired by the time-jumping narrative style of Sara Saab's "Suddenwall," which was in turn inspired by Seth Dickinson's "Morrigan in the Sunglare." I chose that structure because of the way memory—my memory, at least—often presents relationships in blips of specific moments, moments that changed things, joyful moments, moments that ached.

P. DJÈLÍ CLARK is the author of the novel *A Master of Djinn*, and the award-winning and Hugo, Nebula, and Sturgeon–nominated author of the novellas *Ring Shout*, *The Black God's Drums*, and *The Haunting of Tram Car 015*. His short stories have appeared in online venues such as *Tor.com*, *Uncanny*, *Heroic Fantasy Quarterly*, and *Beneath Ceaseless Skies*.

• I've always loved H. G. Wells's *War of the Worlds*. I read the book when I was younger, and I think I've seen just about every filmic adaptation. It was as an adult that I realized the themes of colonization the story represented, which I then began seeing in almost every alien invasion tale imaginable. So, I'd always wanted to play around with these concepts. I started wondering, what if the Martians returned? What if these happenings took place in locations that were not England or the United States? What if instead of microbes, we needed something else to defeat them? Magic seemed a perfect substitute. As I began to think about how that might change the world—perhaps even more than the invasion itself—the story began taking shape. In many ways, it's about what comes after these events that reshape the global order. How have we been changed and what does it mean for how we treat those we defeated? As I wrote, I tried not to concern myself with genre or boundaries. Alien invasion. Haitian vodun. Geopolitical intrigue. Human-ish rights. It's all in there. Because, who says it can't be?

KEL COLEMAN is an author, editor, and stay-at-home mom. Their fiction has appeared in *FIYAH, Anathema: Spec from the Margins, Apparition Lit*, and others. Though Kel is a Marylander at heart, they currently reside in the Philadelphia area with their husband, tiny human, and stuffed dragon named Pen. You can find them at kelcoleman.com and on Twitter at @kcolemanwrites.

• "Delete Your First Memory for Free" started with a one-word prompt: mindless. It also started with a darker premise, one that followed the more common approach to memory deletion, with the character slowly losing themselves along with their recollections. But as someone who deals with a lot of the same anxieties as Devin, the hopelessness of it gnawed at me. I wanted better for both of us.

So, I reimagined it as an almost slice-of-life, just an average day taking a weird but ultimately wonderful turn. As the character's journey changed, so too did the technology. It's easy to imagine all the ways new technology might cause harm, so it was challenging and rewarding to think of a way something so potentially nightmarish as memory deletion could have a positive impact. I left things open-ended, excited by the possibilities rather than a concrete resolution; but I like to think even if the relationship doesn't work out, Devin's life will be a little better for having opened themselves up to it.

MARIA DONG is known for writing across various forms and genres. Her stories, articles, essays, and poetry have appeared in such places as *Lightspeed, Apex, Augur, Fantasy, Apparition, khōréō, Kaleidotrope*, and *Nightmare*, among many others. Her debut novel, *Liar, Dreamer, Thief*, a speculative-leaning psychological suspense, comes out from Grand Central Publishing in January of 2023.

Although she's currently a computer programmer, in her previous lives, Maria's held a variety of diverse careers, including property manager, English teacher, and occupational therapist. She lives with her partner in southwest Michigan, in a centenarian saltbox that is almost certainly haunted, watching K-dramas and drinking Bell's beer.

• This story took eight years to move from its initial draft to the version that sold to *khōréō*. In its original iteration, it was a strictly sci-fi story that followed a team of scientists who build a replicating machine, only to discover they've accidentally launched a viral pandemic. It wasn't very good, and I quit trying to sell it when I gave up writing for the third(?) time—I was making minimum wage and living in precarious circumstances, and I was ashamed of the "frivolity" of the dream of making art when I could barely feed myself.

Years later, after I finished graduate school and had a "big-girl career," I found that despite my newfound security, my mental health was disintegrating, and the longing to write something returned. I brushed through my old work to see if any of it was any good—it wasn't, but I sensed the seed of something important in this story, even if I didn't yet know what it was or what the story was trying to say. I also knew it couldn't be about a virus anymore—not with what had happened in the world.

One theme I had been thinking a lot about at that time was generational trauma, which is often personified for Koreans in the emotion of *han*—a word that is often translated to mean grief, but which goes so much deeper than that. Once I realized that *han* was the linchpin of this story, everything unspiraled easily from there (though the story took a *long* time to find a home).

I guess what I'm trying to say is that this story taught me a valuable lesson. Sometimes, in order to finish a story, you have to become a new person.

MEG ELISON is a Philip K. Dick and Locus Award–winning author, as well as a finalist for Hugo, Nebula, Sturgeon, and Otherwise Awards. A prolific short-story writer and essayist, Elison has been published in *Slate*, *McSweeney's*, *Fantasy & Science Fiction*, *Fangoria*, *Uncanny*, *Lightspeed*, *Nightmare*, and many other places. Elison is a high school dropout and a graduate of UC Berkeley.

• I have a highly involved marinara recipe. It has taken me years to adapt and perfect it, and I've only gotten fussier about the exact right ingredients over that time. While I was making it one day, I was thinking about the recipe cards I've seen in my friends' hands; yellowed and laminated, written in some finishing-school handwriting that looks as archaic as the lettering in a medieval manuscript. I thought for just a moment about cooking this same food in space, working so hard to find and grow and cultivate everything that goes into the red sauce we pour over noodles. "The Pizza Boy" grew up around that problem: How do we make this recipe in another time, under different conditions? How do we make someone understand the time and effort that went into it? If they taste it, they'll understand. If there are mushrooms on their pie, they might think for a minute about the life and death that goes into the circle of every pizza, every life.

NALO HOPKINSON was born in Jamaica in 1960. She lived in Jamaica, Guyana, the United States, and Trinidad before moving to Canada in 1977 at sixteen years of age. In 1997 she won the Warner Aspect First Novel Contest, which resulted in the 1998 publication of her novel, *Brown Girl in the Ring*. She has published six novels, two collections of her short fiction, and numerous short stories. She has written and co-written the comics series "House of Whispers" in DC's Sandman universe. She has received the Ontario Arts Council Foundation Award, the John W. Campbell and Locus

Awards, the World Fantasy Award, Canada's Aurora Award, and the Sunburst Award for Canadian Literature of the Fantastic. In 2018, Eagle-Con gave her the Octavia E. Butler Memorial Award in recognition of impactful contributions to the world of science fiction, fantasy, and speculative fiction. In 2021, Science Fiction Writers of America made her its thirty-seventh Damon Knight Memorial "Grand Master"—a lifetime achievement award in recognition of her writing, teaching, and mentorship. She is the award's youngest recipient, as well as being the first woman of African descent, and the first Caribbean author to receive it. She currently lives in Vancouver, Canada, where she is a professor in the School of Creative Writing at the University of British Columbia.

• I'm Caribbean, so rising sea levels and damage to the oceans and coastlines are very much on my mind nowadays. Jamaican scientist Dr. Thomas Goreau, president of the Global Coral Reef Alliance for coral reef protection and sustainable management, once told me that the rising ocean levels won't happen incrementally as our models currently show; it's more likely it will be exponential, thus so much higher and so much faster than we're imagining. That's terrifying to this island girl. Humans can fix this damage we've done, or at least make it less catastrophic than it will otherwise be. We still have time. Just. This story came out of my fears, but even so, the humans in it are still using all their ingenuity to survive, and some of them are still trying to figure out ways to mend the damage. "Broad Dutty Water" is the basis for a media treatment my partner and I have co-written, set in the same world with the same protagonist, and of course the singing pig.

JOSÉ PABLO Iriarte is a Cuban American writer and teacher who lives in Central Florida. Their fiction can be found in magazines such as *Lightspeed, Uncanny, Strange Horizons,* and others, and has been reprinted in numerous best-of-the-year anthologies. Their novelette, "The Substance of My Lives, the Accidents of Our Births," was a Nebula Award finalist for 2018 and longlisted for the Otherwise (Tiptree) Award, while their short story "Proof by Induction" was a Nebula and Hugo Award finalist for 2021. José is on the board of directors of the Science Fiction and Fantasy Writers of America, and their longer work is represented by the Donald Maass Literary Agency. Learn more at labyrinthrat.com, or follow José on Twitter @labyrinthrat.

• I won't cop to how long it took, but it wasn't long after my father died that the thought crossed my mind, "Welp, guess I'll never prove I'm a real writer." I was already published by then, but he had never viewed my writing as anything but a childish pretense. He'd never read my publications, never told anybody else about them, never introduced me as a writer, never indicated he was proud. That's pretty cliché, I suppose, to write about how you'll never impress your old man, but for all his faults, my father was brilliant, gregarious, and loud. He was widely admired, the life of the party, and he loomed large in my life. I always wanted him to find something in me worth valuing other than my SAT score. To see that my passions weren't his but that I was accomplishing things that mattered to me.

So I wrote an early version of this story, of Paulie reliving my walk through the hospital, and of Paulie trying to have the conversations that were off-limits to me now, only to find that his father couldn't give him any more satisfaction than mine could give me, because it wasn't in either of their nature. Damn, that's bitter, no?

Indeed, that first draft was way too raw. I put it away for a couple of years and let my subconscious work on it. Over that time, the other half of this story emerged, a bit of an ode to mathematics, to mathematical enthusiasm and excitement. I name-checked a lot of my favorite teachers and professors here—sort of my intellectual parental figures.

Since "Proof by Induction" came out, other people have shared their reads on it, and they're not all as bitter as my first inspiration, and they're not wrong either. Grief is complicated, and sometimes I still miss my father.

STEPHEN GRAHAM JONES is the *New York Times* bestselling author of more than thirty novels and collections, and there's some novellas and comic books in there as well. Most recent are *My Heart Is a Chainsaw* and *Earthdivers*. Up next is *Don't Fear the Reaper*. Stephen's been awarded the *Los Angeles Times* Ray Bradbury Prize, the Mark Twain American Voice in Literature Award, four This is Horror Awards, four Bram Stoker Awards, two Shirley Jackson Awards, the Texas Institute of Letters Jesse Jones Award, the Western Literature Association's Distinguished Achievement Award, an NEA fellowship, and more. Stephen lives and teaches in Boulder, Colorado.

• Growing up in Greenwood, Texas, we'd sometimes catch rides into Midland—the big city, the tall city. At Midland Park Mall was the Gold Mine, the arcade we spent all our quarters at. But you had to be careful, because there were kids older than you there, and . . . things could get ugly fast, with only the attendant to monitor stuff. You didn't go alone, I mean, and you were always ready to run and run. Made it hard to high-score when you're always watching the reflection on the screen of your game rather than the game—not there was never any real chance I was going to ever get to tap my initials in. I never had the steely nerves and fierce concentration Rance has, in this story. I could only see it in others, that this game *mattered* to them in a way it never did for me. It felt like they were actually fighting for something, I mean, where it was always just lights and sounds, as far as I could tell. But, my pockets empty, just walking around to look over shoulders at what other kids were doing with their quarters,

I always wondered what it would be like to hide behind a bank of games, and see what happened in this place at night. I guess now I know, sort of? It's not all bad, and it's not all good. It's just growing up.

JUSTIN C. KEY is a speculative-fiction writer and psychiatrist whose short stories have appeared in *The Magazine of Fantasy & Science Fiction*, *Strange Horizons*, *Tor.com*, *Escape Pod*, and *Lightspeed*. A graduate of Clarion West, his debut short story collection is forthcoming from HarperCollins. When Justin isn't writing, working with patients, or exploring Los Angeles with his wife, he's chasing after his three young (and energetic!) children.

• Psychiatry is a fascinating field of medicine. The ability to help people craft and understand their own stories while offering evidence-based tools is an opportunity I don't take lightly. Yet we are still in the infancy of neuroscience and mental healthcare. As we learn more and more about the brain and develop new ways to treat it, I hope to see exciting developments over the span of my career. But everything comes with a cost. What richness of life might we lose with the ability to regulate our emotions with a mobile app, for example? How might we weigh the pros and cons of replacing a physician's intuition with a cold, "unbiased" (but actually biased) computer program? "The Algorithm Will See You Now" explores both my hope and fears for the future.

RICH LARSON was born in Galmi, Niger, has lived in Spain and the Czech Republic, and currently writes from Montreal, Canada. He is the author of the novels *Ymir* and *Annex*, as well as more than two hundred short stories—some of the best of which can be found in the collections *Harbingers* and *Tomorrow Factory*. His fiction has been translated into more than a dozen languages, including Polish, French, Romanian, and Japanese, and adapted into an Emmy-winning episode of *Love, Death + Robots*.

• "Tripping Through Time" is a pandemic story, written during Prague's first hard lockdown. It arrived almost fully formed, via vivid dream, and was probably my subconscious processing quarantine privilege, Anthropocene anxiety, and culpability. Was nearly titled "Pop."

TONYA LIBURD shares a birthday with Simeon Daniel and Ray Bradbury, which may tell you a little something about her. She is a 2017 and 2018 Rhysling nominee and has been longlisted in the 2015 Carter V. Cooper (Vanderbilt)/Exile Short Fiction Competition. Her fiction is used in Nisi Shawl's workshops, and in Tananarive Due's black horror course at UCLA (the latter of which featured Jordan Peele as a guest lecturer!) to demonstrate "code-switching." Her fiction has been praised by *Publishers Weekly*, Barnes & Noble's SF Blog, and by *Tor.com*. (She also has had the honor of having "10 Steps to a Whole New You" read by Alan Neal of CBC Ottawa's

All in a Day show—and he bemoaned the fact that he read it "in the pitch-dark, in the middle of the night . . .") She has been the recipient of the Ontario Arts Council's 2020 writers' grant and the 2021 Horror Writers Association's Diversity Grant. She is also an editor at *The Expanse Magazine.* You can find her blogging at Tonya.ca or on Twitter at @somesillywowzer, or you can join her Patreon at Patreon.com/TonyaLiburd.

• This story's background info is sourced from a portion of my novel that details Azelice's origin story; her partner-in-crime is an East Indian Trinidadian woman who was turned by a Western vampire. However, there's nowhere near the extensive code-switching in the novel that occurs in this piece.

What I remember of my decision to incorporate Patois and Western Standard English in the narrative is that I had originally conceived of this story walking back from rescuing an injured starling and handing it in to the Humane Society, around the middle of December 2020, and planned to do this story as an assignment as part of Richard Thomas's Short Story Mechanics class. Based on how the course was designed, that didn't work out. I still wanted to work on it, seeing as I had never done a story in this way before. Writing a story in complete Patois had been done; writing small segments of a story in Patois I'd done in "The Ace of Knives," my first ever published story. I hadn't seen actively switching between standard English and Patois done yet. So I'm assuming that's how it got started, because I'm always striving to do something I hadn't done previously in my work.

What continues to draw Azelice in, when she seems poised to back away but doesn't, is fascination, and the carrot dangled before her: a chance out. She was a tolerated "madwoman on the street" then. Mental deterioration's my worst fear: losing control of my mind. I worked that into the story.

Ultimately, Azelice was misled, and it's only by going through the process of transformation does she realize the lies she was told. She's forever altered, and she can't go back; but, based on the transformation she's endured, it becomes clear that she doesn't want to.

KELLY LINK is the author of five collections, including the forthcoming *White Cat, Black Dog* (Random House, 2023). She and her husband, Gavin J. Grant, are the co-founders of Small Beer Press, and publish the twice-yearly zine *Lady Churchill's Rosebud Wristlet.* She lives in Western Massachusetts and owns the bookstore Book Moon. You can find her online at twitter.com/haszombiesinit.

• For the last seven or so years, I've been wrestling with an extremely long novel. Occasionally I had the chance to work on a short story—"Skinder's Veil" is the last story written concurrent with this novel, now more or less finished. All of my recent short stories are engaged in conversation with various fairy tales—"Rose White and Rose Red" is one, here, and "The Juniper Tree" is the other. A few other notes—Andy's feeling about his dissertation no doubt bear some relationship to my own feelings about large projects (a novel, say). There's also something of the experience of writing during a pandemic: pre-2020, my usual working life was to meet up with other writer friends and work in company rather than isolation. Once or twice a year, we meet up in rental houses in larger groups, and again, get a great deal of work done. The house that Andy goes to is in many ways the kind of space where I've often gotten writing done, and working on this story was a door into that kind of magical space, the only one available at the time. Andy's visitors are stranger than the writers I've sometimes hung out with, but not always by all that much. Because I couldn't work with friends, I emailed my friend Holly Black when I was near to done with "Skinder's Veil," because I felt I had very little sense—for the first time in a long time—of whether what I had written was a story at all, let alone whether or not it was one that would make sense to any reader other than myself. I owe her a lot of thanks for putting her finger on what was still left to explore in "Skinder's Veil," and thanks to Ellen Datlow and Shirley Jackson, who are the two remaining lodestars for this particular story.

SAM J. MILLER's books have been called "must-reads" and "bests of the year" by *USA Today*, *Entertainment Weekly*, NPR, and *O: The Oprah Magazine*, among others. He is the Nebula Award–winning author of *Blackfish City*, which has been translated into six languages and won the hopefully-soon-to-be-renamed John W. Campbell Memorial Award. Sam's short stories have been nominated for the World Fantasy, Theodore Sturgeon, and Locus Awards, and reprinted in dozens of anthologies. He's also the last in a long line of butchers. He lives in New York City, and at samjmiller.com.

• "Starman" is my favorite David Bowie song, and it's always seemed like a perfect science-fiction story—two outcasts bonding over mysterious broadcasts from outer space; an extraterrestrial message of peace and hope that our (terrible) world is not ready for. This was my attempt to capture some of how that song makes me feel, mixed up with the lonely, painful, beautiful magic of being young and queer and in love in the middle of nowhere in the age before the internet. It's part of a pentaptych of stories based on my five favorite songs—preceded by "It Was Saturday Night, I Guess That Makes It Alright," about Prince's "Little Red Corvette" (included in the fabulous anthology *A People's Future of the United States*); "A Love That Burns Hot Enough to Last," about Whitney Houston's "I Wanna Dance With Somebody" (published in *Apex Magazine*); to be followed at some point soon with stories about Madonna's "Like a Prayer" and the Clash's "Straight to Hell."

AIMEE OGDEN is the author of three novellas, including Nebula finalist "Sun-Daughters, Sea-Daughters" and "Emergent Properties," which is forthcoming in 2023. Her short fiction has appeared in publications such as *Lightspeed, Clarkesworld,* and *Beneath Ceaseless Skies.* She also co-edits *Translunar Travelers Lounge,* a magazine of fun and optimistic speculative fiction.

• This story was always meant as an answer to "The Cold Equations," but I struggled with early drafts—I was unable to imagine a solution that John Campbell wouldn't have just tossed aside as he did with Tom Godwin's earlier versions of the ending. It wasn't until I identified Campbell with corporate powers-that-be—killing with the stroke of a pen, trying to hide flawed human choices behind a curtain of "pure" mathematics—that it felt obvious to me that the solution lay outside of the parameters established by the original story. We do this together, we do it for each other, or it doesn't get done at all.

KAREN RUSSELL is the author of three story collections, most recently *Orange World and Other Stories,* the novella *Sleep Donation,* and the novel *Swamplandia!,* winner of the New York Public Library Young Lions Award and a finalist for the Pulitzer Prize. She has received a MacArthur Fellowship and a Guggenheim Fellowship, the Bard Fiction Prize, and a Shirley Jackson Award. Born and raised in Miami, Florida, she now lives in Portland, Oregon, with her family.

• Since earliest childhood, I have wanted to write a story about a unicorn. One of my first memories is of watching the cartoon adaptation of Peter S. Beagle's fantasy masterpiece, *The Last Unicorn,* with my Grandma Viola in her sunny Miami Springs living room. The moment that haunted me as a child—even more than the Red Bull!—was the immortal unicorn's horror at finding herself trapped inside the burning house of a human body, aging in time. "I can feel this body dying all around me!" she cries. (Grandma Vi, drinking Lipton Iced Tea beside me, was unperturbed). On the night before I went into labor with my son, I remember staring at a human model of a skeleton on the opposite end of a dark room, thinking about how much the pelvis looked like an hourglass, and what a shocking translation it is to take human form, to be born—to pass out of nothingness and into time.

This story is not autobiographical, but I did draw on some of the most painful, terrifying, and beautiful experiences of my pregnancies to imagine my way into Mauve's character. Those panda-like raccoons really do hang out in our backyard. And I continue to be a salt freak. I am so grateful to the wonderful editor Bradford Morrow and to *Conjunctions,* and wildly honored to be part of this anthology.

PENG SHEPHERD is the bestselling author of the novels *The Cartographers* and *The Book of M,* and the novelette "The Future Library." Her second novel, *The Cartographers*, was a *USA Today* bestseller, a national Independent Bookstores bestseller, and was named a Best Book of March by *The Washington Post*, as well as a Pick of the Month by *Good Morning America*, Amazon, Apple, and Goodreads. Her first novel, *The Book of M*, won the 2019 Neukom Institute for Literary Arts Award for Debut Speculative Fiction, and was chosen as a Best Book of the Year by Amazon, *Elle*, *Refinery29*, and *The Verge*, a Best Book of the Summer by *Today* and *NPR On Point*, and has been optioned for television. Peng is also a graduate of New York University's MFA program, and the recipient of a fellowship from the National Endowment for the Arts. She was born and raised in Phoenix, Arizona, where she rode horses and trained in classical ballet, and has lived in Beijing, Kuala Lumpur, London, Los Angeles, Washington, DC, New York, and Mexico City. When not writing, she can be found planning her next trip or haunting local bookstores.

• I first heard about the real Future Library, Framtidsbibliotekct—the long-term environmental and public art project currently under way in the Norwegian wilderness—many years ago, and its strange beauty has stayed with me ever since. But it wasn't until the 2020 devastating wildfire season in the United States, when it felt like the entire West Coast was burning, and the air tasted like ash and the skies were red and black for days at a time, that this story began to take shape in my mind. I was heartbroken at how much forest we were losing, and how powerless I felt to help. So, I did the only thing I could, and picked up my pen. "The Future Library" is about books, trees, our relationship to nature, and also about how love and hope can persist through stories, even long after we're gone.

FARGO TBAKHI is a queer Palestinian performance artist, a Taurus, and a cool breeze. Find more at fargotbakhi.com.

• "Root Rot" haunted me then and haunts me still. The voice of its nameless narrator emerged first in a poem I wrote, and then refused to leave me. So I listened longer and deeper. What came then was a story about failure and loss and giving up, about those who will be left behind within the liberated futures we imagine, and about the entrenchment and extension of colonial technologies. I wrote this story to honor the spaces of loss which must also animate our visions of futurity, alongside and intertwined with the spaces of freedom, joy, and love. And so we move, in certainty and wonder, towards a free Palestine and a freer world.

CATHERYNNE M. VALENTE is the *New York Times* and *USA Today* bestselling author of over forty works of speculative fiction, poetry, and criticism, including the Fairyland novels, *Space Opera*, *Deathless*, The Orphan's Tales, and *Palimpsest*. She is the winner of the Hugo, Nebula, Locus, Lambda, Sturgeon, Mythopoeic, and Tiptree (now Otherwise) Awards, among others. She lives on a small island off the coast of Maine with her partner, child, and a cat who will not stand for being overlooked in biographies.

• "L'Esprit de L'Escalier" began as the barest seed of an idea years ago, one of those classic "what if" questions: what if Orpheus actually managed to do the one thing anyone asked of him and got Eurydice home? Having always been of the opinion that Orpheus is awful, my kneejerk answer was that it would not be the happy ending the mythological setup assumes is on the table. Eurydice has so little presence in the original story, it's not even clear who her parents are or where she came from. All the focus is on Orpheus, as it is in most retellings. He is the romantic hero, after all, risking everything for true love. Isn't he? Isn't that the core of who he is? And yet I could never shake the feelings that this whole story was about no one asking a woman what she actually wanted, over and over again until she died of it.

As a former classicist, gender roles in the ancient world has always been a fascination of mine, and I wanted to bring this myth fully into the modern day, examining the ways in which heterosexual romance has and hasn't changed at all since the days of staircases and serpents. But the gods and the old ways still peek through, in the words Calliope knits into her sweaters, in innocent-seeming dogs out for a walk, in Eurydice's physical needs, which reflect the hungers of the dead in *The Odyssey*. This is an old story and a new one. Of a woman occluded by her husband, her father, and the legend they have both made of her life without even knowing her, a woman for whom death was an escape snatched away from her at the last moment. I really so rarely delve into Greek myth in my work, despite having spent years of my academic life in the classical mines. I suppose I waited until I really felt I had something new to add—this tale, this spirit of the staircase, the ghost of a girl who drowned in the men around her, the words she wanted to say but only thought of so much later, when it was far too late.

CAROLINE M. YOACHIM is a three-time Hugo and six-time Nebula Award finalist. Her short stories have been translated into several languages and reprinted in multiple best-of anthologies, including four times in *Best American Science Fiction and Fantasy*. Yoachim's short story collection *Seven Wonders of a Once and Future World & Other Stories* and the print chapbook of her novelette *The Archronology of Love* are available from Fairwood Press. For more, check out her website at carolineyoachim.com.

• A key bit of inspiration for "Colors of the Immortal Palette" was Sondheim's *Sunday in the Park with George*—a musical that was, in turn, inspired by the Georges Seurat painting *A Sunday Afternoon on the Island of La Grande Jatte*. One of the many things I find interesting about *Sunday in the Park with George* is the relationship between the artist and his model.

I went down a research rabbit hole looking for more information about the models who had posed in famous paintings, many of whom are not named by the painters. One model that I was able to dig deeper into, however, was Victorine Meurent. She was both a model and a painter, best known for appearing in several works by Manet. Unfortunately her own paintings have largely been lost, though a handful remain, including a self-portrait she painted in 1876.

Self-portraits are fairly common amongst painters, and as I was doing this research I started thinking about self-insertion stories as sort of a literary parallel to the self-portrait. There are a lot of ways in which the protagonist of "Colors of the Immortal Palette" is decidedly not me, but this is probably the closest thing to a self-insertion story that I will ever write. I even gave the protagonist my middle name: Mariko. Putting a biracial half-Japanese half-white woman into Impressionist-era Paris changed the shape of the story and forced me to grapple with my own relationship to Japanese culture. It made the story deeply personal.

At its heart, "Colors of the Immortal Palette" is a story about art, identity, and truth. It is about marginalized voices, for all of us who have ever been told that our art is too complicated or confusing simply because it comes from our perspective. It is about the struggle to be seen and remembered. I'm deeply grateful for how well it has been received.

Other Notable Science Fiction and Fantasy Stories of 2021

SELECTED BY JOHN JOSEPH ADAMS

Hicks, Micah Dean
"Fatherly," *Gulf Coast*, Summer/Fall
Hopkinson, Nalo
"Clap Back," in *Black Stars: A Galaxy of New Worlds* (Amazon Original Stories)
Jones, Stephen Graham
"How to Break into a Hotel Room," *Nightmare*, January
Key, Justin C.
"Balancing the Equation," *Escape Pod*, January
Key, Justin C.
"Now You See Me," *Lightspeed*, August
Kress, Nancy
"Little Animals," *Clarkesworld*, June
Larson, Rich
"Complete Exhaustion of the Organism," *Lightspeed*, April
LaValle, Victor
"We Travel the Spaceways," in *Black Stars: A Galaxy of New Worlds* (Amazon Original Stories)
Lavery, Daniel M.
"How, after Long Fighting, Galehaut Was Overcome by Lancelot Yet Was Not Slain and Made Great Speed to Yield to Friendship; Or, Galehaut, the Knight of the Forfeit," in *Sword Stone Table*, ed. Swapna Krishna, Jenn Northington (Vintage)
Lee, P H
"Frost's Boy," *Lightspeed*, January
Leong, Sloane
"Mouth & Marsh, Silver & Song," *Fireside*, January
Lethem, Jonathan
"The Crooked House," *The New Yorker*, March
Lewis, L. D.
"From Witch to Queen and God," *Mermaids Monthly*, January
Loyer, Jessie
"Marked by Bears," *Apex* #126

Machado, Carmen Maria
"A Hundred Miles and a Mile," in *When Things Get Dark*, ed. Ellen Datlow (Titan Books)
Mason, Everdeen
"Miss the Zen, but Miss You More," *Lightspeed*, July
McGuire, Seanan
"Riparian," *Mermaids Monthly*, June
McGuire, Seanan
"In the Deep Woods; the Light Is Different There," in *When Things Get Dark*, ed. Ellen Datlow (Titan Books)
Miller, Sam J.
"A Love That Burns Hot Enough to Last: Deleted Scenes from a Documentary," *Apex* #122
Minton, D. Thomas
"The Memory Plague," *Lightspeed*, January
Mohanraj, Mary Anne
"Among the Marithei," *Asimov's*, May/June
Moles, David
"The Metric," *Asimov's*, May/June
Nayler, Ray
"Sarcophagus," *Clarkesworld*, April
Newitz, Annalee
"#Selfcare," *Tor.com*, January
Okorafor, Nnedi
"The Black Pages," in *Black Stars: A Galaxy of New Worlds* (Amazon Original Stories)
Older, Malka
"The Badger's Digestion; or The First First-Hand Description of Deneskan Beastcraft by an Aouwan Researcher," *Constelación*, #1
Palmer, Suzanne
"Bots of the Lost Ark," *Clarkesworld*, June
Petricone, E. A.
"We, the Girls Who Did Not Make It," *Nightmare*, February

EXPLORE THE REST OF THE SERIES!

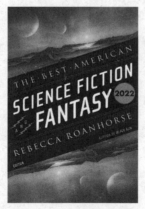
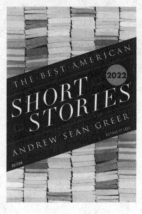